THE SEASONS OF TROUBLE

Rohini Mohan is a political journalist based in Bangalore. She has won prestigious recognition for her work, including the Charles Wallace Fellowship 2013, London; the ICRC Humanitarian Reporting Award 2012, New Delhi; the Sanskriti-Prabha Dutt Fellowship 2012, New Delhi; and the South Asian Journalists Association Award 2011, New York. She has written for *Tehelka*, the *Caravan*, *Outlook*, the *Hindu*, *Al Jazeera* and the *New York Times*. She has an MA in political journalism from Columbia University, New York.

Praise for *The Seasons of Trouble*

'Rohini Mohan's book digs so deep that it touches your heart—and unsettles it.'

—***Mint***

'Mohan has a writer's eye for the telling detail, psychological or sensuous.'

—***Caravan***

'Mohan … chooses to tell the stories of her protagonists with a pleasing directness. She offers context where appropriate, but clever pacing ensures we always return again and again to the people at the heart of the book.'

—***OPEN***

'[A] remarkable book — epic in scale, utterly compelling in detail.'

—***Hindu Business Line***

'Throughout the book, the author delivers a narrative as fluid as fiction in the delineation of these scarred lives. Mohan demonstrates an accessible, engaging method of relaying a difficult, violent history.'

—***Kirkus Reviews***

'*The Seasons of Trouble* focuses on the humanity of those caught up in the horrors. As a result, despite the violence its characters endure, it retains a poetic tone that helps Ms Mohan produce a thoroughly absorbing book.'

—***The Economist***

'Instead of quick portraits, we get to see entire narratives such as the fifteen-year career arc Mohan exquisitely depicts of a soldier who willfully enlistments as a child only to become disillusioned as her own children become endangered … Mohan combines years of superb journalism with a novelist's touch to give a vividly brutal and beautiful look at humans surviving the still-violent aftermath of a civil war.'

—**Editor's Pick List, *Guernica***

'A penetrating account of the stories of Tamil survivors of the conflict.'

—***LA Review of Books***

'Gripping and profoundly moving … Rohini Mohan has produced an astonishing feat of reportage.'

—Charles Mahtesian, *NPR* ("2014's Great Reads")

'Extraordinary rendering of the brutal denouement of the war between the Sri Lankan state and the Tamil rebels … The effect of these three interwoven narratives is haunting, and *The Seasons of Trouble* is a work of daring empathy. Mohan manages to give us direct access to the worldview of impoverished Tamil villagers and the seemingly Faustian choices they face … This is Sri Lanka's tragedy, but it is also Mohan's triumph.'

—Anand Gopal, *Bookforum*

'Governments seriously contemplating Sri Lanka's model would be wise to read *The Seasons of Trouble*. It isn't a traditional political study, but Mohan doesn't intend it to be. Instead, by focusing intimately on the lives of three individuals—their daily struggles, the shared hurt and trauma—she has produced an ambitious, thoroughly engrossing work that informs the mind while simultaneously unsettling the heart.'

—The American Interest

'A significant, though heartrending, account.'

—Alan Moores, *Booklist*

'There is never a dull moment in the book as Rohini skilfully and sensitively segues between the lives of the principal characters, unveiling before the reader the human cost of the war and the brutality of the state while clearly steering clear of an accidental pro-LTTE stand. It's engaging, painful and so intimate. Her attention to the socio-political and cultural context of Sri Lanka is immaculate.'

—First Post

'The book reminds us that in every conflict, no side is completely innocent or blameless. Mohan subtly reminds us that although winners may be declared, wars are always lost.'

—The Aerogram

'Rohini writes with such beauty and violence.'

—Molly Crabapple, author of *Drawing Blood*

THE SEASONS OF TROUBLE

Life Amid the Ruins of Sri Lanka's Civil War

ROHINI MOHAN

HarperCollins *Publishers* India

First published in hardback in India in 2014 by
HarperCollins *Publishers* India

First published in paperback in 2016 by
HarperCollins *Publishers* India

HarperCollins *Publishers* India, Cyber City, Building 10-A, Gurugram,
Haryana – 122002, India

P-ISBN: 978-93-5264-113-0
E-ISBN: 978-93-5136-959-2

2 4 6 8 10 9 7 5 3 1

Typeset in electra by MJ & n Gavan, Truro, Cornwall

Printed and bound at
Repro India Ltd.

HarperCollins *Publishers*, Macken House, 39/40 Mayor Street Upper,
Dublin 1, D01 C9W8, Ireland

To Thatha, for birthing an obsession,
and to Sanjaya, for nurturing another

Contents

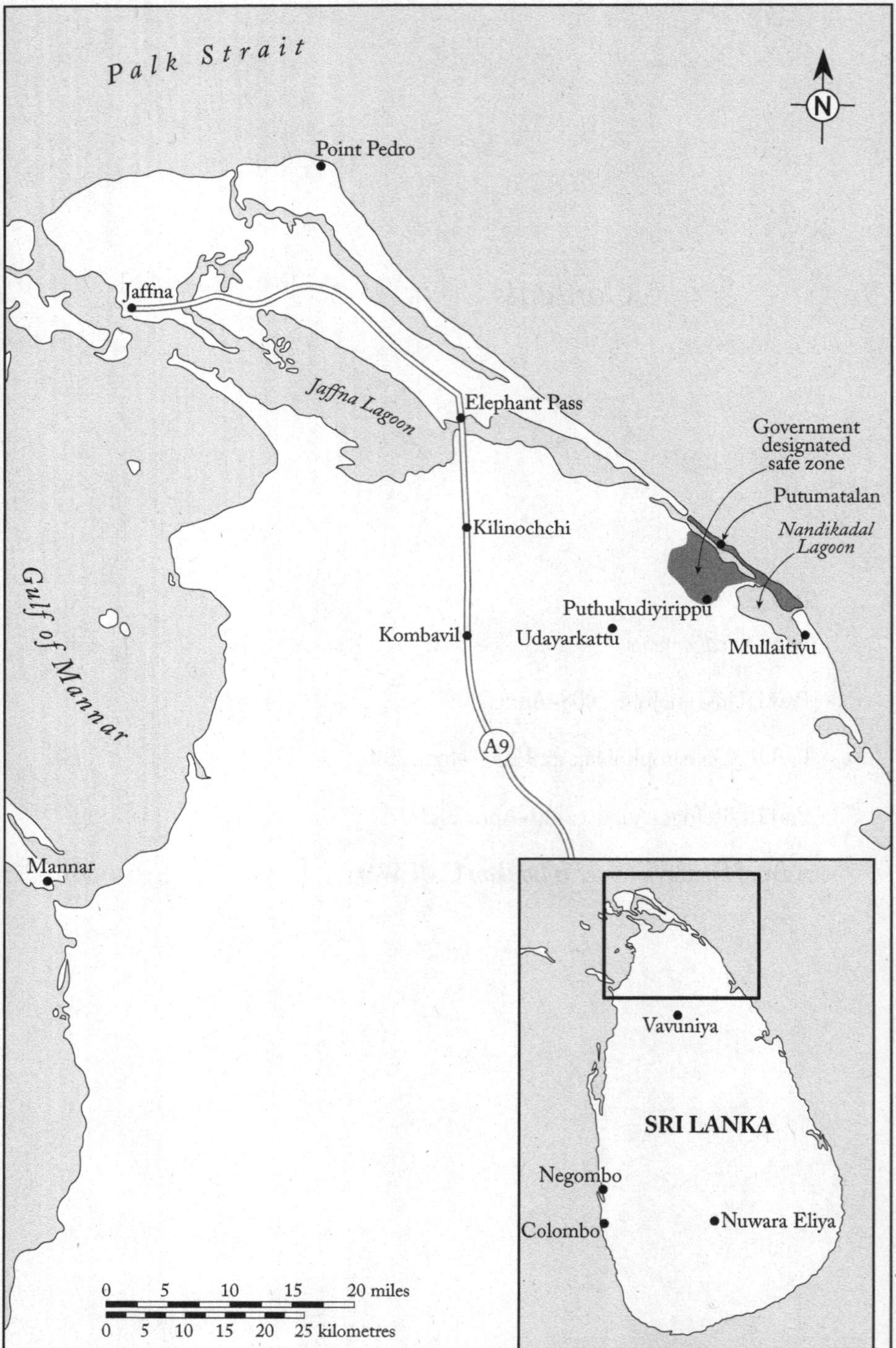
Palk Strait
N
Point Pedro
Jaffna
Jaffna Lagoon
Elephant Pass
Government designated safe zone
Putumatalan
Nandikadal Lagoon
Kilinochchi
Puthukudiyirippu
Udayarkattu
Kombavil
Mullaitivu
Gulf of Mannar
A9
Mannar
Vavuniya
SRI LANKA
Negombo
Colombo
Nuwara Eliya
0 5 10 15 20 miles
0 5 10 15 20 25 kilometres

Preface

IN LATE 2009, I met the first of the three people whose stories are told in this book. After a hurried five-minute interview under a soldier's watch in a dank refugee camp, the gaunt young Tamil woman challenged me. 'I'm sure you'll never return to see us,' she said. In the next five years, I went back to her repeatedly. In these pages, she is Mugil. That same year, a middle-aged woman in a middle-class neighbourhood in Colombo told me of her bewildering search for a disappeared son. I call her Indra here. Her son, who finally reached England after several tumultuous years, is able to tell his story in his own name: Sarva.

Over five years, the three let me into their lives and innermost thoughts. During this time, I lived in Sri Lanka for a total of ten months, and in England for another three. The rest of the time, I kept in touch with them through weekly phone calls from India. It was a journey that took us from mutual mistrust to confidence, as we negotiated the pitfalls of memory, bias, history and trauma. We talked in Tamil, without an interpreter, which somewhat helped overcome our differences of country, gender and class. The reportorial rigour of scrutinising documents, photographs and maps, listening to silences, repeating questions and revisiting locations provides the foundation for the events described in this book.

I conducted dozens of other interviews at length, some with people who had met more tragic fates or lucky ends than Indra,

Sarva and Mugil. But the words, decisions and silences of these three articulated better than most how the effects of a conflict can persist for a year, five or decades after. Their compelling stories also spoke to the Tamil community's struggle with its past. They showed me the indelible nature of the violence and nationalism that reached deep into language and relationships, and crept into their futures. These stories challenged my notions of victimhood, patriotism and community.

My goal here is to tell their narrative as honestly and engagingly as they did, to show the changes they experienced among the wreckage of civil war and the mundane omnipresence of conflict. Being present through these people's setbacks and challenges in the aftermath of this war, I was privy to incidents and emotions they subsequently and frequently blocked out, reframed or remembered differently—in order to cope, because of oppressive fears, or simply to satisfy the human need for closure. As they attempted to define their lives on their own terms, they went from narrating their experiences as a series of events, to a series of responses, to a spiral of melancholy and aspiration.

Apart from the inaccuracy or absence of official data, crackdowns on media, and restrictions on mobility, this is what makes war so hard to report on, and for those in Sri Lanka to live through and move on from: loose ends rarely tie up. Incompleteness and dread are as tangible as the deaths and destruction.

The protracted civil war changed the nature of being Sinhalese, Tamil or Muslim in Sri Lanka, and political sides have often tried to solidify these identities into exclusive, warring blocs. None of the people in this book are entirely representative of Sri Lanka or the communities they belong to, but they inherit the same conflict and its after-effects. Their points of view, prejudices and contradictions push and pull at the ethnic stereotypes the conflict has created.

As the world grapples with new democracies and old hate, these three lives are a grim caution. Mugil says her experience is a warning for the next marginalised group that refuses to assimilate. Sarva sees the war as a permanent obstacle to love and happiness. Indra, his mother, calls it destiny.

July 2014

Acknowledgements

DURING MY RESEARCH and writing, a number of people advised, scolded, cheered, sheltered, fed and read me. My earliest and steadiest guides in Sri Lanka were Ruki Fernando and Ahilan Kadirgamar. V.V. Ganeshananthan fine-tuned my ideas and words from the earliest drafts to the last one. Their generosity and honesty kept me from giving up when roads closed or concepts knotted up.

After every field trip, seeking an even perspective, I turned by habit to Sithie Tiruchelvam. For long conversations about then and now, I'm grateful to Jayadeva Uyangoda, Seelan Kadirgamar, Muttukrishna Sarvananthan, Nirmala Rajasingham, Valentine Daniel, Michael Roberts and Radhika Coomaraswamy.

Colombo became home thanks to the warmth of Zainab Ibrahim, Aminna (Turin Abeysekera) and the kitchen magic of Rasamma. At another time, Tahseen Alam gave me shelter. In Trincomalee, my hosts, Mr and Mrs Laxmanan, never flinched when I dropped in without notice. In Jaffna and the Vanni, P.S.A. and T. shared their humble rooms with me. In Mannar, Father Jeyabalan Croos always had enough room for a tired traveller. All of them not only offered survival tips but also glimpses of daily life in Sri Lanka.

I am thankful to Mirak Raheem, Bhavani Fonseka and the

Centre for Policy Alternatives, Colombo, for their stellar record of state/government initiatives in the north and east; to everyone at the INFORM human rights documentation centre; to Sanjana Hattotuwa for the journalistic force that is Groundviews; and to Ponnudurai Thambirajah for the silence and well-stocked brilliance of his library at the International Centre for Ethnic Studies. Deanne Uyangoda, Dinidu de Alwis, Ananda Galapatti, Sumathy Sivamohan, Guruparan Kumaravadivel, Meera Srinivsan, Namini Wijedasa, Murali Reddy, Father Ravi, N. Singham, Elangovan Chandrahasan, Vel Thanjan, Sanjeev Laxmanan, Sinha Ratnatunga, Manik de Silva, Nishan de Mel, Shireen Saroor, V.K. Shashikumar and S. Anand for their ideas.

It's unfortunate that many Sri Lankans crucial to my research cannot be named, so that they can live without any fear for their life or freedom. I also couldn't have done without the friends in Colombo who helped by just being there, talking of everything but work, inviting me to cricket matches, karaoke nights and family dinners.

I am indebted to my writing partner, Mathangi Subramanian, for her reactions to my early drafts. Dave Swann in Chichester, whose trick for finishing a first draft I'll never forget. Dragan Todorovic, Alex Padamsee, Nandini Nair and Anuj Bhuwania for their encouragement and sharp feedback. Nicholas Lemann, for his precise advice as editor in my first attempt at writing about Sri Lanka at Columbia University, New York; Jonathan Shainin and Vinod K. Jose from the *Caravan* magazine, New Delhi, for enabling my first published piece on it; Basharat Peer for being excited about the project from the start. Shoma Chaudhury and Harinder Baweja in New Delhi; Alexander Stille and Thomas Edsall in New York: teachers in the kind of journalism that still energizes me.

This work would not have been possible without the generous fellowships from Panos South Asia, New Delhi; the Sanskriti Foundation, New Delhi; and the South Asian Journalists' Association, New York. I thank the Charles Wallace India Trust and the University of Kent for the three-month residency at

Canterbury, UK, where I began to write; and Sangam House for the month at Nrityagram, Hessarghatta, India, where I completed the manuscript. In between, Bhagyam aunty and Rajendran uncle in Valparai; Mount Pleasant Artists' Retreat in Reigate; and Joy Guesthouse in Auroville offered perfect writing locations.

Leo Hollis from Verso Books was the kind of encouraging and attentive publisher I did not expect to find in the UK as a first-time author. Mark Martin, tough, but always on my side, closely edited and polished the drafts. I am grateful to Karthika V.K. from HarperCollins India for her enthusiasm about my work. Without Peter Straus, my agent, this book might not have seen the light of day.

Through it all, my parents and friends made up the support team that kept me sane. The not-so-sane moments then fell to my husband, Shailesh Rai, whose admirable ability to read, listen and hold the fort, I know, needed love and more.

Most of all, I am beholden to the protagonists of this book for their patience and trust. Their courage resonates in my life still.

PART ONE

unseen

1.

June 2008

SOMEONE MUST HAVE talked plenty, because on an afternoon in June 2008, Sarvanantha Pereira was detained by men who didn't say who they were. They would call it an arrest. It felt more like an abduction.

Sarva was in a trishaw, his medical report in hand, returning from the doctor's office near the red Cargill building in Colombo. He had just been certified a man of perfect health—no illnesses, no physical weaknesses. It could be no other way; he had spent most of his adult life making sure that the asthma attacks that had plagued his childhood would never return. Growing up, few things had worried him more than his mismatched body and health. With his broad chest, log-like arms and his relative height, he towered over most Sri Lankans—a matter of great pride to him. But his size also signalled an intimidating strength, which, at a boys' school and in the sandbag-punching areas where he lived, was quickly interpreted as a challenge. He learnt to live up to the hype of his tree-trunk body. He ran, did push-ups and ate so competitively that he seemed to have shamed his asthma into submission. All to build a physical confidence to match his appearance.

Two years ago, Sarva had completed a nautical engineering course. His diploma—the first in his family of high school just-pass graduates—was much celebrated. But like all the other young men in his class, Sarva had enrolled for the free travel. With his diploma, he got jobs sailing all over the world on merchant ships. The drab workshops on welding and refuelling had prepared him for an unglamorous job, but once he was actually at sea, it was worse than anything he could have imagined. He spent most of his time inside a damp cabin, greasy up to his elbows, busy with wrenching and oiling, a drudgery broken only for one brief meal a day. He worked almost eighteen hours a day for months on end, learning to swallow the nausea of seasickness, becoming someone smaller and quieter than he thought himself to be. But when the ship docked in a port, there was always a promise of adventure, of unseen countries. He always made sure he scrubbed to the tips of his fingernails and wore his best shirt before stepping out. Who knew what exotic beauty the land would hold, and he didn't want to mar it with his grubbiness. Sarva's journeys to the Maldives and to Thailand had been the best. They were the very landscapes advertised on billboards at home, with footprints in the sand and a pretty couple in shorts and white shirts. Those places convinced him that there was a world somewhere that was worth scrubbing decks for. Now with his health report, he was closer to getting the Greek visa he would need for his next voyage.

The smoke from the trishaw driver's cigarette flew into Sarva's face as they turned past Colombo's world trade centre. His phone rang; it was his father calling from Nuwara Eliya. 'Your aunt tells me you aren't home for lunch yet?' he asked in Tamil.

Sarva looked at his watch. It was already past three o'clock. He was staying at his aunt's house in Colombo and she would expect him for lunch. 'Did Aunty call you?'

'Yes, she has made fish,' his father said, 'your favourite.'

Sarva never tired of his aunt's fish curry, which she made following a traditional Jaffna Tamil recipe: steamed in tamarind extract and seasoned with mustard seeds sputtered in sesame oil. It was the taste of his after-school evenings at her house, where he had stayed with his brother and cousins till the seventh grade.

'Aunty will remember to save me the fish head,' he told his father. He had to go to the recruitment office to hand in the medical report. He would be home by four, he said. His parents, who lived in Nuwara Eliya, had stayed in Colombo till the previous day, for his mother's hernia operation. This was her fifth, but was the first one he had been around for. She had been overjoyed that he had come, which amused Sarva. He was accustomed to thinking of himself as the ignored middle son, always exiled to aunts' houses. Maybe he had acquired this new central position in the family because his older brother, the former favourite, had married a woman his mother disapproved of.

The trishaw drove past the Pettah bus stops, honking and weaving through the hordes of people crossing the road. The recruitment office Sarva wanted was on Armour Street, and they were almost there. There was no reason to hurry; June in Sri Lanka brought on everyone's worst mood. The oppressive humidity and heat seeped right through one's clothes and into one's nerves. The stream of shops selling mobile phones and pirated CDs gave way to fork-lifts, iron scrap and hardware shops. This part of Colombo always looked plundered, the predominance of grey concrete and rusted metal signalling heavy demolitions just beyond view.

The trishaw driver asked Sarva in Sinhala if he was sick. He had seen the stamp of the doctor's office on his papers.

'*Aiyo* no, it's just a check-up,' Sarva replied in Sinhala from the back seat, scooting closer to the driver. 'For a job on a ship.'

When he bent his head to meet the driver's eye in the rear-view mirror, Sarva saw, from under the array of decorations hanging above the windshield, a white van standing near the recruitment office across the road. The trishaw driver didn't seem to notice it. He was making a U-turn around some workers digging up the road. Sarva felt his heart race. This was not good. No white van was ever good.

'Turn around!' Sarva hissed.

The driver looked over his shoulder. 'Huh? Did we miss the place?'

At that moment, four men got out of the van; two of them started to walk towards them.

'Turn around! Turn around!' Sarva was shouting now.

The driver hit his brakes and was just shifting to reverse when the two men from the van caught up and hopped in.

'Who … who are you?' Sarva stammered, trying to squeeze out of the now cramped back seat. One of the men then grabbed Sarva by the trousers, removed his belt, and pushed him out of the vehicle in one motion. They took everything off him—the medical report, his wallet, his mobile phone. They used the belt to tie Sarva's hands at his back. At the wide car park nearby, with traffic still whizzing past, the bigger man threw Sarva on his knees.

Standing above him, the other man screamed questions at him.

'Is your name Sarva?'

'Yes.'

'Do you have three artificial front teeth?'

A pause.

'Yes.'

'Have you been to the Vanni?'

'No. No.'

By now, the trishaw driver had begun to yell, 'Kidnap! Kidnap! Help!' A small crowd of labourers gathered around them. Some people were shouting, '*Aye, aye*! What is happening?' One of the men from the van flashed them an ID—held it high above his head. He was a plainclothes policeman, he said. Pointing to Sarva, he snarled: 'This is a *Kottiya,* a Tiger,' a Tamil militant from the Liberation Tigers of Tamil Eelam. The driver fell silent, the crowd disappeared. Later, Sarva would wonder what happened to the driver after that. Did he drive away—in fear or out of indifference or hate? Did he wait to be paid for helping them set this trap? No one could be trusted.

The men dragged Sarva towards the white van. Its windows were tinted and rolled up. He was made to crouch in front of the passenger seat beside the driver. A man clambered onto the seat and pressed his feet to Sarva's back. The door was slid shut. He counted six or seven men before he was blindfolded.

They drove for about half an hour, perhaps less. Sarva swayed with the sharp turns the van was making. The man above him gripped Sarva's curly hair to keep his balance but did not remove his hand afterwards. Dirty boots dug into his back, and now this hand. Sarva had seen goats taken like this to the slaughterhouse, bleating all the way. A Muslim butcher in Negombo once told him he always killed the noisiest goat first. The quiet ones were smarter, Sarva had decided. Sure, they were still going the same way as the rest, but they managed to stay alive a little longer.

He tried to quieten his thudding heart; he breathed more slowly, he wanted to heighten his other senses. In school, a rich boy who had been kidnapped for ransom had led the police to his kidnappers' lair entirely by retracing the sounds he heard while they drove him blindfolded. Sarva tried that now: inside the van, no one spoke a word. The traffic noise and honking had begun to subside.

He couldn't focus. Why is this happening to me, he wondered. A year ago, he had come close to this: he was with another shipping company and was inside the harbour's customs immigration office to arrange some papers for his Turkish assignment. An officer had seen Sarva's national identity card, which had been issued in Tamil-dominated Jaffna and showed his name in both Tamil and Sinhala. With one look at it, the officer had identified Sarva as Tamil; he took him to a room to ask a lot of questions. Sarva still had the same ID card. As soon as this was over, he decided, he would apply for a new one from Colombo, where his name would be written only in Sinhala and he wouldn't be as easy a target.

The van slowed down for what seemed to be a gate and then stopped. Sarva heard the door open and through his blindfold saw light flood in. He was pulled out of the van and taken up some steps. He heard a ship's horn. That gave him his first piece of real information: he was somewhere near Colombo's harbour.

AT HOME, SARVA'S mother, Indra, waited for him to call once he had reached his aunt's house. It was six already. His father, John, had insisted they take the noon bus from Colombo back home to Nuwara Eliya; that's where John's mind always was, anyway. Now the housemaid was cutting vegetables in the kitchen and John was nodding off while watching a Tamil film award ceremony on TV. As usual, the volume was too high. The obnoxious presenter's voice boomed through the old plantation bungalow. At least they had no neighbours. Uncomplaining tea estates surrounded them.

Indra tried calling Sarva for the fourth or fifth time. An electronic voice said in Sinhala that the number was 'in a no-coverage area'. Sarva never told her where he went all day—none of her three boys did—but it wasn't like him to wander. He was usually home at the time he said he would be. He hadn't had lunch, and he rarely ate out in Colombo. 'I want my sweet aunt's rice and curry,' he always said. Indra suspected he was just buttering up his aunt to win some pampering in return. That fellow would do anything to get attention.

She called him again. This time she heard the phone ring, but there was no answer. 'Good-for-nothing donkey,' she spat, her worst Tamil curse. 'This is what I get for having boys!'

By dinnertime, Indra had called Sarva's phone about thirty times. She wished she had stayed in Colombo. She called her sisters, Rani and Mani, every few minutes. She felt a numbing fear. The newspapers were full of disappearances and shootings, sordid details of an escalating war in the north that was affecting every Tamil—and even some Sinhalese—these days. These were familiar news items; she had been reading them since the nineties. A son missing, a husband stranded in another town because a highway had closed overnight, a sister caught in the crossfire, a neighbour found dead in a ditch, a schoolboy shot by a soldier, another boy joining the Tigers. It all began with these hours of not knowing.

Every wave of battle meant that Tamil families, no matter who they were, expected misfortune. Anything could happen, and few things could be stopped. Indra's mother had once compared the Tamil experience to two million people dressed in white shirts being showered by purple berries falling from a shaken tree. Few would be left unstained. So every time misfortune missed them, Indra was wracked with guilt because she couldn't help but count their escape as a rare blessing. She saw it as a breather until the next wave of consequences.

Finally, Indra phoned the nearby police station to file a missing person's report.

'Who's missing?' the bored voice at the other end asked in Sinhala.

'My son,' Indra said. 'He is a seaman in Colombo,' she added for some reason.

'When did he go missing?'

She said he was supposed to come home for lunch, but she felt something had happened to him. The voice, now annoyed, told her to keep on waiting and hung up.

Indra sat on the threshold of her front door and stared at the darkening sky. Was she panicking unnecessarily? Maybe he'd just gone to a friend's house. But why didn't he answer his phone then? Only Sarva had this ability—to drive her berserk with his neediness and then drop her as if she meant nothing. He had stayed with her through her hernia operation. Maybe she shouldn't have asked him to help change her bedpan. Oh, that was too much for any boy. But no, Sarva had grown up. He was close to his family now. He wasn't footloose any longer. She called her sisters again to check if he was there. He wasn't.

She decided she must do *something* before she lost her mind. She called her usual travel agent and booked two seats on the night bus to Colombo, leaving in two hours. 'Hurry up with that *pittu*!' she shouted to John, who was eating dinner inside.

BY THE TIME she returned to Colombo the next morning, Indra's sisters had roped in her elder son, Deva, to do a round of Sarva's friends' houses on his motorbike. Deva lived with his wife and children just a few streets away from them, and he dropped in for lunch looking crestfallen. 'One day or another, this was going to happen to us, too, Amma,' he said.

In the afternoon, Deva went to the neighbourhood police station to once again try to file a missing person's report. They told him to come back in forty-eight hours. As he was leaving, one of the constables called him to the corner and asked him why he was trying to file a report when his *Kottiya* brother was actually fighting the Sri Lankan army in the Vanni. The constable then grinned broadly. The other constables laughed.

When Deva went home, he told his mother only the part about forty-eight hours.

Indra did not sleep that night. Instead, curled up next to the phone, she pressed redial every few minutes. Her son should never have left her side, she kept telling herself unreasonably.

At around nine the next morning, still in bed, she groped around for her phone and reflexively pressed redial. A man who was not Sarva answered the phone. 'Hello?'

Indra sat bolt upright. 'Where is Sarva? I'm his mother speaking!'

The voice said, in Sinhala, that her son was being questioned. '*Podi vibayak thiyanawa*.' A short interview.

'*Kohadu*? Where? Where!' Indra asked in Sinhala.

'We have him. Stop calling.' He hung up.

Indra had not eaten for twenty-four hours, but this, the tiniest clue about her son's whereabouts, energised her. She quickly washed her tear-streaked face, tied a knot in her wispy white hair, drank half a bottle of water at one go, and called again. And again. The third time, the same man picked up. 'Hello!' he said gruffly. 'Stop calling!'

'Where is he? I want to see him!' Her sister came running from the kitchen, gesturing to Indra to ask who the man speaking was. 'And who are you?'

'We cannot tell you. Stop calling.'

'Please, son, I'm—'

He hung up again.

When she called back immediately, the number had been disabled.

2.

June 1980

INDRA BELIEVED THAT the birth of each of her sons had been accompanied by a sign. The birth of her eldest, Deva, coincided with her husband's promotion from floor manager to factory supervisor at the tea estate: her firstborn had brought prosperity. Carmel, her last son, was delivered by cesarean, which Indra believed made him forever lazy. With Sarva, overnight her cascading black hair showed a thick clutch of grey. He was the child she would struggle most with.

Even at his birth in 1980, as the nurse in Negombo General Hospital had handed Indra the tiny, dark, hairy baby, she was irked that he was not a girl. Of course, a boy meant the continuation of the lineage, a boy would take care of his aged parents, a boy was all any Jaffna Tamil should want. But a girl would have been easy, an infusion of gentleness into Indra's male bastion. Raising a girl would have relieved her anxiety about her own fading youth.

Instead, here was a second boy. Her sisters both had sons, too. Only her brother had two daughters, the lucky man, and it was in his house in which she stayed after Sarva's birth. Her husband was in central Nuwara Eliya, making arrangements for a home in the tea plantation where he'd secured a new job. Indra had refused to stay among the plantation workers in the damp line quarters provided. Instead, she moved in with her younger brother's family in the western fishing town of Negombo. She was ten hours away from John, but she hoped that her absence might expedite his house search.

Indra's brother had a general store in town and a fleet of buses that ran between Negombo and Jaffna in the north. Staying with him was not easy, although his wife was affable enough. He was always mocking Indra's children, saying they had to 'man up'. At the age of one, Sarva had taken to trailing behind his mother, holding on to the bunch of safety pins bundled at the end of her sari fall. The baby spent most of his time in the kitchen dragging pots and pans across the floor. Terrified that she might leave him forever whenever she so much as went to the bathroom, Sarva followed his mother everywhere. At night, he slept sprawled on her stomach, crying if she tried to lift him off or turned on her side.

'You know what happens to such mama's boys in today's world, no?' her brother would ask. 'He is going to be torn into pieces out there.'

Indra was starting to think her brother was a coward. She saw weakness in his voyeuristic obsession with the vivid stories of mass killings and burnings that were splashed daily across the Tamil tabloids. It was difficult to parse fact from fiction, especially when the articles were riddled with bloody descriptions and excruciating detail. Maybe these things actually happened. She didn't know. But they had inspired her brother's *kotthu* metaphor: the noisy shredding, thrashing, and tossing of rotis on hot pans outside little eateries at dusk—a comforting reminder of dinnertime for most Sri Lankans—seemed to suggest to him all the ways a man could be hurt. And the sight of her toddler with his big lips, curly black hair, and shy smile invariably made him bring up the violence of the *kotthu*. Indra would wave her brother off, saying Sarva was only an infant, and if he wasn't allowed to be attached to her now, when would he be? She never said more. She didn't feel she could, not when she lived under her brother's roof.

In Negombo town, Tamils lived among Sinhalese, Muslims and English-speaking Burghers. Her brother had lived there for over fifteen years, spoke fluent Sinhala, and had great friends among his Sinhalese neighbours. If Indra felt slightly ill at ease, she put it down to the pressures of living in a new place and her own rudimentary Sinhala. She had grown up in Jaffna, in an almost entirely Tamil community. She'd later gone to a Tamil convent school in Nuwara Eliya, where she learnt some English from the nuns but no Sinhala. While her younger brothers played cricket with a group of boys drawn from all the local communities, a relative or one of the Tamil tea workers chaperoned her everywhere, even on her walks to the market.

Nevertheless she tried to fit in. Indra believed she could pass as Sinhalese: she was large, round-eyed and fair-skinned. Instead of saris, she took to wearing long skirts and blouses like the Sinhalese and Burgher women. It was a while before she could shake the feeling that she had stepped out of her house in her underclothes. Still, she wasn't sure she blended in; she was unable to speak to people, and she didn't know their ways. She had become terribly conscious of the large red *pottu* on her forehead, something most Tamil Hindu women wore. When she went out on crowded streets, she sensed the circle growing in size with every person who set eyes on it. She felt singled out. She had always considered herself an independent, educated woman—she had practically raised her five siblings singlehanded, and now she helped her brother with his office accounts as well. It was embarrassing to feel so lost.

To add to her discomfort, her brother had begun to hint at a cash crunch, given that he alone was now feeding seven people. To expand his income, he planned to ply buses on new routes. Since his buses went north, his passengers were all Tamils and Muslims. His friends were encouraging him to start buses on southern routes. Negombo was three-quarters Sinhalese, they said; he had to tap the market. It was assumed that few Sinhalese would ever have reason to travel north. None of their families lived there anymore. It was not safe, his friends were always saying, shaking their heads during their tea sessions or drinking bouts. Since the Jaffna library had been burned by Sinhalese policemen in 1981, the militants in the north, some eight groups of them by then, were itching to attack any Sinhalese who ventured there.

The ominous discussions made Indra anxious. She was desperate for John to tell her he was coming to take her to their new home, far from her brother's house. She considered leaving on her own, but people always talked when a husband didn't come to collect his wife from her maiden home after childbirth. John visited his family in Negombo, but so rarely that Indra was sure her second-born would never learn the word *appa*. And he was terrible with phone calls, refusing ever to speak for more than three minutes on the office phone, fearing he'd get into trouble. One evening he called with news that he had found a house a few kilometres away from the line houses, on an elevation, far from gutter waters.

'Why don't you come on your own?' John suggested. 'Why make a round trip, no?'

As if she hadn't even heard John, Indra asked, 'So, when are you coming to take me?'

AFTER THREE YEARS in Negombo, Indra moved with her sons to the house in the hills. While John was thrilled and relieved to see them when they arrived, he did not ask Indra why she had changed her mind and left Negombo on her own. He knew her stubborn ways. She didn't explain in detail why she came so suddenly, merely saying her brother had been attacked by 'some people'. John knew about the riot from the papers and didn't probe further. His family was safe now. It was time to focus on the children and set up the house.

John had been promoted to the rank of assistant manager at the tea estate. In thanks for his loyal service since his days as a line man and then a factory supervisor, the owners looked after him well. He was allotted a white-and-red colonial building that came with a helper and a housemaid. The toilet and bathroom were a bit leaky, but John didn't want to be picky. His favourite thing about the house was that it was a mere five hundred metres from the tea factory. He could walk to work and even come home for lunch and a quick nap.

Sarva's infant attachment to his mother had ceased the minute they left his uncle's house. He spent hours in the overgrown garden of their new bungalow, and as soon as Indra turned her back, he would run for the gate. She often found him two hundred metres away, under the tree where the women who picked tea leaves had left their own infants sleeping in sari cradles. Indra knew he was safe there—she could even see him from the gate—but she made a scene nevertheless. 'Anything could happen,' she would say. 'And then how would we feel?'

For the first couple of days back from Negombo, she had a sick feeling in her stomach, a premonition of some sort. Indra never explained it, so John assumed she just did not want her child, the assistant manager's son, playing with the workers' children. What else could it be? He knew his wife's views of the plantation workers and of his ancestors. Indra was not one to hide her feelings.

Indra and John had entered into a love marriage when they were both in their early twenties. They had fallen for each other, she for his quiet manner and he for her long dark plaits with red school ribbons. Their relationship had been one of stolen glances and smuggled love letters. There wasn't much conversation. Her father, once a soldier in the British army, had been an accountant for a company that owned several tea estates in Hatton. He had lost his fluency of Tamil during his years abroad, and Indra, who read Tamil better than her father, often went along on his auditing rounds. In one of the bigger factories he frequented, they met John, just promoted from labourer to floor manager. 'Young and obedient with a bright future,' Indra's father had announced in English, with a slap to the lanky man's back. John had blushed red, looking at Indra out of the corner of his eye. A year later, she was insisting that her father use his influence with the Sinhalese boss to get John a promotion.

'Because I want to marry him,' she told her father, by way of explanation. 'Don't you want your son-in-law to have a better job?'

When her father objected to John being a Christian, Indra replied with the confidence of a devout Hindu. 'It's not like I'm going to start praying to Mother Mary.'

The bigger bother, however, and one that would plague their marriage, was not immediately apparent, a matter Indra herself had struggled with. In one of their shy ten-minute meetings, in telling her about his childhood, John shared a story his grandfather had often told him. John's great-grandparents were labourers relocated from southern India by the British during the colonial era. His ancestors crossed the Gulf of Mannar in a ship along with almost a thousand others and, from the western coast of Sri Lanka, were forced to walk to the hills at the centre of the island. It took them months, and en route hundreds died of hunger and exhaustion. John's grandfather had been a baby during this mass migration, and yet he often retold the story of how they hacked down the forest to turn it into tea and coffee plantations, women learning to pick leaves and men learning to both farm and serve tea—first for the British estate owners and then for the Sinhalese ones. At the end of the tale, the grandfather would walk to his old metal trunk, and from under his folded dhotis and shirts would fish out the orange cotton sari in which his mother had swaddled him during their arduous journey.

John knew it wasn't an extraordinary story in those parts; everyone in his school in Hatton, a plantation town, told a version of it. But he loved his telling of the story because it ended with the sari; no one else had the sari. For John, it was a piece of truth that had travelled from Trichy in southern India to a damp line house in central Sri Lanka. That fabric was the explanation for his existence, for why he spoke a Tamil different from Indra's. It was the unspoken answer to her query about why he didn't just quit his job at the estate if he hated it so much. He wanted to, but he couldn't.

When John recounted this story, Indra realised that he was a plantation Tamil. She was a Jaffna Tamil, a community that had settled in Sri Lanka centuries ago, and the difference disturbed her. The boy she loved was a labourer. She thought plantation Tamils a poor, uneducated, uncultured lot. But the heroines in Tamil movies loved the handsome, good-hearted labourers, didn't they? And whatever their status, John's father was a doctor. That counted as a rise in class. But could her family accept him, his *background*? Perhaps she herself couldn't. She continued to meet the tall boy with downcast eyes, though with growing trepidation.

After a few more clandestine meetings, however, Indra unearthed a golden nugget from John's history. His mother belonged to the high-caste Vellalar subcommunity of Jaffna Tamils. This freed Indra to imagine a marriage between them, it convinced her disapproving father, and it allowed their differences to—at least temporarily—melt away.

Even after their wedding, John continued to talk about his ancestors as indentured labourers, while Indra focussed on his high-caste mother and doctor father. It was as if they were speaking of two different families. So when Sarva played with the children of the tea pickers and Indra forbade him, John seethed but rarely argued. It had always been this way.

In the spirit of his birth sign, Sarva gave Indra several other things to worry about, too: hiding in the tea bushes, eating from the servant's plate, going into the backyard to look for snakes—he was always doing what he was told not to do. Indra saw a quiet sureness in his actions, rather than defiance. He never sought permission or approval. Indra always rushed to his rescue, partly because she had never shaken off the feeling of dread that had entered her bones when she left Negombo.

That shiver of premonition meant that she was always expecting an imminent catastrophe. And this seemed to manifest itself in Sarva's behaviour. He ate poorly and had stomach upsets. His asthma attacks began to hit at midnight. Indra became surer than ever that these were omens of what was to come.

LATE ONE JULY morning in 1983, a few days after she returned from Negombo, Indra was alone at home in Nuwara Eliya with baby Sarva. John was in Hatton and would return later that week. As she was feeding the child, she heard a commotion down below, near the tea factory. She peeped out her door and heard a few workers shout that they'd seen four busloads of thugs driving towards the plantation. 'They're coming!' they screamed.

It was finally happening. Indra had feared this ever since she had left her brother's house. The feeling had been unshakable, especially when her nights were filled with flashes of the ugliness she had witnessed in Negombo.

She had spoken to no one about the sight of her brother being dragged out of his shop by sweating Sinhalese boys in T-shirts. They had stripped him naked and beaten him with cricket bats. They burned his shop to the ground and strewed the stock on the road. Another mob broke into the house, too, but to Indra's surprise, the Sinhalese neighbours smuggled her family and her brother's out the back door in time to escape.

In the four days the neighbours helped to hide her family, they had exchanged few words. Soft *baila* from the local radio filled their silences, its good-natured thump-thumpity-thump at odds with the menace on the streets. At meals and before going to sleep, Indra's family tuned into the news on BBC Ceylon. It said the Sinhalese mobs were furious about Tamil politicians demanding that a separate nation be carved out from Sri Lanka. Some other accounts said the mobs wanted revenge for the ambush of thirteen army soldiers by the militant Liberation Tigers of Tamil Eelam (LTTE), who were in turn responding to the Sinhalese police's burning of the revered Jaffna Tamil library two years earlier.

The reports were guarded, and the reasons given for the violence seemed speculative. A week earlier, the government banned the press from reporting Tamil militant activities. So Indra and her family had not heard about the immediate reasons for this bloodlust. The Tigers' number two, Seelan, had been killed in Meesalai in Jaffna in a shoot-out with the army. To avenge this, some of the other top leaders had detonated a powerful mine, killing the thirteen soldiers. Eight of the soldiers were under twenty years old.

The ping-pong of murder and counter-attacks in the north turned into mass killings in Colombo. The mobs targeted Tamils who lived among the Sinhalese: on Monday, they cornered and attacked the city-dwellers in Borella and Wellawatte, nestled between the sea and Colombo's busiest bazaars; on Tuesday, it was Kandy, where a deputy inspector general spotted goons with short army crew cuts; on Wednesday, it was Badulla and Negombo, where Sinhalese men burned and beat fishermen and traders; Passara on Thursday. The course of the violence, it seemed, was a wave emanating from Colombo.

The radio anchors predicted that President Jayawardene would order a curfew and that any ruffians found loitering in the streets would be arrested. As the families huddled around the transistor radio, Indra's brother said he wished the curfew would be declared soon. His Sinhala friend clucked. 'Are you crazy?' he asked. 'Then you'll stay inside your house and these madmen on the street will know exactly where to find you.'

Indra shivered. She had not considered this possibility. How could everything turn against them like this? If people had seen this coming, why had they allowed the soldiers' dead bodies to be brought into Colombo? The news said the police had protected Tamils in some places, like in Kurunegala, where an inspector drove away most of the mobs. But overall, the police were mute spectators, even collaborators.

The government was setting up refugee camps for Tamils on the run. Her brother suggested they go there, but his Sinhalese neighbour's wife would have none of it. 'Let's wait till it stops fully,' she said. So for four days they stayed in the neighbour's house, eating rice and week-old *sambol* twice a day. The women took turns putting the children to sleep and washing their soiled clothes. They didn't talk much.

The men drank arrack as if it were their lifeblood, but without their usual banter about how this MP stole that many lakhs and that councillor got this or that person transferred to get his son-in-law a job. Political discussion felt trite at a time like this, when its effects hit so unnervingly close. Red-eyed from sleeplessness and drunkenness, the men cut sorry figures: tragic characters whose gloom could change nothing.

On the day news anchors began to analyse the massacre in the past tense and denials started to pour in from government departments, Indra's brother and wife left with their children for the refugee camp in Colombo. They planned to go from there to Jaffna, where all the Tamils seemed to be fleeing to be among their own. Rather than joining them, Indra had taken her sons on an overcrowded bus to Nuwara Eliya. When she arrived, John maintained a relieved silence; he had listened to the radio and there were, after all, police everywhere. Perhaps he knew. Beyond mentioning her brother's injuries, Indra couldn't bring herself to talk about it either.

A few days later in Nuwara Eliya, as Indra heard the approach of the mob, she realised she had not fled far enough: the violence had reached the hills. There was mayhem in the line houses where the workers stayed. As Indra was feeding Sarva breakfast, she heard two sounds: the mob howling their intention to 'cut up the Tamil dogs' and the plantation workers shouting at her to 'Get away from here! Get lost!'

Neither said why, but Indra understood. Earlier, someone had pleaded for her to leave, saying that if she, a Jaffna Tamil, stayed, they would all be attacked. They had asked her to go up to Tank Hill nearby, but Indra knew she would not survive there with an infant. The Sinhalese owner had given her four minders: one Sinhalese and three plantation Tamils. They were meant to protect her, but when the moment came, they were nowhere to be found.

As soon as she heard the 'get lost', Indra started to run.

She ran to the Sinhalese owner's house for refuge, but he told her to save herself, and shut the door in her face. Indra froze for a second, then ran towards the estate. She tried to climb a tree but couldn't get a handhold.

She heard the buses screech to a halt at the gates. Between the tea shrubs, she put baby Sarva on the ground and lay on top of him, holding her torso up slightly, lizard-like, with one arm. With her free hand, she covered his mouth.

The ground was soggy. Something crawled between her toes. Above, she heard horrific screams, dull whacks and thuds. Women sobbing, begging. A steel utensil clanged and rolled down the steep steps of the line-house colony for what felt like a whole minute. She crouched lower.

Alongside the northern Tamils, the ones the Sinhalese were really pursuing, plantation Tamils were attacked. These workers—poor and largely illiterate, underpaid—were neither the Tamils the LTTE fought for then and claimed to represent nor the ones scholarly Tamil politicians demanded a place for in Parliament.

By noon, a deathly silence had descended over the estate. Gingerly, Indra lifted her head. One of her bodyguards, a young Tamil worker, was lying a hundred metres away, slashed and stabbed. In Indra's still arms, Sarva had fallen asleep.

AS AN ADULT, all Sarva knew of that day in July 1983 was that he had slept through the bloodiest anti-Tamil pogrom, which killed 3,000 people and led hundreds of thousands of Tamil families to flee the country. Even decades later, 'God saved me,' was all his mother wanted to say about that day. She never told him that it was the loneliest moment of her life.

Twenty-five years later, when Sarva disappeared, Indra knew that nothing had changed. Her husband was immobile with worry; her eldest son would help only in his spare time, and her sisters waxed and waned in their support. They all wallowed in the paralysis of grief. Indra was not shy about berating them for it, but this didn't change how alone she felt. With just as little warning, Indra was now once again a petrified mother trying to save her baby from an unseen horror.

Five days after Sarva's disappearance, a man telephoned Indra to say in fluent Tamil that he had found her son. When the caller came to see her a few days later, Indra exploded with inappropriate laughter. The Tamil-speaking man was the whitest American she had ever seen.

3.

October 2008

LOOKING DOWN FROM the mango tree into the abandoned orchard, Mugil cursed herself for having lost her T-56 assault rifle. She hadn't fired it in years; who knew if it still worked, but it gave her an extra swagger: every second step, her hip swung to the left to avoid hitting the rifle slung over her right shoulder. She liked to refer to it as her crab walk.

The T-56, stolen from a burning Sri Lankan army camp in Mullaitivu in 1998, was a souvenir from Mugil's first successful operation in the Tamil Tigers. She was eighteen then, the second-in-command in one of the squadrons. She had been part of a great triumph and had made sure every one of the nine girls she led had come back alive. They had looted everything from the camp complex, taking every item except the Sinhalese books and the pornographic magazines in the soldiers' quarters. They had then cleared the way for the seized army tanks and bulldozers to be driven into Tiger territory. The incredible ambush had made Annan Prabakaran, the supreme leader, call her name out during a formal celebration and shake her hand in front of other combatants; he praised her for being the kind of woman the Tamil homeland needed.

And now she had gone and lost the rifle to the same army, to

Sinhalese boys who looked half her age. Boys she wanted to shoot as she watched them rip the camouflage shirts off five Tiger girls down below. Mugil hoped someone would intervene. But below her only a smouldering garden shed stood mute witness. Bullet holes pocked the mango orchard that had seemed like such a safe hideout just half an hour ago. When the soldiers had arrived, she had clambered up a tree. Now the foliage obstructed Mugil's view of the other girls below her, but she could hear their voices as clearly as shrieking alarms.

The girls were screaming in Tamil, except for one, who was repeating the word *epa* like a loud and shrill chant. That was not how the Sinhala word was usually used, but it was an expression Mugil had often heard Sinhalese policemen and the army lob at civilians. *Epa!* when they didn't want you to sell apples by the road in Jaffna. *Epa!* when you tried to drive on at the checkpoint at Vavuniya. *Epa!* Don't! The girl's voice seemed to ring through all of Kilinochchi. But through the shelling, bombing and chorus of wailing in the forest, no one would hear. Mugil had grown up with war since she was a teenager, but this moment was unlike anything she had experienced before. This latest phase in the conflict had begun two years ago, when the Tigers had forcefully closed the sluice gates of the Mavil Aru waterway on the east coast, cutting off the water supply to some 15,000 villages. In response, the Sri Lankan air force had attacked the Tiger bases. At the time, Mugil had assumed it to be just another stage in the twenty-six-year-long cycle of attacks and counter-attacks between the Sinhalese armed forces and the Tamil Tigers. She had gone about her life unbothered, until August 2008, when the LTTE had sent her to the field after almost a decade of injury-induced retirement. Now, the entire might of the Sri Lankan armed forces, led by President Mahinda Rajapaksa, was engaged with the LTTE across the north and the east. From the unprecedented brutality around her, one thing was clear: the army wasn't just attacking the military might of the LTTE. It was laying siege to the idea of the Tamil homeland, the very inspiration behind the Tigers' leadership.

MUGIL'S FATHER HAD always said that in Sri Lanka there were some districts where the army or government could not hurt even a Tamil fly: Kilinochchi, Mullaitivu, part of Mannar, north Vavuniya, and southern Jaffna—collectively the Vanni. It was the core of the area separatists marked out as Eelam, the separate Tamil homeland that was the dream of most Tamils and the sworn goal of the Tigers. Tamils came to these places to escape the army on the eastern and northern coasts, or the Sinhalese mobs rioting in Colombo and Nuwara Eliya. Here, they hoped, the armed Tamils would shield them from the armed Sinhalese. Her father would say this with dramatic emphasis, bringing his right index finger and thumb together with a tiny gap that represented the Vanni's Tamil fly protected by the Tigers.

As a teen forced to move to the Vanni, Mugil had suspected that this was her father's way of talking up their thatched hut and searing-hot village, named Puthukudiyirippu, or new settlement. She was twelve when they moved there, leaving their harbour-view house in breezy Point Pedro after shrapnel started flying in through the windows. They had left in a rush, but since her mother had packed only two sets of clothes for each of them, Mugil had assumed they would return soon. As they fled, she had seen her first bomb crater: a giant elephant footprint on their street.

They'd taken a shaky crowded boat from across the Kilali lagoon and disembarked at Kilinochchi, where they'd stayed with relatives. Then all of them, including the relatives, had walked for two days to Puthukudiyirippu. It was just a shrubby jungle then, with hundreds of people flowing in like an infestation of ants.

The heat had been unbearable. Mugil was not considered fair-skinned unless compared with her sisters, but the harsh Vanni sun seemed to take that as a challenge. She watched her skin gradually burn to an even coffee char, the hair on her legs grow thicker, and the soil coat her toenails with a permanent shade of rust. Even before she had fully comprehended the place, it had entered her skin and made her one of its own. Like most others who thronged the town then, Mugil's family never left. PTK, as they called it, became home.

Life in the Vanni was an odd combination of freedom and scarcity. They had government post offices and public phones, but except for some Tiger officials, no one had personal satellite or radio telephones. People had plenty of access to food, but because cattle herding was sometimes a border security issue between the Tiger- and government-controlled areas, milk was generally available only in powder form. Many families had bicycles and some had motorbikes, but since fuel was heavily rationed, they often rigged the latter to run on kerosene.

The Tigers—alternatively called the Eelam Movement—became the biggest employers in the region, hiring people for their courts, cooperative societies, banks, vegetable farms, orchards and teak plantations, to work in publishing, filmmaking and engineering, to fish and to drive. If you were a cadre, the movement took care of everything, from your underwear to your housing, and provided for your family if you died in battle. People who established their own shops or garages paid sales taxes to the movement. The Sri Lankan government still ran the schools, registrars, hospitals and ration shops, and these somehow coexisted with the Eelam institutions.

The movement leaders wanted a Tamil homeland in which no one would starve, beg or steal. Thieves were rare in the Vanni, not only because people had few possessions but also because a burglar nabbed by the Tigers' blue-uniformed police would get a public flogging. Within a few months of moving to PTK, Mugil saw a man paraded through the streets: he wore a garland of soiled shoes and slippers, was naked except for briefs, and his head was shorn so badly it was covered in bloody nicks. He'd been caught stealing jewellery from a house. Mugil wasn't allowed to join the crowd that followed the shamefaced man, but her brother and father went. At dinner that night, they reported seeing the burglar tied to a lamppost and whipped with a belt. On the way to school the next day, Mugil took a detour to see the scene for herself. The man's body slumped from the lamppost; he had been beaten to death. A woman, perhaps his mother, sat at his feet, staring blankly into the distance. Mugil had run home crying. When she described what she had seen, her mother said, 'But you are never going to face this situation. No, Mugil? That treatment is only for the bad guys.'

The Tigers controlled everything from discipline to food supply to mobility; but unlike Colombo residents who lived in dread of suicide bombs and air raids, most Vanni Tamils did not consider the militants a presence to fear in the initial years of the movement. Then, the Vanni's people revelled in their relative freedom, and relished promises of more to come. In contrast to the Sinhalese-dominated south, where language parity was the law but not the practice, here everyone on the streets and in the offices spoke, read and wrote Tamil. Vanni Tamils felt no language-based anxiety about going to the police, politicians or government agencies; miscommunication and discrimination were not everyday experiences as they were for Tamils living in the rest of the island. Only a handful here even spoke Sinhala, the national language and the only official one until 1987. Few had even met a Sinhalese person other than the occasional government official.

Here they were among their own. Within these borders, unlike in the Sri Lankan nation, Tamils were the dominant community. In this forested bubble, people largely lived in thatched huts. But they had aspirations, and indeed were confident of equalling Singapore's enviable economic growth, India's cultural vibrancy, and Europe's standard of living.

The Vanni was as much a safe house as a battlefield. By the time she was thirteen, Mugil had learnt that if you heard a howl from the sky, you scurried into the six-by-fourteen-foot bunker in your compound. If you saw streaks of smoke in the air every few days, it would be wise to move several kilometres elsewhere. If the LTTE radio channel announced an expected air raid or there was a siren, parents scooped up their children and fled to the nearest village. They locked their houses and buried their jewellery, expecting to return in a few weeks. Running away never got easier, but it did become routine.

And in September 2008, that is exactly what the people in Kilinochchi did. They evacuated all the villages around the town, from Akkarayankulam in the south to Paranthan on the other side of the highway. By October, Kilinochchi town stood empty. Whole neighbourhoods had gathered their essentials in plastic bags and bedspreads and were now fleeing east from the approaching Sri Lankan army.

Cowering behind the tree's foliage, Mugil thought of her husband Divyan, who would be on the field somewhere, driving the cadre around. How he could be working she didn't know. No one seemed to know whether they were coming or going. Several Tiger high commanders had surrendered to the army, and it was nerve-wracking to keep track of who was trustworthy and who was playing double agent. The counter-attacks, too, seemed vastly disproportionate. One time, Mugil counted the army shoot sixty rounds in reply to a single round of fire from the Tigers.

Her parents were still in PTK. She had been meaning to find out if they were safe; they were also looking after her two sons, whom she hadn't seen in weeks. Maran was three and wouldn't miss her, but Tamizh was barely two. He would bawl if she were gone for more than a few days.

How much might these girls' parents worry about them? Mugil could still hear them screaming and there was nothing she could do. Through the rain-drenched leaves, she watched an army boy snap off the girls' cyanide capsules from around their necks. Another shorter man rammed the butt of his rifle into a girl's hip. As she clutched it and crumpled to the ground in pain, he kicked dry leaves and sand into her face. The front of his boot hit her nose. Writhing in pain, the girl folded her hands towards him. But he was already unzipping himself and pushed her on her back. Mugil looked away. The girls were only as old as she had been when she joined the Tigers, perhaps younger.

ONE AFTERNOON IN 1993, when Mugil was thirteen, her school cancelled the after-lunch classes. Some athletic-looking men and women, wearing long untucked black shirts and trousers, walked into her class. They advised the students to get good grades, and joked about the rotund headmistress. Mugil stared at them in awe, knowing they were the Liberation Tigers.

When they'd lived in Point Pedro, Mugil had only heard about these people. Her father had owned a press there, and he printed pamphlets and notices for the Tigers. He also drove his minivan for them, distributing printed material and other goods to Jaffna, where most of the Eelam groups were then based. He didn't talk about it after they moved to PTK, but Mugil knew that her father had also worked for the People's Liberation Organisation of Tamil Eelam, another militant group. In the late eighties, he had escaped to India for a few years when the LTTE was rooting out and killing those loyal to other militant Tamil groups. Her mother had even ordered the children not to speak to anyone about their father's job or his whereabouts. A middle schooler then, Mugil had been amazed that there were people even her father feared.

Having moved to PTK, Mugil understood his feelings. There was a perfection to the Tigers, a confidence and sincerity that commanded respect even from people much older than the combatants. When her family reached the Vanni, starving, confused and petrified, the Tiger cadres led them to safety. They taught them to build underground bunkers in their home premises and held survival drills in her school. Despite the government's blocking supplies of essentials into the Vanni, the Tigers had managed to smuggle Coca-Cola there. They had guns attached to their hips, but they spoke respectfully even to children. The girls rode motorcycles and wore jeans; they could stand up to any man. A few months into her life in PTK, Mugil started to wave to the older girls when they passed by on bicycles or motorbikes; when the *akka*s waved back or smiled, it made her day.

The Tigers were young, but it was clear to Mugil that they had seen blood and war and knew how to deal with the Sinhalese and Indian soldiers, who seemed to want to eradicate all Sri Lankan Tamils. They would lay their lives down to protect their community. Some people whispered that the Tigers also took lives as easily, but Mugil agreed with those who said that there was no other way this fight could be won. It had to be all or nothing. You couldn't create a separate country by requesting the existing government cede it—otherwise, the old *satyagraha* politicians would have already created an Eelam.

The first Tamil to openly demand a separate nation was not a Tiger. It was C. Suntharalingam, the country's first minister of commerce and trade—a moderate nationalist—whose fury was stoked by a 1956 law that made Sinhala the country's only official language. In protest, this Tamil politician fumed in a letter to the prime minister in 1957, saying the Tamils had been 'tricked and betrayed', and that to 'save themselves from Sinhala colonisation' they had to establish 'an independent Tamil *Ilankai*'. The Sinhalese-dominated parliament paid no heed to Suntharalingam's anger. In the seventies, the government ratified a republican constitution that declared the Sinhalese the original inhabitants of the island, and their greatest duty the protection of Buddhism. Multi-ethnic Sri Lanka, with its Tamils, Muslims, Christians, Burghers and Veddas, was declared a Sinhala–Buddhist country. Tamil politicians again condemned this ethnic oppression by holding fasts, protest marches, sit-ins, and blockades. But the state struck them down.

Mugil knew about Suntharalingam and the peaceful protests, but to her all that was a pointless prelude to the real story—the part where she learnt about the massacres of Tamils, the denial of the jobs and college places they had come to expect. She didn't know, and didn't care to know, that Sinhala Buddhist nationalism was initially a reaction to proselytising Christian missionaries and Westernisation. That when the majority locals felt threatened by British culture, they set up more Buddhist vernacular schools and printed more Sinhala text books. Literature, mass media and political meetings all began to spread the message of Sinhalese superiority, of the need to defend the indigenous culture of the Sinhas, the lion race. The first victims of this new chauvinism were not actually the Tamils, but the Sinhalese Christians in the south and the west; the Muslims were next, then the Indian Tamils who worked in the central tea plantations, the Malayalis, and, finally, the biggest minority, the Sri Lankan Tamils.

Increasing state persecution of Tamils in the seventies inspired the formation of a few small insurgent groups, including the LTTE in 1976. They impatiently challenged the elderly political leadership, but had few recruits. After the July 1983 riots, however, hundreds of enraged young people became radicalised. By the time Mugil was a teenager, the LTTE had emerged as the strongest and most ruthless of the militant groups.

The Tigers were not just real-life heroes to Mugil; they were also the only ones who seemed to be in control. Even Mugil's father, after coming to PTK, started to print pamphlets and run other mysterious errands for them. 'Be loyal to Prabakaran,' he said. 'He will take our people far.'

That afternoon in 1993, the Tigers in Mugil's classroom played some music on a stereo they had brought along. Mugil and most of her classmates had heard the songs before, blaring from speakers on Martyrs' Day or the Tamil New Year. One song described the strong palmyra tree of Jaffna standing upright in all storms except when uprooted and burned by dark hands that resented its growth.

As Mugil hummed to herself, an *akka* ordered her and another girl come to the front of the class. They were asked to perform to a song that rang through the room: *Panirendu vayadhinile tholil thuppaki potukkittu*—Just twelve, she holds the rifle over her shoulder. Mugil marched, danced, and carried a wooden ruler over her shoulder, trying to imagine being on the front line, battling for the freedom of her people, facing the bullets calmly. When she finished, one of the Tiger women patted her on the back. 'The song is about a twelve-year-old. You are thirteen.' Then, in unison, the Tigers said, 'One from every family!'

That evening at home, Mugil swept the yard, burned the fallen leaves, and put the rice on the stove before Mother came home from the neighbours'. 'What is happening here?' Mother teased. 'Who are you? Where is my daughter?'

Mugil didn't bother asking her sentimental mother to take pride in her decision to join the Tigers. Instead, she kept it straightforward. She told Mother that she should not miss her. 'Only one of your children is leaving,' she said. 'You have three others. You won't even know I'm gone.'

A resounding slap left Mugil's cheek burning. 'Are you mad?' her mother yelled, as expected. 'You are a baby! You don't know anything!'

And so it went all evening until her father came home.

Even before he had stepped inside, Mugil ran to the door, and said, 'Appa, I'm joining the movement.' She was sure her father would take her side. Worldlier than her mother, he also understood the Tigers better than anyone she knew. When his friends' son had signed up recently, Father had compared it to the Catholic tradition of giving up one child to God's service.

But now he was silent. Mugil was his firstborn; her loudness and spunk energised him, and made him laugh. One of her sisters had polio, and the other was a touch-me-not, easily startled, her eyes wide with a fear of everything from pressure cooker whistles to cycle bells. 'Lost causes,' he called them. The last one, his only son, was barely seven. Of all his children, it was Mugil he had been hoping he wouldn't lose, even though he had always known she was the most likely to leave.

Her father quietly acquiesced while her mother never stopped berating her, but no one asked Mugil why she had chosen the movement. And so in the tradition of so many youngsters who joined the Tigers, Mugil too left a note at home one day, writing about her desire to go to battle with her generation so that her elders and the children of the future would have a country they could call their own.

Seven girls from the class—including Mugil—had signed up for the movement. Excited, they didn't know how much to pack. Mugil suspected that she would not see her parents for a long time and nicked a black-and-white family photo taken in one of the photo studios in the Jaffna market. It captured her parents looking nattily dressed, perhaps for a wedding at the Nallur temple. Baby Amuda sat on her mother's lap and Mugil, in a silk *paavadai-sattai*, stood morosely in front of her *verti*-clad father. The family appeared awkward, unsmiling, but the fact they had bothered to get this picture taken, and gone to a photographer's studio, meant there had probably been something to celebrate.

None of the girls admitted missing home, though they spent most of their nights swapping stories about their parents' consternation when they announced their decision to become Tigers. Their day started at five in the morning, with a giggly rush to the toilets, and then a run around the grounds. They got three meals, and eight raw eggs per day, and sometimes ice cream, juices and Coca-Cola in the evenings. The trainers were tough, but during break time they told stories about their favourite fights and their beginnings as fighters. 'We are not just your older sisters but your entire family now,' the *akkas* said. 'You can come to us for anything, okay?' Training was gruelling, but at the end of the day, when the girls returned to their dorms and helped apply balm and hot compresses to each other's bruises, they felt like a unit.

After the ten-day programme, all twenty girls in her batch were asked to fall in line under the harsh sun and their superiors cropped their hair. Newly bobbed, Mugil felt she had truly come into her own. Her parents would never have let her wear her hair this short. Some women fighters who were more attached to their hair snake-coiled plaits high on their heads. That was pretty, Mugil thought, but then what was the difference between a commoner and a combatant? She did not have the patience for the time-consuming hair-coil. The bob suited her, she decided, and drew attention to her large black eyes. Through the seven years she was a cadre, the prickly hair on her nape would unfailingly remind her that she was different from other women, braver, with greater purpose. The haircut was her oath as much as the words of loyalty she chanted before she went into battle.

She specialised in GPS operation and navigation, and most of her work was with the Malathi unit. The trainers lectured about shooting, how to cock a gun, how to squeeze the trigger, at what range to fire, which rifles recoiled and by how much, how the elbow had to absorb the impact and come back to position. It was mathematics—angles, multiplication and radii. But the girls asked each other the toughest question at night: do you think you could kill someone? Some girls said perhaps, if the target were not looking them in the eye. They were relieved to be a unit; they would be jointly responsible for the deaths of anyone they killed. They rationalised that they would only shoot or blow up people who wanted their community eliminated. *Azhikkaravanai azhikkarithile pilaye illai,* the senior *akkas* would say: it is not wrong to destroy those who seek to destroy you.

Mugil tried to remember those words a few months later when she joined one of three female units that ambushed an army camp and brought five prisoners back to the LTTE Mullaitivu base. The seniors interrogated the soldiers for a few hours, then called one girl from every unit. Mugil was told to bring a short-barrelled rifle.

Sunlight poured into the room from the holes in the cadjan roof. Five young Sri Lankan soldiers were in a row on their knees, wrists tied behind their backs. They looked beaten, their uniforms torn. Their heads drooped.

A senior commander looked at Mugil and said, 'Shoot the first guy on the left.' She was taken aback; she was only five months into the force and had yet to shoot anyone point-blank. She hesitated and looked at her first supervisor, hoping this was a mistake.

'Did you hear me?' the commander bellowed. She jerked forward and stepped tentatively towards the soldier. Surely he was much older than her, perhaps twenty-one. He looked up at her, his eyes widening at the sight of her gun. He turned to the commander and shook his head. 'No, please, no,' he said softly in English. The other soldiers were shuffling backwards on their knees, huddling together. Mugil stood frozen in front of the soldier, looking at his head, unable to lift her gun. He turned to face her and looked her straight in the eye. She wanted to turn back and run. He was summoning every Tamil and English word he knew: he had an infant child, he was from a poor family, from a tiny village in the south. He begged her to have mercy, cried that he did not hate her. 'Job,' he was saying. 'Job, poor, no money, please, Miss. No.' The commander did not speak, but Mugil felt his glare bore into her back. She lifted her gun, and the soldier shut his eyes tight, still crying but tucking his head into his neck. She pulled the trigger.

Later, she would wonder if she too had closed her eyes.

'Good, next one also,' the commander barked. She moved a step to her right and towards another soldier. He shut his eyes immediately. She heard the body of the first soldier fall to the ground. She shot the second one. Blood dripped down his nose. She realised she was holding her breath. 'Next!' she heard. The third soldier was right there. She stepped nearer him and shot a third time.

Back in her room that night, the first supervisor came to see Mugil. 'You were brave today,' she said. 'Remember, if you had not killed them today, they would have gone back and someone else would be sent to kill you and all of us. On the field next time, it will be easier.'

Mugil didn't believe her that night, but it did become easier. In her seven years in the fighting force, she never held her breath again while pulling the trigger. But new faces did not replace the face of the first soldier in the sunlit room. She would never feel remorse for the killing of anyone, except him.

Over the years, her body, too, was injured in the course of her efforts to harm others. She suffered a broken rib; a dislocated knee; many burns; shrapnel in the abdomen, ankle, forearm; torn ligaments; a smashed toe. Each put her out of action for a few months as she healed, but nothing stopped her from returning until 2000, when her spine was hurt. The Tigers removed her from the fighting unit. She was twenty.

'It is time for you to become responsible, Mugil,' Mother said, when Mugil went home.

Mugil wished her mother would not speak to her as if she was still a child. 'If you mean plait my hair, wear flowers and bangles and prettily wait for a husband, you should know better,' she replied. 'Housework is not what I was born to do.' Too much had changed. She could not go back to sitting in the kitchen. Her life had another purpose, and the movement had helped her pursue it. She couldn't and didn't want to erase the past seven years of her life. The LTTE seemed to echo her thoughts. They offered her a new job: map reading. She would go with the unit into the field, but she would only navigate and provide GPS coordinates for targets. Even as a navigator, she continued to cut her hair. She grew it out only after her wedding five years later. Her mother could not have been happier. 'Finally, you're getting to be a girl,' she said. 'No one to tell you how to wear your hair anymore.' Mother's joy only doubled when Mugil gave birth to two boys, Maran in 2005 and Tamizh in 2007.

Mother did not expect Mugil, now a mother of two, to continue working for the Tigers. But, in 2008, she was asked to join the Films and Communications Division; Colombo newspapers referred to it as the propaganda wing. Her team—eleven people including an LTTE spokesperson—taught map reading, made documentaries and films, took pictures on the front lines and during functions, wrote pamphlets, sent reports to their websites based abroad and issued press releases. Mugil's first job was to photograph the bodies of dead fighters on the battlefield, track down the parents and deliver the news.

At first, she loathed the role—she wanted to fight for her people, not take pictures of corpses. But as the years passed she came to take pride in the work. She believed she was still like a cadre, going to the battlefield, taking the same risks, but making sure she returned alive, with pictures. The closer she got, the better. She accompanied a unit or was driven to the location after the coordinates had been radioed in. If a cadre lost his or her life, she took a frontal shot, two side profiles, and a wide shot. If the body was shredded or burned beyond recognition, she would try to find an identifying mark. If the combatant's ID was found on or near the body, she would catalogue the guerrilla name and code. Then, as soon as she could, she would find the fighter's real name and address and take the photos to the families for identification. She would console the mourning mothers with a short speech she'd perfected with repetition: your child was very brave, he/she had killed a dozen before succumbing to wounds, you have to be brave to honour the memory of your child, we will avenge this death. If the deceased cadre was a girl, Mugil would sometimes add that she wished she could have died in the girl's place.

More often than not, the family would ask for the body. In the gentlest way, Mugil would explain that the body hadn't been found or that it had been blown to pieces. If the body had been brought back, however, the logistics of shipping it for a family funeral were simple. The next step was to print the photos and display them on designated walls, in schools, offices, on trees. (Her father ran one of the printing presses that did this, so Mugil even knew how to work the machines.) Then came the elaborate funeral, which the local community body would organise and pay for. The fighters would be immortalised in graves that the LTTE would maintain. No death is futile, she'd heard Annan say in his annual speeches, if it inspired another to pledge his life for the Tamil homeland.

It was an unpleasant job, but Mugil believed the process brought the bereaved families solace. As she told them, everyone dies, but there is honour in dying for a reason. On Martyrs' Day, the pictures were printed en masse; even from a distance, Mugil could pick her photos out from those of the other photographers. She thought she had a knack—maybe it was an eye for composition or a respect for death—that made her work stand out from the rest.

Mugil did this job for three months in mid 2008, and by October found that she was taking more than ten pictures a day. Her memory cards were full, even the back-ups. Barring the one in her pocket, she had exhausted her entire supply of batteries. She seemed to shoot pictures of nothing but dead new recruits. This was unprecedented. And without a satellite phone and only a stunning silence from her seniors, tracking down all the families of the dead was proving impossible.

In early October 2008, one of the seniors in the political wing asked her to put her media work on hold and navigate the GPS for a group of new recruits. Mugil was torn. Was she back to being a cadre or just filling in? The Tigers didn't generally mix combatant and non-combatant responsibilities and political wing heads giving military instructions felt stranger still. She also didn't understand why they would ask an unfit, limping ex-combatant to lead a young unit. Finally, she assumed it was a one-off mission, coiled her hair on top of her head, and went to join her new unit.

The nine girls in Mugil's charge were about the same age as she had been when she joined the Tigers. They had hastily snipped bobs, and they held their guns as if they were aiming to shoot their own feet. Mugil felt a thick uneasiness in her stomach.

She had felt like this before. Three men from the Tigers had come for her brother Prashant when he had turned fourteen. Mugil had pleaded with them, saying that her husband, father, and she herself had all pledged themselves to the Tigers. Could they not spare Prashant for a few more years? 'How can you speak like this after having been a fighter yourself?' the men had argued. They had continued to turn up for months, quietly eating lunch at her house, making jokes or napping till Prashant returned from school. Mugil would come home every day expecting to find her brother gone. But he left in stages instead of all at once. Prashant began to frequent the LTTE engineering department, hanging out with the men there, and learnt to make bombs, smart mines, and cheap satellite phones. Whenever Mugil objected, her brother's retort was that she had joined when she was thirteen. Later, when he was around nineteen, he finally and officially joined the engineering department.

Age had never mattered, Mugil knew. Vanni natives of five feet or more, boys and girls, became conspicuous if they didn't join up. Sooner or later, they would give in to sweet talk or peer pressure. Since the 2002 ceasefire, the Tigers had even begun forcibly conscripting recruits. When parents rushed to the movement offices to retrieve their sons and daughters, Tiger leaders wrung their hands about a shortage of cadres.

In 2008, the movement numbered somewhere between 5,000 and 11,000 Tigers. The Sri Lankan military, on the other hand, had 200,000 soldiers, and were recruiting more. As the pressure grew, many families in the Vanni, even those right under the Tiger leaders' noses in PTK, hid their teenagers, keeping them from school and in some cases even refusing to let them leave the house. White vans—that dreaded symbol of the unknown—scooped boys off the street. Families arranged marriages for girls barely thirteen to save them from conscription. But the Tigers persisted. They had photographs of almost every family that lived under their authority in the Vanni. They would cross-check the photo with the members of the household, and if anyone, especially an able youngster, were missing, they would take a hostage until the errant youth reappeared.

Some months before she'd been called to fight again, Mugil had read about a Tiger spokesperson denying allegations of child conscription. The United Nations had reported that since 2003 some 6,000 under-fourteens had been recruited—kidnapped from their homes and schools and sent to the front line, sometimes with barely ten days of training. The Tiger spokesman argued that what the UN condemned was only a call for more volunteers. It was everyone's duty to fight, he said; he himself had joined as a teenager. Mugil identified strongly with that.

Even though she'd joined in her teens, Mugil had always considered her recruitment voluntary. She believed that being in the Tigers had given her the kind of experiences a girl like her could only dream of. She'd undergone intense training before she was sent off to fight. She grew into the organisation, and the *akkas* and her fellow trainees were her closest family. She had little time or opportunity to complain. The movement touted a future Tamil homeland, but in the Vanni, they were already citizens, protected and provided for. People like her received monthly salaries of 8,000 to 10,000 rupees and stayed in quarters built specifically for them. When she had her two sons, Mugil sent them to the movement-run crèches, where they were fed and cared for while she went about her work. The Tigers clearly valued her decision to serve with them, and she was grateful every time they considered her qualified for a mission. She'd heard that before her time, people were even allowed to resign from the force. She would not contemplate leaving, though. After all they did for her, when her house was on the land they protected, how could she? How would the men and women she had sworn to protect treat her if she threw up her hands one day and said she was too old or too wounded to go to the battlefield?

But the new recruits under Mugil's command, their eyes fixed on the ground, were not what the movement needed. When she was told to keep a close eye on them, that some of them had repeatedly tried to run away, Mugil had allowed doubt to enter her mind. They were shivering, their faces pale with hunger and fear. They huddled close, as if they were surrounded. Some of them didn't even have standard-issue uniforms or cyanide capsules. Their hair had been cut short not to ease movement but to deter them from escaping. If they deserted the LTTE, they could be spotted anywhere. The bob had become a sign of imprisonment, rather than personal freedom. They didn't want to be there and it was written all over their faces.

These children were being sent to face a real army when they could barely lift their guns. And they were being led by her, a half-able fighter uncertain of her orders. It didn't seem to fit the larger cause. Was this how the Tigers had been fighting in the last few months? Was this how they expected to win? With scared children? They were girls born into the war and its terrors, not its beginnings or causes. In the last decade, they had only watched loved ones die or disappear overnight, their older brothers leave on boats to foreign lands, their schools and roads shut down every few months. When they heard the distinct whistle of a shell, they were primed to run to their bunkers and crouch in the darkness. They did not see why they should fight, Mugil thought, and it was useless to tell them.

MUGIL HAD FALLEN asleep on the tree and woke up coughing furiously. Remembering where she was with a start, she slapped both her hands to her mouth.

It had rained all night. She had not heard from the high command for more than twenty-four hours. The seniors had banned use of the walkie-talkie a few days earlier; there was a suspicion that the army had tapped into their frequency or that there were traitors among them. She had been sent to guard the line with the girls for as long as possible; they would get the next orders to her somehow. Looking down, she wasn't sure what she could do anymore.

Below her, the carnage was over. Five naked girls, their bodies twisted in the last moments of struggle, lay still in the mud. No one had told these girls this could happen.

The soldiers who had raped them had left. Mugil swung down from the tree, looked at her compass, and walked away.

4.

June 2008

SARVA'S ABDUCTORS LEFT him on a seatless chair in the corner of a room. They handcuffed his hands to his back and kept him blindfolded, just as he had been in the van. The darkness pressed close. Outside, ships blew their horns and grunted in what was probably Colombo harbour. In the urine-smelling room, something dripped thickly. It was painfully arrhythmic, but Sarva found himself counting the drops. One to hundred and then back to one, in loops.

He sat in his underwear, simultaneously preparing himself for and ignoring any thought of what was to come. He had vomited a few times, from nervousness and the stink. It was numbing, not being able to see his own hands or touch his own face. It seemed to erase any proof of his being alive. He sensed nothing except the stench of piss reaching into his nostrils. Even the pounding of his heart had dulled.

Once in a while, he made a small soft sound: 'Ah?' It came out of his throat like a question. At first, it was his way of checking if there was anyone else in the room, staring quietly at him. After a while, it began to help confirm his existence. It could have been a few hours or a whole day since he had been brought in. The blackness around him made him unsure of time and its passing.

Nothing had happened yet.

It had to be a strategy. Sometimes a fearful imagination could do what no amount of interrogation could.

Perhaps they would beat him. If Sarva was lucky, they would ask questions. His school friend Kanthan, who now lived in France without speaking a word of French, hadn't been asked anything. They knew everything, they said, and Kanthan only had to sign a sheet of paper. When Kanthan refused, they beat him. Then he agreed to sign it but got the paper all bloody in the process, so they beat him again. A bloody confession paper was not going to work in court.

Sarva fell asleep a few times, sinking into the hole in the chair, and then waking as the exposed nails on the rim cut into his bare thighs. Finally, after cutting himself badly, he realised he didn't *have* to sit on the chair. He heaved his body sideways and fell onto the floor. Vomit and piss drenched the corner. He dragged himself to the centre of the room.

At some point, he fell asleep curled on the floor. A kick to his stomach roused him. They yanked off his blindfold. His eyelids slowly came unglued. In the weak light of a bulb near the open door, he saw two men standing above him. They had closely cropped hair and wore dull blue shirts and shiny grey trousers, like men selling insurance.

Sarva sat up and said, '*Ayya?*' He was glad it was the respectful Sinhala moniker he'd blurted, instead of the Tamil *anna*. These would not be Tamil cops—there were few of those, and they would not be used to interrogate Tamil detainees. Should he have called them a neutral 'Sir', as he had been taught on the ships? But they didn't look like sirs, and he doubted they had the patience for English.

One of the men asked his name.

'Sarvananthan John Pereira, *ayya*.'

'Village?'

'Nuwara Eliya, *ayya*.'

'Not Jaffna?'

'No sir, Nuwara Eliya. In a tea estate, where my father—'

'Okay, okay.'

There was a pause.

Sarva asked why he had been brought here.

They ignored the question and wanted to know if he had ever gone to Vavuniya, a town south of the Vanni, and still under government control.

'Yes, several times.'

'Then, Vanni?'

'No, *ayya*.'

'Fine.'

They put the blindfold back on him. Sarva heard the whoosh of a baton being swung. It landed sharply on his collarbone.

Again, they asked if he'd been to the Vanni.

'No, *ayya*!'

A blow to his back. A few more to his knees.

'Okay!' Sarva screamed. 'I'll tell the truth, please, *ayya*!'

They did not remove the blindfold or ask him the question again. They waited.

'I was in Vanni in 2003,' Sarva said.

'You got training with the LTTE?'

'I was forced, *ayya*.'

They called him a liar. 'You trained in 1993, not 2003. Don't you know?!'

Sarva's brain felt foggy, his legs seemed to be evaporating. He was painfully hungry.

The men were still speaking. 'You have false teeth. You are a spy. You know Sinhala, Tamil and English. How can you not be a spy?'

Sarva couldn't find any meaning to stitch their words together. Everything seemed false and simultaneously true. They were repeating things, changing tiny facts here and there, alleging massive things, screaming, beating. Every time he said, 'It is not me, *ayya*!' the baton came down. The pain was one thing, but the fear befuddled him, made him unsure of what to confess and what to deny.

After what felt like hours, the men left. Before bolting the metal door, one of them said, 'Think about what you're going to say to us when we come back.'

Sarva considered saying yes to everything. But he wasn't sure that would improve his standing with the men. They wanted him to plead guilty so that they could beat him some more, with more reason, greater moral superiority. He didn't want to end up like Kanthan, who had experienced the cowardly shame of accepting all accusations, being spat upon and losing a thumb in the bargain. If the judge had not acquitted him of all charges, his friend would now be rotting in jail, losing more fingers. But even after his release, Kanthan had to be on the run. The court's verdict meant nothing to the cops; it was as if being outside the legal limits of custody, investigation and trials freed the Terrorist Investigation Department to attack Kanthan more severely. Prison might be safer than this secret place. But he wasn't sure that pleading guilty would keep him alive long enough to see the courts. He reminded himself of the things he should not utter.

After some time the men returned. One of them ran at him like a cricket bowler and kicked him in the groin.

They asked why Sarva had only fourteen numbers in his mobile phone. 'That must mean you have all the other numbers of your contacts in your head. You must have memorised them all.' A boot cracked into his face. His mouth filled with blood and he passed out.

He came to with a tight slap to his cheek. Before the high-pitched ringing in his ears subsided, his blindfold was ripped off and a plastic bag pulled down over his head. It was drenched in petrol. Someone tied a rope around his neck, and shook his head hard as if to swirl the petrol around. The fumes funnelled into his nose. Sarva gasped and tried to suck air with his mouth, but that made the fumes sting his trachea. He felt his legs thrash about and flashes of light sliced his head. His eyes were on fire. He was sure all of this meant death.

Finally they took the bag off and left him.

Every few hours, some men returned. They asked him the same questions and he gave the same answers. The petrol bag reappeared. He tried to figure it out, learn to breathe in it, but there was nothing intelligence or patience could do when petroleum flooded your insides.

He was losing track of time, of their words, and where the batons and boots landed on his body. Sometimes he fainted. He pleaded for water, but wasn't given any. The thirst made Sarva retch. Some bile spilled out. He cried, and worried that his tears would finally kill him.

If the white van hadn't got him, he would have been in Greece, in the harbour of Piraeus he'd heard so much about—a place that deserved to be called foreign. What would Athens smell like? Of baked bread or perhaps freshly tarred roads. It would be a vision of valour, power, gladiators.

Sarva had grown up believing that the ghost of one who died unnaturally roamed the earth as an *aavi*, a translucent spirit that held life memories. He felt his *aavi* would surely go to Greece if he thought about it in his final moments. He would like that. Or perhaps he would be happier taking the bus up the tea-leaved hills to his home in Nuwara Eliya, a cool mist spraying gently across his face.

SARVA'S BODY, PERHAPS the only thing he had built himself and treasured, had betrayed him, giving his tormentors power over him. If only he could have willed his spine to be unbreakable, instead of aiding them in shattering his resolve.

He felt daylight piercing his cornea. Against the light stood a uniformed man. Sarva tried to focus on the badge. Silva. He found himself seated at a table opposite Silva.

The inspector set a glass of water down. Sarva's handcuffs were taken off to let him drink. They were in a different room now, and through the window was a clear sky.

The inspector pointed to a man in the corner of the room, near the open window.

'Identify him.'

Sarva looked. The man was short, thin, clean-shaven. He was looking at the floor.

'I don't know him at all,' Sarva said.

'Really? In 1997, did you not learn Sinhala from him?'

Sarva turned to the floor-gazing man again. He asked for more water. He insisted he had never seen the man before. 'I learnt Sinhala because I lived in the hills. Because I was in Colombo. Because … I just learnt it, *ayya*. Even my mother knows it.'

'Does your mother know you were in the LTTE?'

Sarva looked at his interrogator. He was a hefty man. The light from the window behind him gave his balding head a halo but blurred his features. All the earlier baton-wielding men had been leading up to this one. Silva spoke in an unhurried manner, like he could do this, play this game, forever.

Faced with this man, Sarva felt sure his body would shame him with its fragility. All he could control now was his own mind. He had worked to predict the cops' moves, to guess where they would aim their boots or batons. He tried to remember pictures of men showing their scars in Tamil newspapers. Which blow left which mark? But this was pointless. He could not run, he could not dodge, and with handcuffs and no food, he definitely could not defend himself. He would succumb soon, and his back would break. Paralysis? Death? What was in store for him? After the petrol bags, his eyes seemed to both shoot flames and swim in darkness. He thought he heard his baby nephew in the room, the experience so real he could smell a baby scent. His own childhood returned to him in flashes: the day he caught a chameleon and put it on different coloured surfaces to watch its skin adapt. Lights and colours appeared at unpredictable moments, swirling forms that seemed to draw him into exhaustion, into a state of half-life. He was drowning in waves of consciousness; he had to get a grip before he went insane. He had to focus his mind, rein in his fear, vaporise the pain.

He found himself, to his own surprise, thinking of God. Oh well, if that was what his mind wanted. He prayed quietly, trying to recall the words he used to utter as a boy when dragged to the Navali temple. 'The words will cast a *kavacham*, a protective armour around you,' his grandfather would explain. 'You will be like Superman, strong. No harm will come to you.' Sometimes the sacred words came to Sarva. More often he just thought of that moment in the temple when, after all the rituals and must dos, he sat quietly with his grandfather by the mossy temple tank. He focussed on the reassuring taste of the *prasadam* they ate: usually sliced bananas with coconut shavings and jaggery, and the distinct whiff of *tulasi* that made this taste holy.

Silva told Sarva to stand up and bend with his stomach on the table. Even before he was fully down, the baton landed behind his knees, making him buck, throwing his head back. Another officer then cracked his forehead with a pistol. When he fell on his knees, they hit the soles of his feet. Again, when his head flew up, they went for his face. A man swinging at each end, like a morbid seesaw.

As he sobbed on the floor, Silva paced in front of him. 'Let me tell you a story.'

Before he had joined the Terrorist Investigation Department or TID, he said, he had been in the army's intelligence wing. A regular military man, just following orders. It was wartime, but there were rules. Rules the LTTE broke first, he growled. He talked for a while about the LTTE taking him prisoner during the battle for Jaffna town in 1994, and torturing him. He had pleaded that he would cooperate, would tell them what they wanted to know, but they had still beaten him. He said they called him and his people 'savages'. Then moving suddenly closer to Sarva's face, he said, almost smiling, deliberately emphasising each word, 'You people only taught us all this. So don't lie to me.'

Sarva kept silent. He hung on Silva's every word, trying to figure out what the story meant for him. He did not know if he believed the commander, but he was sure this elaborate monologue was leading somewhere horrible.

That same day, more thrashings later, Silva brought a pistol and threw it on the table. 'Didn't you have this in Colombo?' he asked. Sarva shook his head. Silva goaded him, 'You know how to use it, I know. Pick it up, let's see.'

Sarva did not touch the gun. That would be all the evidence they needed, a weapon with his fingerprints on it.

In between bouts of violence and interrogation, Silva sometimes stroked Sarva's head paternally. 'Please understand, *putha*,' he would say, almost apologetically in Sinhala. 'Help me do my job, son. Don't you want to see your family?'

That evening, some men dragged a limp and half-conscious Sarva out of the building to a deserted seaside location. From the raised embankment, he saw the harbour across the sea wall; groups of seamen worked by the sides of ships, hauling ropes. Where he stood, the sand was hollowed by a jagged rock. His eyes burned from the petrol bag, and everything he saw appeared smoky. Then the inspector stood before him, seeming to materialise from the haze. He pushed Sarva down till his bare knees fell on the rock. Silva put a gun to Sarva's head. It was the first time a firearm had been aimed at him since he had been taken.

Silva said he could kill Sarva right now and throw the body into the sea. 'You will be finished,' he said.

To Sarva, it seemed like salvation.

AT AROUND SUNSET—perhaps on the same day the gun was pointed at him, perhaps the next—a constable led Sarva back to the lonely basement. By this time, his left foot was almost useless, and Sarva needed to put his arm around the constable and drag himself forwards. It was slow going, and they stopped often to catch their breath. They had just reached the ground floor corridor when they ran into a white man with a bag stuffed with files.

The cop accompanying Sarva froze. His free hand twirled with the English question before he asked it. 'Hello? Permission?'

The white man nodded calmly. His shirtsleeves were rolled up in typical Sri Lankan style, perfect to keep sticky sweat out of the crooks of arms. His beige chinos were wrinkled. He wouldn't have inspired a second look if not for the circumstances in which he had been spotted. His so very white and untimely presence in the police station and his possession of who-knew-what files would make any cop break into a flop sweat.

'Office closed, sir,' the policeman stammered. He seemed undecided about whether to intimidate this intrusive foreigner or to be cautiously nice to him. Finally, he stretched his lips in a fake smile and said, 'Sir, you wait, okay?' and ran towards the office.

When he was out of sight, the white man walked closer to Sarva and, unexpectedly, addressed him in rapid Tamil.

'Don't worry. I'm with the ICRC?' Sarva had heard of the International Committee of the Red Cross. The man continued, 'I was told by a prisoner I met here earlier that you were brought four days ago. He saw the sacred thread on your hand and recognised you as a Tamil.'

Sarva's frayed sacred thread had been on his right wrist since the previous year. His aunt had tied one for him at home, praying for his employment and divine protection. It had been bright red then. It was a dirty yellow now.

'I speak Tamil, you can talk to me,' said the white man, in case Sarva hadn't cottoned on.

This had to be either a trap or a dream. Sarva wasn't sure how to respond. Had it really been only four days since this madness began?

The man touched his arm. He said he didn't need to ask if they were torturing him. 'I can see it. But did they arrest you?'

Sarva said he didn't know.

'Okay, how did you get here?'

He briefly described being whisked off the street.

'So people at home don't know where you are? Give me your home number, quick.'

Sarva reeled off his aunt's Colombo landline number. 'Please call my mother,' he added. It was the first time since his arrest that he had thought of her.

The cop hadn't returned, but the white man hurried away, muttering something about contacting the family.

That night in the locked basement of the TID, Sarva was occupied with thoughts of his mother. He couldn't be sure how Amma would react to the news of his arrest. She would be worried, of course. But surely she would blame him, too. 'What did you do?' she might ask, as she used to when his grandfather or his aunts mockingly threatened to stop taking care of him. Everybody else had raised him, cajoled him, spoilt him, but Amma had the monopoly on scolding.

5.

July 2008

THE AMERICAN TOOK one sip of the plain tea and set it aside. Pity, it was good tea. John had noticed too, and had already begun his spiel about how people abroad are probably used to a different Ceylon tea, a lighter one that came from the tiniest, youngest leaves sprouting at the tip of the shrubs. Their family always used tea dust, he was saying. He got five kilos free from the factory every month, you see. It had the strongest flavour.

The American smiled apologetically. He was sitting at the very edge of the sofa in Indra's sister's living room. 'It's just that I don't take this much sugar,' he said.

Oh, how good his Tamil was! *Seeni*, how he said it so sweetly. Unbelievable! If not for his extreme perspiration and red face, Indra would have thought this was a Burgher. The American had even known to take his shoes off before coming into the apartment.

Except for John, who was going on about Ceylon tea, everyone stared at the American in silence. After waiting eight days for news of her son, Indra could not bring herself to ask the questions she urgently wanted answered. Where had he seen him? How had he found him? What had happened?

She was hoping he would broach the subject. She asked him where he learnt Tamil.

'I learnt on the job,' he said. 'I'm with the ICRC. Do you know it?'

John looked away. Indra nodded. 'Red Cross, I know it; you give medicines, no?'

'Yes, but as ICRC, we also work with war-affected people, prisoners, missing persons. You understand?'

'Yes, my son is missing; we filed a police complaint,' Indra said. 'But, how did you find us—my number? You called me.'

'Your son gave it to me. What is his name?'

'You know my son, but you don't know his name?'

Indra's sister Rani interrupted with a bottle of Fanta. 'You'll have this, no? Since you're not having tea.' She poured the neon orange drink into a glass.

The American said he would start from the beginning. 'When I went to the Harbour police station a week ago to visit some prisoners we work with, one of them tipped me off about a young man who was quickly hidden in the basement before I got there.'

'What are you saying? The police have him? Why didn't they tell us?!'

'I don't know yet—I just met your son. He was handcuffed.'

Indra's hand flew to her mouth. 'Is he okay?'

'I don't know, he only had time to give me your number.'

John had walked out onto the balcony. Indra sat back in her chair, confused. The American was showing her a form, saying his organisation would keep an eye on her son. If things went well, he would arrange for her to meet him.

'They haven't followed procedure—they haven't informed the family when he was arrested, and I don't think they've put him on the records. That's how they do it.'

'Who?'

'The TID, Terrorist Investigation Department. So first, we need to go ask them why they took your son.'

'Then he can come home?' Indra asked.

The American clicked his pen and looked at the form. 'Shall we start from the beginning? What is your son's full name?'

AFTER THE AMERICAN'S visit, John returned to the Nuwara Eliya estate. When he left, he asked Indra if she'd be okay in Colombo's summer heat. He could've said anything else—if she'd be okay dealing with the police alone, if she had enough money, if she'd prefer him to stay—but he had enquired about the weather. Indra told him she did not like wearing her sister Rani's chiffon skirts, and that when he came next, he should bring her cotton ones.

Every morning, Indra stood on the balcony of Rani's seventh-floor apartment in Wellawatte, staring at the top of the road as if at any moment her son might appear. Occasionally she ran through the kind of abuse she would rain on him when he turned up. She made a deal with Lord Pillaiyar that if her son returned unharmed, she would break 101 coconuts at the temple. Every day, she added another hundred.

Every form she filled in and every document she signed gave her the impression that she was inching closer to her son. But weeks went by. The American would help her, she knew, but she also understood that all he could do was make sure Sarva was not hidden from his family. The wait was tiring, but it seemed obscene to talk or think about anything else.

They'd all grown so independent, her sons, fashioning lives only loosely connected to hers. They had private jokes, secret friends, well-guarded pursuits of which she knew nothing. She, too, thought it best that way. It was daughters who had to be protected; sons had to be free. Otherwise they'd become weak mamma's boys, as her brother had warned long ago.

But now Indra wondered if this moment she faced with Sarva, this black mark on their family, had come because she had at some point decided it was okay to look away. She had repeatedly pulled him out of the worst situations a Tamil boy could get into, but perhaps that wasn't enough. For all the thoughts she wasn't privy to, all the times she knew he had lied to her, all the missed opportunities, she felt an aching guilt.

She pulled out old photo albums to remember the children they had once been, easier to keep from harm. Most of them were black-and-white pictures of Deva, in the crib, in the rice-feeding ceremony, crawling, walking, crying at the ritual head-shaving, going to school in uniform. Sarva's pictures were only a handful, but all in colour: a posed family photo taken in a Negombo studio when he was barely a few days old, a fungus-infested picture with his grandparents in the Jaffna house, and a couple of passport-size photos taken in primary school. By the time Carmel, her last, was born, the family owned a Minolta camera, a gift from her brother, who had emigrated to America. These pictures were in full colour, from Carmel sleeping to his dribbling attempt to eat mangoes; from Carmel running in a temple to his riding an uncle like an elephant. Even her sister's son Darshan, six years younger than Sarva, had baby photos from India, where they had stayed for a bit just after he was born and before his father left for Dubai. Of her grandchildren there were countless pictures, and more filed away on Deva's laptop.

Of all her children, Sarva's childhood had been the hardest to record. Her family had been uprooted again and again while he was growing up, their very existence then under question. How many times had she run with him from the battle and fire that raged around them—dangers from which she could not really protect him? They took photos to celebrate, document, and freeze moments worth remembering—but larger tragic events had upstaged so many of Sarva's milestones. Most of his moments had been unphotographable, happening against a background one didn't want to immortalise in a photograph and amid the disarray of their constant migration.

ABOUT A MONTH after Sarva disappeared, someone who worked with the American's office said they had received permission 'for immediate family to visit the detainee'. Indra asked if she could take Sarva some food. She got his aunt Rani to make a fish curry the way he loved it. All her emotion, she invested in a lunchbox.

Early on 26 July 2008, Indra and Rani went to the Green Pass police station. They did not notice that it was the twenty-fifth anniversary of the July 1983 riots.

In the police station, there were several others like them, the distinct dejection and confusion on their faces setting them apart from other visitors. A social worker, a Tamil from a missing persons' community group, accompanied them. He said Sarva was being brought here from Harbour police station.

At around four o'clock, a circle of policemen brought in a hunched man. He was handcuffed and seemed unable to walk. The policemen were dragging him slightly. When he lifted his eyes to look around, his swollen left eyelid stayed shut.

Indra rushed to him with a wail. Someone held her back and dragged them both to a bench in the corner. She was feeling everything but the relief she had anticipated for weeks.

'What is this, *kanna* …?' she asked, holding his hands. Sarva began to cry. She had brought him the lunchbox, but starvation did not seem to be her son's biggest problem. There were cuts on his face, his hands were bruised, his eyes hardly opened. He was wearing a putrid shirt and someone else's slippers. His feet were turned in.

'Get me out, Amma,' he said. 'Help me.'

Indra looked at the police around her and shouted, 'Are you animals?!' They stared back blankly. Across the room, the social worker, who was riffling through some papers, motioned for her to calm down.

'Get me out, Amma. I can't bear this any longer,' Sarva said.

She wiped his face with both hands, ran her fingers through his hair, and gently touched the gash on his cheekbone. 'Are they hitting you?'

He looked at the floor.

'What are they saying you have done?'

'*Puli*.'

Indra breathed out in exasperation. 'My son is not a *puli*! Catch the real Tigers!' she shouted at the police in Tamil. She thought of how she had almost killed herself six years earlier trying to pull Sarva out from hell to avoid this backlash. But she did not mention it to the police—it would only make things worse.

'Why are you catching my son?' she yelled in Sinhala.

A constable walked towards them. 'That's enough, Amma,' he said.

'Amma, please,' Sarva sobbed. 'Just get me out. Please.'

They dragged him away, leaving Indra and the other parents stranded and disconsolate. Some of them were already asking the police when they could see their sons again. Without a word, everyone was handed more forms.

Indra was furious. She had not raised this child for twenty-eight years so that someone could burn his dreams down in a moment. She had never raised a hand to him, so who were these people to hit her son?

She began filling in a request for the next meeting. The American had explained to her that if Sarva were registered as a detainee, he would be safer. He would still be in prison but out of the secret basement at least.

Marshalling her limited Sinhala, more limited English and full religiosity for her son's cause, Indra tried everything during the next few weeks. She needed to get him out, put him on record everywhere like the NGOs were saying. The government wanted to hide Sarva, make people forget him. But she loudly announced his absence from her life to everyone who would listen and many people who wouldn't.

First, there was the police, but they sent her home with false assurances and insults. Then, the local politician, but he had her wait for three days on a promised appointment before leaving the country on holiday. So she wrote him a letter and left it at his office. She went to Sarva's employers, the ship bosses. She got nothing better than a shrug, and was told they would provide any employment documents she wanted but no more. They advised her to find a lawyer.

The lady from the house at the top of the street told Indra to go to the Kali temple in Mayura Place every day and do an *archanai* there or make an offering of a dozen bananas to destroy the evil eye that afflicted her family. Another mother she met through the Red Cross told her to go to the Sri Lankan Human Rights Commission and register a complaint. Indra didn't ask her how she knew; anyone who was aware of that sort of thing would want to keep details to a minimum.

Indra too was learning not to spill the entire story to anyone until they had shown a commitment to helping her. She'd met six lawyers, based on recommendations from acquaintances and relatives in Colombo and Jaffna, and while they had all heard her out, none had the time to take up Sarva's case. When she left each of their offices, Indra worried about what they would do with the copious notes they'd taken. Even idle gossip could have the burn of malice.

Indra persistently went to the Colombo office of the Sri Lankan Human Rights Commission, trying to work out which ledger she had to fill in before meeting which clerk, whose directions might be genuinely helpful or, more likely, lead to a dead end. She zoned in on one employee who answered a call in Tamil—and assuming that he might be the least ill intentioned, focussed all her energies on him. A week later, he handed her a lot of forms. Some she filled in on her own, reading the Tamil print under the Sinhala and filling in the blanks with neat Tamil letters.

The Sri Lankan government letterhead was the biggest image on the page; its authority gave Indra the jitters. What if she wrote the wrong thing and had to scratch it out? She was relieved when an employee filled in a couple of other forms in a mixture of Sinhala and English. She gave Indra a receipt with a registration number and told her to go home, saying, 'We will call you if something happens.' Indra wondered what that something would be, but she didn't want to ask and risk annoying the clerk.

As she took the bus back, she thought about her recently improved life: her comfortable homes in Colombo and Nuwara Eliya, John's status as manager, Deva's flourishing tourism business and the big dowry and perfect grandchildren his pretty wife had given them (even if the wife herself hadn't been Indra's choice).

Once again, Sarva was the reason things had fallen apart. Yes, there were others like him in the police station. There was a war up north; they got only very limited information about that in the papers, but she remembered that the local Buddhist temple, owned by a ruling-party politician, had celebrated some recent military victory. Something was going on in the Vanni, as it always was, and once again Tamil boys were dropping like flies all over the country. But why did her child have to end up again on the wrong side of fate? When things blew up, he always seemed to be at the epicentre.

Like when Sarva was nine, and Indra had been rushed to the hospital for her third delivery in Jaffna. That night, Sarva had insisted that he be taken, too. But Indra and John had gone first, leaving him behind with his grandfather in her maternal house in Jaffna. It was too dangerous out, and a curfew was in place. The Indian Peace Keeping Forces (IPKF) were fighting the LTTE in the north. The Indian and Sri Lankan governments had signed a treaty to end the insurgency: under pressure from India, Colombo had agreed to merge the Tamil-dominated northern and eastern provinces and give a provincial Tamil government some autonomous governing powers through a constitutional amendment called 13A. In exchange, the Tamil militant groups would disarm. But the Tigers did not agree, so the battle began. They refused to give Jaffna up; it was their headquarters and instead of laying down arms, they trained them on the IPKF. At the time Indra and John needed to go to the hospital, in 1989, the battle was at its peak.

An embargo on diesel and petrol meant that only a few taxis were plying the roads, their engines jerry-rigged to run on kerosene. A *thatha* in the neighbourhood offered to drive them for 3,000 rupees. They survived the bombs that whizzed all the way between Indra's mother's house in Jaffna and the Chavakacheri hospital only because they took stupid risks. Indra barely made it without popping out the baby in the car. When she came to after the caesarean, she saw that her father had caved in to Sarva's tantrum and brought him along. On a bicycle. Everybody, it seemed, was doing foolish things. The child's face was creased with worry, his knees bleeding. Indra could not imagine what he might have seen on the way there.

'You have a sister,' she said. 'But she is not well.' For hours that night, Sarva stared at the odd-looking baby, her forehead swollen with fluid. Nurses had rushed in and out of the room every few hours, prodding the baby's head and whispering to each other in Sinhala. There was only one doctor there that night, and he was tending to the blood-spouting bodies being brought in by injured, shell-shocked people.

The next morning, a few hours after Sarva announced that his sister would be named Doola, the baby was taken away in a shroud.

Days later at home, Sarva would not stop asking when the doctor would send Doola home. Indra had smacked him hard.

Why did he have to be the only boy to have seen a sister who did not survive even twenty-four hours? Even now, decades later, Sarva would correct Indra when she told people she had three sons. 'And a daughter,' he would add. He was wise enough to see how it tore his mother apart, but it was compulsive, his desire to mention Doola, to describe her fluid-filled head.

THAT EVENING AT the Pillaiyar temple, when she ran her hand over the lamp flame, Indra prayed hard. It would take a year of her life, that's all. She could fight for a year if it meant a lifetime of peace.

She tried to focus on the future, a time when her son would be out of jail, back at work, and married with well-dressed children. She believed that imagining a happy time kept her optimistic, gave her energy. She had done this through all the uncontrollable events that had bombarded her life. She would do what she could now, with the unshakable confidence that God would soon reward her efforts.

The priest gave her a *vilvam* leaf and a red hibiscus. 'Any progress?' he asked.

'Not yet, Iyerai,' she replied.

'Your troubles will be over soon, sister. Just have faith,' the priest said, moving on to the woman next to her.

Everyone prayed for something, Indra knew. If not happiness, everyone wanted a trouble-free life of peaceful invisibility. Her mother used to say that when God had a long list of requests, he held a lottery. If you wanted to better your chances of winning, you had to have more tickets in the mix. You had to flood God's ears with daily prayer. Come trouble, temple visits were a given—and not just any temple. You had to choose the most powerful deities.

She had also learnt to be specific about her requests. She didn't ask for 'everything to be all right'; she prayed that all the forms she had filled out would reach someone influential soon, or that the big-time lawyer Deva had contacted would accept Sarva's case. She prayed for her son to get a good night's sleep, for any hand that hurt him to rot and be eaten by maggots. She prayed for her English and Sinhala to improve so she could argue better with the constables and clerks who stood between her and her son.

Indra stuffed 100 rupees down the brass *hundiyal* and marked her forehead with vermilion *kumkumum*. She sat at the base of a corner pillar over-decorated with flowers and heavenly dancers. The sun was setting, and the trainee priests were lighting the rows of oil lamps leading up to the deity. Home seemed much farther than just half a kilometre away.

6.

December 2008

EVER SINCE MUGIL had walked away from Kilinochchi, she had been hearing the thud-thud-thud of missiles crashing in quick succession in the distance behind her. A silence would follow. And then again, the triple thuds.

By New Year's Eve, it looked as if Kilinochchi might fall. For Mugil, this was beyond imagination. Kilinochchi was the Vanni's core, Tamil Eelam's capital. Here were the Eelam courts, the Eelam police headquarters, the Eelam Bank with more gold jewellery than cash, the marriage registrar, the office where Mugil had got her two-wheeler driving licence. Here she had also picked up LTTE stamps to stay in the Vanni and passes to leave it. It had not been captured for more than a decade. At this point, however, it was a gutted town. Only Tigers remained, and they had built a perimeter around the town to deter the advancing army. Every village around it, apart from the one Mugil was leaving, had either been captured by the army or destroyed by the Tigers themselves.

Mugil's safest route home to PTK, avoiding any run-ins with her colleagues or the army, was through the forests. She decided to go eastward and then south. She knew the topography well; in the training camps, they were told that the jungle was another of the Tamil guerrillas' weapons. Defeatingly thick and dotted with booby traps, it was a dangerous place for the Sri Lankan army. But the tropical trees, lagoons and sandbanks were as good as signposts on a highway for Mugil. That said, she had never been inside the jungle alone, and her camouflage was worrying her. If anyone found her walking alone in the bush, she could be shot on sight or could meet the same fate as the girls she had left behind. She needed to get rid of the uniform.

Kombavil village was on the way, and Mugil made for her Aunty Chiththi's house. Her aunt lived there with her eighty-year-old in-laws, one arthritic and the other with a bad heart. They wanted to wait for as long as they could before leaving home. Displacement meant days, sometimes weeks and months, of walking, crouching and thirst. They had worked out the odds: they had a better chance of surviving if they stayed put.

At the mouth of Kombavil, she stood outside the village clinic to catch her breath. The usual fever and blood pressure patients were standing to the side of the entrance, watching injured men and women being carried in and out. Every second person seemed to be bandaged somewhere. Bullet extraction was more or less routine for a clinic of this size, with about thirty beds, but when patients arrived with mine shrapnel lodged in their bones or precariously close to their vital organs, they were sent home with painkillers and bandages. Many spent the rest of their lives carrying the shards of battle within them.

Mugil, too, had carried a piece of metal in her leg for over ten years. It was in a tight fold behind her right calf and sent an ache hurtling up towards her hip whenever she sat down or stood up. The X-ray had shown a tiny crescent-shaped fragment the size of a snipped fingernail in her tibia. The source of her slight limp, it was her most memorable scar—the one that, along with her spinal injury, had coaxed her out of singlehood and into family life.

Mugil's had been the first wedding in the Vanni after the 2004 Asian tsunami. She had spoken to her husband for the first time in 2000, while lying hurt in battle during an operation in the north. A missile chunk had hit her squarely in the abdomen, and after running through brambles for an hour, she collapsed from excessive bleeding. A combatant who happened to pass by lifted the half-conscious Mugil, threw her over his left shoulder, and continued to run, still shooting with his right hand. She was hurting but she was also embarrassed; her clothes were torn from her stomach to her inner thigh.

When she regained consciousness at the Mullaitivu hospital, a man lay in a stretcher next to her. His arms were tanned but his chest was pale. Some short black curls flopped from his crew cut onto his forehead. His shoulder was in a cast, and tiny pieces of shrapnel had punctured almost his entire body. This was the man who had saved her life.

When no one was around, Mugil asked him his name. 'Divyan,' he replied, giving her his Tiger name. His eyes were large and bloodshot.

She had seen him before, at the training camp. He was called Dileepan then, and worked in the long-range shooting team, for whom her own team had often assigned coordinates through GPS. During target practice, he had almost blown the girls' heads off by letting the missile fly in the opposite direction from the coordinates.

That afternoon at the camp lunch, she had walked past his group to deliver her well-practised line. 'With people like you, we don't need the Sri Lankan army,' she had said. Her friends giggled, egging her on.

By Tamil standards, Mugil wasn't much of a beauty. The Vanni's unrelenting sun had burnt her to a coffee brown, and she thought her high cheekbones and cleft chin gave her a masculine look. But she was proud of her thick dark hair, and thought her bob stylish. Her sharp wit and way with words had also made her popular among the girls. Whatever the situation, she had a fitting line. Her big black eyes often twinkled with mischief.

In response to her jibe though, Dileepan—Divyan—had gaped stupidly. No laughter, no comeback. People like this now join us, she had thought of saying, to drive the knife in further. But he'd looked at his feet without a word, and she felt a little sorry for him.

A week later, he had sent her a package through her younger brother Prashant, who by then worked in the engineering department. It was a book of Che Guevara quotations. On the title page, he had inscribed a saying in Tamil: 'Silence is an argument carried out by other means.' He had pressed the pen so hard on the page that the downward curve of the blue-inked *dha* in *vivaadham* had torn through the paper.

She had been grudgingly impressed. Still they didn't speak—it was forbidden to hang around chatting, and anyway, it never occurred to her. Who had time for boys? She and her friends in the women's wing had things to learn, points to prove, muscles to harden. But her brother wouldn't let it go. Whenever she met Prashant, he was always talking about Dileepan, Divyan, whatever his name was.

One day Prashant had come with exciting news. Apparently Divyan was soon going to be on Annan's personal security team.

Mugil hadn't believed it. Please, she had thought, it's impossible. That imbecile among the Tiger chief's black commandos?

But Prashant persevered with his account. He had discovered that Divyan had been learning about Annan's daily routines and his prescription medicines. Later, when her commander confirmed the rumour, Mugil could not look at the fool in the same way again. Maybe his silence did have something to it. Her closest friend in the unit, Mani, told her that maybe it would be wise to apologise. 'He may put in a good word for you with Annan then, should you ever need it.' Mugil, however, wouldn't hear of it. 'You won't get far like that,' Mani had scolded.

In the Mullaitivu hospital, lying in the same ward as he was, Mugil thought she understood now why Annan might appoint a man like that as his bodyguard. Divyan had no regard for his own life. She was overwhelmed with gratitude and wanted to make amends. She couldn't be condescending anymore. She rehearsed her apology silently, editing and rephrasing it in her head. She wanted to say sorry and thanks but also to make light of it all.

Finally, when they were both woken for lunch, she said the words out loud. 'I never meant anything I said, you know, at training.'

'Both of us know you did,' he said quickly, sputtering on his rice gruel a little bit. 'I did think that's not how a woman should talk.'

That irritated Mugil, but she bit back a sharp retort. When the nurse left the hall, Divyan smiled. 'But then I also thought, she's not an ordinary Tamil woman, no? You're a *puli*, a Tiger.'

They ate their gruel quietly. He asked for her guerrilla name. 'Prashant only told me your home name,' he said.

'Thamizhazhagi,' she said. The one who is as beautiful as the Tamil language.

When they were discharged from the hospital, her brother took her home. In a few days, Mugil was called to the office in PTK. She had a spine injury, so she was declared unfit for battle and transferred to the navigation division. She heard later that evening that Divyan, too, had been pulled off the field. He was given driving duty. They were both still cadre but would not carry weapons.

Neither really made a move to meet again, but they continued to exchange books and sometimes letters and poems about love for the country or mythological allusions to courage. When Mugil told Mani about this, her friend was thrilled. Their nickname for Divyan was 'The Fool'. Although most of the girls in the barracks were around twenty, it wasn't easy to talk about boys or love around them. You couldn't tell who would snitch to the commander. Once, when Divyan came to their training facility to drop off supplies, Mugil was so afraid he would make eye contact that she did not leave the gym. She kept track of the operations he was assigned to. It might have been easier if she had asked her brother for more information, but she didn't want to betray any special feelings for Divyan or, for that matter, for any boy. Prashant, not even a fighter yet, was becoming quite a stickler for the movement's rules. And if there was one thing a fighter couldn't do in those days, it was to fall in love.

At the Tigers' inception, Prabakaran had banned marriage, relationships and sexual activity among the cadres. It was part of a rigid disciplinary code for combatants, which included bans on smoking, drinking and gambling. He enforced celibacy ruthlessly; carnal feelings were believed to distract combatants from the call of duty, and family life was considered corrupting, as it would make people selfish. Mugil and Divyan knew that Annan defamed, excommunicated and even killed those who strayed from this rule. They'd heard of couples that had been shot dead. 'Both are not always killed,' Mani had said once. 'One is shot and the other is punished for life.' One of those Prabakaran had executed was a dear friend and a cofounder of the LTTE. He tolerated no debate on the issue.

Mugil and Divyan were finally able to get married only because at some time during the LTTE's growth, Prabakaran himself fell in love. Several versions of this romance swirled through the Vanni, all told with varying degrees of glee and irony but always in a guilty whisper, as if even talking about his personal life might tarnish his titanic persona. According to one version that Mugil swore by, a pretty young girl came to the leader's notice through a newspaper report. She was on a hunger strike to protest the killings of hundreds of Tamils by the Sri Lankan army, and Prabakaran sent his close friends to find out more. Eventually he decided to meet the girl himself. He ended her week-long hunger strike with a glass of juice, and then, struck by her dedication to the Tamil cause, fell in love with her.

Another less popular theory went like this: the girl had accused Prabakaran of not caring enough about his cadres and letting them die like cattle without so much as an apology for their martyrdom. She then challenged him to stop her from fasting unto death. Prabakaran was said to have abducted her to silence the accusations, but when tongues started wagging about the leader living with a girl, he announced a wedding.

Whatever the truth, Prabakaran revoked the anti-marriage rule some years after his own wedding. Still, it was only after a decade or so that several other lovers like Mugil and Divyan could surface at last.

They had a wedding in PTK in early 2005. Mugil was a Hindu and Divyan a Catholic, but both had forsaken religion upon joining the Tigers. In what had become the practice in weddings between cadres, they came to their ceremony in fatigues, and instead of tying a *thaali* or exchanging rings, Divyan tied a thick yellow thread with a golden tiger tooth around Mugil's neck.

This was followed by an oath. 'Even though we're married,' they promised, 'we will place our nation, our Tamil soil, our Tamil people above each other. We will choose the gun over any birthday, family function, or consideration of love and kinship.' It was an oath every Tiger man and woman had to take if they chose to marry while serving. Mugil wore the tiger tooth as a symbol of her marriage to the cause as well as to Divyan. It was to be a promise easier to make than keep.

ON KOMBAVIL'S MAIN road, some courtyards looked abandoned while others were packed to capacity. The chaos of the north-western region had not reached here yet, but some of its residents already had, and they must have brought warnings. While children played, adults rain-proofed bunkers with plastic sheets or sat around talking in hushed voices. They were preparing for air raids and shelling. When Mugil passed by the houses, some people looked at her, puzzled. What was a combatant doing skulking around alone? One or two asked her if 'Kilinochchi was gone,' if what the BBC radio said about the military offensives was true.

One woman came up to Mugil and asked her tenderly if she was looking for her family. 'If they're not here, look near Suthanthirapuram. The army has been driving around with loud-speakers announcing that it's a safe place. Some of our people have gone.'

Mugil had heard rumours of the no-fire zone, but this was the first time a specific location had been mentioned.

'Why didn't you go?'

'Why? Am I a coward?' the woman shot back. 'You will always have us. We won't abandon you.'

A baby wailed from a house nearby. Before the woman turned to run inside, she squeezed Mugil's hand. '*Jeyam namade!* Victory will be ours!'

Mugil's aunt lived a short distance from the main road, across a narrow brick bridge and beyond a row of vegetable plots. Because of the rain, rivulets had cleaved through the mud path that led to the house, and Mugil kept her eyes on the ground. She didn't want to speak to anyone else. There were too many questions, too much speculation. People wanted information but also reassurance. She wasn't the person to provide either.

When she finally got to the fence of palmyra fronds, she looked up. A few hundred metres from the gate, behind the lemon trees,

Mugil saw her great-uncle on a chair on the porch. He was absolutely still, his hands hanging loose at his sides. His eyes were closed and his chin nestled on his collarbone. His sarong had fallen open between his legs, exposing his hollow thighs.

Mugil threw the gate open and ran towards him. She must have screamed, because Chiththi, her aunt, came running to the door from inside, her eyes wide. Following Mugil's gaze, she looked towards the chair.

Chiththi walked slowly towards the old man. 'Appa?' she called softly. Mugil stood frozen in the garden, both hands on her mouth.

'Appa!' Chiththi said once more, louder. She fixed his sarong, making him decent. He didn't stir.

'Appa!' She slapped his shoulder as if he were a child.

Suddenly he sat up, startled, and stared at both of them in confusion.

Finally he smiled crookedly at Mugil. 'Come, come. When did you get here, child?'

Mugil and her aunt looked at each other and burst out laughing.

That night, when they explained to him what they had assumed on seeing his limp body, he sighed. 'It would surely be good to go that peacefully, in my sleep, under the roof my son built for me,' he said. His son, Mugil's uncle, had departed for Germany a decade earlier. Chiththi said he worked as a chef in an Indian hotel there, but that was only what he told her on the phone; they hadn't seen each other since he left.

They ate rice and spinach for dinner, and Chiththi asked if Mugil had seen anything on the way there. 'Anything we should worry about?' Mugil knew that her aunt would never directly ask what the Tigers were planning, what job she was on, or why she was in Kombavil. She must have noticed that Mugil was alone, but she would pretend that nothing was amiss. It was the way of non-fighters in the Vanni.

Mugil replied vaguely. Her aunt, too, let it go. They spent a few hours reminiscing about other battles, as the people of Vanni tended to do, especially when they were waiting out storms such as this. Mugil had grown up listening to these stories, about temples that had become shelters, family enemies who had become saviours, unlikely uncles who grabbed their wives from burning buildings, or aunties who had seen orphans bawling next to their dead parents. Some of them told it beautifully, describing the landscape of destruction, the flies, the way the earth sponged up blood: making miserable poems from sights they could not get out of their minds. A stranger might hitch up a sari or take off a shirt to point to a battle scar and launch into the tale of its origin. These were the common threads that bound the Tamil community: the close shaves, the what-ifs, the recasting of dumb luck as courage, pain as experience, losses as tests of character. Grief could never simply be itself because it was ongoing. As the battles continued, people needed to tell and retell these stories, gather mental energy for more strife, track back reflexive decisions that had saved or killed someone, and glean strategy from them.

As they talked, Mugil refrained from mentioning the mango orchard or the girls. The moment wasn't yet right for that story.

When night fell, they spread the straw mats on the floor to sleep. For as long as Mugil could remember, a few chairs and one wooden kitchen shelf had been the only furniture in this house. Her own house in PTK was the same. Except for some of the most elite families, few in the Vanni bothered furnishing their homes. Plastic chairs were ubiquitous items—cheap to purchase and easy to leave behind.

Mugil wanted to change out of her camouflage shirt, and Chiththi gave her a printed cotton blouse. She didn't sleep well, but it was a relief to lie down on an even floor in a dry place.

Next to her mat was the cloth bag Chiththi had packed with papayas, a pouch each of rice, dal and red chillies, a packet of pickle and *karuvaadu*, salt, sugar, some milk powder, tea, and a Coke bottle filled with well water, just in case Mugil wanted to leave without saying goodbye.

OVER THE NEXT three days Mugil walked, eating the papayas and a few handfuls of the milk powder. She wore Chiththi's blouse over her trousers. When, at the crack of dawn, she had buried her camouflage shirt a few paces away from her aunt's house, she had been grateful for the darkness—she didn't want to see what she was doing. She told herself that if there were army around, she would not be taken prisoner. She wore her plait down instead of bunching it up on her head. She put a *pottu* on her forehead.

She walked till she was close to highway A35. The masses heading for Mullaitivu were camping on either side. When she emerged from the thickets into the crowd, no one even glanced at her. There were lorries and tractors stacked with rice, flour and cereal revving their engines on the narrow roads but only inching forward. These were trucks from the government agent, the chief administrator of Kilinochchi district. They were trying to take supplies to where everyone was going. But hungry and impatient men, women and children were milling around the vehicles already, trying to grab their share before the supplies ran out.

Thousands were trudging eastward, in the same direction she was going. Many others were resting a few metres away from the crowd. It was just before noon, and families were emerging from their bunkers to cook lunch.

She was one of very few women on their own. Most were holding children, sitting beside their husbands, or helping their ailing parents. Many families had radios, which seemed to pick up short-wave frequencies. There was BBC Ceylon and the national station, Swarnavahini. Through the state-run radio channel, the government of Sri Lanka made announcements asking Tigers to surrender for their own good. They assured Tamil civilians that the army would guide them to safety.

Like the Kombavil woman who promised Mugil that the people would stand by the Tigers, come what may, many civilians here, too, were inviting cadres into their bunkers, giving them food, and retying their bandages for them. An aged uncle was offering his own rice gruel to a young fighter, hoping to help him to regain strength, but the youngster was trying to walk away. Mugil remembered this happening to her often when she was a combatant. People were proud of the Tigers, especially the female combatants, and wanted to support them. The movement promised them freedom and an end to the war. What was a cup of tea or a plate of rice in exchange?

Moreover, the cadres had things you could get in return for your kindness. Like the use of their satellite phones, at 1,000 rupees per call, to areas under government control or abroad. Local calls cost 500 rupees, as much as three kilos of rice. The fighters also had more motorbikes than the civilians, and you could hitch a ride if you couldn't walk or had an injured family member. Today, however, people were giving up gold jewellery just for milk powder or drinking water.

Despite these changes and the no-fire-zone announcements, people stuck with the Tigers even if it could lead them to the battlefield. They couldn't yet trust the force that was waging war in their villages. The Tamils couldn't be sure that the army would not just shoot or burn hundreds of them and bury them in mass graves. To Mugil, too, the Chemmani massacre felt like it had happened yesterday. The army's grandstanding about taking over the Vanni territory and decimating the Tigers had been going on for twenty-six years. The Tigers had outwitted them all that time. What could change now?

So despite the surrender orders, Mugil saw people shielding the Tigers among them. Familiar faces dotted the crowd, some in uniform and some not. LTTE bunkers were visible between the civilian tents. Fighters walked in small groups, carrying food supplies on their backs or on the motorbikes or bicycles they pushed. They were like black specks in rice, trying in vain to blend in. It was on their instructions that people were going towards Mullaitivu instead of the places the army suggested.

Mugil began to collect some wood chips and twigs to build a fire before it rained again. She would boil half a fistful of rice, lace it with some crumbs of the fishy, salty *karuvaadu* and eat it with her aunt's gooseberry pickle.

She had barely begun when she heard a deep hum from the sky. Very quickly, it got louder. Others around her were also looking quizzically upwards and at each other. This was not a sound they recognised. It was thicker and deeper than the sound of a plane and not as clattering as a helicopter's. It wasn't a long-range missile's whistle or the crack of a bomb. It was a hum, as if emanating from a wasp the size of a fighter plane.

Reflexively, people ran back into the bunkers. Mugil crouched in one, about fifteen feet long and five feet deep, lined with stumps of coconut trees and covered with their large leaves. Husky coconut halves were holding down flimsy plastic bags that covered the gaps in the leaves. An entire tree had been dissected for this ephemeral safety. The children used to sing a rhyme about this: how generous the coconut tree, how tall it stands, how it sacrifices every part of itself.

Because of the rain, the wet mud was falling in clumps into the bunker, threatening to loosen the tree stumps. A man next to her started to pat the clay back with his palms, pasting it on the wall like cement. He did it slowly, as if he knew the futility of the exercise. His daughter, who looked to be between eight and ten years old, was copying him, patting the clay with her small fingers.

They must have stayed there for an hour, until Mugil heard people on the ground above her. They were coming out again, going back to cooking or fetching water. The danger had passed; there had been no explosion. She heard someone say that it must have been some new technology. 'Not bad, the army is keeping up with us these days,' the man in the bunker said, smiling. 'We'll try to figure it out when it comes next time. Or maybe by then, our boys will have built one of their own and will deliver a fitting reply!' People were laughing, making jokes about the army's dud fireworks.

Mugil smiled, but her mind was on that hum. She wanted to memorise the sound, its length, its timbre. Its newness made her edgy. Sounds from the sky always came with fire. Thunder and lightning. Whistle and blast. What would follow this noise?

After the hum faded, lunch preparations continued. The afternoon sun beat down, and people started to nod off under trees and makeshift tents. The bunkers were unbearably hot, so few went inside. Most children remained at ground level, running around.

A blinding flash and then an explosion; when the missile hit, no one was expecting it. They had ducked from the hum, only to stand around in the open, easy targets for the shelling that followed. They didn't know what it was called then, but the unfamiliar hum had been a drone. The army's eye in the sky. The harbinger of a shower of missiles. The Sri Lankan forces had never used one before.

Mugil stayed in her bunker, only surfacing after an hour. She walked in a daze around the bodies frozen in ugly shapes on the ground. Some who had made a late dash for a bunker were curled halfway near its mouth. The man who had patted down her bunker was calling out for his daughter. Mugil heard the words, but she couldn't internalise the girl's name. Her shin throbbed. Something had ripped into her and stayed inside.

She walked into a cluster of trees, sure only that she wanted to go home. There would be no more stopping, no more talking to people. She felt stupid. The deaths around her seemed ridiculous. Those girls in the mango orchard, their contorted bodies shrieking till death took them, and here, these people dropping face down on their lunch plates. Dying in shameful ways, walking naively into traps. One would think this was a people who had never seen a battle before.

She turned off the A35, wanting to avoid the main roads, and went into the jungle. As she entered the canopy, she took off her chain with the tiger tooth and dumped it in a muddy stream.

7.

July 2008

WHEN THEY DROVE Sarva out of the harbour area in a police van, his single fear was that Silva would bolt out of the station to say there had been a mistake, he was not to be let out yet, there was unfinished business. As they drove further and further away, this fear was replaced by disbelief. By the time the van pulled onto the premises of the Colombo Magistrate's Court, Sarva's relief was bordering on exhilaration. Was this the beginning of his march to freedom? He started to run the events of the past ten days through his mind. He would complain to the judge that justice had been denied him and demand to know why he had not been treated with the respect due to any citizen. He wasn't sure he should name names, however, just in case they sent him back there. He would not raise his voice and would remember to be clear, chronologically correct, and absolutely confident.

The courtroom was at the rear of the building on the ground floor. Sarva and his police escort walked side by side along the corridor, their arms and fingers entwined like lovers. The hand-holding replaced handcuffs, and several accused men stood at the back being similarly intimate with policemen.

At the bottom of a stairwell, Sarva's escort stopped near a lawyer and raised his hand in a gesture somewhere between a friendly hello and a wobbly half salute. The lawyer barely responded. They seemed to converse minimally, using familiar, routine words. Sarva, in his nervousness, missed most of the exchange except the lawyer's bored last words: 'After lunch.'

There was more than an hour to kill. The police escort took him to a tea shack on the first floor. Lawyers, policemen, clerks and legal service vendors stood around the all-purpose shop, slurping tea or biting into rolls. Some of them sat on a couple of benches inside, eating rapidly from rice-and-curry lunch packets. The escort handed Sarva a small glass cup of black tea while he himself tucked into a chicken roti. The tea was just as sweet as Sarva liked it.

They sat there for a while, sipping their tea quietly. It was half past twelve, and the humidity of July was trickling down Sarva's back. His T-shirt, the one he had been wearing the day he was grabbed off the street, displayed overlapping rings of sweat, new and old. He was embarrassed to look so slovenly in a court of law. In the van, he had picked out the dried mud from the sodden hem of the shirt's front, but it hadn't done much good. The police had left him no option but to look like scum, and he would be at a disadvantage from the second the judge set eyes on his T-shirt, hanging shapelessly from his drooping shoulders. His trousers, too, slipped hazardously from his waist.

As Sarva nursed his tea, looking down at his unkempt self, for a brief moment the policeman let go of his hand to pay the cashier. Sarva's heart thudded loudly in his chest. He felt nauseous and stared at the back of the escort's head. The moment seemed to grow longer, as if expecting him to respond, react, do something. He knew he would think of this moment later, in a future where he would not be afraid to run. But now he sat there, heat rising from his neck and his feet stone cold.

The hand gripped his again just as securely as before. It was almost a relief to be spared the responsibility of making a decision.

The buzz around the shack had died down, and they walked to the court downstairs. He had expected the court to be a large hall with wooden benches and an elderly judge who banged a gavel saying, 'Order! Order!' Indeed, an impatient judge did sit atop an elevated wooden podium, and a bored clerk on his left called case numbers and passed him files one after another. When people left the courtroom, they bowed to the judge and walked backwards out the door. Lawyers addressed him as 'Your Honour'. The colonial style was truly preserved, including the architecture of humiliation. Sarva was taken to the far end of the room and thrown into a cage with iron bars painted silver, within which stood all the accused. Family members and visitors sat on rows of benches with their backs to the cage, and occasionally they turned to look at the men behind bars. It was demeaning to make eye contact with strangers this way, so Sarva kept his gaze fixed on the judge.

A lot happened very quickly and with casual finality. The policeman accompanying Sarva gave a sheet of paper to a grubby lawyer, who in turn handed it to the judge. Sarva mentally readied himself for his speech at the three-sided dock, but the judge mumbled an English word and stamped the paper without a second thought. He had not even glanced at Sarva, let alone asked him a question. A decision seemed to have been made. He was led out of the court into another building and dragged a few floors down. The escort was almost running now; he had another accused to go hold hands with. Sarva's head was spinning, and his lower back was shooting arrows of pain down his legs. The stairs seemed to multiply with every step.

Finally, in a dark corridor, his escort let go of Sarva's hand. 'Go inside,' he barked, opening a metal gate. In front of them, a room, ten by twenty feet in size, was packed with men. It looked like all the passengers and hawkers hanging about the Pettah bus stop had been forced in here. There was nowhere to sit. Sarva's legs and back were useless after days of interrogation, and the arrows were now flying from his spine all over his body.

From behind him, the escort's voice boomed, demanding that the comatose men move their asses and make room. They all looked at Sarva but no one moved. Sarva shuffled to the centre of the room and continued to stand. The policeman locked the gate with a clatter.

Some men went back to their conversations while others stared blankly ahead in the dark. That was when Sarva realised there were no windows.

Straight from the solitariness of the police station's basement, through a whirlwind of hope, to a room with men who lay head to toe, packed like beedis: here was a new form of torment for the government's prisoners.

IT WAS HIS second night in the crowded room, and again a cacophony of snores woke him. Immediately he was aware of the sickly sweet smell of sweat laced with ganja smoke. There were feet right in front of his face. They looked surprisingly soft, the feet of one who wore shoes: someone well-to-do or a soldier. He wondered what this man might be in here for. He wanted to turn to his other side to be able to shut out the claustrophobia and fall asleep again, but he didn't want to wake the men sandwiching him. It was a tight squeeze.

Sarva propped himself up on his elbows. The corridor light bulb cast a checkered shadow on the sleeping men, like a blanket of iron bars. He counted the bodies. The previous night, there had been ninety. Today, there were seventy-eight, including himself. There had been a mad scramble for the spots of those who left. Sarva had been ashamed to shove about for a mere place to sit, especially with these men—murderers, smugglers, rapists, thieves of all races, shapes and sizes.

In the day, when they smoked ganja, peed in the open latrine in the corner, and swapped their stories, often proclaiming innocence, Sarva bit back his disgust. He felt he did not deserve to be thrown among these unclean low-lives, these immoral criminals. They didn't even seem bothered by the filth in the room; they were clearly used to seeing flies hover over dried urine in their slums or in other jails. He did not like this forced intimacy, lying among them, feeling their breath on his skin. He shouldn't be here.

'What happened?'

It startled him, this voice from the dark. It came from the owner of the clean foot. The man repeated the question.

Sarva hesitated before asking what was consuming him. Why are we here? Where will they take us next? What did the magistrate do? Did they tell you? Are you Sinhalese or Tamil? What have you done?

He only asked, 'Can you tell me? What is this place?'

The man looked amused. 'You really don't know?'

Sarva did not reply. He regretted having asked.

'This is hell's waiting room,' the man said, chuckling. He seemed to enjoy saying those words, introducing another newbie to a reality only a few were clever enough to decipher. To Sarva, these words meant nothing.

The next evening, Sarva was pulled out of the room along with about twenty others. He mustered up the courage to ask the guard where they were being taken. The guard told them they would be kept at 'CRP'. No one asked what that meant.

IN HIS NEW cell at the Colombo Remand Prison, or CRP, Sarva was holed up with forty other men. He spent the first week speaking to them entirely in Sinhala, easily and fluently. When they replied, he listened for the inflections of a native Tamil speaker. He was hoping to find a companion with whom to swap news and fears, to kill the time that stretched before him without end or purpose.

He hadn't spoken in Tamil since he had met his mother in the police station. He missed it on his tongue, missed seeing its twirls, dots and dashes leap from a page into realms of meaning. He wanted to ask for some literature, but he wasn't sure how many Tamil books the CRP would have or if asking for them would get him into trouble. Maybe some paper and a pen then, although he had never written anything but schoolwork in his life. He wasn't sure what he'd say, but he was dead certain something would come to him. A record of his experiences, just in case he never got out.

Before that, however, Sarva wanted to ask the jailer to have his room cleaned. The cells were less crowded than the one at the court, but they were putrid. The ammonia odour from the latrine in the corner floated through the room. Sarva felt as if someone had peed in his mouth. Others complained about it too, but only among themselves. One of the older inmates, seeing Sarva hold his nose through the day, snapped at him: 'Why, are you too special for this?' he asked. The comment stung. Later, he heard the man narrate the incident to another prisoner, but the quip was modified. It became: 'Why—are your people too special for this?'

Sarva tried to distract himself from the smell, but there was little to occupy the mind. CRP was boredom punctuated by mealtimes and line-ups:

Wake up at six; line up for a breakfast of tea, *sambol* and bread; sometimes rice.

At seven, back to the cell. He was rattled by the practice of prisoners locking the cell gates themselves, pulling the external latch shut from behind the bars. They huddled inside, willing captives doing away with their jailer.

At half past eight they lined up again, this time for a head count, after which they were free to roam the central courtyard. They played football or cricket or read magazines. Sarva didn't like the way most of them played cards, gambling with cigarettes. But since he rarely saw them smoke, he assumed for a long time that the smoking area was a secret, as everything seemed to be. One night, however, he found his sleeping spot in the cell taken by another man who had paid twenty cigarettes for a week of sound sleep.

Cigarettes seemed to buy you anything from a weekly sleeping spot to chilli powder to season the bland meals. Paid to those jail guards whose price was known, the cigarettes could negotiate a family visit on court days or a transfer to a preferred cell. If an apocryphal story were to be believed, a prisoner once even managed to smuggle in a local journalist in exchange for three packs. Beedis were for smoking. Cigarettes were currency.

Sarva deplored gambling—it just wasn't something decent people did—and its combination with cigarettes lowered it several notches. But he needed to get his sleeping spot back. So one morning he tried to join a game of rummy. As soon as he approached, the men sitting in a huddle stiffened. One of them raised his eyebrows at Sarva. Another turned his wrist and pointed behind Sarva, signalling that he'd better go away.

He turned around, feeling his face flush and his stomach constrict. His mother would have skinned him alive if she'd seen him join those gamblers. Why had he done that? Why had he stooped to their level?

He shook his head, berating himself: *Chi*! Shame on me, shame on me! He had given them the power to exclude him, to strip him further of his dignity. Those morally inept gamblers thought he was not good enough for them. *They* had sent *him* away. He started to wish more intensely that he was among his own people.

Although he had been careful not to speak in Tamil, something about him or the guards' attitude towards him had clearly given him away. They knew he was Tamil, and that he was under PTA, as they called it. Being charged under the Prevention of Terrorism Act changed everything. Rules, even if they could be bent, would not apply to a *Kottiya*. It did not matter whether he denied being in the Tigers or said he was trained against his will. In his cell, everyone claimed to be imprisoned for something he hadn't done—even the bug-eyed uncle who was always passing things to the guard during visiting hours. Or the boy whose mother shouted at him for having stolen from their employers. Or the drug addicts shaking violently with abdominal cramps and moaning all night. They all believed they were going to get out of there soon, go back to their wives, mothers, fathers and children. They all believed themselves to be innocent—that no court or police could prove otherwise. Sarva, however, had already been convicted in prison, and this justified his torment.

Even the trishaw driver Sarva played cricket with in the yard—the guy swore he had never beaten his wife and that she had him jailed because she was carrying on with another man—asked him suspiciously about his Sinhala. Where did he pick it up? 'How?' the wife-beater kept asking. 'How did you learn it?' Sarva's bilingualism had become a liability. It was as if he indulged in some deviant behaviour.

The prisoners all ate the same insipid food, endured the same crowded conditions and humiliations, but he could see that they still believed they were a step above him. He was often singled out from the line-ups for a body search. The guards treated them all as convicted criminals, so Sarva didn't expect any better from them. What rankled him was the enmity of his prison companions.

Guilt, innocence, charges, crime, height, age—nothing set apart one man's insults from another's. They stared. Pointed. Made lewd jokes. A scrawny boy once asked his friend loudly if this *Kottiya*—Sarva was doing stretches nearby—would ever have seen a girl naked. The other replied, 'No, no. Their great leader asks them to be celibate, you see! *Paavu*, he is a virgin!' He was the butt of abuse that ranged from the solitary word *Kottiya* spat with revulsion to elaborate comments about his dark skin and invitations to 'take all the Tamils and go back to India'. Some men came to his defence, saving him from bullies by joking with them just in time, or giving him the corner near the wall so that he could rest his aching back. But these small kindnesses did little to allay the all-consuming ugliness of the racism.

He could not sleep from worry that someone would slit his throat as soon as he shut his eyes. He was afraid to be found complaining of something and having that attributed in whispers to his being a national traitor. One afternoon while they were playing catch, the wife-beater casually asked, 'Even if you didn't actually shoot or anything, did you support Prabakaran or not?' He mentioned the name of the dreaded LTTE chief with easy familiarity, as if they were schoolmates. When Sarva was quiet, he wagged his finger, 'Ah, if you didn't oppose him, you supported him.' Sarva fumed that even if he might have, you could not put a person in jail for their thoughts. Their recreation time was becoming more unbearable by the day. In the pecking order of the prison, Sarva was the lowest vermin. He felt utterly alone.

Surprisingly, it was the wife-beater who made things easier. He was the closest thing Sarva had to a friend; they played cricket, taking turns at the bat. He seemed to be on top of all the prison gossip: who did what, said what, which jailer was easiest to bribe, at what times the food supplies came and how milk could be stolen from the kitchen. He also did an entertaining job of using colourful language to describe his wife and her alleged promiscuity. One day he said that if the Tamils hated the Sinhalese enough to become suicide bombers, he would gladly give them a separate state.

'Okay, at least tell me this,' the wife-beater said. 'Did you ever *want* to join the LTTE? I hear they come for you when you're just sprouting a moustache.' It was all he wanted to know about Sarva. Yet he had a silliness that sometimes made the rest of the drudgery tolerable.

Together, Sarva and the wife-beater classified the daily lunch menu as follows:

BROWN DAY (boiled tasteless mutton)
YELLOW DAY (dal and rice)
BROWN ONION DAY (mutton and onions)
RED DAY (sambol)
MUD DAY (an overcooked vegetable)
EGG DAY (boiled)
WHITE DAY (milk rice)

Asking for second helpings was frowned upon, but a handful asked and often got more, albeit with a pronounced scowl. Sarva didn't understand why more people didn't ask for an extra helping. Surely they couldn't be satisfied with just a couple of pieces of bread.

Wife-beater told him he shouldn't draw attention to himself by asking for more. But the question grew and grew in Sarva's mind, until one day, out of curiosity rather than hunger, he gingerly did ask for more.

He was served, but before he had turned around, his fresh portion of *sambol* was splattered on the ground.

A burly fellow prisoner stood before Sarva. 'Just like that?' the guy thundered. 'You will just ask … and take?'

The servers were giggling. Another swipe, and the plate clattered on the ground.

Sarva tried to keep his voice from trembling. 'Why, *ayya*? What did I do wrong?' he asked.

The big guy looked around, took a step back, and dramatically pointed both hands at Sarva, as if to ask the other lunching prisoners if they could believe their ears. Then he looked at the servers, who were prisoners on canteen duty. 'Give the blackie another plate. Aww, he is hungry,' he said, sticking his lower lip out in mock sympathy.

The servers looked unsure what to do.

The thug took a step towards Sarva. 'There are rules here,' he said, his voice a low growl. 'Learn them, *Kottiya*.' His face almost touching Sarva's, he said, 'I know about you.'

Sarva stood motionless.

From among the watching prisoners, a voice yelled, 'He is new. Leave it, Lasith *ayya*!'

Sarva took the cue. He looked at the ground and quickly mumbled, 'I'm new, *ayya*. I didn't know.' It seemed to satisfy the man glowering at him, but Sarva would later regret that it sounded like an apology.

By this time, a jail attendant had walked up, making noises as if he were dispersing sheep blocking a highway, 'Anh, okay, okay. Enough! Get lost!' To Lasith, he was a mildly annoyed parent. 'Whyyyy?' he asked indulgently in Sinhala. Lasith shrugged and lumbered away. Sarva looked for the wife-beater as the prisoners returned to their cells, but he seemed to be keeping his distance.

The consensus in Sarva's cell was that Lasith was a bootlegger. 'He spends more time doing business in jail than he did outside,' they said. If the prison was a den of vice, Lasith was its main supplier.

At three and six in the afternoon, when they were called for the line-up, Sarva scanned the faces for Lasith. He wasn't there. The count was just to check for runaways anyhow. Lasith was far too settled in the CRP to want to escape.

When they were walking back to their cells, the wife-beater emerged suddenly, hurrying towards Sarva. 'Don't go into your cell after the nine o'clock line-up!' he hissed. 'Lasith has it for you tonight.'

'What!' Sarva hissed back.

'Just don't go!'

There was such panic in his friend's voice that Sarva decided to take him seriously. After the evening line-up, he hung back till he was the only one left in the corridor. The guards looked surprised, then yelled for him to get inside. Sarva refused.

'What is this new drama?' a guard said, shoving him.

'No! I won't go in!' Sarva shouted.

A baton fell with a thwack on his already cracked lower back and he dropped to the floor. They dragged him into his cell with a stream of abuse.

That night, as wife-beater had warned, Sarva was awakened by a chaos of fists and feet: three—no, four men. One held him down, stepping on his forearms. The others—none was from his cell—stomped on him, pounded his abdomen, kicked his hips, stood on his chest.

Some prisoners ran to the gate and started to scream for the warden. It was about fifteen minutes before the guards came. By then, Sarva had curled up into a ball and was spitting blood.

The morning after the ambush, when he was brought back to the cell after seeing a doctor, he spat at the men in his cell. 'Cowards!' he yelled in Tamil. They'd shared a room, seen each other piss in a bucket, but none of them had defended him. Even the wife-beater felt like a potential danger now. He might have warned Sarva about the attack, but how had he known it would happen?

Sarva was shaken by the unadulterated hatred that drove the attackers. He had smelled their collective need to mete out punishment, squish the worm he was to them. They clearly thought they had the right to destroy him at will. Every vice Sarva witnessed—the marijuana smoking, the nightly cocaine and cigarette exchanges, the abusive language—he began to associate with the inmates' Sinhala-ness. He resented their lack of fear.

8.

January 2009

MUGIL REACHED PTK by mid-January. She'd spent almost two weeks on a circuitous route from Kilinochchi, which, by the main roads, was only about forty kilometres from PTK. The way was dotted with mines and pocked with shell craters and she feared the Tigers might spot her. Her shin was a dirty yellow and red now, thoroughly infected. The cloth bag that served as a bandage was soaked in blood and smelled rancid. Her head throbbed from thirst.

She had come this close to home. It would be a shameful waste if, at this point, she were pulled back into the Tigers' dwindling ranks. They were desperate now, hunting for people to throw in the lines, if only to hinder the army's progress. Many months ago, the LTTE had given three days of compulsory weapons training to entire villages, including children and the elderly, like her sixty-six-year-old father. Mugil's mother had tried to dissuade the recruiters, reminding them that this old man had printed pamphlets in the eighties for Thileepan's historic fast. Although he had been a Tiger leader, Thileepan had become an icon of nonviolence to the Tamils after he had starved to death protesting the massacres committed by Indian and Sri Lankan armies in Jaffna. Many people who had fasted in solidarity or helped organise Thileepan's protest afterwards laid down their guns. Mugil's father, too, had always said that seeing Thileepan's selfless determination had shifted something inside him. He had tried to explain this to the platoon subcommander rounding up villagers for training. Father asked why he had to train at his age, especially when he had served the Tigers for decades in other ways. He was told curtly that there are times when everyone must pick up a gun.

On the outskirts of town, Mugil waited to make sure the Tigers were not watching. When the torrential rain let up and the armoured trucks moved, she lay stomach-down in a trench. When it poured in sheets, obscuring vision, she dashed into PTK.

In the Vanni, PTK was held up as a model of development, with concrete bungalows, temples and churches, lush parks and good high schools. It was an example of what the Tamil homeland could look like. People often said that if ever there were a mall in Tamil Eelam, there was no doubt it would be in PTK, with Kilinochchi putting up a good fight. When Mugil described her hometown to anyone, she used a popular standard in the Vanni: here, she said, a young woman could walk alone on the streets at night. According to her, for a woman, there was no safer place in Sri Lanka than PTK.

While its residents swore by PTK's modern spirit, it was, before anything else, a town steeped in war. Opposite the government hospital was a United Nations relief office. There were three orphanages, a home for the elderly and destitute, and a vocational centre for the hundreds of men and women—militants and civilians—disabled by the conflict. In the town centre was the Pass Office, where the Tigers gave—and often refused—passes for civilians to leave Vanni for a day, a week, or a few weeks, based on the guarantee of another resident family. Long queues were common outside this office. In the schools, students were given reflex drills and shown how to run to bunkers during air raids. Some seesaws in the playgrounds were shaped like AK-47s. School walls were plastered with pictures of martyrs and grotesque images of Sri Lankan state leaders and presidents grinning over piles of dead Tamils. The children added their touch to the images, drawing devil horns on the politicians' heads. Trees and fences held notices with stencil prints of a burning candle, the symbol of mourning. Every family living in PTK had arrived here after being forcibly displaced by battle or evacuation.

Now PTK was heaving again with thousands of people. This time, there were families hailing from the far west to the east, occupying every inch of space. Those from the eastern provinces had been on the road for more than a year. Most had relocated about two dozen times in less than three months, searching for safety from army bombardment in the shrinking Tiger territory. The Tigers told them to stay calm and move to PTK, to the south of which they held a strongly fortified redoubt, the only one left apart from the units in Mullaitivu. People arrived in droves. They believed Annan had a plan, as he always did, a stunning strategic strike that he would launch at the opportune moment. For now, however, it was mayhem.

By the time Mugil reached her parents' house, the red dusk had darkened. As she approached the doorway, feeling with her feet for craters and bunkers in the courtyard, someone called out, 'Akka!' It was the raspy voice of her younger sister, Amuda. 'Akka! No one's there!'

Amuda had lived in Paranthan, a village in Kilinochchi district, with her husband Siva, who worked with her in the Tigers' farm accounts department. Their son was six and their daughter Kalai was two, born two months after Mugil's second, Tamizh.

Mugil's mother compared the sisters' relationship to that of a snake and a mongoose. Mugil and Amuda were rival siblings; one was always cutting the other down to size. Mugil had been particularly exasperated by Amuda's polio. When they were children, Mugil was expected to do all the housework because Amuda was too weak to sweep, unable to squat to cook by their floor-level stoves, or too embarrassed to go to the market. Mugil and Prashant, the youngest one, were close, and they ganged up against Amuda and the third sibling, Priyamvada, who was a perpetually ill crybaby. Mugil also thought Amuda lazy, even cowardly, for escaping recruitment into the Tigers. It was unfair of her; she knew Amuda was physically challenged, but she couldn't help suspecting that her sister exaggerated her disability to get away with a lot. When Amuda entered a love marriage with Siva, a soft-spoken, artistic, handsome upper-caste man who composed soulful songs for the LTTE's propaganda movies, Mugil had not hidden her surprise. '*Kaakaikki mayil,*' she had joked cruelly, twisting an old saying. A crow gets a peacock.

Amuda, for her part, thought Mugil had grown pompous because of her career with the movement. She liked being a mother and an accountant. 'Everyone helps in their own way,' she would say when they fought openly. 'Don't think you're some great hero just because you wear a uniform.' Mugil, who was in the Malathi unit by the time she was a teenager, would retort, 'It's not about uniform. It's about how much of your life you're willing to sacrifice.'

When Mugil was injured and pulled off the fighting cadre, Amuda picked that moment to tell their mother that her 'arrogant' sister would 'feel the pain now'. Once Mugil learnt about this, they stopped talking altogether. The fights ended, but so did any chance of reconciliation.

Now, the rival sibling approached her, limping slowly. Relief and nervousness made Mugil exclaim as if she'd run into a long-lost friend on the street. 'Amu!' she yelled. 'When did you get here?'

'Come, come, Mother and all are in the bunker,' Amuda said. 'We need to leave. We were waiting for some news from you.'

They walked in silence for a while before Mugil found something to say. 'So? Where is my tiny devil Kalai?'

'Must be playing with her brothers,' Amuda said. She grumbled that Kalai had been throwing too many tantrums. 'We forgot her colour pencil box and she won't stop crying about it.'

'She's a baby. Maybe she's hungry.'

'Everyone's hungry.'

'And Siva? How is your husband?'

'Kfir *adichchadu,*' Amuda said, her face placid. One of the army's Kfir missiles hit him. 'Just as we left Paranthan. He had gone outside the bunker to get the rice gruel and curry we had cooked, and the Kfir hit him. Dead on the spot, gone.'

The Sri Lankan army owned seven Kfir ground-attack fighter aircraft bought from Israel to use against the LTTE. When the Sri Lankan air force dropped long-range missiles on the Vanni from close quarters, hundreds of civilians died with the Tigers.

Amuda continued, 'I just watched him burn. I covered Kalai's eyes. She was his pet.'

Mugil wanted to hold her sister's hand or at least meet her eye to reassure her. But they'd never had that kind of relationship.

'The body?' Mugil asked.

'I left it there and came back. I had to get the children.'

'But you saw the body? You're sure it was him?'

Amuda nodded.

Mugil persisted. 'You're sure he was gone?'

'Yes. I went to his body two days later. It was lying there, piled with eight or ten others on a tractor. I had to take his purse from his pocket. He had all our money and I had to leave. I will never forget that I did that.'

It was the longest conversation they'd had in years. And Mugil had asked about the dead body more than she had consoled her sister. But Mugil had to find out. In their fear and panic, too many people were leaving their loved ones behind, sometimes mistaking a severe injury for a fatal one. She had to make sure her sister had checked.

Amuda led Mugil to the bunker their family shared with a few others. Mugil and Prashant had dug this for their parents years ago and taught them how to add sandbags, repair and waterproof it. It had three levels: the damp ground floor, which was the safest but most suffocating section, a lumpy mezzanine for storing bags, and a breezier upper level for when immediate danger had passed. It also had a small alcove with a dry toilet. They believed it to be one of the more durable underground structures in the area.

Newly arrived families didn't have such bunkers. Many simply dug hasty trenches and covered them with tarpaulin or coconut leaves. Otherwise, they just sat by the roads, in yards, across fields. Mugil could not tell how many there were, but she saw thousands of heads catch the headlights of vehicles, their hair glowing as if on fire.

Mugil found her mother sitting on the bunker's upper level, the roof off, painstakingly cleaning a banana flower. When she saw Mugil, she held it up. 'See! I can't believe this was just hanging on the tree and no one had got their hands on it yet!' Even on good days, Mother was all skin and bones, but now, with no oil in her white hair, her eyes sunken and lips chapped, she looked a hundred years old.

Inside the bunker there were people Mugil didn't recognise. Mother had taken in a distantly related elderly couple, and their very pregnant granddaughter. She looked no older than sixteen.

'Her husband was taken by Pottu Amman,' Mother whispered, pointing to the girl. Pottu Amman, the senior LTTE leader now in charge of PTK, had stepped up the recruitment of underage boys and girls. Several families were going to great lengths to protect their children. Boys and girls hunkered down in bunkers, never venturing out. Parents married them off in their teens, hoping the recruiters would then spare them. The girls were encouraged to get pregnant to escape conscription. Self-preservation had pushed her people to reject practices they'd followed for years.

Mugil said hello to the pregnant girl, and asked how far along she was. 'Five months,' she said. Her voice was high like a child's.

Amuda called Mugil's sons. 'Maran! Tamizh! Look who's come!' Maran emerged from the dark, running towards them. He saw Mugil but coolly turned away and sat next to his grandmother, sucking on the flower pods. If he had missed his mother, he didn't show it.

Tamizh, on the other hand, started to cry uncontrollably. Mugil held her baby, hugging him and, as a distraction, described some birds she had seen on the way there. He felt bony and weightless in her hands. He had only one slipper on, and his eyes were bloodshot. Mother said he had not slept in four days. He just would not close his eyes. Mugil rocked him in her arms, not sure if it would help.

Around them, half-lit people bobbed slowly in the expanse, making supper or getting ready to sleep. The bunker next to theirs, however, was abuzz. Mugil's mother said their neighbours believed that the worst bombing came at night, and they did not want to 'lie down and die for the army'. No one who took shelter in that bunker was allowed to sleep at night.

Wherever it was in the Vanni, each bunker had a character: its own obsessions, its own schedule, its own fears. One large bunker in Uruthurapuram, occupied largely by the elderly, was lined with blue tarpaulin hoarded by the occupants, who felt the rain to be their greatest enemy. The residents of a rectangular trench near what was once the office of the Coir Cooperative Society followed a strict roster to maintain a nightly lookout. A disabled former combatant called Manian enforced this with such fervour that even after pneumonia did him in, the bunker's inmates followed his routine. Next to the Manian bunker was the 'ladies' bunker'. This trench, with eight women and seven young children, had become a kitchen of sorts. They cooked gruel or *paruppu* at every opportunity and distributed it to others in exchange for milk, firewood, medicines or groceries. For survival, they were counting on the men's *uppu kadan*, the moral debt incurred by eating someone else's cooking.

Packed with splintered households and strangers from different villages, the bunkers created new families with every battle. Years afterwards, bunk mates would recognise each other on the street and greet each other with the melancholic joy of survivors. They would ask if that broken limb had healed, if the family was together, if mother had overcome her paranoia, if the army had finally allowed them to go home, if they were planning to go abroad. The raw bonds forged while crouching underground, among people thrown together by catastrophe, would last a lifetime.

MUGIL'S FATHER HAD been out gathering firewood. On his return, he immediately sat down to ask her if she knew what was going on. Military strategy was his preferred topic of conversation, especially with the daughter he always called his 'first son'. When he began the 'battle talk', as Mother used to call it, Amuda walked away.

Father said Divyan and Prashant had come by some days ago, bringing news: Kilinochchi was captured, and the army had crossed Elephant Pass. Mullaitivu was still standing, but Divyan had hinted that they were surrounded there, too. Prashant, however, had assured him that 'something will change and we will hit back'.

Father reported her little brother's assertion with a wry smile. The latest in their family to work with the LTTE, Prashant had the passion of a recent convert. He was good for morale and made a resolute soldier, but Mugil knew it would be years before he learnt to balance obedience with discretion. Father trusted her instinct, however, and wanted to know if their decision to leave PTK was well advised. 'We're being fired at here, so shouldn't we try to leave for Vavuniya or Jaffna by boat?'

Mugil told him what she had seen on the way—the retreat of LTTE units towards PTK. But she felt muddled about what to make of it, unable to judge if being near the Tigers meant they'd be protected or if they'd end up in the line of fire.

In similar situations since the nineties, the LTTE had usually kept the Tamil civilians with them, even forcing them to leave their villages with the movement of cadres. It had led to hundreds of deaths, but had saved many more lives. Exodus was the very foundation of the Vanni. Cadres internalised the practice: if civilians were removed from the picture, the army would have a free hand to bomb the fighters. And if the fighters lost and ceded territory, inch by inch, the dream of a Tamil homeland would go up in smoke. Keeping civilians around them was the way these guerrilla forces fought. It bought them time and, often, resources.

But on the other side of the line now, Mugil was disconcerted. Had the battle followed them or had they been led into the battle? What if she and her father were dragged out to fight? Perhaps it would be worth the risk to defy orders and leave. Would the Tigers ostracise her family if they won the war? Moreover, leaving the area meant they would have to fend for themselves. Here, the Tigers were accompanied by ration lorries, from which you could buy food. Even if a coconut cost 600 rupees, at least it was available. What would be in store for them at the other end, where the army was? She wasn't sure she could abandon the saviour and embrace the attackers. If they were not under the Tigers' care, who could her family turn to? Was it time to tell father about the mango orchard, about her hopelessness? Aloud, she said, 'We've never been surrounded this tightly before. Maybe the leaders know something we don't. Divyan and Prashant are on duty, we should listen to them for now. Let's stay put until they return.'

'Why is Pottu Amman in charge of PTK?' Father asked next. 'What happened to Ratnam Master?'

The supreme leader's special friendship with his right-hand man Pottu Amman had decayed around 2007, when he replaced him with Ratnam Master. If all of Vanni was heading to PTK, her father was puzzled as to why Annan's most trustworthy commander had not been put in charge.

Mugil realised that Father was speaking to her as if she were still privy to the inner workings of the LTTE. She wanted to tell him that she wasn't sure her leaders even had a coherent plan—that if Pottu Amman was dragging unwilling children into war, this was probably the last stage. But her father wouldn't believe that. She wasn't sure she did entirely. So she told him that Pottu Amman was still holding onto PTK while other zones had been captured. 'So maybe it's good we have him here,' she said.

'He'd better not surrender and sing like the others,' Father said.

As soon as he said this, the old man, the pregnant girl's grandfather, seemed to stir awake. 'Don't count on it,' he scoffed, shaking his head in a way that annoyed Mugil. 'There are so many spies and leaks on our side now. It's better the leaders keep their plans close to their chests.'

This was a familiar refrain. Traitors—*throhis*—were the ghosts of Vanni. Everyone believed in them but few had evidence. They were considered the hidden rot in an otherwise perfectly healthy system, and leaders didn't think twice before putting a gun to their heads. Anyone could prove a traitor—it could be a friend, relative, or comrade—and, since there was always the threat of army torture, no one could be sure of not becoming one some day. Every combatant feared succumbing to coercion and divulging strategic secrets. So throughout training, each fighter was warned that a moment of weakness could mean the death of thousands of Tamils, perhaps even his or her family. The fatal cyanide vial, which every cadre carried, was the potent symbol of this dread of the *throhi*. Biting on one, and committing suicide on capture meant you avoided the shame of betraying your community.

Treachery was not solely a matter of divulging secrets to the enemy. Infractions of protocol or convention could prove unforgiveable—a sign of disloyalty, for instance, or a desire to cut ties with the LTTE. Privileging family over the Tamil nation, harbouring personal ambition or merely demonstrating critical thought could damn you. The price for questioning the LTTE's actions was death. Rajini Thiranagama, a former combatant, wrote about the atrocities committed by the Sri Lankan army and the Indian army stationed in the north in the late eighties, as well as similar crimes of the Tamil militias, including the LTTE. It was the Tigers who killed her in 1989. Thiranagama's co-authors, professors from Jaffna University, fled the country, fearing the same fate. The Tigers had always been a tough outfit, but once they had hunted down their competitors among the militants and emerged as the unrivalled leaders in the Vanni, a ruthlessness entered their bones. They didn't tolerate any view that contradicted their propaganda.

Lest their comments be carried to the high command, Vanni's residents largely avoided talking about the workings of the LTTE unless it was to eulogise the movement. Doubt or negativity among civilians, it was said, would hinder the Eelam mission. Death, fear, depression, none of it was considered a good reason for a Tamil to retreat from the Vanni. Prabakaran once said in his annual speech on Martyrs' Day that traitors were 'more dishonourable than enemies'. Lost battles were blamed on betrayal, and considerable energy was spent on rooting out spies and informers.

Her community blamed the ongoing war squarely on someone it considered, as did Mugil, to be the greatest traitor of them all: Colonel Karuna, the eastern wing commander, who had been close to Annan but broke away from the Tigers in 2006. Since then, the Vanni was inching towards decimation.

Mugil was wary of spies, like everyone else, yet reluctant to encourage the gossipy direction of the grandfather's comment.

'They won't all turn out to be like Karuna,' she said. 'We wouldn't have come so far without loyal fighters.' She would have said more but was afraid her recent doubts would become obvious.

'Oho! How could they know of our hideouts if *throhis* hadn't blabbed?' the grandfather argued. 'Oh, how will we win with people stabbing us in the back all the time? We need to support the movement at this time.'

Mugil didn't understand how this man could gabble on about *throhis* and winning the war when his own grandson had so recently been forcibly taken by Pottu Amman. She, too, wanted nothing more than for the Tigers to thrash the army, but she had other ideas about who the real traitors were. She was sure it was the political wing that was stealing the children. No sane military would enlist children if they were serious about winning. She couldn't fathom why the Tiger military leaders weren't sending the children back. Divyan had been saying for months that they were understaffed, but she thought pushing raw recruits out to fight was inefficient. That's why her camera had been full of new faces lying dead throughout the battlefield. That's why the Tigers were retreating like never before. That's why people were ready to abandon the side they had stood by for decades.

Before she could bite it back, the words rolled out of her: 'I'll tell you something, *thatha*. We won't lose because of traitors. We will lose because of five-paisa ideas like sending out baby recruits to fight an army.'

The old man looked at Mugil pointedly. 'How have you escaped fighting and run away?'

'What's it to you?' Mugil snapped. Her mother, listening in silence until now, slapped her thigh to shush her.

'Don't talk like that, *thatha*,' her mother told the old man. 'She has done her duty already. Now she's come home to her children, that's all. My son and son-in-law are still in the field, anyway. We're doing our duty.'

Mother then looked at Mugil pointedly and asked her to serve the food on the leaf plates. She called Amuda and her kids. 'Enough of this useless talk. Shall we eat?'

Quietly, they ate their first meal of the day, digging into the banana flower *poriyal* (made without coconuts or chillies), boiled *kadala paruppu* and rice. Mugil's mother had a lifetime's experience of making do with limited ingredients, but this was a stretch even for her. A UN truck had brought vegetables and rice, but Mugil's father had not even made it through the crowd that milled around the distribution area. Mother had then fallen at strangers' feet, crying about her hungry grandchildren, begging for a share of their supplies. One woman had given in, but only after Mugil's mother handed over a thin gold bangle for five handfuls of rice.

That night, Mugil prepared to sleep on the highest level, her favoured position in any bunker, from which she could keep an eye on the ground. The grandfather, however, announced loudly that it would be better for the ladies to sleep on the lowest level. Mugil had a mixed urge to both laugh and scream. He wouldn't have dared speak this way if she were in uniform or if her husband were there.

Lying down in the bunker was impossible; there were too many people. They made space for the pregnant girl to sleep on her side, and the other women sat upright. Maran curled up with his cousin. Kalai slept across her grandmother and Amuda. Tamizh, still awake, sat listlessly on Mugil's lap. She patted his back. It was cold, but the bodies pressing against each other were comforting. Mugil felt her eyelids shut, even though gunfire rang out at close range.

SHE WAS WOKEN by Maran's soft crying. Between thunderclaps, Mugil heard explosions. Behind them was the continuous crackle of small arms, some of it close. She peeped through the periscope-like tunnel, from which one could see the ground above. White streaks of fire whizzed through the purple sky. People were running, crying, searching for each other, wild with confusion. The old man and her father hurried to the bottom floor. No one talked while her mother's fevered chant of the *kandhar shashti kavacham* prayer wrapped itself around them. This was the bunker's circle of trust, the space they could understand and return to every time the world above turned into a blur of bullets, fire and falling men.

For the next three days, PTK was under siege. The Tigers were engaging the 58th division of the army marching from Viswamadu. The cadre had reverted to guerrilla ways and was constantly changing position, firing at the army and immediately moving to another location. When the army responded with missiles, they would hit only ill-informed villagers. The army was equipped with long-range missile launchers, and as it closed in from the west, it loosed them continuously.

The missiles fell round the clock. On the second day, a piece of red-hot metal nearly sliced open Maran's eye. On the third, the old man went outside during a lull and did not return. Mugil had known him for barely two days. On the fourth day, his granddaughter would not stop saying, 'They will kill my baby.'

At one point, while everyone in the bunker hid their faces between their knees to avoid the flying embers and the shrapnel, a man dove into their huddle, screaming. The children shrieked. His leg was on fire, and he seemed so stiff with panic that for a second Mugil thought he was dead. They scooped some wet sand from the bags and threw it on his burning limb till he fainted. As the smell of burnt flesh filled the bunker, Mugil realised that the man's dive had left a gaping hole in their bunker roof.

When he came to, the man broke down—he was looking for his children and aged parents. He had lost them a few days earlier and had been sure they would be in PTK. Mugil told him to stay in the bunker until the firing ceased; he was now part of their circle. For two days, they nursed his wounds as best they could, but they could not stop his weeping.

As PTK continued to be pulverised, on 21 January, the government announced a no-fire zone along the A35. It was a thirty-five-square-kilometre triangular patch of land, and its points were Suthanthirapuram junction, a yellow bridge and Thevipuram colony. Heavy fighting surrounded it, but the army promised civilians safety there. As the announcement boomed in Sinhala-accented Tamil from the army jeeps fitted with loudspeakers, the burning man didn't wait a moment to announce his decision to leave.

'Will you make it?' Mugil's mother asked, pointing to his rotting leg. She had used her last spare sari to bandage his thigh, and the fabric was soaked with a yellowish secretion.

'I don't want to think about that,' he replied. 'I can't sleep, eat or breathe. You are all fortunate you're still together.'

The burning man left their bunker early the next morning, after touching Mother's feet. Mugil would never know if he made it out PTK.

AFTER SEVERAL WET days, sunshine lit the bunker in patches. No bombers had come that morning, nor had the rain. For the first time in months, Mugil heard birds sing. After sunrise, on 29 January, the Sri Lankan government had announced a forty-eight-hour safe-passage window to allow civilians to move into the Thevipuram no-fire zone.

The streets filled with families, bicycles and motorbikes, tractors, trishaws and bullock carts loaded with possessions double their weight. It was almost impossible to move, and time was ticking away. In half a day, most people travelled just a few metres. Simmering impatience exploded into futile fights: a story did the rounds that a man had slit the throat of a motorist who ran over his foot.

People were desperate to get out of the town, but most couldn't. Tiger units forbade them to seek protection from the army. Mother wanted to leave for the no-fire zone, fearing she would go the same way as the old man, but Father could not make up his mind. If they left before Divyan got in touch, it would be difficult to find each other later. Others in the bunker were ready to cross over to the army's side, but it was clear that first the pregnant girl would have to be calmed down. She was now borderline hysterical. She was sure her child had died inside her womb. 'See, *akka*? See? There is no movement. Touch and see!'

Mugil decided to take the girl to the town hospital and have her own badly infected shin examined. Mother asked her to get food on the way, or at least water, lemon and salt. The children were wilting with dehydration. Kalai was sucking her thumb and clawing at Amuda's dry breast.

The road to the hospital was not as treacherous as Mugil expected; the firing had stopped for a few hours and the town was streaked with bloody sludge. Families leaving for the no-fire zone had removed mud-caked bodies from the road and placed them by the side, so their tractors, vans, bikes and cycles could pass. Almost skidding on an abandoned slipper, Mugil had an odd thought—that there must be twice as many desolate slippers as dead people.

The PTK government hospital looked like a crowded market for wounds and flies. There were people moving through the gate, through the compound and up the steps. Others had spread straw mats or saris and lay on them in the heat, waiting for a doctor to call or come by. Insects buzzed everywhere. A toddler was sitting on a bench outside, his left eye bandaged, his right teary. Someone had given him some candy, which he ate dreamily.

She had expected there to be blood everywhere, but all she saw were several colours of infection. Very few had fresh wounds; most were days, weeks, months old, often with fraying temporary bandages. The usual hospital smell of antiseptic was overpowered by the putrid stench of decay.

When they entered the corridor, they saw a grieving man throw himself on a small shrouded body. A child's feet, wearing thick silver anklets, stuck out from under the dirty bed sheet. A woman crouched next to the child, looking away. A doctor, his once-white coat smeared with many shades of rust, stood with a pad and pen in his hands. A man and three women were hassling him, pulling him in different directions. He walked to an old woman sitting below a window, her eyes closed. He sat down next to her, holding his back as he did so. That's when Mugil noticed a long piece of bark lodged in the woman's side. Her abdomen seemed to have closed in around it, as if trying to digest it. Mugil watched the doctor talk continuously to the woman in Tamil while his orderly yanked the bark out in one motion. Anticipating the woman's scream, Mugil clapped her hands to her ears and turned away.

Doctors were operating in open rooms or right there in the corridors. There was no electricity, so large vats of water were being boiled in the backyard on wood fires. The medical staff just dipped the steel clamps, knives and other surgical implements in cloudy hot water before plunging them into people. They were already rationing supplies of gauze, asking people to rip up their own clothes and use them as bandages. As hundreds came for treatment every day, the doctors worked for long stretches without sleep, sometimes forgetting to take a break or eat until they fainted.

Behind Mugil was a doctor whose fingers poked inside a man's forearm. A woman who acted like a nurse but wasn't dressed in white fed the patient a few spoonfuls of glucose. Mugil went up to her with the pregnant girl and asked if she could tell whether the baby was dead. When she was done with the male patient, without a word, the nurse touched the girl's belly and put a stethoscope to her wrist and neck.

'It is alive, but the heartbeat is very faint. Maybe it has twisted itself in the umbilical cord. Leave her here, we'll see,' the nurse said.

Mugil looked at the pregnant girl, who nodded that she would be okay in the hospital. 'Just send my grandmother here when you get home.' She'd referred to the bunker they'd shared as home.

Mugil then pointed to her own shin. 'I can't walk. Will the infection spread? Will this go away?' she said to the nurse, trying to speak fast and clear.

'Is there something inside?'

'I felt around. Something might be there. I'm not sure.'

'You have some antiseptic or hot water? Or sugar?' the nurse asked.

Mugil smiled. 'No, I only have an X-ray machine in my bunker,' she said.

The nurse responded with a tired smile. 'Okay, here,' she said, handing Mugil half a strip of headache tablets. Mugil asked if she really had nothing else. The nurse swivelled her head, inviting Mugil to look around. 'Army is not letting the ICRC or UN people bring in the proper medicines,' she said. The government didn't want the Tigers accessing emergency painkillers like ketamine for their battle-injured fighters. Because of the embargo on fuel, cold storage sections in the hospital were not able to preserve blood or store oxygen either. The nurse hurriedly showed Mugil how to place a splint on the back of her leg and tie it on with a bandage. 'It'll help you walk. There's nothing else I can do for you.'

Outside, for a few hundred rupees, from the Tigers' cooperative lorry, Mugil bought a piece of pumpkin, 100 grams of milk powder and a bottle of supposedly clean water, which had tiny things floating in it. The supplies came from the UN and the Indian government, but somehow it was the Tiger cadre that was distributing them. They didn't have any lemons. A handful of salt, dirty and wet, was 1,000 rupees. Mugil wished she had kept the Tiger tooth. It was gold-plated.

She hobbled back to the bunker and sent the pregnant girl's grandmother to the hospital. They hugged and said they would meet sometime soon, when all this was over.

The next day, on 1 February, the Sri Lankan army rained artillery shells on the PTK hospital for more than four hours.

9.

February 2009

NO ONE WAS held responsible, no one was punished or even questioned. After all, everything could be denied.

Sarva had written a letter describing the prisoners' attack on him, begging to be moved out of the CRP; he had posted it blindly to 'The Honourable President Mahinda Rajapakse, Sri Lanka'. Two months later, Sarva had been finally shifted to the Welikada New Magazine Prison on the outskirts of Colombo city. It was the largest in the country. He couldn't be sure if this was in response to his request or simply the turning of the system's unseen wheels. In any case, the transfer hadn't come a day too soon.

The G Cell of the H Ward, where he was now, was exclusively for political prisoners: social workers, politicians, union leaders, protesters, even some army deserters. But the majority were suspected of being Tamil Tigers or their sympathisers. When Sarva was escorted inside, the inmates were lining up to go back to their cells after yard time. He saw most of them take their slippers off outside their cell gates. He felt weak with relief.

Among these men, Sarva spoke in Tamil freely, even to excess. An ageing prisoner from his cell once asked why Sarva 'jabbered away like someone had turned on a tap inside him'. The places the prisoners came from, their schools, their wives' villages, their favourite foods—anything would suffice for Sarva to find a connection. During the very first week in his cell, he swapped notes with twenty-nine-year-old Rooban about their idyllic childhoods. The stealing of mangoes in summer, the anger on losing one's precious marbles or wickets to a bully, the devouring of stories in Tamil literature textbooks even before classes began. Rooban used to work in a rice mill. He had a handsome face and lustrous hair, but it was his timidity that was his most pronounced physical characteristic.

When Sarva was brought to the cell, Rooban saw him wincing while sitting on the floor. 'I can't sit down either,' he said. 'Is it only your lower back or your feet, too?'

'Feet also,' Sarva replied.

Rooban said he was from Valaignarmadam, in Mullaitivu in the north. 'Where are you from?'

'Nuwara Eliya,' Sarva had said first, but then added, 'My mother's side is from the north.'

Like Sarva, Rooban had been pulled off a street, but in Vavuniya, a city in the north that was under government control. He was detained in a cow shed for about six months along with three strangers he had not heard of since. When his bladder had ruptured from a severe kicking, he was moved to a hospital in Colombo and then to the TID basement. He was cagey about the details of what happened to him there except for mentioning once that he was suspended from the ceiling by his ankles for half a day with a bucket of petrol evaporating slowly beneath his head. His interrogators had asked him to sing the national anthem in Sinhala, and he had only known the Tamil version learnt in school. It was a state-approved Tamil translation of the Sri Lankan anthem that government schools all over the north taught, but in a dark room with the anti-terrorism police, nothing was innocuous.

In prison, Sarva saw Rooban struggle to comprehend Sinhala instructions and get into tight spots with officials who didn't speak Tamil. He wasn't 'one of those separatists' who didn't want to learn Sinhala, Rooban said. In his part of the country, he had never needed more than Tamil. Sarva told him not to bother learning Sinhala. After all, Sarva spoke Sinhala, and he was accused of espionage.

During a morning assembly in their ward a few months later, when the national anthem was being sung, Rooban and Sarva broke into the Tamil rendition, hoping to get caught so that they could retort that the Tamil anthem wasn't outlawed. No one noticed, however, until, in desperation, they switched to the dirty version passed on for generations by older boys to high school kids. This variant moved a few words around, turning patriotic descriptions of Mother Sri Lanka into a tribute from hormonal teenagers to a curvaceous woman. When the part about 'thou, laden with luscious fruit' set off the giggles among a whole section of inmates, the friends were finally punished with sweeping duty for a week. A week later, they did it again.

They spread silly rumours about prisoners: that the gruff cellmate had a mellifluous voice, the vegetarian had taken to meat, the cricketer Muthiah Muralitharan was soon to visit. When the day prison officials gave in to the G Cell's demand for a Pillaiyar statue for prayer, Rooban and Sarva suggested smuggling mobile phones in through the statue's pot belly. They got a parent to seal a phone on the inside of the papier mâché idol and deliver it covered in garlands during visiting hours. Another prisoner bribed a guard so he wouldn't run a metal detector over the idol, but Sarva and Rooban always took credit for the idea. They behaved as if they were in school, rebelling against suffocating rules and routines in small, entertaining ways. Sarva told Rooban that with him around, he sometimes forgot that he was in prison for the worst crime in the country.

If there was a brutal reminder of where they were, it was the ritual they underwent every fortnight. Neither Sarva nor Rooban were told why they were taken to a basement every fifteen days in batches of sixty, a metal chain looping through the cuffs on their wrists and ankles. It was a long human snake, the distance between the prisoners shortening towards the end. Barely five inches separated the last of the chained men, and as they walked down three flights of stairs to a dark basement, they shuffled and bumped into each other. Once, a prisoner tripped and about fifty-five of them tumbled with him. As if the broken ribs, chipped teeth and injuries were not enough, the guards immediately swung batons at them, accusing them of deliberately delaying the procedure by creating a ruckus. Rooban, who found himself underneath two other prisoners, fractured his forearm.

In this basement, a man of authority sat on an old wooden chair at a metal table covered with files. In the sick white glow of a humming fluorescent light, he scanned the files and called out names or numbers. As the prisoner called came forward, the seated figure glanced up almost imperceptibly and stamped a sheet of paper. Next!

The process took a whole day, as several chains of prisoners were brought in and took turns going to the front. Through it all, the chains stayed on their wrists. No toilet breaks were allowed, all meals for the day were cancelled, no talking was tolerated. It was a soul-deadening exercise, exhausting and disorienting. Every time, Sarva imagined that the stamp was on his neck, like red-hot metal branding cattle. The prisoners called this *paathalam*, the hell underground.

Only after months did Sarva and Rooban realise that the *paathalam* was the prison's court and the stamp a fortnightly extension of their detention. The anti-terrorism law they were arrested under allowed the Investigation Department to keep them in remand prison or in a police station for three months without being charged, even before they had a shred of evidence against them. Once the three months were up, the police asked for more time to gather evidence for a charge sheet, and they kept doing so every two weeks. These extensions, under the PTA, could allow for endless detention and more harassment of the prisoner. Charges were filed in very few cases; eventually detainees would have spent anywhere from six months to several years wasting away in jail, still unclear as to what they were being accused of.

Sarva understood some of this only after Amma hired a lawyer in January 2009. The advocate on record, Mr Vel, visited only once, and Sarva was too intimidated to ask the various whys, whats, and hows he was bursting with. He knew he was being accused of terrorism, of having worked for the LTTE as a spy. But he didn't get why he was moved from prison to prison, what he was waiting for, what remand meant, why the lawyer said he could do nothing until the police actually filed charges, 'which could be anytime or never'. It was only after Mr Vel's junior lawyer, a young, cherubic woman called Sumati, started to visit Sarva that his situation became slightly clearer.

Sumati's arrival always caused a tizzy among Sarva's cellmates. 'What! You get babes visiting you, you lucky fellow,' one of them whistled. For kicks, Sarva let them believe the pretty, chipper woman was his girlfriend. She always draped her saris professionally and carried lots of files; Rooban asked if she was a teacher and congratulated Sarva on scoring a girlfriend with a government job. When Sumati came, she usually asked for a private conversation in the visitors' room, a privilege lawyers were sometimes allowed. There, she patiently dissected for Sarva the legal web he was caught in.

Sarva was arrested under the 1979 Prevention of Terrorism Act, or PTA, originally passed as a temporary law to fight communist insurgents, mostly rural Sinhalese youth. It was made permanent in 1982, by which time the state was under attack not only from regrouped insurgents in the south but also Tamil militants in the north. By the early nineties, the leftist insurgency was quelled, with about 7,000 members detained under the PTA and emergency laws. After that, the law was used to arrest Tiger sympathisers, largely Tamils, but also some Sinhalese and Muslims.

Sumati said that Sarva was luckier than most because he was arrested directly under the PTA. The more common practice was to arrest people under the Emergency Regulations, which had been in place longer than the PTA, and nearly continuously from 1971. In these decades the police had perfected the systematic abuse of detainees. They would be detained without charge for up to two years under emergency law, and then have the PTA slapped on them, extending the detention by another eighteen months. This explained why Rooban, who was detained in mid-2006, was still in prison when Sarva got there in 2008. The double stranglehold of the Emergency Regulations and the PTA could keep a person in custody for up to fifteen years based on mere suspicion, without being charged. No evidence was necessary.

Sumati warned Sarva not to sign any statements the police showed him. The PTA was Sri Lanka's only law under which confessions made to the police during custody were admissible as evidence in court. Sumati said three of the four PTA detainees she had represented had succumbed to threats and admitted to crimes they did not commit. She asked him to recall whatever got him through the TID torture. 'Confession is suicide,' she said.

Sarva knew he was fortunate just to have a legal representative. Amma had pulled many strings to find these lawyers, and was digging through John's retirement fund to pay them. Most prisoners could not afford this. Rooban did not have a lawyer either, but Sumati advised him free of charge on occasion. Despite the desperate situation, with a better understanding of his situation, Sarva began to nurse a little hope. With a privilege such as an advocate, perhaps the odds, however tiny, could turn in his favour.

This optimism was only bolstered when J. S. Tissainayagam was brought to Sarva's ward. A reputable English-language journalist, Tissa, as he was known, was booked under the PTA for allegedly inciting communal hatred through his articles and aiding terrorism by collecting funds for his magazine. The other prisoners were heartened to have Tissa in their midst, eating the same bland food, walking the same grey corridors, and bearing the brunt of the same unfair law. Those who chatted with him raved about his simplicity and good humour. A celebrity who was just like them.

Sarva had not come across Tissa's articles but had read reports on him since his detention. He knew Tissa was arrested three months before he was. When Tissa was brought to the same cell, Sarva mentioned to Rooban, for the first time, his appetite for news reportage. He had begun to imagine that his destiny was interlinked with Tissa's.

In truth, however, their trajectories couldn't have been more different. Although he was imprisoned with the rest, Tissa was a VIP, watched closely both by the guards within and his fraternity outside. Every political prisoner yearned for the kind of raucous support the journalist had. The liberal elites of Sri Lanka demanded his release, condemned the government for targeting the free press, and questioned the practice of labelling any dissenter a terrorist.

'Release Tissa' posters, with his gaunt, bespectacled face printed in stark red and black, challenged postwar state authoritarianism. The campaign, spearheaded by Sri Lankan activists and scaled up by the Tamil diaspora, had begun to have global impact. President Barack Obama had mentioned Tissa on the 2009 World Press Freedom Day as 'an emblematic example' of the persecution of journalists. The battle to free Sarva, on the other hand, was fought only by his mother.

10.

February 2009

ALTHOUGH ONLY A handful in the Vanni had any reliable information about what was happening around them, it was not difficult for Mugil and the others, in the yawning time between the shelling and their meals, to stitch together a coherent story from conversations. All the recent talk was about the hospital bombings; fact and conjecture began to dissolve into each other.

In Mugil's experience, the army had never before targeted hospitals in the Vanni. But all that had changed now. The Kilinochchi and Mullaitivu general hospitals were hit in December. Long-range missiles came dangerously close to several makeshift clinics and a shower of flying metal hit the patients. A month earlier, twelve people had died and sixty-eight were injured in the bombardment of the Vallipuram and Udayarkattu hospitals. In some of these cases, the Sri Lankan government claimed that the army had credible intelligence that Tiger cadres were hiding in the clinics. At other times, they talked about collateral damage—civilians simply happened to be in the way.

The February attacks on the PTK hospital, however, fitted neither explanation. As the war intensified, millions of Tamils were displaced from across the north and east, and the hospital premises became a safe haven for the gravely injured and their families. It was one of the few areas in which the government permitted Red Cross workers to treat civilians. It was also common knowledge that there was a highly visible Red Cross sign on the hospital's terrace, marking it as a medical facility to be avoided by bombers flying overhead.

In the first three days of February, the army shelled the PTK general hospital repeatedly. Since the centre of the building was bombed and not the annex or side wings, it was unlikely to have been hit in error. Over seventy-two hours, six separate air attacks rained shells over the women's ward, paediatric ward, staff quarters, operation theatres and about 500 civilians seeking treatment. As the medical staff and Red Cross workers tried to evacuate some 200 patients and fifty severely injured children from the war zone, the shelling moved to a private medical facility in the town, the Ponnambalam Memorial Hospital. Sixty people died in and around it.

Every day since the hospitals were hit, Mugil had thought about the pregnant girl and her grandmother. They would have been in the women and children's ward. Mugil hoped they escaped with a few bruises. She imagined them walking away in safety, a healthy baby cradled in her mother's arms. She imagined she would run into them suddenly, around a corner, two recognisable faces among the thousands. She imagined they would not blame her for leaving them to die at the hospital.

A week after the attacks, the government held a press conference in Colombo to deny that hospitals had been targeted. To a room full of journalists, Ministry of Defence officials displayed satellite images of the PTK hospital. In the photos, the building was intact. 'There has been no attack on the hospital,' said one official. Questions about whether the picture was taken before the date of attack were not answered. Around the same time, Brigadier Udaya Nanayakkara, the military spokesperson, stated, 'We don't fire shells on that area. There is no requirement for us to fire into there.' Then, contradicting the press conference claim that the hospital was untouched, he said the hospitals had indeed been hit, but by the Tigers. 'It must be LTTE shells, as they are desperately firing.'

Few among the Tamil locals and international aid workers in PTK had any doubt who was firing on the hospital. It was clear that the shells came from the southern end, where the 57th Sri Lankan army was stationed.

Every statement from the government contradicted some earlier pronouncement. The Ponnambalam hospital, which was known to treat both civilians and cadres, was said to have been hit because it housed militants. Indeed, of the sixty who died when it was shelled, fourteen were Tamil Tigers. If Brigadier Nanayakkara's argument held, why would the Tigers bomb themselves? Moreover, in PTK hospital, there was no proof that Tigers outnumbered civilians to such an extent that the air force had no option but to attack.

Even in the worst of times, the Tamils had not expected the Sri Lankan army to shell the sick and dying. But as the bombings continued, and the Red Cross workers left the hospital with the severely injured, disbelief was a luxury no one could afford.

Mugil's father began to believe that the army's intentions went beyond defeating the Tigers, or winning back territory. 'I get it now,' Father said, a new conviction gripping him. 'What do you do when you can't deal with locusts? You burn the field. That's what they're doing—eradicating as many Tamils as possible.'

The PTK bunkers were rife with arguments about the hospital shelling, the rising number of injuries, the food shortages and displaced and separated families. But the hardest developments to digest were conscription and the loss of confidence in the Tiger leaders. Pottu Amman, people said, had all but lost PTK. Since January, Tamil villagers had been appalled at the Tigers' casual neglect of people's safety in the battle zone. They did not inform villages about sieges and set off landmines on approach roads. Cadres camped among the civilians in bunkers, exposing people to both LTTE fire and retaliations from the military.

Because of the Tigers' callousness, many began to look for ways to shield themselves from the onslaught. Over the radio and over loudspeakers, the Sri Lankan military was promising shelter to civilians in the Thevipuram no-fire zone. 'If you stay in your villages, we cannot guarantee your safety,' they announced. 'Go to the no-fire zone. Move with your families there. There is food, water, and security there.' Panic-stricken thousands rose from the bunkers and filled the roads that led away from PTK.

Above Mugil's bunker, feet ran helter-skelter. People were packing to leave. 'I didn't think I would be alive to see this happen in the Vanni,' Father said. 'Putting our heads willingly into the lion's mouth ... Has it come to this?'

Leaving, however, was not proving easy. Just as the Tigers had done in the nineties with the Jaffna exodus and often in the Vanni thereafter, they were ordering the civilians to stay or move with them during battle. Mother reported seeing a young man loudly berate the LTTE for turning against their own. They had lit tall fires around exits from PTK, he screamed, preventing people leaving for the no-fire zone.

One evening, when Divyan came to see them, he described seeing charred bodies all around PTK, contorted in the last moments of failed escape. Taking her aside, he admitted to Mugil that disenchantment had crept into the forces. 'This time is different,' he said. 'Since Kilinochchi fell, some cadres are not sure what they're fighting for. They still fight like machines, but in the breaks they talk about surrender.' That thousands of civilians were making it to the no-fire zone, defying the LTTE rules and trusting the enemy, was to him a sign of both their desperation and defeat.

There were still thousands who stayed in the Tiger-held areas—from injury, allegiance to their leaders or fear. Criticism of the LTTE was not easy for most; loyalty was not just a generations-old habit but also considered a duty in guerrilla war. Some were sure the Tigers would have a reasonable explanation for what seemed like utter betrayal. Mugil heard it said over and over again: 'They *must* have a strategy they have kept secret from us. We must stick with them.'

Mugil's family was clear on one thing: they could not bring themselves to trust the army, especially after the hospital bombing. Going to the no-fire zone, they felt, was a sure way to die at the enemy's hands. Mugil was also certain the young soldiers would not spare her and Amuda.

Having a member of the family serving in the movement made leaving doubly difficult. Divyan had to return to duty that night and didn't want his family to act without him. 'Stay in the bunker,' he said. 'I'll try to get a driving assignment at Vattapalai.' He would get in touch with Prashant, too, and let him know that's where they would go next. 'Give me a few days.'

FOR PEOPLE IN PTK, days and nights passed in phases of cowering from rain or missiles, foraging for food and repairing bunkers—actions to which there was no other purpose than to prolong survival. More than a month had passed since Kilinochchi was captured, and taking shelter was becoming dreary. Dulled by the routine and tired of crouching underground, people began to test their limits. In dry afternoons, they walked far from their bunkers to stretch their legs, stopping to chat with acquaintances and leisurely going about life-threatening tasks.

Both rumours and facts were exchanged as bunker room *vetti pechu*, or idle talk. Telephone lines were down and satellite phones were rarely available; gossip was the primary source of information. People gleaned lessons from new arrivals who told horrific tales from other places and of the miracle of their escape. They hung on the words of barefoot analysts conversant in military strategy, seeking to understand the impact of losses and wins. If a long-range missile hit a school at quarter to two in the afternoon, how long before another was launched? If a pellet from a cluster bomb lodged itself in your leg, why would amputation be the only option?

Children ran around near the sandbags, playing hide and seek, hopscotch and war games, shooting each other with twigs. A Catholic pastor who was among them held daily prayers for the Christians; many Hindus attended for the solace of swaying in group prayer and for the comforting sound of the pastor's beautifully crafted words.

At one such gathering, Amuda met a schoolmate who, since her wedding, had moved to Vadduvakal, near Mullaitivu town. This woman had returned to PTK a day earlier, having left Mullaitivu when it fell to the Sri Lankan army. She described how her family had tried to take a boat out of Mullaitivu and into Vavuniya or Jaffna. But the missiles had come from the sea, too, killing her teenage son, parents-in-law, and most of the twenty-odd people on the boat.

Amuda was shaken. She related this to Mugil back at the bunker: 'What I can't believe is that Mullaitivu has fallen to the army, and we find out only now, after ten days! Which world are we in? Next, our mother will die, and we won't know the date on which it happened.' It was perhaps an idle comment but it alarmed Mugil. How could chronology be possible when minutes became weeks in the darkness of bunkers and a day was lost in a moment's explosion? She had to regain her grip on time. She tore a long strip from her mother's already ripped sari and turned it into her version of a tally bar. Beginning with 25 January, the day Mullaitivu fell, she tied one knot for every sunset. A count of every day they survived.

But the knots would not record how hard it was to make it through every single day. Death and serious injury were becoming more familiar, but the most dreaded killer was hunger. Mugil hated its slow onset and the maddening paralysis it brought. Malnourished children and famished adults shrivelled. To put out the burning in their stomachs, they made rash decisions and took risks. They fought over morsels, dove into burning jungles and rushed frantically to food supply lines, wherever they were.

When Mugil heard that some officials from the government agent's office were distributing *paruppu*, salt and pumpkins in an Iranpalai school, she spent half a day crossing the dangerous A35 highway to get there. As she stood in the food queue, she scanned the hands of those coming back from the counter. Each carried a small pyramid of yellow pumpkin spotted with brown fungus. A newspaper packet held 250 grams of pale *kadala paruppu*—one look and she knew it would be hard as pebbles. The precious salt was packed in pages of used school notebooks, like thumb-sized sachets of holy ash from a temple. She had expected much more; she had brought an aluminium bucket.

'Come on, give us coconuts!' yelled a man from the queue, a futile demand that came at least once in every food line. From behind him, a woman's assertive voice heckled the distributors. 'You should have told us it was rotten Indian rations; we wouldn't have bothered to come!' she shouted. That won a few tired laughs.

The heckler then asked sarcastically if it hadn't occurred to the government agent to send drinking water. 'Or maybe you expect us to drink the seawater!' More nervous laughter.

Mugil watched as the woman marched past her to the front of the queue and grabbed a few food packets. No one protested; the woman wore pants and a shirt. As she walked back, she lifted the rations for everyone to see. 'It's running out!' she said cruelly. Several people broke the line to rush to the counter. That's when Mugil recognised the heckler's cocky grin and intimidating broad shoulders. The woman had been one of her first unit commanders.

'Devayani *akka*!' Mugil called out.

The woman turned around. 'Selvi!' she shouted, using Mugil's old nom de guerre. She pulled her former protégé out of the queue and hugged her. '*Sugama irukkeerhala*? Is your family well?' she asked. The greeting had survived their region's many battles; its evocation of family, health and happiness reinforced what they held most dear.

'Only as well as everybody else,' Mugil said.

'Where is that Divyan? Aren't all of you together?'

'Most of us. Divyan is on duty. Prashant—I don't know where he is,' Mugil said. Did Devayani *akka* have a way to find out? Did she still have a satellite phone?

'No, I don't have my phone. Anyway I'm not waiting for orders anymore. I'm done.'

Mugil was taken aback by her senior's candour. 'Won't the main office come after you?'

Devayani *akka* responded with a hollow laugh. 'Who will they kill if I'm dead?' she asked. Then, pulling Mugil away from the queue, she lowered her voice. 'We're crumbling, Selvi, we're fighting with each other about what to do next.' The commander admitted that the Tigers' weapons were fast running out and that she had let some young recruits escape when she was put in charge of them. She railed against the LTTE political wing for recruiting 'just anybody off the street, by giving them two slaps'. Her niece was killed at the front, she said, and so was her brother. She was weary of the arguments among the leaders, their collapsing unity. 'I'm still in uniform,' she said. 'But that's just for show.'

Mugil listened to Devayani *akka*, but half her attention was on the queue. She was annoyed at having lost her place. So when the commander paused, Mugil seized the opportunity. 'Can I ask you something? Where do you think Prashant might be?'

Devayani *akka* looked confused, so Mugil continued. 'You remember him? Prashant? My little brother? The eager boy? He was in the bomb-making unit, not on the front lines. I'm afraid he won't survive all this.'

The commander seemed to pull herself together. She said that just a week earlier she had heard a rumour that many Tiger boys had been sent to an area near Valipunam, which had been a no-fire zone since late January. While one section of the LTTE had tried to stop the masses from relocating, some other leaders sent social workers, engineering department boys and Tiger doctors there to help set up tents, carry luggage or treat the wounded. She suggested that Mugil's brother had perhaps also been sent there. 'I'm not sure, okay? It's what I've heard,' she said.

Mugil began to thank Devayani *akka* when the latter slipped the food packets into Mugil's bucket. 'You know how the Sinhalese chaps are trying to win, right?' she whispered. 'By starving all of us. That way, they won't have to waste ammunition.' She patted Mugil's stomach. 'You beat their game and eat as much as possible, okay?'

'You?' Mugil asked, but Devayani *akka* was already walking back to the counter.

Late that evening in PTK, the family mulled over Devayani *akka*'s tip-off about Prashant. Father didn't entirely believe it; he had decided from Mugil's narration of events that the former commander had all but gone cuckoo. But it was more information than they had had in weeks, and Valipunam didn't seem too far off. Mugil could make a quick trip there to search for her brother.

The decision made, they began to cook their first meal in two days, and Mugil opened the tiny sachet. Inside was not salt but the crushed dust of a few dried fish, salted by the sea air.

MUGIL LEFT FOR Valipunam before dawn, before Tamizh could wake up and throw a fit. He was too attached now, always wanting to be carried, refusing to leave her hip. Maran was lying half awake, and when she stepped over him in the bunker, he mumbled deliriously that he wanted some water. 'Not one glass, I want a full bottle, *amma*.' She shushed him.

Valipunam was across the highway, which the army patrolled. On the other side, in the section of the no-fire zone close to the A35, the Tigers were hiding in bunkers and firing at passing army trucks and tankers. She zigzagged across the road, using the vehicles as cover, and walked through the jungle and beyond to the cleared areas, in the opposite direction to the mass of people heading for safety.

As she approached Valipunam, the smell of burnt flesh made her retch. An eerie silence pressed on her ears. The houses were abandoned, their roofs blown off, and the palmyra trees were decapitated. Tents smoked. Hastily dug and discarded bunkers were collapsing wetly into themselves. She tried to find her way to the middle school, which the Red Cross had converted into a temporary hospital for civilians. Perhaps Prashant was there, helping.

The place looked nothing like she remembered. The once lush paddy fields were barren. Plastic bags, bits of clothing, toothbrushes, combs, toys and utensils stuck out from the soil, household items overtaking the land like weeds. Through the thick smoke, in the distance, she saw a woman rocking on her knees, her hands on a small boy's body. Her shrill *oppari* pierced the air.

Swollen bodies lay in the streams of rainwater. A few hundred metres away, some boys were straightening the corpses, fixing the clothes of dead girls, moving the bodies away from the centre of the road, where they could get run over by tankers or jeeps. Mugil guessed they were workers from the Tamil Rehabilitation Organisation, or TRO, a local NGO attached to the Tigers. This was their way of preserving the dignity of the dead.

By the looks of it, Valipunam, touted as a no-fire zone, had been hit by repeated air raids. Mugil hoped she wouldn't find her brother here. But if not here, where could he be? She was unable to process the sights and smells. Fallen trees were still smouldering. The shelling was past, but the burning present. She held her hand to her nose and mouth. Below her, the body of a young man, face down in a culvert, bobbed slightly. His camouflage shirt was torn and his sarong ballooned. In panic, Mugil took a step closer and turned the body on its back. The boy's thin chest hair was clogged with blood, grass and mud. Below it, where his stomach should have been, was a large cavity that was still bleeding. It was only then that she looked at the boy's face. Just a second ago, she could have sworn it was Prashant.

She turned around and ran.

It took a day for Mugil to reach her family. They were preparing to leave for Matalan. Divyan had apparently sent word that he would meet them on the way there. He still couldn't trace Prashant but assured them he would soon.

'We told him you've gone to look for your brother,' Mother said.

Mugil said she had been unable to find her way to Valipunam.

'Really?' Mother asked incredulously. 'You took a whole day to get lost?'

'Be glad that at least she came back alive,' Father mumbled.

As they packed small bags, mostly with food rations and firewood, Father put his arm around Mugil's shoulder. 'I meant to ask you … Do you have a skirt, Mugil?'

Mugil knew what he meant. She was wearing a pair of faded jeans and a long blouse. She was dressed like a Tiger.

'No skirt,' she said. 'But I will find something else.' She undid an old housecoat that Amuda had wrapped around some vessels and pulled it on. The longish housecoat not only hid her sinewy calves and scars but also changed who she was in the eyes of the world. In a series of impulses, she had gradually shed the façade—the gun, the cyanide, the tiger tooth and now the uniform. Each act had taken only a few seconds, but eventually the effect was like shedding her skin. She was setting aside the only life she had known since she was a teenager.

As the family left their bunker, their neighbours stared at Mugil. After fifteen years, the proud female cadre among them had changed into civilian clothes. The men and women Mugil had grown up with seemed to judge her, their eyes smiling and their lips curling in vindication at her eventual hypocrisy. Here is that woman, their eyes seemed to say, that great combatant who just a few years ago hunted down traitors and deserters, and now a deserter herself. Here is the limping combatant who was so disgusted with her sister for refusing to join the Tigers. Where are her morals now?

Nothing in the Vanni was valued quite like self-sacrifice. In this regard, Divyan and Mugil had been role models for the youngsters at every opportunity. They had always walked a few steps above the ground. She had visited her neighbours' homes and lectured their sons and daughters, speaking of the virtues of serving Annan, selling them the dream of Eelam before they ever thought about engineering, teaching or accounting. 'Take part in the making of a better tomorrow'—how many times must Mugil have uttered those words to wide-eyed teenagers? Of course the others would avenge themselves with their stares in this moment.

'Ignore them,' her father said, sensing her shame. 'This is no time for self-pity.' He thrust a coughing Tamizh into her hands. 'Look at his face every time you feel some doubt. Now it is all about family, that's all.'

11.

February 2009

INDRA HAD WOKEN up before everybody else. She made herself some black tea with three spoonfuls of sugar. She opened the balcony door to let in some cool air. Colombo was hot even at sunrise, even in February. Her sister Rani was still in bed. She had better wake up soon. If they wanted to get the food to Sarva by lunchtime, they had to leave for the prison in two hours.

She downed her tea, soaked some rice in a pot of water, and put some *paruppu* in the pressure cooker. She made another cup of tea, covered it with a saucer and got ready for a shower. As she passed the bedroom, she pulled Rani's toes, which stuck out from under the blanket.

By the time Indra was out of the bathroom, Rani was sitting on the balcony sipping her tea. 'Shall we take some mussels, too? I heard the fish vendor call from the street.'

'Good idea. Remind me to make some buttermilk as well.'

Rani asked if Indra had slept well. 'Just take those sleeping pills, *akka*.' Rani said. 'I don't know why you won't.'

Indra had spent the previous day at the lawyer's office and then visited several pawnbrokers to see how much they would lend against her gold bangles. She had returned exhausted and gone straight to bed but had tossed and turned till dawn. The sleeping pills would have helped, but she felt somewhat guilty taking them. How could a mother sleep soundly when her son was still in prison, lying on a hard floor every night? 'I got a few hours, it should do,' she said feebly. In the puja corner, she lit an oil lamp and smeared some holy ash on her forehead. These days she cooked only after a bath and a prayer, pious habits of her own mother that Indra believed would bring good luck to her family.

Sarva's lunch menu had been decided the previous evening: mutton curry, *mallum*, *rasam* and rice. Rani had prepared the mutton before she went to sleep. She had roasted and ground coriander, cumin and dried red chillies and massaged the mixture into the mutton. She added salt, turmeric, cinnamon powder and crushed cardamom pods, as well as tomato puree to cut through the fat. The meat had been marinating in the fridge all night.

In the morning, Indra took over. She added oil to a clay pot—Sarva could always tell when she cooked meat in this vessel, he said he smelled its earthiness. She threw in chopped onions and garlic, ginger for the zing, and slit green chillies for heat. She roughly tore—never cut—curry leaves and pandan leaves and they hopped in the oil. Immediately the aroma sharpened, and she knew the curry would be perfect.

Her mother had taught her cooking like a science—flip the *dosai* when brown, cut the meat in the direction of the muscle, lift the ladle against light to see if it is steaming, add the iron-packed spinach water to the lentils, slam the garlic cloves flat and pull the skin—and Indra had fortified it with her own philosophy. To her, there were no shortcuts and no do-overs; the fate of a dish was determined right at the beginning, when the onions were sliced and the first ingredients chosen. If something was forgotten then or a step was missed, nothing could save the dish in the end. Some cooks might think clever substitutes or new techniques could fix anything, but not Indra. If the curry was not sour enough, you couldn't add more tamarind bit by bit; you had to accept that you made a mediocre curry that day. Once you burned the oil, everything you put in it would reek of your mistake. She was aware of the possibility for error and she focussed with the intensity of a trapeze artist to avoid it.

The mutton went in. Water was added, the pot closed with a lid, the flame reduced. She checked the curry every five minutes, gave it a stir, waited till the oil surfaced. After half an hour, she added fresh silken coconut milk. Many in Sri Lanka used Maggi instant coconut milk powder, but Indra despised it on principle. The powder did the job all right, gave density to the curry and moistened the meat, but it lacked the sweetness of freshly squeezed coconut milk. Extracting it was a labour of love, but so what? This mutton curry—meat on the bone—was the favourite of both mother and son. There could be no shortcuts.

Rani had gone downstairs to buy mussels, an indulgent addition to the menu. The large fleshy ones were expensive, so she got a handful of the pebble-sized ones. The sisters worked quietly, never having to taste or measure at any point, both led by the memory of their mother's recipe. As Indra slit the beans and *bajji molaga*, Rani steamed the mussels. They were fresh, and the purple-ringed shells snapped open in minutes. She sautéed them with the long strips of beans and *molaga* as well as some spicy chilli and tamarind extract. Indra then cooked some rice and made a quick green salad with chopped mallum leaves, small onions, green chillies, lemon and shredded coconut. *Rasam* was served every day, so Indra had bottled a thick concentrate of tamarind, pepper, cumin, turmeric and garlic and stored it in the fridge to last a week. Now, to a spoonful of the concentrate, she simply added hot water and curry leaves sputtered with mustard seeds. In a big steel tiffin carrier, Indra packed all this food and poured the *rasam* and buttermilk into small polyethylene bags.

The bus to Borella was at 7:10 a.m., so the sisters were out the door by seven. Rani's son, who had woken up as they were leaving, asked if there was any food left. There is a plate with rice and rasam on the dining table, they said. Next to it was a small bowl of mutton curry for him, without any of the meat.

After changing buses three times, they reached New Magazine prison at eight. As they entered the gates, a guard checked their belongings and noted their national ID numbers. Then they joined the long queue of relatives, mostly mothers and wives. The prison officials would let in visitors only after eleven thirty, but everyone came early to find a spot in the queue. During the long idle wait, mothers exchanged pleasantries and worries. There were many familiar faces ahead of Indra, women she had been seeing for months now. She had befriended a handful whose sons were in the same cell as Sarva. One of these women, Grace, walked over.

'So, is it meat day or vegetarian day?' Grace asked. Indra knew Sarva shared his lunch with some of the inmates, including Grace's son. 'Mutton,' Indra replied. 'Ah, *that* Sarva won't share with anyone!' said Grace with a smile.

For some time, Grace had come on these visits with her pregnant daughter-in-law, but a month earlier the police had arrested her, too. She was with the TID for interrogation now, and family were not allowed to visit. The daughter-in-law was in her second trimester when she was detained and had already developed some complications. Worried sick, Grace had been struggling to find a lawyer and an NGO to help secure a release as soon as possible on medical grounds. 'I hear you found Sarva a good lawyer,' she said to Indra, and asked for the number.

Indra found Mr Vel's office number in the palm-sized diary she always had with her. Usually it was in her handbag, but since phones and handbags weren't allowed inside the prison, she would stuff money and the diary inside her bra. The tattered pages were filled with numbers, names and addresses for every office, commission, activist, lawyer, politician and journalist Indra had met in the year since Sarva had been arrested. It was mostly her own large Tamil letters leaping over the lines, but some people had written their details for her in English as well. Between the pages, several business cards stuck out, collected in compulsive hope. On the central pages, Indra had written the dates and times of every intimidating visit the plainclothes police had made to her house. Ever since she had understood the deniability built into everything the police did to her son, she had started to make lists, note things down, put everything on record. They wouldn't give her a single document, so she created her own. She had learnt to be meticulous, because as in her kitchen, here too there were no second chances.

When the gates opened, there was the usual push. The guards sometimes shut the gates midway through lunchtime, citing some security lapse or a breach of discipline. So people shoved to enter the visitors' hall, only to be held back by shouting guards. It happened every day, and each time, Indra felt ashamed. The people in the queue, in coming to see their loved ones behind bars, shed every ounce of dignity. She saw elderly women sob and throw themselves at the feet of guards half their age, begging them to reopen the gates. Only few like Indra spoke Sinhalese and had homes in Colombo. Most others had come from places as far away as Kytes Island in the north or Batticaloa in the east and were living in cheap lodges or rented houses, just so that they could bring food to their sons or husbands every day.

In the corridor leading to the visitors' hall, two guards stood on either side of the queue, each with a bench in front of him. They wielded a steel spoon each. The approaching women had to place their lunchboxes or steel carriers on the bench and display the contents. The guards would then run their spoons through the containers, one by one, checking for banned substances hidden in the curries and rice.

Indra bristled. Everything inside the lunchboxes had been prepared with care, love and even prayer, and in one moment it was defiled. It made her retch to see the same unwashed spoon going into every box, touching yoghurt to *rasam*, rice to *puttu*, dregs and droplets moving from one box to another. On Fridays, Saturdays and Tuesdays, her family was vegetarian because she visited the temple. On those days, as the spoon rose from other people's meat dishes and plunged into her vegetables, she uttered an apology to God. Sometimes the guards had a mug of water next to them to clean the spoon, but once she saw the oily brown liquid inside the mug, she wondered whether the daily lunchbox was worth all this trouble, and why her son could not just eat prison food.

She entered the visitors' hall, and saw Sarva waving behind the wire mesh. A guard took the tiffin box and passed it through a shaft to another guard on the other side of the mesh, who handed the lunch to Sarva. Immediately her son put his nose to it. A grin lit his face. Over the din of other men thanking their respective mothers and wives, sending loud desperate love to their children, Sarva shouted, 'Amma!' and gestured as if he were cracking a bone with his teeth and sucking the marrow, the way she had taught him to eat the best part of the mutton.

There, that is why she spent eight or nine hours of her day to bring him one meal. To give him that memory. To make him do things normally just as he used to, like greedily smelling his lunch-box. He had earlier tried to save some of it for dinner, too, but when it had spoiled one day, he had been unable to forgive himself. Indra believed the smell and taste of home, the sight of his aunt or mother once a day, kept him motivated and hopeful. For her, it was an opportunity to ensure his good health and safety. In the CRP, he had been beaten brutally and she had not known for weeks. That could not happen again.

It was almost three o'clock when Indra and Rani got back home. They absently ate some leftovers, did the laundry, watched some news and started to prepare for the next day.

SARVA'S BROTHERS HAD begun to complain that he had taken over their lives. 'You have every freedom, no one has put you in jail, no one has broken your bones,' Rani once scolded her son Darshan, who was unemployed after completing a filmmaking course in India. 'Go fix your life. You have no excuses.'

The energy and finances of the entire household were focussed on Sarva and his well-being. He consumed so much attention that, on 7 February 2009, when Indra's daughter-in-law Priya called her to say some plainclothesmen were dragging Indra's son out and arresting him, she was confused. 'Inside prison?' she asked.

'They're taking Deva, Amma!' Priya yelled.

Her other son. Someone was kidnapping her firstborn. Indra rushed to Deva's apartment a few streets up. Three men were pulling him into a van. Priya stood frozen on the street, tears streaming down her face.

Indra ran to the men. 'Please don't do anything to him,' she cried. 'He's just a travel agent. Please!' One nightmare was unfolding to reveal another. 'Stop please, tell me what it is!'

Ignoring her appeals, the men thrust Deva's head inside, closed the van door, and sped away.

Upstairs in the apartment, Deva's children sat dumbfounded on the sofa. The house was a mess, chairs pulled out of place, curtains torn down, shattered glass on the floor. Priya stood over the debris looking crushed. Her right hand gripped the bottom of her bump, and Indra thought her daughter-in-law would go into labour right then and there.

'Are you okay?' Indra asked. Priya did not reply. She was in a trance, pointing around the house, describing the men doing their search, throwing stuff around. They had taken Deva's laptop. They knew about Sarva's detention. They said they suspected Deva's involvement and wanted to ask him some questions.

Priya looked straight at Indra. 'It's your stupid jailbird son's fault!' she said. Her voice was harsh. 'He is dragging everyone down with him.'

Indra had been hearing this ever since Deva's wedding, when she had run off to rescue Sarva from the trouble she rarely spoke about. She wanted to erase the memory of those days, but Deva and his wife would not let it go. They insisted that she only cared for her middle son, an accusation impossible to counter. Shall we weigh my love for each of my sons on a scale, Indra would ask. She had hoped that her sons would look out for each other as she had for them, but over the years they had grown more detached. Indra blamed the rich, demanding daughter-in-law for tearing the family apart. Deva always told his mother that she was being dramatic, but Priya knew exactly what Indra thought of her. Every time Indra asked Deva for money to pay Sarva's lawyers' fees or to buy Nuwara Eliya-to-Colombo bus tickets, Priya had raised questions.

'Mother and son together are killing the whole family!' Priya was shouting now.

Indra knew how powerless Priya must feel at this moment, but couldn't she see that as Deva's mother, she too was upset? Still, Indra began to apologise, saying she was only doing what she was supposed to do with Sarva, she hadn't anticipated all of this, she loved all her sons equally.

'Enough, stop it! I've heard all this a hundred times before, what is the point now?' Priya said. 'At least you have done this before. Tell me what we should do now.'

Together they went to the Wellawatte police station. By this time the cops recognised Indra and knew that one of her sons was in jail under PTA. 'Hmm, now what happened?' asked the first policeman she met.

Indra had a feeling they already knew the answer.

'They have detained my first son.'

'Who has?' the cop asked. The others were staring.

'The TID, who else?'

They laughed, just as they had when Sarva was taken. 'He must be a *Kottiya*,' one of them said. 'His place is in jail.'

'He's just a travel agent—he has done nothing wrong!'

A policeman said he saw Deva 'stylishly walking around', driving a car, taking millions from people to get them visas for trips abroad. 'How come he's so rich?' They were implying that Deva's agency was a front for smuggling and other fundraising businesses.

Indra started to sob. One of them said it was her fault. Raise two terrorists and then cry, he said.

For the next few days Indra asked her sisters to take lunch to Sarva and threw herself into the search for Deva. She spent the nights at Priya's house and sent the children to Rani's. She told Carmel, her youngest, to stay at a friend's house and not venture out. She was sure he would be next. It would be relentless; she would be running again from prison to police station, lawyer to activist; in the end, nothing she did would ever be enough. She was fighting a force she could not comprehend.

Indra's lawyer had his juniors call the TID office. They were told that no Deva was being detained there. But that's what they always say, insisted Indra. The lawyer suggested that Deva might not have been taken to the TID office yet. As was the practice in such illegal abductions, the victim would be kept in an abandoned house or garage, where interrogation could occur without the restrictions of custodial rules. Indra had come to understand that these unrecorded hours were when the most brutal torture occurred. And because there were no witnesses other than the police, the incident could be entirely denied.

The country had seen abductions for recruitment or vendetta since the southern insurgency and during the LTTE period. But one didn't exist today and the other was crumbling in the north; it didn't stop youths from dying or disappearing. Had she not seen the men dragging Deva away, Indra might have suspected both the TID and LTTE. As it was, the Tamil militants were losing the war in the north, and the state had launched a covert operation to sweep for sympathisers and cadres everywhere else in the country. Since 2006, these kidnappings, especially of Tamil boys, had increased exponentially: the UN had recorded some 10,000 cases but many more went unreported. Indra herself knew many mothers who beat their chests for years over vanished sons. They had seen unknown men take their kids away, but once a police report had been filed, the mothers had discovered that the investigating authority was usually the same TID or army department suspected of the kidnap. These agencies said no one was arrested, no one was tortured, no one was held in custody secretly. A court could only go by evidence, and when that was obliterated, all that was left was a family member demanding truth, investigations and other rights that were a nuisance to a military-backed government prioritising national security concerns above everything else.

Enforced disappearances, the NGOs called these cases. To Indra, it was simply a fight against a spectre of lies. She imagined that soon her picture, too, would be in the newspapers, with dishevelled hair and a tear-streaked face, holding passport photographs of her sons, showing the world that they existed, that she was not insane.

Four days after Deva went missing, Priya received a call from an unknown number. The voice asked her to pay 2 million rupees, failing which they would hurt her husband. Indra had not expected this. She instructed Priya not to pay because that would still not guarantee Deva's safety.

The lawyers had connected Indra with an NGO that provided protection to civilians under threat of state violence. She told them about Deva, but the activists said they were flooded with such requests and needed more time to do background checks. They suspected that while Deva's kidnap was intended to look like classic detention, it could also be an attempt at extortion. The demand for money was a dead giveaway, they said, and it had happened to several other aggrieved families.

Indra felt lost, spinning out of control. She kept the news of Deva's disappearance from Sarva; she didn't want to make him feel unduly guilty. If this were indeed extortion, perhaps they should pay? She had no one but Priya to discuss this with, but her daughter-in-law was already shutting her out, saying she didn't want to have anything to do with Indra or with Sarva's case.

On the eighth day, Indra heard that Deva was back home. She rushed to his flat. His forehead was bleeding, his chest black and blue. That morning, Priya had paid 2 million rupees to the kidnappers and they had sent Deva home. Indra was not told any more.

'We'd better do things separately now,' Deva said, not meeting Indra's eye. 'You deal with your son, I'll deal with my life. We don't have to all sink in the same boat.'

12.

March 2009

MUGIL WALKED TOWARDS the coast, one child in each arm—a dot in a sea of people inching along laboriously. Heat rose from the earth, burning her bare feet. It was almost two months since she had left PTK. As monsoon turned to summer, the displaced families around her had trebled. Some two million had abandoned the first no-fire zone in Suthanthirapuram after it was shelled by the Sri Lankan military. As they fled, the army declared a second safe zone on 12 February. This one was on the north-eastern coast, a narrow strip of fourteen square kilometres stretching from Putumutalan down to just before Mullaitivu town. Loudspeakers every few kilometres promised safety and food, as they had for the first no-fire zone. The government announcer, perhaps an army man, said, 'Go to Putumatalan! There will be no shooting there.'

Few bought what he was saying. The first safe zone had turned into a battle zone and potential relief had led to further trauma. Yet with nowhere else to go, the swarm—including Mugil and her family—trudged on towards Putumatalan. Mugil was merely following whoever was in front of her. Charting a route wasn't possible, especially with the little information they had. But even as she stuck to the herd, she could not shake off the thought that she was walking into a trap. She recalled what she saw in Valipunam, at the tip of the first no-fire zone: the burning flesh, the woman crying in grief, the disbelief. The army had killed thousands of innocents, claiming to target the Tigers hiding among them.

Several cadres had indeed exchanged their uniforms for sarongs and shirts and had mingled with the families. But were they still a threat?

The man who gave Mugil directions to Valipunam, for instance, was a combatant until three years ago, when he contracted tuberculosis. He wasn't even armed anymore. Did the army consider him an active Tiger and someone to be targeted? Devayani *akka* was still in uniform, but she had given up the cause—how would they define her?

Mugil herself had trained as a teenager, but her longest stint in the LTTE had been as a photographer. Her father printed pamphlets for the militants but had not carried a gun once in his sixty-six years. Her mother had quite possibly fed every hungry cadre who knocked on her door. Their PTK neighbours, two middle-aged doctors, had skipped the basic ten-day arms training compulsory for Vanni people, but they had saved the lives of innumerable fighters. It seemed as if the army now considered non-combatant, sometime supporters, such as Mugil's parents and their neighbours, as part of the Tigers' military operation.

How far back would the army go in the twenty-six years of conflict, how broad a brush would they apply? The children conscripted in the final hour, having trained for just a day or two; the women pretending to take part to deter sexual predators; the men posing as fighters to get rations—they were all terrorists, the president claimed. Were they so dangerous as to warrant shelling them in a safe zone, along with those who were unarguably civilians? The boundary between civilian and militant had always been difficult to discern in the Vanni. Mugil herself was often not sure where the line should be drawn. But that doubt, in the mind of a Sinhalese soldier or general steeped in generations of hatred and with heavy weaponry at his disposal, was bound to wreak havoc.

So here they all were, paying the price for that indefinable difference. People were dying around her, sometimes in a second, sometimes after excruciating weeks of suffering. The survivors—their families and friends—moved with the gait of people who knew they weren't far behind. No longer did Mugil feel that initial frenzied need to survive. She simply wanted it to end.

The year 2009 was supposed to be when her son enrolled in a school. Instead, here was Maran attached to her right index finger, flopping to the ground, holding a single packet of wet biscuits, hearing her yell that he was to eat only one a day. She had left Maran's new school uniform behind in PTK and also forgotten Tamizh's milk bottle. Every time they moved to a new place, they had to leave pieces of their life behind.

Mugil had been walking longer than her family, from the mango orchard in Kilinochchi. Her limp was getting worse. At every step, the piece of shell lodged in her shin seemed to come alive and shoot flames right up to her chest. The wounds from before had felt like trophies—bodily commitment to Annan, to a freedom and autonomy her community dreamt of. Even in the scream of the most blinding pain, there had been an equally physical satisfaction: I lost blood for a reason. All those times, she had felt deeply that she had moved everyone closer to the heaven they were dreaming of. She could experience it, swallow it, taste it. She bore each new scar with pride.

But this sharp, alien shard in her shin inflicted a pain that was not attached to a purpose. Maybe that was why everyone around her was screaming so much, wailing like babies. Maybe deep down, everyone knew there was going to be no reward for what was happening. Not tomorrow, not any time.

She wondered if her obsession with her two boys had made her a coward, lowered her threshold for pain. No, no weakness today. Just one more day, she told herself, only half-believing. For months now, she had been trying to silence these doubts, dispel the fog of exhaustion that was blurring the future she had always seen so clearly.

To keep from giving up, Mugil tuned her limp to the rhythm of the pain—short left step, long right step, short left, long right. Tha-dhaa tha-dhaa. It was a tactic her first firearms trainer had taught her. 'Make it a game,' she would say. 'Don't make it a life-or-death situation when it's actually happening.'

Her mother would not stop nagging Mugil to go to a hospital. Look around, Mugil kept telling her, look at all these people. *Nondi, kurudu, oonam*—limp, blind, half-human beings. Many more are dead. At least her family was whole, their hearts still beating. Had her mother not witnessed what the army did to PTK and to the people in Thevipuram? Had she forgotten the pregnant girl and her grandmother? There was more danger in looking for a safe place than in running. Mugil knew that at some point she would have to sit her mother down, hold her face, and say slowly and directly to her: we need to run.

From what, they all knew. But where? To what?

MUGIL REACHED AN earthwork, on the other side of which was Nandikadal lagoon and beyond that Matalan; from there the northern end of the Putumatalan no-fire zone was only a few kilometres away. The army was rumoured to be taking families to refugee camps from there. All along the vertical east of the no-fire zone was the Indian Ocean, from where some refugees hoped to escape on boats to India or Jaffna. Still others were making it across Putumatalan and going further south towards Mullivaikal.

On the thin tract of open land before the embankment, with Amuda's help, Mugil propped up a tarpaulin tent. Under it they would dig a bunker, just as deep as the shifting sand would allow, just as wide as their family of eight needed to sit. Other families were doing the same, to break the long walk through perilous forests and bombed-out villages before they took to the water. The Nandikadal lagoon lay ahead of them, bloated after the two-month downpour. Straight across it was the only route left to Matalan. The road was impassable; it was being shelled by both the army and the Tigers.

They stayed here for about a week, biding their time and regaining strength before the next bout of displacement. At times, bursts of bullets and mortar shells whizzed around them, and the shudder of explosions shook the ground where they sat. At least one thing was clear: Divyan had promised to join them at Matalan. Again, Mother had asked him if he had reached Prashant at all. The more certain she became that her youngest was alive, the more she believed she was alone in her optimism. 'You lot just want to move on, to have one less mouth to feed,' she berated her daughters. 'But I'm a mother. A mother never gives up.'

Mugil didn't pay Mother any heed, and tried in vain to bring the *paruppu* to a boil in the seawater. The vessel was caked with mineral scum, which had to be scraped off every few minutes. Ahead of her, families were swaddling their most precious belongings—school certificates, land documents, medicines, family photographs—in plastic bags, preparing to cross the water. A little further away, Amuda kept an eye on the kids. Kalai was drawing with her fingers in the sand, and the boys were staring at the coal-dark smoke spiralling from the villages they left behind. Explosions lit the sky every few minutes.

Suddenly Prashant ran into Mugil's line of sight, shouting, 'Akka!' Mother was the first to reach him. She hugged him in triumph, as if she had somehow conjured him up. 'See? I knew my boy would not leave me like that.' She wiped his face with her palms and kissed her fingertips. Prashant laughed, basking in the attention and taking in his sisters' stunned faces.

Amuda, not big on goodbyes or greetings, said, 'Ah, sir has arrived.'

'Where's Siva *anna*?'

Amuda gave the one-word answer she had been using to everyone: 'Kfir.'

His eyes widened. 'Those savages! We'll get them back! We'll kill them all!'

'Yes, go tell that to all the widows.' Amuda's tone was acidic, and she walked away.

'Poor Amuda.' Prashant sighed. Mugil pulled her hand back and slapped his face hard. 'What did I do?' he yelped.

Mugil was furious. Why hadn't he bothered to reach out, send one message through Divyan or any of the cadres? The floating boy with the absent stomach had appeared often in her dreams, and he always wore her brother's face.

Prashant took his favourite sister's hand and mockingly slapped his other cheek with it. 'I'm here now, no?' he said softly.

'Don't talk to us like we're children. You're not a big hero, okay?' Mugil shouted. 'Where the hell were you?'

It turned out that Prashant, whose expertise in the LTTE was building missile and shell cases, had been out of work for a few weeks. In 2007, even before the land forces moved in on Kilinochchi, the task forces and naval divisions had captured three of the LTTE's floating armouries. The ships carried approximately 4,000 tonnes of military cargo, including dismantled light aircraft, artillery shells, mortar rounds and speedboats. All of it was simply sunk in the sea. Still, there was enough ammunition hidden in other places to last till early 2009. Now, however, as the battles intensified and the Tigers cadres exhausted their bullets and missiles, the engineering wing, too, ran out of supplies to manufacture more. Since December, Prashant had been manning the line outside PTK.

So why didn't he tell the family this? 'Selfish, selfish!' Mugil screamed.

'I was doing my job, and now I have got permission to come check on my family,' Prashant said, unfazed. He walked up to the boiling pot. 'What's your plan? Where are you headed? Our boys are there in Mullivaikal. You will be protected there.'

Mugil didn't reply. She doubted if their protection was her brother's foremost concern. The Tigers' defences were nearby, and she knew they had built high sandbag walls along some parts of the lagoon. They launched shells from behind these, but the walls seemed to have a second purpose in hampering the movement of civilians. A few days earlier, Mugil had seen hundreds of civilians bound for Matalan clash at the walls with a large group of Tigers. The trouble brewed for hours as the cadres tried to dissuade people from leaving. They appealed to the civilians' loyalty to the homeland and to the trust they had once placed in the Tigers. They scared them with fearsome reminders of what the army was capable of and the government's historic discrimination against Tamils. They painted demonic pictures of the majority community the Tamils would have to live with if they left. They talked about how the Sinhalese would make the Tamil children their servants and rape their mothers and sisters.

Tamil civilians had heard these warnings for decades; the Tigers were playing on justified fears fed by people's experiences of personal discrimination and violence, and by their disconnection from the Sinhalese by language and geography. But the urgent reality today was the five months of unabated shelling and starvation. It had replaced every other demon.

That day, Mugil watched the argument escalate into violence. People pushed the armed Tigers aside and clambered over the earthworks. The Tigers, in turn, pulled them down, beat them with palmyra branches and chased them back to their tents. Horrified, Mother declared that the apocalypse had come. '*Kaliyugam*, this is *kaliyugam* we're witnessing.'

Mugil suspected that Prashant's sudden arrival, too, was meant to encourage them to stay. He didn't have a palmyra stick, of course, but he did have his words.

MUGIL WOKE UP at dawn while it was just getting light and left her tarpaulin tent to find a quiet spot to relieve herself. Lately peeing had become excruciatingly painful: there was an intense burn and barely a trickle. Severe dehydration had led to an infection.

At this time of day, if there were no air raids, only women tended to be up. Bunker life erased all privacy, so pre-dawn was when women chose to urinate or, if they were menstruating, change the cloth in their underwear. Every time battle broke out, Mugil felt the world forgot about menstrual cycles. As Amuda commented once, with everything else in total disarray, it was a surprise to have anything arrive on time, especially something as inconvenient as a woman's period. Female combatants on operations took pills that postponed the bleeding. Hospitals stored sanitary napkins for civilians; the UN, Médecins Sans Frontières and the Red Cross had given them out before being banished from the Vanni. But as the war continued and hospitals, clinics and makeshift dispensaries ran out of dressing wool and cotton, they used sanitary napkins to dress wounds. So, like other women, Mugil and Amuda had ripped up the last of their old saris to use as pads.

Mugil didn't find her quiet spot. Instead, around her, hundreds had already begun their journey to Matalan and Putumatalan. It was mid-April now, and the water level had fallen slightly. People waded through the muddy water that shuddered as if to consume them. The early crossers used the thin sandbanks as bridges, but there was no room now, and they had to walk through water. Women's skirts and saris ballooned as they entered the lagoon gingerly. They sank deeper, to the knee, the waist, the neck. Thousands soon pushed their hips against the waves, finding their feet in the sand bed, and found it futile to use their hands for anything but to hold on to what was most precious. Parents carried their children on their shoulders and heads. Adults held hands and groped for shoulders to keep their balance.

Everything else was left behind on the long shore. The mountains of discarded bags, baskets, clothes, motorbikes and trishaws grew. If utensils, TVs, books and bags had made it this far, they were now tied to trees and vehicles in the hope of being retrieved later. Some bicycles and tractors were retained till the very last minute to take the disabled or severely wounded through the water.

The best time to cross Nandikadal was before noon, during low tide. The water level was manageable at this time, but the gunfire was often at its worst. The collapsing shallow bunkers in Matalan were, however, no safer than the water. So despite the barrage from the sky, leave they had to.

The route chosen was behind the most crowded section of the lagoon; the deserted parts were bound to be deeper. At around ten in the morning, Mugil's family—her father, mother, brother, and sister, carrying the four children on their shoulders—waded into the water. The further they went, the more the water and crowds separated the group. Balls of fire ripped through the air like arrows and fell into the water, diffusing loudly, throwing people off course.

In minutes, her family had scattered. When Mugil ducked into the water to avoid the gunfire and emerged, Amuda was way ahead of her, Mother to her right. Maran had lost his balance and almost took another woman's hand by mistake. Mugil began to panic. A matter of seconds was enough to break up families. Some days earlier, she had seen a woman trying to cross the chest-high water with a toddler on each shoulder. The woman lost her footing and crashed into the water, surfacing with only one of her sons. She screamed, whipped her head around, begged people to go under and look for her baby. Some did, but it didn't help. The wailing woman had to give up and cross to save her other child.

Mugil tied Tamizh tightly to her chest with a sari and her hands gripped Maran's ankles tight to keep his body fixed on her shoulders. Throughout the six long hours it took to reach the expanse of sand before Matalan, she could not stop thinking of the drowned toddler.

At the shore, Prashant propped up the blue tarpaulin again. Near it, Mugil and he struggled to dig a bunker. Trying to build one in the sand was like sailing against the wind. With the lagoon only a few hundred metres away, the groundwater leached in quickly, destroying the walls.

Just as they managed a shallow trench and sat down to rest, Divyan arrived. Maran and Tamizh ran to their father. Mugil noticed a hobble. The armoured jeep Divyan drove had been thrown into the air by the force of a mine blast. He had landed on his back and dislodged a few discs. A white rope, which doubled as a sling for his left arm, securing it into his shoulder, was layered with coagulated blood and mud. His left thighbone had a hairline fracture. He had been recovering in the Matalan Tiger dispensary and had come straight from there. He was still unable to walk straight and was in a lot of pain. A strip of hair on the left side of his head was shaved off, exposing an ugly stitch. His boys wanted to be carried, but Divyan sat down slowly and told them, 'Appa is hurt. He will carry you once he is better.'

'Tomorrow?' Maran asked.

'No, not so soon!' Divyan laughed.

'Day after, then?'

'You tell me when it is the day after tomorrow, and I'll carry you,' he said, to Maran's satisfaction.

Mugil asked her husband when he would have to go back. He said he would not; he was here for good.

The small tent had only enough space for the children, Amuda and Mother. After dark, the others lay down outside, the wet sand soaking their clothes. Mugil stared at the night sky, at stars she knew well and had counted on whenever she was lost. Between the stars, explosions glittered and lightning flashed. Immense fires burned beyond Nandikadal. Smoke and the smell of gunpowder and burning flesh stung her nose.

Suddenly, sharp whistles and crackles foregrounded the thuds and hums. Mugil moved fast and woke Divyan. The attacks were coming closer. Amuda shoved the children into the bunker and the rest of the family jumped in. Between the long whine of shells, they could hear cluster bombs detonating.

Mugil had first seen a cluster bomb go off in PTK a few months ago. She had looked up from eating a roti in the bunker and stared, mesmerised by how pretty the explosion was. In time, she'd learnt that this bomb was like any other when launched. But about a thousand feet from the ground it let out a loud soda pop–like sound, throwing out bomblets. This made a para-para-para noise, like a drum roll, before the multiple blasts.

In Matalan, people who were just settling down to sleep had heard that same popping. They ran out of their tents and into the water and bunkers, screaming, '*Kotthu gundu*! Cluster bomb!' This rarely helped. It was near impossible to avoid being hit. Each cluster bomb contained eighty-eight or seventy-two bomblets—depending on the type—and they travelled up to a kilometre from where they were discharged from the cluster.

Soon after the drumming stopped, people crawled out of the futile sand bunkers where they'd been cowering. People were holding burst cheeks or bleeding feet and arms. The survivors knew that after every ten minutes of onslaught, there would always be a ten-to-fifteen-minute gap. This breather was their only chance to dart from tree to tree, go grab some food packets, or pull into the bunker a lost child or wounded man frozen in fear. In contrast, Divyan shuffled rapidly to one of the scattered bomblets.

When he was in the Putumatalan clinic, he had seen a teenager with a bomblet lodged in the back of her thigh. The doctors had amputated her leg at the hip and the nurse had run out to discard the limb far from the hospital. Since then, he had been curious to see what these bomblets looked like; he needed to understand them and what they could do.

He peered closely at the one on the sand, careful not to touch it. It was bell-shaped and smaller than his palm.

He looked back at their tent and hurriedly called Maran and Tamizh over. Mugil ran over, too.

He pointed. 'Do you see this?' Maran instantly tried to grab the shiny thing. Mugil held his hand back.

'That is exactly what you should not do, okay? Will you listen to Appa? This is bad, it will go boom, and then you will die. You will see these everywhere, but don't touch them, kick them or pick them up,' Divyan said. 'It is not a ball.' The boys nodded. 'He called it the machine gun of bombs.'

When they rushed back to the bunker, the attacks resumed. The children nodded off but woke startled when the cluster bombs rattled.

During a lull, Divyan spoke softly. 'Mugil, maybe I should just surrender.'

Throughout the journey from PTK, the loudspeakers guiding, instructing and ordering the displaced had also been urging the Tigers among the Tamils to surrender. 'Give yourselves up!' the army said. 'Why do you women want to wear trousers and hold guns when you can wear a beautiful sari, and have bangles and flowers in your hair? Why do you men not want to have a peaceful life of business or farming? Choose peace. Surrender!'

Mugil was sure her husband would consider it. Still, she was taken aback. 'Why? Are you not able to walk anymore? Is it hurting that much?'

Divyan didn't answer.

'Have you forgotten what you are capable of?' She reminded him that he had once run with shrapnel peppering his body and that, another time, he had stayed on the front line with a busted kneecap.

'Each time makes you weaker, not stronger,' he said.

She offered to rebandage his wounds. 'I'll carry the boys from here on, or we'll hire a tractor.' She was using every argument she could think of.

He shook his head, saying that their leaders, too, had started surrendering or leaving the country. Others were trying to reach the

UN through the Norwegian foreign ministry to negotiate a ceasefire. But Divyan didn't think it would work. 'No one is coming, even the aid agencies are gone,' he said.

The bombing had ceased—they could hear loud talking outside.

'I say you should take a boat and leave for India with the kids.' The commotion almost drowned his voice. He seemed to imply he wouldn't join her.

Even as they spoke, people were leaving the island, choosing the dangers of sailing a small boat on a rough sea over enduring the war. A boat journey to India could take days, even weeks, and navy patrols were looking to apprehend refugees. Long stretches of swimming were often required, too, because the boats couldn't get all the way into shore. The boatmen would not allow food or any supplies on board, wanting to fill their vessels with as many people as possible to maximise their profits. Divyan was weak and would probably not survive such a journey. The circle of red on his bandages had now spread from his thigh to his hip. 'You take the kids and your parents,' he said.

'Is it right to leave at this time?' Mugil asked.

'Stop it! None of that matters now,' Divyan said, getting up. 'I'm going to ask how much it costs to arrange a boat. Are you coming?' This was not the man Mugil knew. This man, always the voice of morality in his family, always reassuring with his black-and-white principles in the greyest of days, was too weary even to think through the biggest decision of their lives.

As the night darkened Mugil looked at the mass of people running madly into the warm black sea. The shelling had stopped for a while, but it was on everyone's mind. They were scrambling onto the nearest boats. Some were toppling over, pushed, pushing. Water flooded everything: their eyes, mouths, bags, boats, engines.

Mugil would have to run to the boats, too, to join those going to India. There were thirty people in a boat that usually held ten, sailing away, fleeing. The going rate was 60,000 rupees per head, but they knew a boatman, a handicapped ex-fighter. She could give him Divyan's gun, some kerosene she had stashed and 30,000 rupees.

Should she really go? Divyan repeated that he wouldn't survive a night-long motorboat ride, even to Jaffna. He assured the family that his best chance of survival was to surrender. It was risky, but the army had promised to be lenient to those who gave themselves up. The family should go on, he insisted. After a few years, they would find each other. It wouldn't do to let the children see their homeland in this state. He spoke fast, but every word seemed to have been rehearsed.

Divyan fished in his shirt for some money. 'You should go now, while the shelling's stopped,' he said. He would take Mother and the others across the lagoon and then surrender.

Mugil couldn't think clearly; her mind was flying far into the future and yet unable to dig out of the clamour around her. It was the first time she would ever leave Sri Lanka. She would go first to Rameshwaram in India, and then from there to Malaysia, then maybe seek asylum in Canada. People had done it before. When her childhood friend Shakti had decided to leave the country seven years earlier and Mugil had asked her why, the girl could not answer. 'Perhaps because I have the chance,' she had said. But later, when she wrote from Germany, raving about the generosity of the people but missing coconut and spice in her food, she had recalled Mugil's question. 'I know the answer now, my sister,' she wrote. 'Here, I can stop caring about others all the time. I can be happily self-centred.'

Perhaps this was not a bad idea. Mother was encouraging her to go, Amuda said she had been considering it herself, Father reminded her of extended family in India. Prashant, however, threw a fit. 'How can you leave?' he yelled. 'You'd abandon your people?'

His indignation cleared Mugil's mind. 'I have children, Prashant,' she said calmly.

'You'll be a traitor if you leave,' he growled. 'If all of us leave, there will never be an Eelam. All the people who died for it will have died in vain.'

'This is not the time …' She stood up to go to the water's edge.

'Then when? When you're sitting on a sofa with your belly full, in an air-conditioned room in America?'

Amuda tried to help. 'Look, we're all so hungry.'

'Food. All you people can think about is eating! What about all those years when Annan fed us? Are you going to turn your back on the people who cared for you?' He looked at Divyan, who was quietly packing a polythene bag. 'Divyan *anna*, why aren't you stopping your wife?'

Mugil took the bag and started to walk towards the sea. Maran followed.

Prashant grabbed Mugil's elbow. 'Is this what you'll teach your son?'

'At least he will be alive!' She was almost running now, with Prashant following.

'If you try to go, I will take a rifle and shoot you, you *throhi*!'

Mugil felt the water lap at her feet, and Maran holding her finger. Her parents rushed to her with Tamizh. Amuda followed behind them. Divyan watched in silence. If Mugil left, didn't it have to be with all of them? Did this make sense? Leaving Divyan behind with the army? Taking on a long journey they might not even see through to the end?

Prashant continued to curse her. 'Traitor! Go! That's what you were anyway, a traitor! Go, all of you! Go then! Where is my rifle?'

Mugil had done as she was told for most of her life; she had sworn on the Tamil soil perhaps a million times. She had worked for something she loved and hoped that it would make sense later. By the light of faraway bombs, hundreds were running haphazardly towards boats bobbing in the water. The horizon was bathed in darkness. It made her stomach churn. It felt endless. Circuitous, spiralling. A tiring, nauseating forever. Guilt-ridden, she turned back.

PART TWO

claustrophobia

13.

April 2009

IN PUTUMATALAN, MUGIL was unable to tell which way the war would swing. There was every sign that the Tigers were losing, but their supporters remained hopeful. What stood out, however, was the new, quiet confidence of the army. It frightened her.

As thousands of Tamils crossed the Nandikadal lagoon, Sri Lankan soldiers came to help them out of the water into Putumatalan. They took the children by the hand and carried the elderly. People filled the narrow beach, sitting with barely an inch between them. Soldiers distributed food to eager refugees. 'We will take all civilians to a camp until the battle is over,' they said over the loudspeakers. 'But anyone who has spent even a day in the LTTE should surrender to us first. We will take them to another camp. Come of your own accord, it will be better for you.' They didn't say *Kottiya*, or terrorist, as they usually did.

Everyone was given bananas, biscuits, a meal packet, and a cup of black tea. There was rice, the tea was hot, the bananas were ripe: luxuries after five months of living like animals. It seemed to promise an end to their trials.

The young soldier ushering them around referred to Mother as *amma* and Father as *ayya*.

'These boys are so respectful,' Mother said, at once suspicious and pleasantly surprised.

'They give you tea, and you instantly change sides, old woman?' Father scolded. 'The real test is how they treat their enemies.'

From every batch of civilians the army received in the no-fire zone and brought to the refugee camps, it first sifted out the combatants. Many men and women gave themselves up. As the families sat on the ground under the eyes of the army, the former combatants hugged their relatives, stepped away from the crowd and placed themselves in front of a soldier.

Mugil watched, knowing her husband, too, would do this soon. She sat next to Divyan, who held his thigh with one hand and Tamizh with the other. His mind was made up even before they reached Putumatalan. As hundreds surrendered now, he seemed to be talking himself into it once again. Mugil searched the soldiers' faces for the expression she had seen in the mango orchard, when they kicked the LTTE girls. She looked for signs of hate or condescension, but she saw only fatigue.

The battle continued within earshot; the Sri Lankan armed forces were still fighting the Tamil Tigers. To change sides, the combatants had to overcome a reality formed over generations in less than a day. Mother supported Divyan's decision to surrender. Like many at this time, she no longer trusted the Tigers to take care of them. Those who had been beaten up by the LTTE cadre while trying to cross the Nandikadal shook with disillusionment and anger. 'Those we knew and trusted have failed us!' a man cried. 'What do we have to lose now?'

'I don't want to say it, but everything is over anyway,' Father said softly. 'We should accept this defeat.'

He said he didn't remember the last time he had felt cornered like this. The Tigers were behaving like thugs. So many Tiger leaders had died. Innumerable stories were doing the rounds: about where Annan was, what he was planning, whether he was alive. But none of them were credible. And now their bravest were giving up. What could this be if not the end?

Prashant, too, decided to surrender along with Divyan. 'Why should I hide?' he said. 'There is honour in surrender.'

Mugil was taken aback at his hypocritical turnaround. When she had wanted to leave on the boat to India, Prashant had demanded adherence to the LTTE at any cost. 'Oh, now it is honour!' she shouted. 'What happened to your great loyalty?'

'Do you want me to be ashamed of having fought for Eelam? Why should I hide it?'

'You just want to be a big hero!'

Prashant shrugged.

'You are the traitor now,' she said.

Prashant smiled cloyingly. 'Go and tell that to your husband first.'

Mugil wanted to slap the smirk off his face. 'You are small, tiny, an insect in front of Divyan. Don't use his name!'

'Let him go, *akka*,' Amuda said, pulling her away. 'If he doesn't surrender, he'll be found out in two minutes.'

Father was saying that Divyan and Prashant could look out for each other. Perhaps it was better there were two of them now.

'Yes, he'll give keep me company on the way to hell,' Divyan added, as a weak joke.

'If they're going to shoot all of you point-blank, just push this idiot in front of you,' Mugil replied. They laughed nervously. This was the way they used to banter before an operation—belittling imminent danger, belittling their own fears.

Finally, Divyan pushed Tamizh to Mugil, looked her straight in the eyes and said, 'Look for me if you hear nothing for a long time.' He then walked up to the soldier, and Prashant followed.

Mugil would recall that moment for years. The sky glowed orange on the horizon, a woman's voice behind her pleaded with someone not to go, and Tamizh was digging his nails into her neck. Divyan's instruction filled her with dread. Find him if she heard nothing.

Prashant's words, too, left a bad taste in her mouth. He didn't want to hide who he was. But she would have to hide. As the surrendered combatants were taken away, Mugil joined the wider stream of families being led by the military to buses that would take them to the civilian camps.

She was going on as a civilian with her sons, while Prashant and Divyan would be the soldiers of a cause, even though they had surrendered. This is how it would go down in history: she was the parent; they were the fighters. She understood why she had to do it, but nevertheless her indignation was as real as the wound festering in her leg. They claimed honour in surrender. She would have only the ignominy of hiding.

MORE THAN A month later, on 19 May 2009, a day that would change her life forever, Mugil skipped the camp's afternoon queue for lunch and hung back in her tent. In summer the camp was so hot a broken egg would fry on the ground. Although May temperatures were not new to her, never had she felt so helpless before this onslaught. It was like something immovable, solid and invisible, weakening not just body but soul, too. She didn't know which was worse: the shaded slow cook inside the oven-like tent or the blaze outside. Red dust coated everything: the grass, the tents, the food, even the people. When Mugil licked her dry lips, she felt the soft grains on her tongue. The halo of Amuda's unruly curls glowed red. The ends of most children's hair were blond, their eyes a dull yellow. With their rust-red dry skin, they looked like small mud devils.

Mugil's family was taking shelter in Ramanathan zone, better known as Zone 2, in a white tarpaulin tent with eight other people. That morning, like every morning, her parents, sister and all the four children had woken to hunger an hour before breakfast time and left to secure a place in the line. And now it was lunch. The queue would be unbearably long.

With 76,000 people when Mugil got there, Zone 2 was the largest and most overpopulated of the eight zones that made up the 700-acre Manik Farm camp run by the Sri Lankan army just outside Vavuniya town. Much of the area was once forest, and growing up, Mugil had known it as Karadipokku, the Route of the Bear. Not a tree was in sight now, all hacked down to shelter thousands of Tamils pouring out of the combat zone. From the Vanni, the army took people to closed camps in Mannar, Jaffna, Trincomalee, and mostly to Manik Farm. In just the last ten days of April 2009, about

110,000 people had entered Zone 2. Soon they replaced the vegetation entirely. Mugil had rechristened the place *ahadi-pokku*, the Route of the Refugee. 'How long will we be here?' Amuda had asked a soldier less than a month ago when they entered the camp. He was writing their names down, and they had realised that the camp was ringed with barbed wire. Their induction took place at the end of a long disorienting bus journey with the army from Putumatalan. The official had continued to fire questions about their native town and the size of the family. Another refugee behind them had repeated the question in broken Sinhala. 'How long here? How long?'

When they had boarded the bus in Putumatalan, they were relieved to say goodbye to the shelling, displacement and starvation. But as they drove through destroyed villages occupied by army battalions and a desolate shoreline of discarded bicycles, chairs, bags and slippers—so many slippers—they felt nauseous with something like guilt. When they were stopped at five army checkpoints—the same checkpoints the Tigers had used earlier—for full-body searches by uniformed soldiers who had just hours before rained ammunition on them, Mugil felt the first sting of humiliation.

'You'll be here just till we figure everything out,' a soldier at the camp office had finally replied, with a weak smile. 'What, what did he say?' someone behind them asked, his question echoing among the other arrivals. The soldier's manner was reassuring but his words meaningless.

The real answer—and it was likely even the soldier did not know it—was this: beyond getting the Tamils into the camps, there were no plans. Mugil learnt this only two weeks in, on the day Aunty Sumathi visited her from Vavuniya with some fresh clothes for the family. As they waited their turn outside the visitors' centre—shouting across the barbed wire ('How are the children? Is it very hot? Have you eaten?')—Mugil noticed a middle-aged man in expensive clothes. He wore sunglasses and stood near his imported SUV, a few steps from the press of visitors. Other inmates seemed to have noticed him, too, and they craned their necks to see which internee he might have come to visit.

When it was Mugil's turn in the centre, she barely listened to her aunt from behind the wooden bars. Only waist-high tin sheets separated the inmates, and a private conversation was impossible. To Aunty Sumathi's left was the well-to-do SUV man, speaking to an elderly woman on Mugil's side. He addressed the old lady as *amma*, and from the way he spoke about her grandchildren, in tender respectful Tamil, Mugil guessed he was her son. But how could it be? The old lady looked like she was squeezed dry, her sparse grey hair leaping off her scalp and her hands shaking involuntarily. Her sari was faded and tattered from the Vanni months. A bloody bandage covered her ear. Like most other inmates, she was barefoot.

The son cried softly as his mother babbled about having been in the toilet when her name was announced over the loudspeaker and how she had almost missed hearing it and seeing him. He then looked at the soldier standing by and asked in authoritative Sinhala about the procedure to take his mother home to Colombo. The soldier waved his hand in the air dismissively. No one could leave, he was saying. Not even if they had homes and family outside.

That was when it finally dawned on Mugil; it would not be a few weeks or months here. They would keep them in this enclosed space patrolled by armed guards for as long as they could. Many requests of transfer to relatives' homes in Jaffna, Vavuniya, Colombo and even abroad had been rejected. The camp for civilians was no different from an open-air prison.

The ways of the camp became easier to comprehend once she understood the situation. Ten or more people occupied each tent, assigned to their beds by camp officials. Food was served three times a day, and you had to queue alongside thousands of men, women and children waiting with their plates and cups. Inmates got thirty litres of water per day for washing, bathing and drinking, but if the water truck didn't bring enough one day or you couldn't collect the water because you were lining up for medicines, your loss would not be compensated the next day.

Pit latrines, separate ones for men and women, lined the corners of the zones. Some hundred people would use a latrine meant for twenty. They were always blocked and rarely cleaned. When the summer sandstorms blew mud into the air, the tang of urine and faeces wafted throughout the camp on the wind. Flies buzzed everywhere, and mosquitoes bred in the dirty drains cut along the tent rows.

Complaining about all this was impossible; in all the applications, forms and affidavits they had to submit, all the permits and passes they had to get, there was never any space for complaints or feedback. Communication went only one way. When the speaker boomed with orders and instructions, people responded mockingly, 'God's voice! Listen!'

Speaking directly to a soldier was inadvisable. One enterprising neighbour had created a spot of shade in front of his tent with spare wood poles and a piece of tarpaulin. It stood for barely two days before a soldier kicked it down, saying the pathway between rows of tents had to be kept clear.

'Why are you doing this? I only wanted some shade, and all of us used it,' her neighbour argued.

As Mugil watched, the soldier's eyes bulged. He took a menacing step towards the man and bellowed what sounded like rules in rapid Sinhala. The neighbour stared blankly for a bit and then looked at his feet. For the next few days, the soldier would swing by to check if anyone had dared raise the sunshade again. 'Why couldn't you just shut your mouth?' Father asked the neighbour. 'Every time he comes, he's checking us out to see if something else is amiss.'

Visitors could not enter the camp. They could meet inmates, as Aunty Sumathi did, at the visitors' centre by the camp entrance, the cubicles separated by tin sheets, for not more than twenty minutes, and under the watch of an armed soldier. When the workers from the UN Refugee Agency or World Food Programme came with aid packages, you couldn't talk to them or ask for what you really wanted: sanitary napkins, milk, medicines, a clean toilet. Mobile phones were banned. Inmates were allowed a three-minute telephone call from the landline in the camp office, but the wait for this often lasted two days. Also inmates were not allowed to travel between zones; zones 2 and 3 were separated by a gravel road and a high barbed-wire fence. If there was one rule people defied most, it was this. The barbed wire was repeatedly breached all along the fence. The army thrashed someone for it every few days.

Mugil sometimes wondered why she didn't feel more grateful for what the Sri Lankan government gave her. For a moment—when she thought of the battle raging just two hours away by road from where she stood and remembered that thousands were still trapped in the conflict—she would acknowledge that there was food, water and shelter in the camp, just as promised. Her family was together, all alive; they didn't have to move home every few days, and there was a shed school for the children. The Bank of Ceylon had opened a branch inside the camp, and she had been able to deposit 6,000 of the 10,000 rupees that remained with her family. The aid agencies were not being kept away as they had been in January. Mugil whined about their under-salted, under-cooked, insufficient meals, but when she heard others complain, she was embarrassed. Did she too sound that petty? She had heard that the NGOs would soon bring dry rations and allow people to do their own cooking. Perhaps the government did care about their health.

The same military that was bombing their villages less than a hundred kilometres away, that shelled no-fire zones with impunity, was running this refugee camp. As the inmates settled into the routine, they learnt to coexist with the army, sharing the same putrid space, and their interaction changed. When the soldiers used polite words or smiled, or when they were quick to explode into a rage, an elder might forgivingly say, 'They are just young boys following orders.' A few faces became familiar, the leniency or gruffness of some well known, but Mugil still stiffened when one of them passed by. Some of the soldiers were considerate, even generous; one of them slipped Amuda's baby daughter a packet of biscuits or a toffee once in a while. Mother befriended a tall one called Krishan after he helped her carry her water buckets. Krishan had been recruited just a year earlier, which meant he was fresh from his first experience of war.

'Look, not even a moustache has sprouted on their lips yet' was both an abuse and a free pass. Some of the soldiers had Sinhala–Tamil phrasebooks, but this unnerved the inmates more than it pleased them. 'Oh, they won't let on that they understand us,' Mugil's sunshade neighbour had whispered. He believed, like most people, that the soldiers' language classes were meant to help them flirt with the Tamil girls or to spy.

The rule Mugil detested most was the one that forbade them from working outside the camp. This was really why she couldn't feel real gratitude towards the army, only anger or mistrust. Every waking moment was spent asking for something. Life was a series of agonising queues for food, water or the latrine. They were reduced to tearing at each other for essentials; at the end of April, two children were crushed to death in a stampede for food. Everything was a handout to the conquered people, not a right. 'We survived all that to become beggars and thieves,' Mugil often said. Internees chased water lorries and smuggled in vegetables wrapped in saris, not because they were incapable of working for a living but because they were not allowed to. One could work for food inside the camp, however, and when Amuda joined the camp accounts office, she signed Mugil up as a part-time Tamil teacher at the makeshift school. Every week, they got oil, soap, powdered milk and three kilograms of rice. The payment was paltry for the work they did, but the jobs gave the sisters some dignity.

Mugil loved the few hours she spent teaching. Even with the shortage of textbooks, benches, pencils and chalk, the tin-shed school was a sanctuary of optimism. It was one of the first facilities to be set up in Manik Farm; inmates had demanded it even before they asked for a medical clinic.

For the Sri Lankan Tamil community, education maintained its cultural heritage. Even in pre-independence Sri Lanka, or Ceylon as it was once known, school and college enrolment among Tamils exceeded that of other ethnicities in the country. Gradually, differences in educational attainment came to form the identities of the Tamil and Sinhalese communities, which grew into separate ethnic blocs, each of which considered itself wronged by the other. When an anti-colonial revolution swept the country, the south and west focussed on a resurgence of Sinhala, while the Tamil-dominated north saw the proliferation of American missionary-run English-language schools alongside anti-British movements. In the coming decades, however, Tamil and Sinhalese political leaders selectively highlighted certain facts of colonial history to exaggerate ethnic distinctions and justify violence. Aided by propaganda and politics, a particular narrative gained popularity. It maintained that when the British hired English-speaking locals, Tamils, who were 12 per cent of the population, held about 60 per cent of government jobs. That '60 per cent' is much contested, but was a powerful inspiration behind discriminatory state laws and the Tamil militancy, and continues to encourage the perception among the Sinhalese that they are a sidelined majority. The idea of colonial bias was one of the earliest causes of tension in independent Sri Lanka. Sinhalese-led elected governments passed Sinhala-only language laws and admission policies, claiming that this was affirmative action designed to help youngsters from backwards rural areas, but they were widely seen as a way to undo the predominance of minorities in universities. As middle-class Tamil applicants were refused college places, they rallied against a state that blocked the advance of a prosperous, more literate people—these were the perceptions on which the Tamil militancy was mobilised. Thousands left to study abroad and poorer, frustrated Tamils went on to join separatist groups. Politicised in this way, education became both a marker of a besieged identity and an aspiration for the Tamils.

In the camp, too, determined students from six to sixteen years old thronged the makeshift school, gratified simply to spend a few hours in a classroom. Many of them had carefully wrapped their school certificates in plastic sheets to protect them from exposure to the elements, hoping to continue their studies when stability returned. Now, a few months after the school was set up, high schoolers began to take their OL and AL exams in the camp.

That morning in Zone 2, Mugil had supervised a batch of eighty OL students taking mathematics exams missed during the war. At half past twelve, she was back in her tent. Since everyone else was queuing up for lunch, she decided to use the privacy to change the bandage on her leg. She could hear the distant metal clang of the server's ladle hit the plates to a predictable beat, serving gruel or rice and *sodhi*. There would be no vegetables or fish or chicken except in the name of the dish. As soon as she opened her bandage, flies started to hover around it. She used one hand to swat them while the other slowly unwound the gauze.

The camp clinic had determined that a piece of shrapnel was lodged in her shin, but not having an X-ray machine, they had referred her to the Vavuniya general hospital. She had wanted to take her sons, too. Maran's neck and arms had broken out in itchy pink patches that grew larger as he sweated and scratched. Tamizh had a wheezy cough, and a camp doctor had said it was bronchitis, from which almost three-quarters of the inmates suffered. Mugil meant to ask the doctor how her son contracted it, but he only spoke Sinhala, and in the two minutes stipulated for each patient, there wasn't time for a discussion to be carried on through the interpreter (a Tamil inmate whose Sinhala was so halting that worried patients elaborately mimed their ailments for the doctor).

Even with the doctor's letter, it had taken a week for the camp's administrator, Brigadier Weerakoon, to give Mugil a day pass for the town hospital. She was not permitted to take her sons. 'Then you'll just run away happily,' said the soldier distributing the passes at the front office. He had said it in Sinhala, but he jeered, and his fingers had done a fast run.

As she had walked through the camp gates for the general hospital ten days earlier, Mugil looked down at herself. She was wearing the skirt her aunt gave her. Her fingertips were white with the chalk she had used on the school blackboard earlier that day. She had bitten back the words that rushed to her mouth, eager to respond to the soldier. She had already run far from everything she held dear.

At the hospital, the verdict had been as expected. The shrapnel would have to remain where it was. Painkillers were given, and the external infection cleaned and bandaged. Mugil had enquired about Maran's sores, and the Tamil nurse asked if she was living in the camp. 'Malnutrition, and probably ringworm, then,' the nurse said. 'All that shit floating around, I hear. Once you're in your own home, the sores will disappear.'

On the way back to camp, Mugil had scratched the itch of defiance building up inside her. She stopped at a shop and bought a used Nokia mobile phone for 3,000 rupees. It would be perfect for the phone card Aunty Sumathi had smuggled hidden in the hem of the sari.

Now in her tent, having redone her bandage, Mugil fished out the phone parts she had hidden all over the tent. The back cover from under the mats, the keypad in the folds of the tarpaulin, the plastic-wrapped battery in the clay under the wood poles. She assembled them and switched on the phone. It beeped almost instantly with a text message.

It was from the government of Sri Lanka's information department, and had been sent at 1:20 p.m., 19 May 2009. Addressed to all Sri Lankans, it proclaimed, in Sinhala—a language she could not read—that LTTE chief Velupillai Prabakaran had been killed on the battlefield.

MUGIL STARED AT her mobile phone, unable to make sense of the swirls, dots and exclamation marks of the Sinhala text. It spooked her. Something really big must have happened.

When her tent-mates returned, she showed the text to Bhuvi, a young man who had worked in the Kilinochchi government agent's office and knew some Sinhala. He squinted at the phone a long time.

'No wonder they served *kiri bath* today,' he finally said. It was rice cooked in milk, a Sinhalese dish made for celebrations and festivals.

He translated the text.

Mother gasped. 'It is a lie,' Father said. 'They are lying.' Mugil thought it was the worst kind of propaganda. That evening, when it was announced on the camp loudspeaker, people stopped in their tracks.

LTTE chief Prabakaran had been killed by the army in Mullivaikal the previous day, 18 May 2009. The government TV channel, Rupavahini, showed pictures of his portly body lying on the ground, his eyes closed, face swollen, a smear of blood on his head under his camouflage cap. President Mahinda Rajapaksa cut short an official trip to Jordan and the government media showed him kissing the ground when he landed. The next day he announced that the death of Prabakaran marked the end of terrorism in Sri Lanka. Speaking from Parliament in his trademark white kurta and maroon shawl, Rajapaksa said, 'Today is a day which is very, very significant—not only to us Sri Lankans but to the entire world. Today, we have been able to liberate the entire country from the clutches of terrorism.' The war, he added, was a stage in a larger, nobler task: that of assimilating the Tamils into Sri Lanka as part of a unified national identity. The terrorists were gone now. Peace would prevail; warring Sinhalese and Tamil identities would be reconciled. 'We should live in this country as children of one mother,' he said. His voice was triumphant. In just his first term as president, he had succeeded where eleven heads of state before him had failed.

The streets of Colombo erupted in celebration. The inmates of Manik Farm were cloaked in gloom. Prabakaran's death meant the same thing to both groups: the end of the LTTE.

That night in Zone 2, some people organised a candlelight vigil. They lit hurricane lamps and candles in a clearing near the tents and gathered around it in silence. In barely five minutes, shouting interrupted the ceremony. The inmates expected Sri Lankan soldiers and had prepared their cover story: they were mourning not Prabakaran but the thousands of civilians who died in the Vanni.

But the voices spoke in Tamil. '*Aye*! So eager to celebrate Annan's death, *anh*?' they yelled. 'Get out! Scram, you traitors!' It was a small group of men, loud and brash, their eyes wild with despair. 'You have no respect!'

An elderly woman tried to mediate. 'It is only an *anjali*, a memorial, don't you have eyes to see?' she said, with the authority her age gave around men young enough to be her grandsons. 'What is the despair in this?'

No one paid attention to her. A beefy man blew out the candles in a huff. The others kicked over the kerosene lamps. This was the image of 19 May that would endure in Mugil's mind: the pathetic aggression of these men, their blowing out of candles as if they were throwing punches, the way they looked at the teary mourners and said, 'You're all Sinhalese ass-lickers!'

For her, the news was like the shattering of glass on a silent night. She had never thought of the day Annan would be gone. He was her hero, the man whose words and mission had directed most of her life. He had taught her, her sister, her brother, her husband, to keep a firm eye on the future they wanted and let it shape the present. All the decisions she thought she had made of her own volition—her proud rebellion – were made for the dream he had designed. She told her father, without reserve, that she felt orphaned. He understood; it was likely he felt the same way.

Mugil wasn't sure why she'd thought Prabakaran immortal. She had rarely seen the leader after the cherished felicitation ceremony, except when he gave the annual Martyrs' Day address. Yet, somehow she was devoted, always conscious of his presence. This face appeared on every poster and film; the fifty-four-year-old had never looked older than forty. Few knew more about his personal life than that his aged parents lived in Valvettithurai and that he had two sons, the first a commander of the eponymous Charles unit and the second eleven years old. Tales from his youth were symbolic narratives of imminent greatness or innate brutality—he shot small animals with a catapult; he hated the discipline of school; he moved from petty theft to bank robberies to fund the fledgling LTTE; the first person he assassinated was the mayor of Jaffna.

A handful of trusted associates had earned his trust by demonstrating intense loyalty, a crucial test of which was keeping quiet. When Divyan had trained as Annan's bodyguard and spent most of the day tagging along with the leader, he was sworn to a code of silence. Even to Mugil he had allowed himself only two anecdotes, both adding to the leader's aura of power and benevolence. One was about the time when Annan, in bed with a fever and headache, asked Divyan to bring him some headache tablets. Fumbling with the foil packaging, Divyan dropped a pill on the dusty floor and began to extract another one. But the leader stopped him. 'Someone must have risked his life to smuggle that pill into the Vanni,' he apparently said. 'Let us not waste his sacrifice. Give me the Panadol that you dropped.'

On another occasion, Divyan was called to accompany Annan to an impromptu meeting. As the bodyguards ran in, the leader's wife said they had not eaten lunch. Divyan would describe how the leader had taken the plate of rice and curry, balled it up into mouthfuls and fed his bodyguards 'with his own hands'. 'I felt like Annan was my mother,' he would say.

Mugil wondered if Divyan, wherever he was, knew about 19 May. He would be heartbroken. Those in the camp who struggled most with the news were conjuring conspiracy theories about a faked death. The tales of Prabakaran's escapes to India when he was hunted in Sri Lanka were resurrected to illustrate how he always had a trick up his sleeve. A woman in the camp's water queue told Mugil that her son believed Annan would spring a surprise and turn up in a foreign country. For thirty years he was not even caught, the son said, now suddenly he is killed? A generation that had known only one leader believed he was invincible, gifted with unmatched military cunning, even divine foresight. Bhuvi's cousin, a boy from the political wing, pointed out that since the global proscription of the LTTE in the nineties, Prabakaran had been a wanted man. 'Even India and all the western powers couldn't catch him. How can this new Rajapaksa and his army do it?' The cousin was sure Prabakaran had escaped, tapping into the legendary intercontinental network of LTTE supporters and covert sponsors.

A song called *Thalaivar sahavillai*—the leader is not dead—was all over the Internet. Many Tamils were arrested just for listening to the song. Mugil had received the song on her phone, the powerful words and rousing tune playing over file pictures of Prabakaran. It came with an instruction to 'forward and delete as soon as you watch'. Another photo became a popular meme: originally published in an Indian Tamil magazine, it showed a laughing Prabakaran watching a report of his death on TV. It was captioned, 'Far away in an unknown location, he laughs. The leader is not dead! Long Live Tamil! Long Live Eelam!'

When the inchoate theories grew into rumours that Prabakaran had escaped in a secret tunnel from Mullivaikal to India and that the dead body left behind was a secret double, Mugil was disgusted. 'They are all talking as if this is a movie!' she complained to Amuda, who was weak with wheezing and counted on Mugil for all the latest updates.

Mugil, in turn, relied on Bhuvi and schoolmaster Sanjeevan, whom she called 'newsreaders'. At every opportunity they were glued to their radio transistors, tuning into the BBC, India's NDTV, and several Tamil stations. They ignored the frequencies playing music except when they tuned into one during the news bulletin. Their email inboxes and phones were full of articles and reports, and Bhuvi was so well connected to his government colleagues in Vavuniya and Colombo that Mugil was sometimes afraid he might be a spy. On the day he showed her the UN satellite map of the no-fire zone and the craters caused by shelling, however, she banished any such doubt. With Prashant away, Bhuvi easily filled the role of Mugil's younger brother. She did not share this familial intimacy with Sanjeevan, who taught mathematics in the makeshift school, but he had impressed her with a sullen demeanour that would not tolerate nonsense. He was a useful person to know.

Weeks passed and the camp expanded. In the wider world, only shreds of information floated around about the last stages of the war, and even less was known in the camps. In fact, different groups—the Sinhalese and Tamils, the English-reading and the vernacular-reading Sri Lankans, the diaspora Tamils and the Tamils still in Sri Lanka—were consuming their news from completely different sources, rendered in their native language and each with its own bias. Among the cacophony of denials and argument between the Sri Lankan government, the UN, and global human rights groups, divergent narratives of the war's end emerged.

Bhuvi and Sanjeevan, with their obsessive lapping-up of news, were able to fit some pieces of the puzzle together. In May 2009, by the Nandikadal, in an area only slightly larger than a football field, Prabakaran and some top LTTE leaders had hidden in bunkers holding thousands of civilian Tamils hostage (the UN estimated 5,000, but the number is always debated). They were cornered, with the army to the north and south, the navy on the eastern coast, and the lagoon to the west. After the military captured the rest of the Vanni it encircled Mullivaikal. This third no-fire zone was identified as a Civilian Safe Zone, a technical change of nomenclature that legally allowed the army to attack it. Here, the Ministry of Defence launched what it called a humanitarian rescue mission to evacuate the civilians. Simultaneously, the army rained shells into this tight circle. The Tigers resisted with suicide attacks on the army's 59th Division in Karayamullivaikal and Wadduval shore. Hundreds of civilians died in the mortar shelling and crossfire, and thousands burst out and left the area by sea, going to islands near Jaffna or to Mullaitivu beaches, from where the army took them to the camps. Meanwhile, a group of Tiger leaders raised white flags in surrender but were shot nonetheless. A team led by Prabakaran's son Charles was shelled. Finally, Prabakaran, with a number of leaders, including the political wing head, was killed while attempting to escape in an ambulance via Nandikadal. As one of the only surviving Tigers close to Prabakaran, the surrendered Tiger spokesman Daya Master was flown into Mullivaikal by the air force to identify the body. A tag marked 001, a T-56 rifle—the same kind Mugil had lost in Kilinochchi—two pistols, a satellite phone and a canister containing diabetes medicines were found along with the body.

About 282,000 Tamils from almost five districts were now housed in Manik Farm and a few other camps. Families were separated across camp zones, but the army maintained its ban on travelling between them. On 28 June 2009, Sanjeevan participated in a massive protest against this prohibition; his sister was among those trapped in Mullivaikal and now in Zone 4. Despite Mother having forbidden her, Mugil went along with Sanjeevan to the demonstration. Shouting slogans by the barbed wire between zones 2 and 3 and then again in front of the camp office, she saw her quiet friend yell till he was red in the face. Each time he shook his fists in the air, his anger was renewed and his soft voice went up in pitch. 'I feel like I'm hitting my head against a wall,' said Sanjeevan. She, too, felt a tightness in her chest, as if she were suffocating. If Sanjeevan needed to see whether his sister was safe, if he wanted to meet her after months of separation, why should the army stop him? Everyone in the camp was a survivor. They had seen horrors and lost loved ones—some dead, some left behind, some missing. Tears had been shed and replaced with the burn of helplessness and a collective desire for closure.

After the protest, the rules were mildly relaxed. Zone 4 remained a high-security area, but sometimes, on the army's whim, relatives would be allowed in. By this time, soldiers were also taking bribes to bend the rules. In mid-July, Sanjeevan was finally able to meet his sister—he had paid 10,000 rupees. Mugil saw him sitting with Bhuvi the next day, wearing his silence like armour. She waited for a week before she asked him how the visit had gone.

'My sister has lost an eye,' Sanjeevan said. 'She wishes she had lost her life.' The Tigers had kept high earthworks around them and shot at the civilians who tried to leave. His sister's husband and their daughter had not survived. 'I know we shouldn't speak ill of the dead,' Sanjeevan said. 'But if our leader needed to use innocent people to protect himself, then he was dead long before they killed him.'

14.

May 2009

COLOMBO HAD BEEN transformed. The passengers on the bus seemed less burdened, more relaxed, as if it were a holiday. Relief was writ large on their faces. People looked at each other and smiled knowingly. The demons had been conquered. The lurking tension of the everyday was gone. There would be no more suicide bombers on school buses or trains. Airports and markets were safe.

Indra's own days were unchanged, most of them spent between home and prison, in a perpetual state of suspension. From the bus on the way to see Sarva one day, she saw some middle-aged men pump the hands of young soldiers stationed at checkpoints that had been there for years. They were thanking them for their service, perhaps also hoping to see less of them in their city from now on.

Months after the killing of Prabakaran, Indra saw more Sri Lankan flags flutter on storefronts, rooftops and lampposts. Patriotic songs went on sale and were played incessantly on loudspeakers. Pettah market sold toy soldiers dressed in Sri Lankan army uniforms alongside military guns and kids' clothes in camouflage prints. We love our country, everyone seemed to be saying.

Sri Lankans had suffered conflict after conflict since independence. The first insurgency occurred in 1971, in response to an economic crisis. Unemployed Sinhalese youth formed a socialist militia called the Janatha Vimukthi Peramuna, or JVP. They led an armed revolt across the rural south and central provinces, but in three weeks the government cracked down, killing around 15,000 insurgents, many of them poor teenagers. By the eighties, militants had emerged in the north, too—young Tamil men and women demanding a separate state. The 1983 riots which Indra had narrowly escaped—when urban Sinhala mobs ran amok, killing more than 3,000—were the beginning of the bloodiest decade in Sri Lankan history.

By the late eighties, the Tigers were locked in a struggle with the Indian army, which had been deployed to disarm Tamil militant groups. At the same time in the south, the JVP struck again; over two years, the militia and the army butchered thousands of Sinhala Buddhist peasants and young lower-middle-class men. Every group in the conflict engaged in revenge killing, and youths all over the island were murdered in gruesome ways. It was common to see corpses dumped in rivers and beheaded bodies publicly displayed. Boys were chased in broad daylight and their throats slit. Families found bodies with burning tyres around their necks. Indra's sister Rani, who lived in Colombo then, had seen three Sinhalese boys hanged from a tree in the city centre. Uncounted young men had disappeared, thousands were murdered and more than 10,000 thrown in jail under terrorism charges. Violence and destruction had become mundane. Even after the Sinhalese militia was subdued in 1989, the Tigers kept up the violence, ruling the north and terrorising the south. The Sinhalese public abhorred them doubly for this.

The perpetual state of war incrementally polarised the country. Through the bloody years, successive governments fanned ethnic hatred and even the surviving JVP socialist leaders turned their outfit into an ultra-nationalist Sinhala Buddhist political party. Tamil complaints about discrimination and their call for autonomy found no support among most Sinhalese, who had endured checkpoints, economic instability and a culture of fear for too long. So when the LTTE was eliminated in May 2009, the people on the streets responded by embracing an era of hope and rejoicing that an ethnic war had finally been won.

The festive mood in Colombo made Indra uneasy. She, too, was rid of something that had wrecked her life, but she did not share the elation of those around her. The celebrations were alienating. Somewhere in the texture of the victory was the tense fibre of her defeat. She sensed it among the revellers but also felt it twist inside her. She felt exposed, more vulnerable than before.

In prison, the women in the visitors' queue discussed the end of the war. They brought up what they read in the papers or heard from relatives about the thousands killed, about the bullet through Prabakaran's forehead, about the zoo-like refugee camps. They analysed what it meant for their loved ones inside jail: release, detention, a life sentence. Or did it change nothing? There was much to say, but when guards passed, they changed the subject. It was dangerous to express doubt or question the cost of victory.

Indra could not even imagine how it would be inside prison. She was told only in August that the Tamil prisoners, during assembly a day after Prabakaran's death, had attempted to observe two minutes of silence but were admonished and forbidden to do so. They had finally done it a week later at night, in their cells. Indra often advised Sarva to keep a low profile and not agitate the guards. He had a stock reply: my behaviour has nothing to do with how they treat me.

In August 2009, when the journalist Tissa was charged with terrorism and sentenced to twenty years in jail, Sarva plunged into depression. He had tied his fate to Tissa's, the prisoner he thought most likely to bust his way out and throw the gates open for the others. When Tissa was sentenced, Sarva was inconsolable. 'They really spare no one,' he told Indra.

Around the same time, the TID accused him of having been a member of the Tigers' intelligence wing; they claimed he had confessed to his involvement. When Sarva's trial began, his lawyers argued that he had been tortured in custody and that the TID had no evidence to support their allegations. Indra gave a statement that her son had been forced into the LTTE. Even though she followed nothing of the exchange between judges and lawyers, she went to every hearing in court. She had relinquished nearly all her possessions to pay the lawyers and she only hoped they were making some progress. Showing up was all she could do.

The intimidation had now reached her doorstep. Every other week, plainclothes policemen and soldiers visited Indra's Nuwara Eliya tea estate bungalow or her sister's apartment in Colombo. They searched the house and questioned the family about Sarva's whereabouts, as if they didn't know he was in jail. Some of them even followed Indra and her sisters when they took the bus to prison.

Fear sapped Indra of energy. After a long day at the court once, when she walked to the bus stop, she fainted. When she came to, a young soldier from a guardhouse nearby offered her a bottle of water. She pushed it away, asking if he was trying to poison her. 'How can *I* trust *you*?' she asked in Sinhala. The soldier looked hurt. He said she was like his mother. Could she think of him as her son? She had sipped the water, but not swallowed the mistrust.

After the sixteenth visit from the plainclothesmen, Sarva's lawyers recommended that Indra approach an NGO for help. She met a group called the Nonviolent Peaceforce, an international NGO working to protect civilians from political violence. In just a few days, the NGO confirmed that Indra's movements were being watched. They asked her to keep them informed about her activities, and offered to help deliver food to Sarva in prison occasionally.

But Indra continued to visit the prison—it was her way of keeping an eye on her son. If she needed proof that her persistence was worthwhile, she got it on 13 November 2009. It was one of those days when the prison guards would just not open the gate. Relatives had been queuing up since seven in the morning as usual, but noon came and went and still the gates remained shut. No explanation was given. People were losing their patience and hurling abuse. Indra and some others were pleading; one woman even offered a bribe. But the guards would not relent.

Finally, at three o'clock, the gates opened. Visiting relatives charged inside. Indra dashed to the wire mesh, her eyes scanning the faces for Sarva. She spotted Rooban, who she knew was Sarva's best friend. She was about to wave when she noticed something odd about his face. His forehead seemed squashed from the top. Then she saw the other prisoners pushing against the wire mesh and bars. Many of their clothes were ripped. She caught a woman pointing at her husband's nose in horror. He touched it, wincing—it had snapped to the left.

When she finally saw Sarva, Indra screamed. His shirtsleeves were spotted with blood. He was supporting his lower back with one hand and clutching his abdomen with the other, as if midway through making a wobbly bow. When he looked down, saliva dribbled down his mouth; he seemed unable to close his lips. The visitors were asking what had happened. Indra couldn't string together a coherent answer from what she heard of the replies.

Indra called the lawyers' office as soon as she got home. A few meetings later, it became clear what had happened, why the guards had not opened the gates. After breakfast, when the Tamil prisoners had returned to their cells, Sinhalese prisoners had stormed the Tamil section and the door was locked from the outside. More than 200 Sinhalese inmates wielding clubs, hockey sticks, metal rods and chains attacked about 130 unarmed Tamils. When the Tamil prisoners grabbed the sticks and rocks being used to attack them, a full-scale riot ensued. The sinhalese prisoners stripped and beat a middle-aged man. They stuffed another's face into the toilet bowl for so long he lost consciousness. Someone almost bludgeoned a partially sighted prisoner to death with a stone. Many inmates banged on the gates, shouting for the guards, begging them to stop the assault. More than an hour after the violence began, prison officers turned up and took the Sinhalese prisoners away without a word. The Tamil prisoners remained behind bars.

Ten minutes later, a guard called the names of seven Tamil inmates. Five of them, including Sarva, came forward, only to be set upon again by about fifty Sinhalese prisoners in the courtyard. One attacker held Sarva down by his neck and another pounded his lower spine and stomach with a hockey stick. The five Tamils were dragged to the office, and there it was the prison staff's turn to beat them. 'You have the balls to create a riot?!' one baton-wielding officer shouted.

Outraged, Sarva told his lawyers that he wanted to file a fundamental rights petition accusing the prison authorities of colluding with the Sinhalese inmates to deliberately target Tamil prisoners.

Indra, too, wanted the prison officers to be punished, but could not help feeling that a petition would be futile. She knew that Sarva had learnt from Tissa that he had the right to file such a complaint. She didn't want to discourage her son, but a petition hadn't protected a VIP prisoner like Tissa. Any legal attacks mother and son launched would only be arrow after arrow loosed against a bulldozer.

15.

September 2009

WITH THE RAINS, a bloodless battle began. August flooded the refugee camp with sludge and disease. Tents in low-lying areas of Zone 2 billowed in the gush of dirty rainwater and sewage.

By September, Father was bedridden with diarrhoea. He lay on a straw mat in the tent, half-conscious, exhausted. The frequent visits to the toilet were agonising; he had to lean on someone and drag himself there. Mugil accompanied him until the day he couldn't hold it in and went all over himself. Embarrassed, he had fallen on his knees, held his face, and sobbed as Mugil had never seen. Now Bhuvi or Sanjeevan took him or, if they weren't around, Mother did, on a rusty wheelbarrow she had smuggled in by bribing the soldier Krishan with 500 rupees. More often than not, Father didn't last until the latrine area, and he burst into tears.

Mother, on the other hand, had hardened. She was always scolding Father, asking why he waited until the very last minute before saying he had to go. All the caretaking expected of her had calcified into a loveless efficiency. She snorted, spat and complained, walking away as if on cue when one of the children asked for food or water. In the muggy afternoons, when activity dulled in the camp and people rested, she sat outside their tent, hugging her knees, still and unmoving, not even waving away the flies from her face.

'Are you praying?' Mugil asked once.

'You think our house in Point Pedro still exists?' Mother said in a trance, as if she had not heard her daughter. 'Remember the coconut trees in the backyard?' Mugil had walked away, but later she wished she had hugged her mother, or taken part in her daydreams.

At the beginning, Father's illness had seemed simple to deal with. But their visits to the camp's primary health centre demonstrated it was much more serious. While the disease was commonplace, here in the camp its cure was not. If the doctor was in, the line wound long and looped through the tent rows. Fights broke out when someone tried to cut in. Please, it is an emergency, someone would always say. This is an emergency, too, another would reply, perhaps adding sarcastically that some people had nothing better to do than stand in line to be treated for a cold or cough. Each would point to their sick relatives and try to outdo the other's symptoms. Eventually a soldier would appear to end the squabble and throw both families out. More often than not, only half the queue made it as far as the doctor's office before it closed for the day.

It took Mugil four attempts to get in. Father couldn't stand in the queue, so she waited in line and, when it was near her turn, she called Bhuvi and hung up before he answered, the signal that he should bring Father fast. As soon as the doctor saw Father, grey and drooping, he wrote a prescription. He handed it over without a word and waved them on.

'Diarrhoea?' the medical dispenser asked when Mugil handed her the prescription. In front of her, stacks of tablets and capsules had collapsed on a white table.

'Yes,' Mugil said, although what she really wanted was to scream, 'Can't you see?'

'The prescription is not going to help. Give him lime juice and *kanji* to get his strength up,' she said. 'And fruits. Give him lots of fruits. Except mango and banana.'

Mugil couldn't believe the woman. Lime juice? Rice gruel? Fruits? Who had access to all of that in the camp? Trucks from the Multi-purpose Cooperative Societies were allowed inside camp now, and they sold sugar, tea, biscuits, brooms, plastic mugs, rope and other items the refugees might need. But the inmates had noticed with much consternation that most of the traders—Sinhalese and some Muslim—were selling essentials at a huge profit. A supermarket had opened, too, run by the Sathosa chain of stores, and it sold, to Mugil's bewilderment, largely ice cream and soda. Vegetables, fruit and milk powder were rarely available, and inmates who somehow managed to get their hands on a banana or some rice resold it—illegally, as they weren't allowed to set up shops—to make a few extra rupees. This, too, was gone in minutes, its disappearance usually coinciding with the arrival of a soldier. An orange or watermelon, even a lemon, was a luxury.

'Where am I going to get fruit?' Mugil snapped. 'All we give him now is tea. We don't even have sugar to add to it all the time.'

The lady didn't seem to care.

'Just give me the pills,' Mugil said, the fight in her fading.

'That's what I'm trying to tell you ... We don't have the medicine in stock.'

By the end of 2009, more than half of Zone 2 had diarrhoea, triggered by abysmal hygiene and poor nutrition. The toilets overflowed, and the filthier they got, the sicker people became.

Back in the tent, Mugil tried to feed her father watery gruel, but most of it dribbled down his chin. He could not swallow; perhaps he didn't want to. He mumbled gibberish all night and all day, and cried quietly about being a burden. They bought a tarpaulin sheet from a Sinhalese trader and laid Father on top of it. This reduced the number of trips to the toilet, but the tent smelled of shit and piss. Mugil asked the grandchildren to cheer him up, but he was too tired and bored them. 'Periamma, is Thatha going to die?' Amuda's son asked Mugil. Kalai refused to sit beside him because 'he smelt of *kakka*' and scared her. His gaunt face looked nothing like her smiling grandfather.

Mugil needed to take her father to the Vavuniya general hospital, but as the applications for day passes to the hospital increased, the camp office grew stricter. She looked at the soldiers, busy with desk jobs, carrying firewood, even cleaning the overflowing toilets. Surely when they signed up for the Sri Lankan military, this was not what they had in mind? They would indeed always be the men who defeated the LTTE—they would tell their grandchildren that—but they also sat in the camps for months looking into the eyes of emaciated, imprisoned men and women who loathed them in return.

In the south, however, the armed forces were heroes and the 2010 presidential election, just a few months away, was being fought in their name. The incumbent president was riding high on his historic victory over terrorism. His opponent was his former army general Sarath Fonseka, who had led the military against the LTTE, but had been fired for saying that the army had committed 'war crimes'. Global NGOs and the Sri Lankan Tamil diaspora demanded an independent international enquiry.

'War crimes' was not a phrase Mugil was familiar with. Sanjeevan said it could be about the attacks on civilian areas, the shelling of hospitals and no-fire zones, maybe even the army's use of cluster bombs.

'What about the rape of our women?' Mugil asked.

Sanjeevan winced ever so slightly. Mugil was a little taken aback herself. The word rape was not usually used, in Tamil or English. Even when inmates spoke openly about it, they used euphemisms like 'took her honour' or 'insulted' or 'left our women unable to show their face in public'. It irritated her every time, this dancing around the act, as if it were not a crime but just an embarrassing secret. She had used the English word *rape*, with the strong *r*, and it hung in the air. Emboldened and somewhat proud of herself, she prepared to come clean to Sanjeevan about the rapes she had witnessed in the Kilinochchi mango orchard.

'I don't think the NGOs will care about rapes, especially of Tiger girls,' Sanjeevan said.

She hadn't anticipated this. 'Why? That, too, is breaking the rules of war, no? Like burning hospitals?'

'But it was our fault that we had women in our militia. Otherwise this would not have happened at all. See how the army doesn't have women? They knew that would be a weakness.'

Mugil stared at him, heat rising from her neck. He was facing the other way, stitching a patch on his shirtsleeve, and he continued, his voice unemotional as ever: 'I am also upset that it happened, *enna*, but it is distracting us from the real issues. The army is taking our land, men from detention camp have just disappeared, they're trying to cover up all the evidence in Nandikadal ...'

He went on, offering clever, interesting opinions, ideas she had admired earlier. It was Sanjeevan who had once said, 'I know now how the Muslims must have felt when the Tigers forced them out of the north.' He had called them the oldest displaced community in the country, expelled entirely from Jaffna, Mullaitivu and Kilinochchi in October 1990 by the Tigers. About 72,000 people were given two hours to leave the homes they had inhabited for generations, allowed to leave with only what they could carry. Most had walked to Puttalam, a Muslim-dominated western town, where locals had taken them in. Many still lived in settlement villages. It was unusual for a Tamil man to mention this, especially one who grew up in the Vanni. Mugil had wondered how Sanjeevan was able to acknowledge the suffering of the smaller minority group at the hands of his leaders when his own community was wrapped up in its victimhood. How had he held onto that unselfish thought? How did he preserve his empathy? Listening to Sanjeevan became Mugil's way of seeing through the muddle of her own emotions about the movement and the Tigers.

Now she thought, looking at his lean, bearded face, that he was just like a newsreader—just saying things, feeling nothing. Rape was not a 'real issue' for him. What if it happened to men, she wanted to ask. Don't you see that this is also a way of subjugating our community? What if they raped civilian girls? What if someone did that to your sister? There were so many what ifs. But what was the use?

Suddenly all the months of analysis, of finding out what was happening, what had happened, how many were killed, who was a Tiger, who was a civilian, all of it was irrelevant. All Mugil wanted was certainty. She wanted a roof over her head, a life. She wanted to go home.

Everyone wanted to go home. Protests broke out regularly at queues, where the crowd gave people the anonymity they needed to speak up without direct consequences. Why does the government still lock people up in camps, they asked. By July 2009 only about 4,300 had been sent home, mostly people with specific needs, including the sick, university students, pregnant women and the elderly. Only about 9,000 more were cleared to leave, from close to three million refugees. Politicians from the Tamil National Alliance spoke out in Parliament and even came to Zone 2, in pristine white outfits, bringing cartons of bottled water and food. They patiently heard the inmates' pleas. But everyone in the camp was aware that the politicians had no power. No one did except the president and his army.

Most of the Tamils in the camps hated President Mahinda Rajapaksa; they had never voted for him. He became president when the LTTE made the grave mistake of enforcing a boycott on the 2005 elections, which he subsequently won in a landslide, defeating a candidate more sympathetic to the Tamils. Mahinda then launched a three-year-long war on them, and his brother Gotabaya, as the defence secretary, had a blank cheque and the liberty to conduct the battle however he thought best. Surprisingly, in May 2009, after the end of the LTTE, President Rajapaksa's speeches had stirred many Tamils. They had been startled to hear words few state leaders had ever used before; he called them equal citizens and spoke of inclusion. He recognised the often ignored distinction between the LTTE and the Tamil people. If he seemed sympathetic enough to realise that not all Tamils were terrorists, they thought, maybe things would get better. Father had once even made excuses for the president, recalling that the Tigers had once attempted to assassinate both Rajapaksas. 'And they took their revenge,' he had said, as if it was the most natural thing in the world.

But as the months wore on, apologists like Father wondered if they had been gullible. The president continued to make promises about rehabilitation and resettlement, but as they suffocated under his rule, these words rang hollow. Posters with his photo—a clean face and toothy grin—littered the camp. Mugil felt as if he was physically there, actually turning every knob, pressing every button, controlling every move of the Vanni Tamils.

An emergency had been declared and extended indefinitely by Parliament, and it was the president who now called the shots. The presidential task force directed the activities of Manik Farm and other camps, determining matters such as how aid agencies could engage with the displaced. It was dominated by high-level defence officials and was chaired by another of the Rajapaksa brothers, Basil, who was also the minister for nation building. Tamil- and Muslim-dominated districts were run not by the elected legislators but by the Sinhalese central executive, appointed by the president. On 12 July 2009, Major General C. A. Chandrasiri replaced Dixon Dela, a civil administrator, as governor of the northern province, which included the Vanni and Jaffna. Of the country's nine provinces, only the northern and eastern ones—where most minorities lived—were governed by retired army officers. These appointees and the president's office said that the refugees would have to wait until their villages were entirely cleared of mines before they could go home. The army, meanwhile, was moving into these evacuated areas, gradually establishing military bases in Mullaitivu, Vavuniya, Kilinochchi and Mannar.

Mugil felt caged in the claustrophobic half-truths of the president's rhetoric, which only seemed to intensify following international pressure to resettle the displaced Tamils. With the visits of global leaders, the inmates' emotions surged in waves of hope and despair. On the days when the United Nations teams came and went, the inmates prepared to chant Secretary General Ban Ki Moon's name in case he approached their tents. But he had visited only the 'showcase area', as the inmates named the misleadingly habitable model rows of Zone 3.

Then the politicians from India arrived, mostly from the southern state of Tamil Nadu. They shed tears, recited moving Tamil verses, professed anger at the ill treatment of their ethnic kin. Mother was not just dismissive of them, she saw in their goodwill a bad omen. 'We will not hold garlands and stand up for the Indians again,' she said, remembering the late eighties, when the ecstatic welcome of the Indian army into northern Sri Lanka spiralled over the next two years into a bitter war with the LTTE. To the Tamils, the Indian army was synonymous with rapists and torturers, and the Indian government was a selfish and unreliable big brother. They expected more from Tamil Nadu, but it became apparent after 2009 that these politicians were only play-acting an old friendship.

In July, the president had pledged to release and resettle up to 60 per cent of the displaced Tamils in the camp by November: 'That is our plan. In 180 days, we want to settle most of these people,' he said, but then clarified, 'It's not a promise, it's a target.'

'How much they talk!' Bhuvi said. 'Words, words, words. If this was food, our stomachs would explode.' Most Tamils in the camp had been lashed by some moment in the history of racial hatred and discrimination—a riot, a murder, a rejected college application, a whizzing bullet, a death, a lost eye, a dead child or parent—but this now was a whole community trapped together, three million people, with no options. Never before had they felt walled in by indifference like this.

MUGIL HAD BEEN in the camp seven months when the presidential election was announced, a choice between two candidates who filled her with dismay. The Tamil National Alliance strategically threw its weight behind Fonseka, the former army general, in exchange for guarantees to end military rule and relieve those affected by the war. Most Tamils wanted to cast their votes in favour of the TNA, the only Tamil alliance in the fray—other than the largely mistrusted pro-government Eelam People's Democratic Party—but they didn't expect a free or fair election. The state assured the inmates that it would install voting booths inside the refugee camps; the men who robbed the refugee Tamils of freedom now wanted to bestow upon them the right to vote.

Only a few thousand internees had been sent home, largely to the north of Mannar. The largest contingent from the Vanni remained in the camp, wading in knee-deep water. Mugil's tent leaked, and while they were allowed to cook for themselves now, dry firewood was hard to come by. A throbbing headache had lasted so long she had forgotten how she felt without it.

Tamizh's bronchitis worsened in the damp tent, and he had wheezing attacks every other night. Mugil had nightmares about waking to find her child's body cold and blue in the morning. In her row, five out of ten children had died of respiratory tract infections in the previous month. Amuda had managed to get some medicine from the camp dispensary for her own wheezing and shared half the tablets with her nephew. At this rate, neither would get well, Mother said. Every time someone in the camp said, 'Oh at least your children are alive,' Mugil bit her tongue, crossed her hands to her ears, as she would at a temple, and hoped that Pullaiyar hadn't entirely forsaken them.

But divine compassion was in short supply. Almost every week some Tamils were arrested, sometimes dragged out of the camp, for allegedly having served in the LTTE. Young men simply disappeared. 'There are eyes everywhere,' Bhuvi would say. Inmates informed on each other to the army or police in exchange for small freedoms: a few weeks of unmonitored peace or an extra packet of rations. Bhuvi's cousin had been taken away by the TID. He said a woman in his tent had betrayed him so she could speak to her husband in the detention camp.

Mugil was sure she'd be disappeared, too, any day now. She had been careful not to reminisce aloud about the Tigers or let on that she had the skills of a trained combatant. To keep the lie as close to the truth as possible, she admitted to being a photographer in the communications wing. 'Those who recognise you,' Amuda consoled her, 'are probably hiding themselves, so there's nothing to be afraid of.' But the fear of being found out remained. One day, when Mugil hopped over a puddle without breaking her stride, Bhuvi quipped that she was as agile as a tigress. Her heart started to thud loudly, and she made a bad joke about being a lame tigress. How much did Bhuvi guess?

Mugil was concerned about Divyan and Prashant, too. When they surrendered, the army said they would be taken to a special camp for ex-combatants; but there had been no word since then. In July, along with hundreds of others, she had submitted a request for information about surrendered relatives. Every week, when the army produced a list of 'surrenderees' held in detention camps, Mugil returned disappointed. She was now afraid that her comment to Divyan about being shot point-blank had been too close to the truth.

IT WAS MARAN who discovered that grandfather was dead. He had gone inside their tent to look for the steel cup he liked to play with. The old man lay on his mat, turned to the left like always. As Maran stepped over him, his foot hit a hand, and something in the way it fell made the child scream.

It was 17 November and no one else was in the tent. Mother was outside, picking out lice from Kalai's hair. Amuda was in the water queue. Bhuvi had been admitted to the Vavuniya hospital for jaundice a week earlier and had not returned. Mugil was returning from the camp office with a letter that gave her Prashant's location in a Vavuniya detention camp. Her family would be reassured by this rare good news.

She was near her row when she heard Maran shriek. Her mind immediately conjured up an image of Tamizh's dead body, lying in the sewage. She ran into the tent. When she saw her father, relief and guilt fought within her. She cried for hours. Grief, irritation, nostalgia and so many things burned away in her mind till all she was left with was rage. In another place, in another time, he could so easily have survived.

'The good man, he died in his sleep,' people said, as if the months before his death had nothing to do with it.

'At least he did not die under a bomb, he will go to God,' they said, as if a humiliating disease was a peaceful way to go.

It would cost 10,000 rupees, including bribes, for the body to be taken to Vavuniya for burial, and another 10,000 rupees for the funeral. Amuda said she would get a loan, at interest, from one of the richer camp inmates, but Mother forbade it. 'We have too much debt already,' she said. There was nothing else to discuss.

And so they buried Father on the camp's periphery, at the bottom of the barbed wire fence. Other bereaved families seemed to have made this choice, too; there were many mounds, close together, at various angles, almost overlapping, and Mugil was afraid the men she had paid to dig would hack into a decomposing body. A family three tent rows away from Mugil's had guided them here. Soon after arriving at the camp, their daughter had died of an intestinal rupture caused by shrapnel. She was young, 'fair and just twenty-six', the mother had said, and engaged to marry a boy from their village before they were displaced by war.

The death of the young was considered more tragic, which depressed Mugil because it implied that her father's time had come. It had not, she wanted to tell them. Your daughter was going to start a family, while my father had one. Why was the potential greater than the actual? He was once healthy enough to take his grandchildren to school, to expect to see them attend college. He could scoop them up and jump into a bunker. She wanted to say she felt rudderless and alone. But she said nothing because she was the person who had not known where to bury her father.

An armed soldier hovered nearby as they dug the grave and Amuda abused him under her breath. They would have to get a death certificate soon, and this soldier would be the witness. This was something else the family of the twenty-six-year-old had told them. In a register, the girl's parents had entered the date of death as well as the age and identification marks of the deceased, but the cause of death, usually filled in by a doctor, was added by the soldier.

'Bomb attack,' the dead young woman's mother had said.

'From unknown causes,' the soldier had written.

The dig took two hours. Mugil's family stood watching. Everyone was crying except Mother.

When they were about to lower the body, they noticed a small shroud lying unattended nearby. The bedsheet bore a Red Cross logo.

Mother went over to it and slowly opened the flap. Under it was the grey face of a boy not older than six. She threw her hands up and let out a howl.

'Take everybody!' she wailed, looking skywards and beating her chest. 'Oh the things my eyes have to see …'

The soldier slipped away. Without a word, the gravediggers started on another grave, this one only three and a half feet long.

When they returned to the tent that afternoon, muddy and defeated, Mother ripped to shreds the tarpaulin sheet Father had slept on and burnt it on their stove. A month later, in December 2009, a pass system would be officially introduced, allowing people to leave the camp for up to thirty days for medical reasons.

16.

June 2010

AMMA'S WORDS WERE brief. 'Don't be afraid,' she said. 'Someone will pick you up outside the court.' The plan was spare, but it could be no other way.

As soon as Sarva left the court building, still handcuffed, he walked with the guards towards the prison bus. From the corner of his eye, he saw his brother's yellow car parked a few feet ahead, its licence plate removed. Near the bus door, as soon as the prison officer turned the key in the handcuffs, Sarva ran for the car.

He shouldn't have had to run. A few days earlier on 22 June 2010, Sarva had been acquitted of all charges of terrorism. It was a miracle: Amma and the lawyer had somehow managed this feat in twenty-four months, while many others arrested under the PTA frequently remained imprisoned for much longer. After the upheaval of the past few months, it was unnerving to think that a signature and a stamp would soon allow him to emerge from the labyrinth. He was still in prison, but a formality would soon release him. Rooban had got out a month earlier, and Sarva knew that he was freed thanks to the desperate payment of 400,000 rupees to the attorney general. Sarva had wondered if Amma, too, had paid a bribe, whether his acquittal had been entirely legal. Amma brushed his scepticism aside with a simple question: 'Where would I have found all that money?'

Sarva was uneasy about being declared innocent. He wasn't sure if being a man on the street made him more vulnerable to the TID. Free men disappeared all the time. His lawyer seemed to have the same concern. After his acquittal, he advised Sarva to withdraw the fundamental rights plea they had filed against the Colombo New Magazine prison for the 2009 attack on Tamil inmates. Sarva wanted justice for his friends, but it was dangerous to aggravate the government any further. And so, while Sarva sat on the bench in Court No. 2, his lawyer declared his client's intention to withdraw the case against the prison. The judge had taken note and called a lunch break. She had then called Sarva to her office. 'Why do you want to withdraw the case?' she had asked in Sinhala. The question was perhaps a routine one, a matter of protocol, but for a moment Sarva felt the guards accompanying him bristle.

Accusing the authorities that held him was not safe, he wanted to say. I have had enough of these dark walls and dreary hopeless days, he might have said. But she was a judge. He was not able to form these words in her presence. 'Miss, I just want to go home' was all he managed.

The judge scratched her head and said, 'Okay, *haari, mudaar.*' Release him.

When they left the court, Sarva knew what he had to do next.

Some days ago in the prison waiting room, the lawyer had explained why Sarva was in jail despite his acquittal. The TID claimed not to have received Sarva's release certificate from the attorney general, and insisted on keeping him in custody until then. This was a frequent ploy to delay release, the lawyer said. 'They will never receive it, of course,' Amma had fumed. 'I've had enough of their theatrics. We're going to get you out.' There were no charges against him and he'd won all the big fights; now that freedom was so close and yet denied, even his mother had lost patience. She would stage a getaway. 'Next time after the court visit, okay?' she had said.

As he ran to the car, Sarva was afraid. He wanted to see if the police were chasing him, but he did not dare look. He imagined

TID officers watching him from the shadows, lunging at him, pulling him into a dark corner and beating him with batons. He imagined how he would suffer in silence, committing himself to one day taking vengeance. He knew he must be deranged to be so paranoid, to need the fantasy of his silent heroism, to be unable to feel an emotion as simple as relief when he shut the car door on what had been the worst year of his life.

SARVA'S OLDER BROTHER, Deva, was in the driver's seat and Amma sat beside him. They turned around to see Sarva slide in. 'Shut the door properly,' Deva said urgently and hit the accelerator. They were so sure of being pursued that no one actually bothered to see if they were.

Sharing the back seat with Sarva was a burly man with a wide, dark face and shoulder-length curly hair glistening with styling gel. 'Hello, brother,' he said, as if he were inviting him into a party. Sarva knew this was Randy, who worked for the NGO protecting Amma from the plainclothesmen harassing her. He was the only one in the car who did not look harried.

'Is it done?' Sarva asked anxiously. Deva was driving like a madman, and Amma was staring at the road ahead with an intensity that could only be prayer.

'Don't worry!' Randy reassured. Here they were stealing Sarva away from custody, and Randy looked as if he was sitting behind a counter in a bank. What a laid-back chap, Sarva thought. If the police had followed them, they were not doing so anymore. Sarva tried to relax.

They drove directly to the beach in Wellawatte, but at a safe distance from Aunty Rani's house, and parked opposite the railway station. Amma said they couldn't go home; the TID had been at the end of the street when she left for court that morning.

It was about an hour after noon. Sarva, Amma, Deva and Randy crossed the railway tracks and walked onto the beach. 'Have a bath,' Amma said, handing Sarva a bar of soap. It was Lux, the fragrant soap his mother always bought and which her sons thought too feminine but could not be bothered to make the effort to replace;

it was the family soap. She also had a small travel bag in her hand with his clothes from home, washed, neatly folded and pressed.

Sarva took off his rotten cotton trousers and faded T-shirt and walked into the waves. He bathed in the sea, his mind empty. When he finished, he put on the fresh shirt and trousers Amma gave him.

'You must be hungry, but we should go to the NP office straightaway,' said Randy. Amma would not accompany them. She was going home with Deva. She had planned this rescue, arranged for Randy's NGO to help, done everything for Sarva since his detention. She had gone beyond what she thought herself capable of, singlehandedly seeing Sarva through two years of uncertainty. He knew that without her he would not have left the first basement he was taken to. Without the reassurance of her lunchbox of rice and mutton curry and sweet-and-sour brinjal, he might have lost his mind in prison. But now, as he stood in front of her, she seemed too tired to linger over the reunion. She left without her characteristic teary goodbye or long hug. Before going, she awkwardly apologised for forgetting to bring him a change of slippers.

RANDY DROVE SARVA to the Nonviolent Peaceforce office in Colombo 3, talking all the way. He wore a shiny shirt, and the hair near his temples was drenched in sweat. His voice was surprising: soft, childlike. He spoke Tamil, and said he was a field officer at the Sri Lanka office of the NP, a risky job with a constant threat of violence from powerful quarters. A Burgher of Portuguese descent, he joked that he looked 'like a black bear', which made Sarva laugh. In the next few months, as they got to know each other better, Sarva would come to depend on Randy's humour in the darkest moments.

At the NP office, Randy introduced Sarva to Isabel, a tall, warrior-like woman. As soon as he met her, Sarva was rattled. Other than his lawyer Sumathi, this was the first young woman he had met in more than a year. She was pretty, and her smile had the warmth of welcome. He became suddenly conscious of his appearance. What she saw would not be the muscular, broad-shouldered, well-dressed man he once was. In prison, he had aged rapidly; Isabel would be looking at a patchy face, thinning hair, black rings under his eyes.

These days, he slouched when he walked. The once round cheeks were sunken. His thick pink lips, once striking against his dark skin—the hallmark of the men in his family—were chapped. To make things worse, the shirt Amma had given him was oversized, bought at a time when he ate three helpings of rice at a meal and lifted weights.

He thought Isabel was white at first, but when she sat next to him on a sofa, he saw that her skin was a golden brown. Later Randy told him she was 'maybe South American or Mexican'.

Isabel said Sarva's mother had briefed them about his 'situation with the TID'. NP would first find a safe place for him to stay. Sarva understood only some of what she said; it had been ages since he had heard English, and it was hard to follow in a foreign accent. Apprehensive, he replied in Tamil, and Randy and Devi, another field officer, translated. As he listened to Devi, impressed with her fluent English, he became intensely aware that he did not sit with this group as an equal but as a victim seeking help.

Isabel said she needed to know specifics—dates, names, whatever he could remember. 'I apologise in advance for having to ask you some sensitive questions, okay?'

'Yes, miss.'

'Please, call me Isabel.'

'Okay.' Of course he would not call her Isabel.

'At any time, if you want a break, please tell me to stop, okay?'

Sarva nodded. He was astounded an interview could even be conducted this way. He marvelled at Isabel, her even tone, her liquid eyes and the effort she made to put him at ease. He told her everything from the beginning, narrating his kidnap, detention, court cases and prison time in detail. He was describing the ordeal to another person for the first time. He mixed up the chronology and could not recall names. Isabel and Randy gently prodded him for dates.

As soon as he said the English word 'torture', Isabel shook her head in distress. It's always the same nonsense, she said, but looked stricken enough for him to think this was the first case of torture she had encountered.

'My lower back, it's broken. Paining,' Sarva said. He was

searching for phrases in English, attempting to level the ground, to establish a more direct connection than was possible through an interpreter. 'My eyes, dull. Burning. Petrol bag.'

Isabel gasped. 'Really ...' she said, jerking her neck back. When he said, 'They beat me', he watched her eyes widen in anger and her mouth twist, contorting her pretty face. She was hanging on his every word. Had he become so inured to pain that he could not react as she did? Isabel must be terribly large-hearted, he thought, if she felt such personal emotions as rage and disappointment for everyone she met. Or she must be soft, a lightweight. He pitied how easily she was mortified but was nonetheless grateful. When he described being chained and handcuffed in the prison's underground remand court, it was her unconcealed horror that told him it was inhumane. He was learning to judge his treatment for the first time through her eyes and to classify the seamless string of brutalities he'd endured on the scale of human suffering. Although Isabel repeated a lot of questions in the three-hour interview, by the end he felt unburdened.

'Thank you for being so patient with me,' Isabel said, as if it were he who was doing her a favour. She squeezed her hands together on her lap. If he were a woman, he was sure she would have hugged him. 'I asked so many questions because we have to be careful, you know,' she added. 'We can't take on ... doubtful cases.' She let that statement hang in the air, allowing Sarva a final chance to come clean as to whether he had served in the LTTE. 'The court has discharged me,' he said. 'I have papers.' For now, that was the legal truth that mattered.

When Isabel went to her desk, Randy and the other staff explained to Sarva what NP did. The NGO protected journalists, human rights defenders, whistleblowers and any civilian under threat from violence. They were headquartered in Brussels, with offices in conflict areas around the world. They specialised in unarmed protection, which meant keeping civilians in safe houses, providing security, and sometimes helping them secure political asylum in European countries. Sympathetic immigration authorities, embassies, civil servants and locals helped them anonymously, and there was always the fear of repercussions from the government, ranging from cancelled visas to arrests or even physical harm. The staff admitted that since 2008 they had been on shaky ground in Sri Lanka. Their director, Tiffany Easthom, a Canadian national, had been deported just a few months earlier, and they knew they were all under state surveillance.

A recent experience had made the NP more jittery. Someone named Senthil had sought protection, claiming the TID had tortured him. The man had been in prison for six months. But after Randy did a background check and Isabel interviewed him, they discovered that Senthil was a TID mole, planted to observe their methods, expose their safe houses and uncover their network. The infiltration had sent a ripple of panic through the organisation, as they realised they'd almost taken on a spy. It would have greatly endangered not only the employees but also the people they helped.

Ever since the war intensified in the north, the government had wielded sedition and anti-terrorism laws against humanitarian agencies. NGOs like the NP worked under outrageous constraints: their projects were subject to approval and monitored at every stage by the state or armed forces, the very bodies they were often taking on. Since 2007, the principal threat had come from the state and its armed forces. Farcically, the Ministry of Defence and the presidential task force appointed themselves regulators of groups documenting this violence. The threat of deportation hung over their every move, hampering their work. NGO licences were cancelled, and the visas of aid workers were revoked. The NP was thus wary of helping those accused of being linked to the LTTE. One ill-chosen case would be enough for them to get kicked out of the country.

As Isabel put it, 'The situation was complex.' She sifted through Sarva's story for fact and fiction, analysing the risks of taking on a man once accused of terrorism. She believed Sarva's account of being tortured, but was ambivalent about his vague claims about service in the LTTE. Militancy spread far and wide, often in indiscernible ways. There were fighting cadre, spies, political workers, fundraisers, forced recruits and sympathisers—a shade card of the movement's reach. The Rajapaksa regime tarred them all with the same brush, but some NGOs knew better.

NP was not short of legitimate reasons to offer Sarva protection. His arrest had been illegal, like hundreds of others in Sri Lanka: the country saw the second-highest rate of illegal detention in the world, after Iraq. Sarva's still-visible wounds were proof of horrific custodial torture. Even after his acquittal, the police continued to harass his family. They threatened to detain him again. In addition, Sarva's case was well documented. The Red Cross had registered Sarva's detention after that chance meeting in the TID basement. They had made sure that a police arrest report was drawn up, after which his detention was on record, a rare piece of luck that helped the NP substantiate his claims.

Despite her doubts, Isabel was persuaded by Sarva's acquittal. The court's declaration of his innocence—exoneration by a body that was rarely lenient or sympathetic to an accused terrorist—was the NP's best insurance policy.

As Isabel and Randy arranged a safe house for their new case, Sarva sipped hot sweet tea in the back of the office. It was remarkable that the NP agreed to help him. He credited it to Amma and the force of her conviction. His iron-willed mother had pulled him out of ditches innumerable times, and how quickly he always forgot. He did not deserve her.

'Shall we go, men? What are you dreaming about?' Randy asked.

'It must be cool to have a boss like Isabel,' Sarva said, grinning.

'Okay, okay, lover boy,' Randy said. 'You're my competition! This is why I have to send you away to Bataramulla.' That's when Sarva saw that Randy was holding two helmets.

Bataramulla was a suburb just outside Colombo, and had they taken a bus, they would have reached the safe house in two hours. But Randy was wary of army checkpoints and the police on main roads, so they rode on his motorbike. Throughout the one-hour journey, Randy spoke loudly, making jokes, telling Sarva to think of this as an adventure. Sarva concentrated on not screaming in pain. His crushed lower back felt the impact of every bump on the crooked routes off the highway.

'How long will I have to stay in Bataramulla before going home?' Sarva shouted over the revving of the motorbike.

'Let's see,' Randy said. 'Till it's safe for you, till they stop tormenting your family.'

'Okay, around a month then, I guess.' He had no inkling then that it would snowball into eighteen months, enough time for him to lose all sense of where or who he was.

SARVA'S SLOW ERASURE began in a church in Bataramulla. A dour head priest handed Sarva to a young brother, Hendrick, to be shown around.

'You're not Catholic?' the friar asked first. 'But you're a Pereira?'

'My father was Catholic but I was brought up as a Hindu,' Sarva said, unsure if this would make things difficult. But Brother Hendrick didn't seem to care either way. He was jovial, smelled of soap, and said he was hooked on Facebook. Several Tamil-speaking boys in the same parish were studying to be ordained as Catholic priests, but he advised Sarva to keep a low profile. 'The more you share with people, the more you expose yourself,' he warned in all seriousness, and then repeated the word *expose* with mock shock and a little giggle.

Sarva had been given a room near the kitchen, at the back of the parish house. His own space, a soft bed, a clean bathroom. He was thrilled. He picked flowers and put them by his window. Next to the Bible, on a cupboard, he placed a small idol of Pullaiyar, which Amma had put in his backpack.

He wasn't allowed to have his own phone and had to call his family on Randy's. The NP suspected that Amma's phones were tapped and did not want the safe house to be exposed.

Isabel and Randy visited occasionally, bringing news from home. Plainclothes policemen had visited Sarva's Nuwara Eliya house again, and Amma had challenged them, demanding to know why they were looking for a man who had been freed by the courts. Ignoring her, the men repeated the same questions: 'Where is Sarvananthan? Where is his passport?' As Amma berated them, they searched every nook and cranny in the house. Aunty Rani had also reported a suspicious man who had tried to chat up the security guard at her Wellawatte apartment, asking whether Sarva had been to see his aunts.

'Things are not going as we hoped,' Isabel said. 'You might have to stay away from home for longer than we expected, Sarva.'

The head priest suggested that Sarva occupy himself at the parish house. 'Don't simply sit around waiting,' he said. 'You can help out around here.'

So Sarva offered to cook lunch for the ten or so residents, but he didn't last for long. They didn't seem to like his cooking and were especially annoyed that the meals weren't ready on time. Brother Hendrick asked if Sarva had used the whole bottle of chilli powder in the curries. Sarva was mildly offended but told himself that they didn't appreciate his culinary experiments because they were simple men of God who wanted only bread and sambol or bland rice and curry.

After a couple of months, Isabel asked Sarva to think about going abroad. The way she said it reminded him of his mother's attempts five years earlier to get him to leave the country. She had been frightened about his future and wanted him to get out before he was drawn into the war. Her Negombo brother who had moved to Long Beach, New York, had been ready to sponsor his visa. But Sarva was adamant. 'What is there for me in America?' he asked. He didn't want to live off an uncle who was himself struggling to educate his daughters. When he finally landed his shipping job and started to travel around the globe, Amma was satisfied somewhat, hoping the foreign air would seduce him one day into settling abroad. A few years later, when relations with her US brother soured over a land dispute, Amma complained that Sarva had wasted a golden opportunity.

Ever since he had first been locked up, Sarva too had regretted not having emigrated when he had the chance. Desperate to get out of jail, he was preoccupied with thoughts of leaving Sri Lanka. He imagined the furthest place he could go to, beyond the whitewashed prison walls, beyond Colombo, away from Sri Lanka, beyond South Asia—somewhere far, far away. With his lawyer's help, in early 2009 he made an asylum application to the Swiss embassy. He now told Isabel of this and she checked on its progress. She wanted to get him an interview as soon as she could, but ever since the army had started its offensives in the east and north, asylum applications from Tamils had soared; the waiting list was insurmountable.

Switzerland was the only country to half-process applications for political asylum at its consulate in Colombo and issue preliminary visas for travel. For Sri Lankans, a Swiss visa was an alternative to illegal emigration. The NP had worked closely with the Swiss in emergency situations before, getting people under threat across borders on short notice. But since their director had been deported, the NP's clout had weakened considerably. Randy kept telling Sarva to wait, that things would surely work out soon.

Another month passed. There was a burglary at the Bataramulla parish house. Very little was stolen—only a laptop and some silver-plated candlesticks—but the break-in shook everyone. 'Why would any thief waste his time with a poor church?' Isabel asked on the phone, her voice thick with suspicion. She came the very next day and drove Sarva to a safe house in Batticaloa, in the east of the country.

There, a Father Peter welcomed them to a retreat and counselling centre. It was called The Cuckoo's Nest. Isabel's eyes danced with amusement at the name, but Sarva didn't see what was so funny.

'You know? The book?' she asked. He didn't.

'The movie?' No.

'Jack Nicholson, the actor?'

Sarva smiled, feigning recognition to end this attempt at bonhomie. He knew Isabel was trying hard to help him, but he was sick of waiting. In prison, he had seen his mother every day and had been allowed to speak to other people. Hiding out was different. Unlike prison, it did not kill his dream of freedom entirely but cruelly postponed it, day by day, crisis by crisis. Three months of self-imposed solitary confinement, and now, another hiding place at another seminary that required discipline, silence and obedience. His affection for Isabel was eroding fast.

The Cuckoo's Nest was busier than the previous safe house. It sheltered more than fifty poor men and women, taught them tailoring or carpentry, and fed them three meals a day. Sarva's room was in the men's dormitory, and was basic—a washbasin, a wall shelf, a bed with a mosquito net. The women were in another building, and a lady warden sat on the veranda between the two hostels, her face severe and eyes hawk-like.

Men and women were discouraged from interacting and sat separately in the dining hall. The meals were bland and under-seasoned, and Sarva felt that the spice had been leached from his life. He was the oldest there and was formally addressed as *anna*, in a way that isolated him. Father Peter always spoke tenderly to him, but Sarva sensed that this was not exclusive. He craved his aunt's fish curry and his mother's doting. When the parish sweeper once brought her toddler over, he played with the child incessantly to somehow satiate the need to see his fat little nephew and hazel-eyed niece. It was surprising how much he missed them all; he had spent most of his life negotiating more independence for himself. He felt unseen now and locked in. Days would go by without his speaking to a single person. Once, when it rained, he ran out of his room to feel the drops on his face, to sink into their coolness and feel like himself again. In this place, with its impersonal kindness, Sarva felt inanimate; a thing to be protected, fed and ignored.

Then Randy came by one day and said the government had revoked the visas of several more NP employees. They had deported Isabel. 'She wanted you to know that she will always remember you, *machan*,' Randy said. And just when Sarva thought this was another of his friend's jokes, he continued, 'You were her last case in Sri Lanka.' Randy said NP's days in Sri Lanka were numbered. They would pass Sarva's case file to another NGO and hoped to do a handover. All of this, to Sarva, meant only that he would be hiding for even longer. He did not respond and refused Randy's usual offer of a glass of arrack.

Perhaps Randy realised that Sarva was depressed, because on his next visit he brought a phone and three SIM cards from Amma. It was not safe, he warned, but since Sarva was so lonely, they could make an exception. Change the number as often as possible, Randy instructed.

'And I should speak only for a few minutes each time, right? Three minutes, no?' Sarva asked, perking up, recalling some trivia about phone tapping.

Randy guffawed. They had discovered ways around that now, he said, 'But yes, do that if you want. Or just text, man.'

Sarva wasn't sure later if it was the phone that had normalised his life or if he had adjusted to anonymity. He began to wake early and go for a walk within the campus to exercise his weak spine. He learnt to associate food with sustenance rather than taste, and his appetite improved. He called his family every morning and night. His littlest nephew was starting to speak and because he was told his grandmother lived in Nuwara Eliya, he called her Noorie. Sarva's younger brother, Carmel, was into Snoop Dog and Jay-Z and wrote Tamil hip-hop songs about girls and gangs.

Although Sarva loved hearing their voices, the conversations with his parents always upset him. The plainclothesmen still came. His father had quit his job and found another as manager in a small private tea estate in Maskeliya. Amma was in the process of moving there, spending time between the two houses. Thus, fortunately, it was often the housemaid who answered the door to the TID or police. Amma had instructed her to say, 'I don't know', 'Amma has gone to town', 'I will tell them you came', alternating between the phrases, and never to open the chain lock on the door.

The men continued to visit Aunty Rani's Colombo house, too, and once even forced open her front door. Typical of Aunty, she narrated it vividly enough for him to picture what happened: she had been at the post office and her middle-aged tenant had called her, flustered and high-pitched. Some men had shoved around the apartment building's watchman, taken the elevator to the seventh floor, and burst into the house. The tenant had screamed for several minutes and then fainted. Before that, she had registered this much: there were six or seven well-built men wearing crew cuts and sky-blue shirts tucked into grey trousers. They had asked for Sarva and Indra. Aunty said she was now noting the dates, times and details of all raids on her home in a diary.

Almost four months had passed since Sarva had been acquitted and the release papers sent to the TID, but the situation was now well beyond documents and courts. He was helplessly wracked with guilt about his family's continued harassment. He often wondered if he should have just stayed in prison till the paperwork was complete, but his unending backache reminded him why he had bolted. The pain had grown and spread to his legs. A doctor prescribed some painkillers over the phone.

Sarva also had unexpected blackouts and would come to with bloodshot eyes. It burned when he peed, and every few days there were drops of blood in his urine. Shifting between sitting and standing was agonising. Sarva needed to visit a doctor for proper treatment, but the NP had been unable to convince a government doctor to see, much less treat, Sarva.

'Any bloody doctor will be able to tell that your injuries are from torture, and the fucking cowards don't want to get involved.' When Randy was frustrated, expletives poured out. 'Even if they'll treat you, the bastards are too scared to put their signature on a damn certificate.' The NP needed such a certificate for the asylum application, and it was proving impossible to get. It was urgent because soon the baton marks and chain impressions on Sarva's body would fade. For now, the NP had given the Swiss embassy photographs of his injuries and his medical report from the prison attack.

Sarva spent afternoons on his phone, reading interviews with the lucky few who had escaped from the north and made their way to England or Canada. Within Sri Lanka, former combatants were arrested or had surrendered; the government had close to 11,000 men and women in detention camps, but gave no explanation for the 15,780 missing. Sarva's life had led him along a different route: torture, trial and an acquittal. He had privileges—his distance from the war, a middle-class family with access to lawyers and some money, and a bilingual mother. Even so, his future was uncertain.

More than a year had passed since the end of the war, and the re-elected president was amassing more power. Rajapaksa had won six million votes, handily defeating General Fonseka, whose four million votes drew in most of the electorate in the minority-dominated northern and eastern provinces. The very next month, the president had Fonseka arrested for 'military offences'. Over 100 military policemen burst into his house, threatened his family and dragged him away. It was the start of a stronger clampdown on all opposition, including the muzzling of press freedom.

Censorship and the threat of violence hung heavy over the media. Murder, kidnapping, violence against property and journalists, financial restrictions and control—all these techniques were employed to limit what could be published or broadcast. The government-run TV channel and papers ran propaganda and, fearing harassment, much of the private media learnt to practise self-censorship. Sri Lanka sat 162nd in the index of press freedom compiled by Reporters Without Borders, making it the lowest-ranked parliamentary democracy.

On websites and in foreign media, undercover journalists and activists published front-line reports and eyewitness accounts of the army shelling no-fire zones, using cluster bombs, grabbing land and harassing freed combatants. A year after the end of the LTTE, the missing pieces of the war gradually emerged, unveiling the fabrications of a government eager to claim victory but keen to deny the number of fatalities. Every time the state claimed the army caused zero casualties and that all killings were the LTTE's responsibility, the Sri Lankan diaspora, including covert Tiger sympathisers, accused the state of sponsoring genocide. The truth lay in the gulf between claim and counterclaim. In the cacophony of different accounts, attempts to measure the cost of the conflict—the counting of the dead, lost, disappeared, raped or displaced; their names and addresses; the dates and locations of war crimes; the number of soldiers deployed, killed or injured; the battle methods of the army and the LTTE—became fraught with motives and desired ends. Propaganda eclipsed facts, denial extinguished compassion. The war's end produced two aggressive parallel narratives, which ran fast and strong, never meeting, like the dual histories of the warring peoples themselves.

Sarva was far away from all the action. Yet he felt a kinship with the Vanni Tamils, a shared suffering. He envied them their closure. The long war had torn their lives apart but had also ended in front of their eyes. What he fought with were the ghosts from the same war: how long would they haunt him?

Sarva read Tamil and Sinhalese dailies cover to cover, including the obituaries, with a growing dread of finding the name of someone he knew—a classmate Malainathan from Chavakacheri or cycling buddy Frederick, who had moved to Mullaitivu—until he realised that such deaths would be kept out of the papers. People disappeared; they did not die.

After a while, he stopped bothering with the Sinhalese papers; they were filled with excited bloviating and overwrought praise for the president. Their optimism and convenient blindness made his blood boil. They wrote about the inauguration of new Tamil-language schools in the Vanni but didn't mention that the earlier school buildings had been bombed. His own high school had been shelled and his primary school turned into a camp for the displaced. By and by, the helpless pathos of Tamil papers wore him out, too. His life was no different from that of the millions of Tamils they wrote about; his fate was inextricably linked to theirs.

The more he thought about this, the further Sarva sank into himself. Beside a small stream behind the Batticaloa seminary, he watched tortoises flop around, paddling into the water, onto the mud, into the water, onto the mud, a game without end, until the twisting current pulled them away.

If someone had told him how much longer he would have to stay at the seminary, Sarva might have fared better. Instead, the incremental extension of this period of hiding chipped away at him, the uncertainty leaving him breathless. What he didn't know was that the months ahead would be a blur of locations and new identities. He would be desperate to be visible, numb with solitude, and constantly on the verge of nervous collapse, until an unexpected love affair, irrational and all-consuming, would resuscitate him.

PART THREE

refuge

17.

August 2010

'YOU HAVE AN interview at the Swiss embassy tomorrow!' Randy shouted on the phone. He was already on his way to Batticaloa to pick Sarva up.

Why he wasn't given more notice Sarva couldn't imagine, but he started to prepare mentally. Four months had passed since he left prison and he was sure his brain had atrophied. He would never forget Inspector Silva, but the other names were fading. At least remember the dates, remember the order, he told himself throughout the van journey to Colombo.

They drove through the night without stopping. Sarva didn't sleep a wink. At dawn he was groggy and feverish; his nerves were shot. He brushed his teeth, rinsing from a bottle of water, and changed his shirt in the van. They entered through the back gate of the embassy. Later, when he would overanalyse what had happened and superstitiously attach meaning to every minor event, he would consider this the first bad sign, an omen that his life would soon be ruined: you never enter through the back door.

Then he was annoyed about having to give his statement to a Muslim official. They speak a different type of Tamil, Sarva hissed to Randy. 'He might write things wrong—wrong on purpose, I mean—and misrepresent me!' The second-largest minority group in the country, Sri Lankan Muslims also spoke Tamil, and their vocabulary was indeed slightly different from Sarva's Jaffna Tamil. But so was that of plantation Tamils and Indian Tamils, and Sarva would never have become suspicious so quickly of someone from those communities. This was another of the Tigers' unfortunate legacies to the Tamils. Even a Colombo boy like Sarva could buy in to this unfair stereotype of the backstabbing Muslim.

Randy just whispered to Sarva that he'd better shut up because he had no choice here. 'I'm sure the interview will be all right,' he added, more reassuringly.

The interview couldn't have gone worse. Sarva's nerves made him mix up the dates, contradict himself, and forget crucial details. He was a babbling mess, and even as he exited the office, he knew he would not get an asylum visa. He found Randy waiting outside in the van. '*Kote vittiten*,' Sarva said, choking on the phrase, one he used in school when he failed an exam.

'Leave it!' Randy said. 'We'll go to the office and you can meet Elizabeth,' he added with a wink, forcing Sarva to laugh.

Elizabeth Ogave turned out to be a tough South African woman, stout and as tall as Sarva, with a manner that screamed efficiency. As soon as he saw her, Sarva felt better. She was the election project coordinator at NP and was confidence personified. She spoke compassionately, and her quick manner shrank any obstacle into a petty nuisance. Sarva imagined she would beat up any number of people for him. 'What a woman!' he whistled to Randy when she was out of earshot. By the time it was five in the evening, and Sarva was already falling for Elizabeth, she decided to send him back to the Bataramulla seminary.

'Is that okay?' she asked, and he liked her for pretending that he had any say in the matter.

Brother Hendrick was happy to have Sarva back, and threw him a welcome-home party with the rest of the residents. 'No drinks,' he said, 'except tea.' Sarva told a rapt Brother Hendrick about Elizabeth, exaggerating her good looks and his own smooth talk. He forgot for a few hours why he was there until someone fished out a camera to take photographs; then he left hurriedly with an unconvincing lie about hearing his phone ring.

A few days later, Randy came by with a long face. The Sri Lankan immigration authorities had deported Elizabeth, too. Sarva's heart sank. The NP was hurtling towards shutdown.

'You may be out of job soon,' he told Randy.

'Yes, man, and you may be dead soon.'

That night, Randy smuggled a bottle of Old Reserve arrack into the seminary, and Sarva got plastered for the first time since his shipping days. The only line he recalled from that night was Randy assuring him, 'There are others, don't worry!' He might have meant other NGOs, but it could as well have been about other women.

And sure enough, in a week, Sarva had reason to feel hopeful. Randy said a local NGO had agreed to take on Sarva's case, and one of their employees would come to the seminary to meet him. The NGO was Colombo-based and worked on press freedom, illegal detentions and disappearances. It had recently started campaigning for the release of some high-profile detainees.

This was uplifting news, but did he really have to face another interview? 'They speak Tamil?' a tired Sarva asked Randy. 'Will you be coming to translate?'

'No, the woman is Sinhalese,' Randy said. 'Her name is Miss Shirleen. You can talk to her in Sinhala directly.'

'*Aiyo*, she is Sinhalese?' He wasn't sure anymore if this NGO woman was a safe bet.

Soon after his meeting with Miss Shirleen the next day, however, Sarva dialled Randy. 'I expected an old lady, but who did you send, man?! My eyes popped out!'

Randy burst out laughing. 'Yes, of course. This is our special treatment for torture victims.'

Shirleen was breathtaking, and Sarva was smitten the minute he saw her walk into the seminary in a stylishly worn sari. That she was also a young lawyer and activist and would be accepting his case immediately made her an angel fashioned by God especially for him. He found her polite and was flattered by how attentively she listened. Throughout the interview he had to hold down a fit of boyish giggles. She called him 'Sharva', with an *h*, and he swore to himself never to correct her.

Shirleen took copious notes as he told his story, and he was able to give a clear account of events this time. What a relief not to have an interpreter, he gushed to her, and tried to downplay his unease while describing in Sinhala the racism he had experienced.

She had already met with his mother, and judging from the way they'd been harassed, Shirleen surmised that it would not be safe for Sarva to stay in Sri Lanka. He told her about his failure at the Swiss embassy, and she assured him she would think of alternatives.

That night, Sarva dreamt of America. It just came to him, for no specific reason, that if there was a place he should live other than his home country, it had to be the USA. He hadn't ever been there, but it already felt familiar somehow. Long Beach, where his uncle was, sounded inviting. Or perhaps New York, where all the superhero movies were set, where King Kong had clambered up that tall building with the pointy antenna at the top. His uncle's daughters said the taste of food at McDonald's was different in the US; people ate it casually for lunch and dinner, they said, while in Colombo it was a treat, something for a special occasion. The only western music Sarva had ever known was Michael Jackson and he had obsessed over *Thriller* as a teenager, squealing and shrieking in the room he shared with his brothers and doing the moonwalk for the entertainment of visiting relatives. He was in jail when Jackson died, and Sarva had consumed the obituaries and pictures of the funeral in newspapers in the prison library, feeling connected to thousands of mourning American fans. He was sure he could make a good life there.

When Shirleen came back to meet him a few days later, another beautiful woman accompanied her. He was all in a tizzy. Were all social workers stunning, or was Randy playing a prank on him? The new activist would help Sarva with applications for an engineering course in Denmark. Sarva hadn't been to Denmark but knew they spoke Danish there. He asked if he wouldn't stand a better chance of education and employment if he went to an English-speaking country. Say, America? No, he was told, America and England were some of the toughest countries to get into.

Sarva sought out Brother Hendrick at dinner that night. 'Why can't Sri Lankans be let into America?' he asked. The string hoppers he ate were dry, and he drenched them in spiced coconut milk and squashed them in frustration.

'Calm down, man!' Brother Hendrick said. 'Lots of Sri Lankan Tamils have already gone and maybe they filled the quota.' Since the 1983 riots, thousands of middle-class Tamils had fled to the US, armed with their English-language education, and were now a sizeable diaspora, owning businesses and working in multinational corporations and hospitals. The recent wave of emigration was of poorer, less-educated Tamils. This development coincided with the US government toughening immigration laws and enhancing screening procedures for asylum seekers from all over the world. It was further exacerbated after the US, Canada and Australia invested significant resources in intercepting the *MV Sun Sea*, a ship carrying 492 Sri Lankan Tamil refugees, including women, children and many who might have been linked to the LTTE. In August, when the ship docked in British Columbia, all the adults, except the mothers of minors, were detained.

It irritated Sarva that his destiny was dependent on such events. On his phone that night, he googled 'Immigration Sri Lanka USA' and spent hours reading articles. He tried the English ones first, but struggled. Angry with himself, he moved on to Tamil websites. One featured a harrowing interview with an anonymous Sri Lankan Tamil—an undocumented immigrant working under a fake social security number and constantly afraid of getting caught.

Sarva clicked on another. A report said that fewer Tamil immigrants were being given asylum after the LTTE had been proscribed as a terrorist group and the front organisations funding it from America had been shut down. Another blogger wrote that the US government didn't want its own neighbours, the Mexicans, crossing the border. How were people from the other side of the world meant to get in?

American elections were won and lost depending on how a capricious majority decided to define a minority population—no different from Sri Lanka. In Sarva's homeland, the hard-driven Tamil plantation worker was deemed okay but not the Tamil university student protesting discrimination. The happy-go-lucky Burgher with his glass of whiskey passed muster, but not the Burgher with a government job. The trading Muslim was fine, but not the praying Muslim. The devout Sinhala Buddhist was all right, but not the inquisitive, sceptical one. These groups had to fit in, flow into the crevices the majoritarian state created for them.

Even when he thought he'd shed all distinctions that could identify him, Sarva was still recognisably a Tamil. Three years earlier in Negombo, when he ran the video parlour with Deva, a young customer had enquired about their videography packages for his sister's wedding. Sarva gave the customer the rate card. Admitting that he had only shot Tamil weddings, Sarva had asked the customer how many hours a Sinhala Buddhist wedding would go on for and what rituals were most important to capture. The customer looked surprised. 'Where are you from?' he asked. 'Pereira? You're not Sinhalese?'

'Nuwara Eliya—Tamil,' Sarva said. It had not taken long for the customer to mutter that he'd get back to him and walk out.

The question of who came from where had always burned with implications in Sri Lanka and, as Sarva was learning, everywhere else, too. It stood in his way, reminding him that however hard he might try to break away, his identity would always limit his options.

Sarva's English wasn't good enough to fill in the Danish college applications or write his statement of purpose, so Shirleen did it for him. The image of the top of her head, bent over the paperwork, was etched in his mind. Her dark hair, which she usually tied back in a bun, was streaked with grey.

Sarva was baffled by Shirleen. Why did this Sinhalese help him, a Tamil? He didn't see why an educated, privileged, gorgeous woman would walk through the heat and dust to help a nobody like him. She worked hard for Sarva's safety, for no payment, taking great risks to do so. Her compassion was sincere, and most of all she believed him. Sarva could have sworn that every Sinhalese possessed a *thveshagunam*, an evil spirit of vengeance. But in Shirleen's presence he felt guilty thinking that way. He tried to trust her—there was no real reason not to—but the scepticism was unshakable.

In the following months, he would meet another Sinhalese who challenged his stereotypes. Jehaan was Shirleen's senior colleague and the one Randy had been petitioning to take Sarva's case. More people from the NP were being expelled, and the staff were feeling the heat. The TID raided Randy's house in Colombo, and he had come back home to find his wife furious and daughters in tears. A week after that, Randy drove Sarva from his safe house to Colombo and booked him into a posh hotel in Mount Lavinia. 'I have to go underground,' he said. 'I will hand your case over to Jehaan.'

Sarva was upset, but he had seen this coming. He asked if the new person would be Tamil.

'No, Sinhalese. But you can trust him more than me,' Randy said.

When Sarva first met Jehaan in the hotel room, his mind flew to the phrase 'simple living, high thinking', a maxim of his father's. Jehaan was slight of build, shorter than Sarva by half a foot. He was in his mid-thirties: his head was shaved, masking a receding hairline. He wore a thigh-length half-sleeved kurta and cotton pyjamas; his sturdy sandals were frayed with walking; and his canvas bag seemed stuffed beyond capacity with papers. Jehaan was also on crutches, and this muddled Sarva's assessment of him. He was relieved to learn that the disability was temporary, the result of a bad fall.

Jehaan had brought along a reed-thin man aged about fifty to act as translator if needed. But they ended up speaking entirely, and comfortably, in Sinhala. Randy talked Jehaan up, explaining that he was responsible for launching the global campaign for the journalist Tissa's release from prison. It was thanks to Jehaan that several civilians, journalists and activists who had been attacked were able to leave the country unharmed and get political asylum in Europe. He was an expert at documentation, an underrated skill that turned neglected local cases into global issues.

Everything about Sarva was on file, Jehaan said, and he had been briefed by Shirleen: 'She said yours was a genuine case and that your life is truly at risk.'

Sarva would stay at the hotel at NP's expense for several more days until Jehaan could arrange a new safe house. His days passed with a great deal of eating and TV-watching. Randy forbade Sarva to contact his family and friends even if they were in the same city.

But Sarva broke the rule once and called an old classmate who ran a computer shop. Before he left the hotel, his friend sent him a used Dell laptop and an Airtel data card. It might be years before he could emerge from hiding, and even a man on the run needed entertainment.

JEHAAN ACCOMPANIED SARVA to his next safe house, leading him along routes that were treacherous and unpaved yet beautiful. It was obvious he used these roads often, with others who depended on him just as Sarva did. As they wound their way over a forested hill, Sarva became petrified of getting lost. He was frantic about what would happen if they had a flat tyre or if an elephant crossed their track. Most of his injuries had healed, except for the occasional pulsing that coursed down his lower back, through his legs and to his feet when he sat or stood for too long.

Sensing Sarva's restlessness, Jehaan asked the driver to stop at a clearing. He asked Sarva if he would like to stretch his legs. They stepped out and walked a bit until Sarva saw that Jehaan was struggling with his broken leg.

'We don't have to do this,' Sarva said.

'We have to,' Jehaan said. 'I want to show you the stream at the top.'

'In that case, let me help you.' Sarva carried Jehaan in his arms for some of the way. It could've been embarrassing, but Jehaan's obvious awe at Sarva's strength made them both laugh.

Sarva heard the stream before he saw it, gurgling, swishing and crashing. He heard animals grunt and birds shriek, and for a second imagined something terrifying coming out the woods—a wild animal, a nameless creature, a soldier. But in a few minutes his breath became less laboured. For what felt like hours, he sat in the stream quietly, letting the cold water push past him. Jehaan sat on the bank, his feet in the water. His face was still, lit with pure joy.

When they talked, Sarva was uninhibited. He poured out everything that was on his mind except the persistent question of why Jehaan was helping him—why he didn't hate or fear Sarva for what he was accused of doing.

Had he asked, Jehaan would have explained that his organisation had indeed been worried about taking on clients who were accused of being Tigers; but he had persevered, because Sarva had been acquitted in court. Jehaan might even have confessed to what was considered blasphemy in Sri Lankan humanitarian work: that if Sarva were a Tiger, protection would still be his due; no human deserved the torture he had undergone.

For more than a decade, Jehaan had protected victims irrespective of their identity. As he was helping Sarva, he was also assisting Sinhalese journalists, Muslim activists and Tamil women, but Sinhalese acquaintances often asked why he was 'into protecting *Kottiyas*'. He would say it was sad that he needed to give reasons for defending someone's basic rights, to question the need for violence, or to ask for greater accountability from an elected government.

Initially it had disturbed Sarva that, unlike Randy, Jehaan, who was in all regards friendly, rarely spoke about his private life. He knew that Jehaan was only a few years older than him, was Sinhalese, and could not speak a word of Tamil, though he knew the alleys of Sri Lanka's smallest towns, including those in the Vanni. But that was the extent of Sarva's knowledge of the man. He did not know that Jehaan had gone to an exclusive boys' convent school, that he had not changed jobs in years, that he lived with his parents and loved his evening glass of arrack. He had friends in the military and argued fervently with them till he left in a huff, but kept in touch with them and returned to the subject another day. He hated interviewing torture victims—that was why he had sent Shirleen to Sarva—he was obsessed with train travel, and he did not like talking about love. Nothing, however, was more personal to Jehaan than his work. He was motivated by deep moral forces: his Christian faith, his need to fight the good fight, and his unshakeable Sri Lankan pride.

Just like Sarva, Jehaan was running. But whereas Sarva's flight would stop eventually, presumably after a few years, and he would be free to live his life, Jehaan would accompany other fugitives through forests to safe houses again and again, till the Sinhalese-dominated state, incensed at the defiance of one of their own, turned its wrath on him.

18.

October 2010 to May 2011

BEING INVISIBLE WAS exhausting. In less than a year, Jehaan took Sarva to eight different safe houses: Bataramulla, Hatton, Madulsima, Colombo, Kalaeliya, Dikoya and two other locations Sarva couldn't even name. A succession of priests opened their doors to him. When he met the love of his life later that same year, he would tell her God must have approved of his hanging round His premises.

In truth, Sarva had not been entirely passive during all that time spent in churches. Though his father's Catholicism had made little impression on him as a child, now, with nothing else to do, he gave religion a shot. One just had to go through the motions, he decided, the deliberate, slow string of ritualistic actions. The soft one-knee genuflection, the loud amen, the mumbled amen, the choral amen, the sign of the cross over one's chest, the sitting and standing for choir, the saying of grace before a meal, the unfussy silent use of the fork and spoon—he wanted to master it all and fit in.

Sometimes, out of boredom and also gratitude, he attended daily mass. On Sunday, it pleased him to see well-dressed families occupying the pews sway to the choir, nod to familiar faces, and mumble parts of the prayer they had memorised. Afterwards, they would elbow each other, lining up for juice and snacks. People left their shoes outside, as he would do in a temple; he had never noticed this before. They were quieter than visitors to Hindu temples, and he wondered how devotion could be so muted. He liked worship to leave him buzzing, to overwhelm his senses and to leave its camphor smell on his clothes.

When he said this to a young priest in Badulla, the man laughed: 'You just want to break coconuts and scramble to get a piece!'

Sarva agreed. 'There is joy in getting even half a banana from the temple priest!'

'Okay, okay. But let me see a Hindu temple putting up a fugitive like you.'

It was only a joke, but to Sarva it rang true. He saw many broken people seeking shelter at these churches. Journalists and aid workers would stay the night, and social workers delivered documents, food and money intended for people stranded in zones cordoned off by the army. It was almost self-destructive how much the priests risked simply by allowing human rights work to be conducted on their premises.

Sarva stayed for almost four months in a seminary in Hatton. Here he met Father R., a thirty-something priest with whom he formed a strong bond. After dinner, they would have long philosophical conversations about duty, morality and what it meant to have faith when your world was crumbling. Father R. said that, in his experience, suffering was as likely to make someone reject God as turn to Him for comfort. But they all grappled with the same questions: why is this happening to me? What have I done to deserve this? The greatest challenge of his life, Father R. said, had not been finding God but reconciling his spirituality with the violence of war. He was a Tamil, raised in a village near Jaffna, and, after being ordained, had worked for two decades in the Vanni areas, teaching and counselling youngsters. After several years, he found that he had taken sides and chosen to support the Tamil separatist movement. He abhorred their violent ways but had begun to wonder if there was any other way to fight generations of discrimination, and decided it was impossible to work in such a polarised society without taking a political stance.

'Then what is the difference between you and a Tiger?' Sarva asked.

'Maybe as much difference as there is between a Tamil and a Tiger,' the priest said. He did not speak Sinhalese and believed that without his cassock he was no less vulnerable than an ordinary Tamil civilian. The army rarely stopped his church van, but he was always terrified of harassment. Once, in Colombo, he had been out without his vestments, wearing trousers and a shirt, on his way to meet his relatives. The soldiers had not believed he was a priest even after he had showed them his ID card. They had strip-searched him and he spent the night in a police station cell. Since then, he never left the church without his cassock.

For the priests and nuns, their vestments were armour. Their robes commanded respect from the armed forces, some of whom were Christian. Buddhist soldiers, many of them rural boys brought up to venerate saffron-clad Buddhist priests, often extended the same courtesy to members of the Christian clergy. This gave nuns and priests greater access to closed spaces like refugee camps and detention centres. Father R., in addition, made maximum use of the privileges his church gave him: chauffeur-driven cars, access to village authorities, an international network of contacts, even the church's usually large premises. In heavily patrolled regions, church and temple compounds tended to become hangouts for friends, venues for NGO meetings, places with secure boundaries where people could sit alone in silence.

Many people who knocked on the parish door needed more than prayer. They suffered from post-traumatic stress and as the presidential task force rarely approved NGO projects for psychological counselling in war-affected areas, church group sessions were frequently the only therapy on offer.

Public funerals and memorials were banned, leaving thousands with no way to deal with loss. In May 2011 Jehaan and some of the priests had organised a silent prayer for one of their number who had died in the war. It was held in Kilinochchi, the deceased's birthplace, but refugees from all across the north came to the renovated church where the ceremony was held. As the priest prayed for the souls of those who died in pain, there was the rare spectacle of people bursting into tears, mourning for the first time in public.

Exercising this privilege was not without risks. One of Father R.'s colleagues from Jaffna, a priest who ran an NGO focussed on the rights and safety of war widows, received death threats on a weekly basis, and he heard the giveaway clicks on his office landline and mobile phone indicating that they had been tapped. A western province priest who had accompanied some foreign journalists to a camp woke one morning to find navy booths on either side of his street, keeping watch on him. Some priests delivered straightforward, apolitical religious sermons, helping people find peace without controversy through God and family. When Sarva stayed with such priests, he noticed their deliberate indifference towards him, his story, or the reason he was hiding. But they fed him, gave him shelter, and did not give him away.

ONE NIGHT AFTER dinner, Sarva told Father R. about Malar, the source of an obsessive love that had preserved his sanity through the long months of hiding. Malar had entered his life at a time of crisis. After Shirleen and her friend had applied on Sarva's behalf to a Danish university, a grave technical mistake occurred. He gained admission, and the fee had to be paid in advance, which Amma did, but the money didn't reach the university on time and his student visa was not approved. He would have to wait another semester to apply again. That meant six more dreadful months in hiding. And that was when Amma had mentioned Malar.

Amma and Malar had met at a convention in Nuwara Eliya on studying abroad. Malar was a schoolteacher and had spent a year in Switzerland and Germany on an exchange programme. To Amma, she looked kind and respectful. She wore her chiffon sari modestly, neatly pinned to her blouse. Her fingers were patchy with blue ink. She spoke English and Tamil and said she could understand 'a little Swiss'. Amma had trusted her with Sarva's story, and she had agreed to give him some tips on applying for courses abroad.

After this, every time Sarva called Amma, she insisted that he speak to this lovely girl, Malar, to learn more about opportunities in Switzerland. Amma adored Shirleen but unfairly blamed her for the rejection of Sarva's visa. 'They don't know about these things,' she said, and gave him Malar's number. 'She is very smart, so don't try your broken English with her,' Amma added.

He called her. She didn't pick up but called back at night. They talked till dawn.

The next day he messaged her in transliterated Tamil. 'Thank you for stealing my sleep!'

'I'm sure you're used to it!' she replied, with a wink and a question mark.

'This has never happened to me before,' he typed, adding a smiley. 'I swear on my mother's life.'

They spoke again that evening, after Malar got home from school. He explained his situation and she shared hers—her brother had taken a boat to Canada but was struggling to get asylum as the country was tougher with refugees than it used to be. Her parents were retired, her mother was ill. She was the only breadwinner in her family.

A week later, he admitted to her that it was 'love at first sight'. She cried.

For months, as he went from safe house to safe house, they spoke on the phone. About what, he couldn't say, but it was not about Switzerland or universities. Amma knew that much when she got his monstrous mobile phone bill. He asked Malar to get a SIM card from the same mobile company so that they could talk for longer. It would be cheaper if they were both using Dialog.

While he marvelled at their compatibility—they were late risers, both put family above everything else, loved movies, liked travelling and the hills—he would ask her why she had chosen him over other men. She said it had started with shock at his experiences, and amazement at his survival. It might have begun with sympathy, but this wasn't pity-love, she assured him. She liked his childlike nature, his ability to joke at the worst of times, his greed for joy, his strength. Yet, she felt like caring for him, shielding him from the elements.

When Sarva was housed in Kottayena, Jehaan told him he would be moved to Hatton next. Excitedly, Sarva told Malar that he would be getting closer to her.

'I think you're beautiful,' he texted later that night. 'I want to know if I'm right.'

She did not reply for two days. For those forty-eight hours, every morsel of food was mud, everyone he saw was ugly, boring, annoying. Was she insulted? Had he blown it? 'Sorry,' he texted in transliterated Tamil. 'Was that out of line? Please, I'm a decent guy, don't misunderstand me.'

The third day, as he dragged himself to breakfast, the phone beeped. Her picture. A yellow floral-print sari. Long wavy hair with a shiny clasp. A toothy smile that was simultaneously shy and mischievous. She stood near a window, and her head reached the curtain rod.

'You are tall!' he typed. He was impressed. *He* was tall. This was perfect.

'???' she replied.

'It is a compliment! You are more angelic than I imagined.' And so on. All day, he raved about her beauty. He sent her YouTube links to ballads by A. R. Rahman.

Finally, her reply: 'Can I see you?'

He had sent her an old photograph of his, posing in front of his house, healthy and wearing his best trousers. In a few minutes, guiltily, he sent her a recent one, taken by Randy near a waterfall on one of their trips between safe houses.

She called at night and they chatted for hours. The proctor who had a room next to Sarva's knocked hard on his door: 'Quiet!' The lovers giggled uncontrollably. The next day, Sarva jumped the parish walls and bought her two saris, one cream and another maroon. He cut his palm scaling the wall on his way back.

Hatton, his next destination, the closest he'd come yet to Malar, was where he had gone to high school. As if association worked some magic on him, he became a teenager in love, single-minded and relentless. Sarva loved being in love with Malar. He felt like his old self: playful and always in a good mood. The jitters left him, his appetite returned. His eyes were always wandering to his phone, hoping to find an incoming message. He was happily distracted, and reeling with a sensation he hadn't savoured for ages. After more than a year in hiding, he was tired of being tortured, hunted, of being the man with medical problems and no family. Malar made him handsome, funny, normal. She knew what they had done to him in the basement. She understood that if Sarva did not heal entirely, the two of them could probably never have children. She loved him nonetheless. She was everything he needed.

Without Randy around, Sarva couldn't think of anyone to confide in. But the moment he blurted out her name to Father R., the priest unexpectedly squealed with delight. From then on, Malar was all they really talked about. It was Father R. who convinced him to meet her.

It was arranged for the second of the month. Sarva and Father R. took a van and parked it opposite the Hatton bus stop. Her Nuwara Eliya bus would arrive that afternoon. She had told her family she was visiting a school friend in Hatton.

The first time he saw her, she was standing near the petrol pump, attempting to cross the road as buses wound this way and that, people milled and trishaws meandered, their drivers hoping to pick up a fare. She towered above them all. She was so tall.

He was running across the road. He was grabbing her hand. '*Vaa di!*' he was saying in front of everyone. 'Come!' He was pulling her to the van. She turned crimson.

The priest left them alone in the van and went off to buy groceries. Sarva held Malar and could not let go. They were hugging hard, speaking at the same time, hearing nothing, laughing nervously but feeling a floating inner calm. They held hands tight. 'Why are you squeezing me?' she asked. 'I'll also squeeze you.'

Meet my wife, Sarva said, when Father R. came back.

They spent the day walking around the seminary, sitting in the church, or taking shade under the mango tree near the poultry. They wondered if they should get engaged. But before a conclusion could be reached, two o'clock rolled around and she had to leave to get home for dinner. He gave her the saris and showed her the cut on his palm. She scolded him, then cried.

When Father R. and he dropped her off, Sarva kissed her forehead before opening the door of the van. As she walked to the bus and waved, Father R. said, 'What? You kissed her like she was your daughter.'

Sarva was still in a trance. 'How can it be that this is the first time we have met?'

A COUPLE OF months later, in May 2011, Sarva decided to leave the country. Malar had helped him make up his mind. 'Follow your dreams,' she had said. 'Go to America. You're smart enough to find a job there and manage.' Later, she could apply to study for a Master's and join him.

He would travel with a fake passport. His brother Deva's friend would smuggle him out of Sri Lanka with about ten others. The guy owed Deva a favour, so the fee came at a discount. Sarva would pay 2.5 million rupees instead of 4 million. It was all working out.

Shirleen and Jehaan were appalled. They visited Amma and Deva, trying to make them see reason. It was dangerous, they said, and there was no assurance Sarva would eventually get asylum. Amma sobbed as she explained that they just couldn't wait any longer, living separately, never seeing each other, knowing that Sarva was wasting his life. Deva did not say much.

'We cannot help you any longer if you decide on the illegal route,' Shirleen told Sarva. How could he trust a stranger, a human smuggler, with his life? Jehaan explained the risks. Sarva could be deported from the airport as soon as he arrived—he didn't even know where that would be. If he were sent back, the TID would arrest him the moment his plane landed at Colombo. His nightmare would begin all over again.

Sarva understood. But he was done with the safe houses. He had found the woman he wanted to marry and he wanted to get his life in order. He had given so many people control over his decisions, so many strangers had walked in and out. He needed to try it his way. He would trust his brother.

On 4 May 2011, Sarva left.

19.

January 2011

MUGIL AND HER family were finally getting out of Manik Farm. Without explanation, an official in the refugee camp office handed her a release notice and told her to prepare to leave. She couldn't read the form, which was written in Sinhala, and was too afraid to ask for a translation and risk triggering a familiar tirade about how it was high time the inmates learnt the first language of Sri Lanka. What she understood from the form was that she was being sent home—but the wrong home. The army was sending her to Point Pedro, the town of her childhood, not to PTK.

Confused, Mugil went to Harini Akka, a woman from the row closest to the camp office. Harini Akka spoke some Sinhala and overheard things. Mugil had buttered her up for months, always stopping to chat and listening patiently to her complain about her mother-in-law. Akka was a Dalit and her husband, an upper-caste doctor with a Jaffna University degree; his family had stridently opposed the match and disowned them when they married. In the thick of battle in early 2009, Akka had seen the doctor being picked up by the army, which now denied ever detaining him. Akka and her mother-in-law had been compelled to join forces in their hunt for him, though each took every opportunity to blame the other for their family's misfortunes. They shared nothing but the conviction that the doctor was alive and being kept hidden by the military. Mugil thought it was more likely he had been summarily executed, but she was not one to dash their hopes.

Mugil found Harini Akka sitting outside her tent in the mud, her legs stretched out under her frayed housecoat. She was removing black specks of dirt from a plate of rice gruel. Mugil showed her the release notice.

'Oh, Parutithurai for you!' Akka squealed, using the old Tamil name for Point Pedro. 'I was praying for you to get some good news.'

'This is not good news, Akka! Why Parutithurai? I don't understand. I was expecting to go to PTK.'

'Don't nitpick, be like me. Just take the chance and get out of here.'

'Where are you going?'

'Jaffna.'

'But you're from Viswamadu, no? Why are they sending you to Jaffna? I don't know what is going on.'

Akka said the army told her that Viswamadu was not yet cleared of mines. 'So I'll have to live at my mother-in-law's for a while. It's a pain, but what to do?'

Mugil sat down next to her and started to shave the skin off some plantain.

'Is PTK also not yet cleared of mines?' she asked. 'Is that why I have got Parutithurai?' The town had not been directly affected in the most recent battle.

Akka shrugged. 'The army has fallen in love with our Vanni now. They want it all for themselves.'

Then, dropping her voice, she added, 'Those places … there are memories there. This government does not like that.'

The release was a fraud, Mugil thought. Bussing people to strange places instead of their homes was hardly granting them their freedom.

The camps had been open for almost two years now, but few Vanni residents had been released; the official reason was that the inmates needed to be screened for Tiger cadres and the war zone had to be demined. There had always been mines in the Vanni, but in the last stages of the war, both the army and the Tigers had laid many more haphazardly, without keeping records. Global demining agencies had worked painstakingly slowly with former combatants and the military, and cleared several villages for habitation on the Mannar coast and on the peripheries of Kilinochchi and Mullaitivu. But it was only the army and navy that had moved in there, expanding their military presence while the villagers were imprisoned in refugee camps. Even after they had started releasing a few hundred inmates every month under international pressure, most villages remained out of bounds.

Harini Akka had been chatting to people who got their notice to leave camp and had noticed a trend. A lot of families were being sent to the residential addresses they had listed on electoral registers twenty-eight years earlier, in 1982, when the last election was held in the north. These lists were the last official record because there had been no census in these parts since—owing to the violence and the government's lack of access. The dramatic changes in the region's demography and population had gone unrecorded. The Tigers had forced out over 75,000 Muslims and a smaller number of Sinhalese since the eighties, whittling the northern province into a proto-Tamil state. They had initially compelled Tamils from elsewhere to move into the region; but in time, millions persecuted by the state had also rushed to find safety among their own. It was a migratory pattern layered over three decades; if a diagram were drawn to depict it, the mesh of intersecting lines might form a spiderweb, at the centre of which was the Vanni. The state readopted the 1982 records because these helped legitimise the return of Sinhalese and Muslim families to lands that Tamils had occupied since, thus diluting the Tamil population in the Vanni and preventing any future claims to a separate Tamil homeland. It was a strategic decision for the government, but for the Tamils, greatly disorientating.

Because the 1982 records linked people to villages they had long left, or had been forced to leave, Mugil's family was registered in Point Pedro. But they had moved twelve times since, before finally settling in PTK. That was her home, however convoluted the process that led to her living there. She didn't want to be sent back to the beginning. Moreover, in Chundukuli Junction in PTK she owned a house that she had built with Divyan after their wedding. She mentioned this to Harini Akka, who laughed bitterly. '*Anh*, good luck getting it back from our new army landlords!' she said.

'Can I move out of Point Pedro after they send me there?'

'They apparently register us with the village office and keep an eye on our activities. So just stay put for a while.'

Akka seemed to have resigned herself to her allotted destination (she had once mentioned that Viswamadu, where she last stayed, reminded her only of death), but Mugil felt cornered. Why didn't the resettlement ministry just ask the refugee families where they wanted to go? To value out-of-date records over individual or community choice was to pretend these last twenty-eight years of dislocation had not happened. The government was rewinding to a time before the war, before she met her husband and had her sons, before her rebellion at thirteen, before the worst riots the Tamils had ever experienced, before even the first thought of Eelam existed in Sri Lankan history. It seemed her family was not simply being sent to Point Pedro but back in time.

A few days after her conversation with Akka, a convoy of buses drove Mugil, her family and about 150 others out of the camp. She did not look back, but the miles of barbed wire seemed etched on her retinas. She shut her eyes, and it was still there. The departure was a year too late; they were three people short.

Along the A9 highway to Point Pedro, the bus dropped off other families at several points. Some were taken to their villages and accommodated in schools and churches. Others were simply let off at the start of a road, accompanied by a couple of soldiers. At noon, when one such group was dropped off just after the Omanthai checkpoint, Mugil roused herself to look out the window, Tamizh snoozing on her lap. There was no sign of life outside, and the only indication the area had ever been inhabited was the imprint of a demolished house on the ground. Its cracked red-oxide floor traced the layout of a sandy living room, two other rooms and a kitchen. A few metres away, two concrete steps stood orphaned from the threshold. Thorny shrubs had overtaken everything else, including the mud trail that led to the village the former inmates were now supposed to walk to. As the bus groaned and moved ahead, a one-armed man who had just alighted with his daughter stared back, as if he were considering getting back on. His lost eyes caught Mugil's for a moment, and then the bus pulled her away.

FOR MOST OF the journey to Point Pedro, Mugil's head was out the open window, trying to take everything in. Mother sat next to her holding Maran, and Tamizh sat on Mugil's lap. Amuda and her children were in the seats behind them. There were mostly women on the bus.

They were on the A9, the main highway connecting the south and north, the Sinhalese and the Tamils. The more the communities were polarised by war, politics and language, the greater the A9's inaccessibility. It was a physical manifestation of the growing gulf between peoples. It was closed for long periods during the conflict, and Mugil remembered how news of its opening would excite villagers in the north. Immediately, they would plan family visits, think about shopping in the more developed central and southern towns, or attempt to tend to long-delayed chores.

Anyone travelling on the A9 was subject to intense scrutiny. A Tamil getting out of the Vanni needed a pass from the Tigers. All the way to the south, the army checkpoints would ask where that person was going, why, what she was carrying, and when she would return. When she reached the south, she would have to register her national ID at the nearest police station and state how long she intended to stay. On her return northwards, the Tiger checkpoints would do the same, ask the same questions, charge heavy taxes on alcohol purchased, and not allow more than two litres of precious petrol per head to be taken into the Vanni. The journey from Vavuniya to Jaffna, which used to take four hours, would end up taking more than a day.

The A9 shut overnight during wartime, and remained closed for long periods. People were unable to get home for years because of the closures. Since 2006, when the military launched its final attack, the highway had been shut down completely, and the Tamils in the north were caged in, darting about in a panic within a limited, threatened space.

Just before the presidential elections in January 2010, the A9 had been finally cleared for traffic; it had been open for a year now. But instead of the usual NGO cars and Tamils on bicycles and scooters, the postwar highway was chock-a-block with army vans and tourist buses from Colombo. There was a festive air. The coaches played videos to entertain the passengers and large families—grandparents, mothers, fathers, uncles, children—squeezed picnic baskets onto the crowded seats and the luggage racks.

The bus of refugees passed Kilinochchi, where three years ago Mugil had forsaken the girls and her own life as a Tiger. The town was now a trail of burnt wooden cots, broken ceramic toilets and smashed cars. They passed rows of dilapidated buildings with their roofs caved in, Tamil signboards blacked out, vans lying stripped and burnt. The police headquarters, court complex, market, temples, were all in ruins. Among a group of tourists, a man snapped a picture of one such half-building plastered with posters displaying the president's grinning face. Mugil and her mother looked at each other.

'How can they celebrate like this?' Mugil whispered. 'Why don't they care?'

Mother placed a hand on her thigh. 'Tch, leave it, Mugil! Our problem is ours. Their problem is over and they want to enjoy themselves.'

It had been a quarter-century since Sri Lankans from the south had set eyes on the north. The Tigers were hated, feared, held responsible for the terrorism that rocked ordinary lives. Their end led to an explosion of relief among southerners: they were finally free to move around and even to go north if they wanted. They burst upon the A9, claiming it as their own, rejoicing at the end of their nightmare.

The A9 now showcased victory. A glossy new white statue of the Buddha towered over the ruins; near it was a broken-down Hindu temple. A few hundred feet from the statue stood a tall bronze lotus, a Buddhist symbol, growing out of a wall cracked by a giant projectile. Before Elephant Pass, an armoured Tiger vehicle—a truck modified to serve as a tank—was displayed as a monument to the sacrifice of a Sri Lankan soldier, Corporal Gamini Kularatne, who died attacking it on 1 July 1991. Next to the tank was a war souvenir shop.

The final checkpoint was at Elephant Pass, the thin strip of road where the A9 ended and the Jaffna Peninsula began. There, soldiers entered Mugil's bus and checked the refugees' meagre belongings. Many were being frisked but Mugil was spared. She stiffened in her seat and stared ahead blankly, humiliation stinging her eyes. When the bus moved again, turning towards Jaffna, the sign with the name 'Yalpanam' in Tamil script was missing. In its place, was a new sign—'Yapanaya', the Sinhalese name for Jaffna. Round the bend, a freshly painted yellow concrete sign read, 'One Nation, One Country'.

By dusk, they reached the Point Pedro bus stop. The bus emptied and about twenty families got down along with two soldiers. They walked to the nearby Amman temple. This was a Tamil area, but shopkeepers stared and shoppers froze nonetheless. What did they see? Mugil wondered. The noticeable absence of men? The lack of footwear? Their haggard appearance, worn-out clothes, and white-and-blue UNHCR plastic bags? The distended stomachs of the kids? The families huddled closer.

The Amman temple was small but housed an enormous pillared hall. Its young priest was at first taken aback to see the families, but he went about his duties without a word; temples and churches had always been default refugee shelters. He brought out straw mats for them to sleep on and distributed bananas to the children.

POINT PEDRO HAD no special point and commemorated no one named Pedro. Yet that was its official name on documents, road signs and buses. Conductors dangling from the bus doors chanted, 'Parutithurai! Parutithurai!' Mugil, too, knew it by that old Tamil name. Paruti-thurai, with the crackle and snap in every *r* and *t*, with the harbour and the cotton fields, with the deep-fried *vadais* crispier than anywhere else in the country.

It was the windswept coastal town her father had loved, that her family had called home till they abandoned it in a rain of shells for the forests of the Vanni. The town before the bombardment was a moving photograph in her memory: sandpapery tobacco leaves bundled on market-bound pushcarts, anchored catamarans jerking in the waves, everything bleached by bright sunlight except the cobalt blue of the sea and the fluorescent green moss on the walls. Against that image from her childhood, this Point Pedro was surprisingly grey. It seemed scrubbed clean and simultaneously abandoned. A boat left too long in the sun. They were returning to it after sixteen years.

They slept in the Amman temple for the first few nights. Every morning, the priest arrived earlier than sunrise, waking them before the six o'clock prayer. He gave them jugs of water with which to wash their faces. When the devotees broke coconuts as divine offerings, adult refugees scurried like children to pick up the shattered pieces.

After five days, the village officer arrived with a posse of soldiers to take down the families' names. 'Register *panni-panniye azhich-chiduvaangal,*' one of the refugees in the queue mumbled: they will kill us with this incessant registering. It took all day, and they had only the temple offerings of a few banana slices and coconut shavings to eat. When the registrations were done, the soldiers left with the village officer. They said the UNHCR would come by in a few days to distribute tin sheets, shovels and building material. Until then, the refugees were left to fend for themselves. Most of them had only a little luggage.

On the bus, Mother had declared her intention to find their old house again, the one that was her dowry when she married Father, the one they had fled. 'It was a house with *raasi,*' she said, it brought prosperity to the family. So after the registration, they went looking for this dowry house, Mother gingerly retracing steps taken more than a decade ago. The family followed her quietly, a few paces behind. Mother was sort of under a spell, squealing in surprise once in a while or mumbling at a closed road or new lane that offended her by challenging her memory. It was almost eight in the evening and the darkness was perplexing. Shops were closing their shutters. A few flickering street lamps came on, and insects threw themselves at the bulbs. The porches of most of the houses were dark. Mugil hadn't been out on a residential street at night for close to two years. It felt illicit. Miraculous.

Finally, turning left from a tobacco field and going past a T-junction and temple, Mother stopped dead in the middle of the road. 'It was here,' she said, swinging her head left and right. 'Where has it gone?' On her left was a crumbling wall. By the dim streetlights, Mugil saw that someone had drawn a charcoal door and window on it. 'Is it really gone?' Mother's voice was shaking. She crouched on the road and held her head. 'There was a beautiful idol of Saraswati on the archway in front; even that is nothing but dust!'

They went back to the temple courtyard. Mother couldn't sleep. She wished that she had come back to see the house at least once in all the years since they left. She had expected to find squatters or to deal with some rain damage, some bullet holes. She had not imagined her home's complete destruction.

Maran woke Mugil up the next morning, screaming that his stomach was 'saying gurr gurr'. They walked to the closest cool bar for bread and tea. Amuda asked for glasses of iced water. As they sipped in silence, shrinking under the gaze of the other customers, the middle-aged owner left the counter and came up to their table. '*Sugama*? All well?' he asked, smiling kindly. He smelt of holy ash, and his neatly parted hair shone with coconut oil.

The server brought a plate of short eats, buns and roti. 'Eat well,' the owner said. 'Don't worry about it.' As he went back to the counter, Mugil wondered how many refugees he had fed this way. She asked for some milk. It was hot, frothy, thick and sugary. The children drank up.

As they left the shop, Mugil stopped to thank the owner and fished out her slim purse. As she'd expected, he waved the money away. They hoped to see him again soon, she said. He patted Kalai's head and said goodbye.

Outside, Mother said she was going to look for her house again. 'There is some light now. I'm sure I made a mistake last night.'

Mugil went another way, to recharge her phone card. There was a shop ten minutes away, near the beach. Barbed wire curled all along the coastline; the military now regulated fishing in these parts. You needed a day pass to go into the sea; to get the pass you needed a national ID card, and to get the ID card, you needed the navy or army to clear you.

Towards the north, in the distance, the navy camp was a black block. There was not a boat in sight. At this time of day, the waves were bright overlapping sheets of silver. The sand was white, fine. Through squinted eyes, Mugil saw a slim silhouette on the shore, facing the sea. Thin legs stuck out from under a folded sarong. A hand extended forward and remained there motionless, wrist bent forward, the index finger and thumb pinching something. Whatever it was, it was invisible from where Mugil stood. But she knew the man's pose, knew the trance he was in. He was holding a fishing line, waiting for a bite.

As she walked away, thoughts of Father and his fishing stories came to her in a rush. The large sardines he caught for the market and the tiny sprats he asked Mother to fry for the children. The smell of engine diesel on his shirts. The yarns he wove about monsters at sea when she begged to go with him on night expeditions. His teasing her for shunning eel because she thought it was a poisonous snake. Parutithurai, or Point Pedro, was Mother's birthplace, but it was Father who had brought it alive.

Mugil took a long route back, now eager to see what the town was like. She turned into a narrow lane along the side wall of a hospital. The first two houses were bordered by new cadjan fences, woven from palmyra leaves, and she heard pots clatter inside. The next had a concrete wall covered in moss. She peeped in through the gate. A goat was tethered to a tree, a couple of chickens pecked about. The next compound was overgrown with weeds, but it had a well. Before she could stop herself, Mugil went in through the arched gate and drew some water from the well. She cupped some in her palm and sipped. It was sweet on her tongue. To one side was the bungalow, unlocked. Mugil walked in. The first thing she noticed was the framed pictures of three Hindu deities high on the wall, the trio of prosperity: Saraswati, Pillaiyer and Mahalakshmi. Next to them was the black-and-white face of a clean-shaven man in a turban and dark suit. Mugil peered closer. It was a painting, the fine brushstrokes imitating a photograph. A well-to-do ancestor, a lawyer perhaps, or an accountant. If the residents left him behind, they must have been in a hurry, she thought. Everything else seemed to have been looted. The walls were pistachio green and the kitchen looked unused. There were no cobwebs but small piles of sand everywhere. The wind tugged and pushed the metal door of the backyard toilet. She stood in the living room for a while, pressing her soles to the cool floor, noticing absences. No shutters on the windows. No furniture. No residents.

She knew then that she did not want to go back to her mother's house or what was left of it. She would move here, to this house with the sea wind.

THE HOUSE IN Point Pedro changed Mugil. With six rooms and an indoor kitchen, it was almost palatial, the biggest place she had ever lived in. Time expanded with the extra space. Her toddlers couldn't get enough of the half-moon well in the side yard. Every morning, they eagerly kicked off their shorts and ran out for their bath. Mugil didn't allow them to clamber up the sides when she yanked the rope. Their anticipation of the cold, crisp splash was stretched so taut that when the pulley whirred loose and the metal bucket hit the water below, they yelped with delight. Drenched from head to toe and shivering, Maran once told her with extravagant joy that it was as if they were back at their old house.

But their old house in PTK was nothing like this. They had lived in the basic quarters the Tamil Tigers had given them—two rooms and a kitchen. All around, people blown there by conflict or loyalty from places as far afield as Colombo and Jaffna lived just like them, in equal-sized houses with thatched roofs and no electricity or running water. They had been surrounded by the forest, sharp and unforgiving in the summer, bountiful but mosquito-infested during the rains. They had known everyone in the neighbourhood; everyone spoke Tamil. Maran, had he been old enough, would have walked with the neighbour's son to the government primary school five minutes from home. People were attached to the little there was because they had built it with their own hands.

This house, in the northernmost town of Sri Lanka, was so close to the Arabian Sea that the wind howled through its rooms. It had a yard of pearly sand, bald coconut trees and lantana shrubs. Its compound wall, whose green and pink patterns had dulled in the salty air, hid them from the street. She cleaned the rooms inside and removed the portrait of the glowering ancestor. The deities continued to watch over her. The skid marks on the red oxide floor suggested that there had once been some chairs and tables, but they had probably been stolen or cut up for use as fuel during the conflict. Even the front door was missing.

Mugil didn't need a door; the roof alone was more good luck than she had dared hope for. If she wished for something else, the little she had might be snatched from her. She prayed that the owners, descendants of the man in the portrait, would not abruptly return and throw them out. Mother vaguely remembered an affluent family residing here but didn't know why they left or who they were. She and Amuda moved in with Mugil but insisted it was temporary. The UNHCR gave them a resettlement kit—25,000 rupees, some tin sheets, a bag of cement, rope, basic household items like bed sheets, jerry cans, kitchen utensils and construction tools—and Mother was determined to rebuild what was left of her old house. 'Why take someone else's?' she asked Mugil.

'Because they are gone and we are here,' Mugil replied.

Ever since she discovered this house, abandoned, littered with the muck the seasons had swept in, Mugil had felt optimistic. The tension from the press of queues and the constraints of tent living left her body; the urgency of bare survival melted away. It was so simple to buy cheap fish and gather firewood, start the stove, boil some rice, eat a filling meal, sleep. Mugil imagined Divyan released from detention, arriving at this house, praising her for her decision. Her boys would be going to school in smart uniforms. Drumstick, mangoes and jackfruit would hang from healthy trees in the yard. Perhaps the years of fear would end at this house.

20.

May 2011

SINCE JANUARY, MUGIL had done little apart from care for her home and family. By summer, Maran and Tamizh had lost their beaten look and the house was more or less in order. She made her own front door: she wove a cadjan mat, mounted it on a wooden frame and used a stick and rope loop as the latch. It would not stop thieves—what was there to steal?—but it gave her some privacy. She knocked the rust off the backyard toilet door and bought a bucket, mug and plastic drum to fill with well water. There was no electricity, so she purchased kerosene lamps and candles. Mother and Amuda had moved out to their old property; they had fixed what was left of that house, but the roof repairs were stalled for lack of funds. It was comfortable enough to live beneath the sky in the summer months, but the roof would have to be fixed by June, before the rains.

Mugil did not remember things ever being this expensive. The compensation they had received from the government, a one-off payment, had evaporated in the first month. The cost of living had escalated since the end of the war, an effect of the sharp rise in demand from refugees and the still ailing economy. Non-refugee locals seemed to struggle, too, because incomes had not caught up with expenses. For families from the Vanni, the market rates were doubly shocking; the price of essentials had been regulated under the Tigers, which muted market fluctuations. Staples like milk powder, oil and coconut now tripled in price.

It was annoying, having to buy food they once caught or grew. Coastal households with men around managed to make fish curry twice a day. Even though the navy rationed day passes for fishing and occasionally banned it, when they did go to sea, the men said, 'Fish is free, the sea charges nothing for it.' Only the garlic, tamarind, oil, salt and chilli powder needed to be bought.

When Mugil bought seafood, she wondered if the fish seller realised there was no man in her house. Sometimes she returned from the market with an empty bag, indignant about paying money for vegetables and lentils that she could have grown on her acre of land in PTK. But even those who still had some land, like the farmers closer to Jaffna, were seeing disappointing crops, especially in the rice paddies. When some of them came to the Point Pedro market to sell produce, Mugil asked if they needed farmhands; she needed to earn a living and she had experience. But they were too deep in debt to pay for labour. As a cooperative, they were working on coconut, plantain and mango orchards, but the soil was poor and they had other obstacles to deal with. The saplings needed tending, but what with travel restrictions, sudden curfews and a tight budget, they were invariably falling behind. If the rainfall in June were low, they'd be in trouble. Life was precarious for everyone, and over time, expenses piled high: medical treatment, education, loans. Without a reliable income, people had to be creative. A refugee family that still lived in the Amman temple sold their tin sheets and used the money for their daughters' tuition fees. Another sold their government-issue rice bags to buy supplies for their newborn. Mugil gave her rice bags to a mill for pounding, a method that expanded each kilo by half. She made gruel for meals, retaining the starchy water; this way, her rice lasted for several more weeks.

Every visit to the Point Pedro village office to complete some bureaucratic formality cost Mugil 53 rupees for bus fare. So she combined such trips with visits to one of Divyan's aunts who lived nearby. She would sit with the family and chat aimlessly for an hour. When it was time to say goodbye, the aunt would run into her yard and pack a few papayas, pumpkins or coconuts for Mugil to take home. If she were lucky, there would be a half sack of lentils or rice, too.

Saris became curtains, unnamed leaves made it onto the dinner plate, buckets of well water were bartered for firewood. When Amuda passed a broken wall somewhere, she brought home some of the bricks. Discarded fragments of fibreglass boats from the beach became part of a fence. A rusted bike wheel became a laundry hanger; pieces of its tyre were door stops, and the tube was stretched across Mugil's bicycle bar to hang baskets. The sisters were turning into scrap geniuses.

Mother pawned her gold bracelet, two rings and her thick silver anklets. This sustained them for another two months. Mugil had lost her distaste for her community's compulsive accumulation of gold, having seen so many people sell their jewellery during the war. She was never attracted to the thick, clunky designs people bought, and she herself wore only small hexagonal ear studs. She disapproved of gold as a marker of status, but were it not for the hoarded jewellery, many families would have been without food or shelter. For the displaced, it was invariably the currency of distress, the most portable thing of value. Mugil had owned a house and farmland, but when she ran for her life, they were lost. How easily trinkets, coins and chains could be bundled into a handkerchief and tucked into sari petticoats or underclothes. One by one, they would be pawned or sold—for utensils, an operation, some poultry or goats.

But pawning gold was never a simple transaction. For the Tamils, it was a tragic, sentimental shedding of prosperity. Acquired on auspicious days, worn to weddings, child-naming and coming-of-age ceremonies, each piece of jewellery had a value far exceeding its cash price.

Mother had pawned everything since Father passed away, giving a different melodramatic reason each time: she was embracing widowhood, ageing, or their new poverty. She sometimes broached the subject of selling her wedding chain. 'What use is the *thaali* without him?' she would say. 'We need the money.' Mugil wouldn't hear of her selling the *thaali*. Even if it curled unused at the bottom of a metal trunk, it was evidence Father had once existed. If it came to selling this, Mugil would have failed as the head of the family; she would have pushed them to shed their last ounce of dignity. 'Keep it for when we're worse off,' she told Mother.

It was May 2011, and Mugil needed a job. She did not have much of a formal education but could ride a motorbike, use a camera, even climb a coconut tree. She was fluent in Tamil, good with numbers, and had a way with people. But she had begun to have misgivings about displaying these skills lest she be identified as a former combatant. Things had shifted inside her. Her life was no longer dedicated to the movement, but the state would not see that. The TID and army would find little to distinguish the unrepentant from the transformed and give her no credit for deserting the Tigers. She would be pushed back to the edge. She knew that hiding was perhaps unfair to those who had surrendered, like her own husband. But there was Maran and Tamizh, and the need to raise them overrode all other moral concerns.

It wasn't easy to be invisible. She knew the rules but hadn't absorbed them. Oh no, Mother would say, good family women don't go to the market after dusk. They don't sit near a man on the bus. They don't draw attention. A loud voice, short temper or confident walk was enough to get one into trouble. Amuda knew of a primary school teacher in Thevipuram who organised a sports day without following the recent practice of inviting an army official as the guest of honour. She was banned from leaving her village without military permission. A young man, an acquaintance of Mugil's from Valvettithurai, went missing after he turned down a soldier's offer of a beer. 'I don't have such habits,' the customers in the tea shop heard him say. Only a former combatant, the powers that be seemed to surmise, would have the prepossession to both refuse alcohol and do so looking a solider in the eye. It did not help that the young man belonged to Prabakaran's hometown.

Being female itself invited danger. Mugil knew seven women in her neighbourhood who had become more vulnerable after the killing or kidnapping of their husbands. They told her in whispers how the soldiers used the investigation into the missing man as a pretext to come by after dark or to summon the women to the army office alone. One of them had been asked to send her teenage daughter. The soldiers, only a few years older than the girl, did not touch her but teased and flirted till she was in tears.

A woman could do no right. If she spoke to soldiers, she was easy. If she did not speak to them, she was rude or had something to hide. They were harassed for information or amusement. The mother of one of Maran's friends told Mugil that late one night a soldier walked in (she, too, had no door) and 'slept next to her'. Mugil knew that phrase to mean she had been raped.

It was all as real as it was bizarre. There was no use going to the police, even if they were Tamils; they had been neutered. The military ruled the north—one soldier for every eleven civilians. The government said this presence was necessary to weed out Tigers, separatists and antisocial elements. Those categories included anybody who didn't cower in fear of the military: former Tigers, of course, but also journalists, priests, association leaders, wisecracking boys, women who recoiled from flirtation.

The consequences of being picked out by the army were far-reaching and permanent. You could be detained for a long time. You could be prosecuted under the PTA, and who knew where that would lead. It felt dramatic and over the top at times, this dread of oppression, especially for those who had never experienced it before. The army's presence in Colombo had made the Sinhalese feel safe, and many asked why Tamils were so resistant to it—they are there for the Tamils' own good, they would say.

But every time Mugil passed a soldier, her pulse raced, her palms sweated and a terrifying image of her boys, orphaned and wailing alone, flashed through her mind. She imagined being plucked off the street and plunged into darkness. She sometimes scoffed at her fear, told herself it was paranoia, but it still gripped her. It had happened to others, too many innocent others. She fought to subdue her confident stride and straight back. Kept her voice soft. Did not run as fast as she could to catch a bus. She would hoist one of her sons on her hip when approaching a checkpoint. It was not enough that she was harmless; she needed to be seen to be harmless.

It was not just the army's watchful eyes she had to worry about. The Tamil community was unforgiving to combatants after the war, calling them traitors. They accused the Tigers of stealing from civilians on the run. For many, the former cadre were the lowest scum of society, the reason the army was apprehending innocent people and a force whose decrees had robbed families of their children, whose decades of promises came to nothing. Some people swung wildly between feeling betrayed by the Tigers and nostalgic for the era they represented, but the old loyalty had entirely dissipated. Ex-combatants were dreaded, avoided like the plague. Any association with them was considered too risky. Most people would give them up to the army without hesitation. The ones who went through rehabilitation were suspected of being government spies. No one wanted to employ them.

Female ex-cadre faced the worst stigma. Those who were single were deemed unsuitable for marriage; they were too independent, too dangerous for any family. In gossip, their unwilling visits to army camps were recast as sexual liaisons. The older women—married or widowed—were held to unforgivingly high standards of femininity and obedience.

This was why, when Mugil mounted her bicycle, she kept her legs together, her eyes on the ground. She did not argue with men. She shrank. She acted frail for the comfort of others.

And so it was that Mugil chose what she felt was a traditional woman's job. In May, she and Mother started a small business with their neighbour Sangeeta, making snacks. Mugil, as the worst cook but fastest talker in the group, made deliveries to the market on a bicycle donated by the Dutch Refugee Council. The kind cool-bar owner was their most dependable customer, and he recommended their delicious fish rolls and patties to other shops, too. They made between 500 to 1,000 rupees every day. Some of this they set aside to keep the business running, and the rest they split evenly between them. At first they naively bought groceries at retail, but in time Mugil cut wholesale deals. Some evenings, she scoured the shops for day-old vegetables or oddly cut fish that sold at half-price and tasted just as good.

Her pretence of innocence made Mugil feel like a criminal. 'I'm acting so much like a helpless mother that I forget that I *am* a helpless mother!' She felt hemmed in, but the snack business worked.

She earned just about enough and, given the circumstances, it was the most feminine, unthreatening job she could be seen doing.

Amuda had something marginally better on the horizon. An international NGO had offered her an interest-free loan, and she was considering setting up a knick-knack shop. With the loan, she would be able to afford a solar panel and a used fridge, so she could stock milk and yogurt. 'And I could chill soft drinks and water,' she declared, knowing the demand for cool beverages in households with NGO visitors. 'Nothing like a chilled glass of Necto or Sunquick to get hot and bothered people into a giving mood.'

Mugil, too, had applied for the loan; she didn't like not being chosen. When Amuda signed the papers a few weeks later, Mugil read the certificate. 'Special Livelihood Loan,' it said at the top of the page. In the checklist of borrower eligibility, there was a tick next to 'Disabled' and 'Widow'. Mugil swallowed the resentment that rose like bile in her throat.

Later, she asked Mother why Amuda was always the more deserving one. 'She has always got stuff because of her limp, and now she's a widow, too,' she said.

Mother didn't look at her. 'She is your sister,' she said.

Mugil continued: 'Fine, I guess she deserves help, but why are others like me left out? I'm also alone, without my husband.'

A few days later, their snack business partner, Sangeeta, arrived to settle the previous week's accounts. She went straight into Mugil's kitchen and made two tumblers of black coffee. Not finding any sugar, she added more water to make the brew less bitter.

They sat on the porch. Mugil sipped, and let out an appreciative sigh. 'You added coriander seeds?'

'You like it?'

Mugil nodded vigorously and sipped some more. She could never make coffee like this. 'What was I *doing* in the past?'

'Again this? It's okay, *akka*, you can change now, start anew,' Sangeeta said.

'How? They won't even give me a loan.'

Sangeeta cocked her head. 'I didn't get one either, *akka*.'

Mugil was not surprised. For all her optimism and toiling, twenty-nine-year-old Sangeeta was a difficult one for NGOs to slot.

She had been living in Point Pedro for a decade, having moved here after her marriage to Daya, a fisherman. The woman wore too much powder on her face, and too much oil in her glorious long braid. She had three boys. Her youngest, six-year-old Madhusan, was the one who had told Mugil his father was dead. In time, as the two women struck up a friendship, Sangeeta told her how Daya died. She remembered that day as a series of pictures and sounds, the connections and context emerging from years of retelling the story to the police.

In January 2007, Daya had stopped at Point Pedro market after work to buy kites for his sons. The army had already begun to capture parts of the Vanni, and security had been ramped up in all Tamil districts. The military dotted every corner of the market. One soldier asked Daya for his ID, glanced at it and handed it back. Daya came home and gave the older boys their kites. Remembering something else he wanted to buy, he decided to go back to the market on his motorbike. Madhusan, then two, asked for a ride, so Daya put the boy on the petrol tank in front of him and drove off.

Within minutes, Sangeeta, who was inside the house, heard gunshots. She ran out the door and down the street. Daya was on the road, lying on his side. The bike was on its side, too, still whirring. A few people rushed out of their houses. Sangeeta saw a stunned Madhusan in a stranger's arms. She threw herself down near Daya. Under his head, a puddle of blood was growing. His eyes were half open, his breathing sketchy but definitely there. She tried to stem the blood, but his curly hair was thick and she was panicking. She couldn't find the bullet hole, and the red just kept flowing. Under him, under her, under the bike. She suddenly heard the revving of a motorbike in the distance. When it reached them, she saw it carried two helmeted men. They rode around her and Daya, circling like vultures. People made noises, waved their fists. That was when Sangeeta found her voice. 'Why don't you shoot us, too!' The men sped away.

Some of their neighbours took Daya to a hospital, but the doctors could not save him. The police had taken days to respond to Sangeeta's complaint, and when they finally took the body to conduct a post-mortem, they refused to share the report. The police buried the body, despite Sangeeta's request for a family ceremony and a Hindu cremation. Madhusan had been inconsolable, speechless for days after and then crying for weeks. His cousin distracted him by spinning a 2-rupee coin, the only way anyone was able to get through to the boy.

That was four years ago, but the experience still haunted Sangeeta's family. The couple had never worked for the LTTE, but since Daya's killing that fact mattered little. After the case was transferred to the army for investigation, a team had raided Sangeeta's house. Locking her in, they had demanded to know who she thought shot Daya. With armed soldiers in her house, she had been unable to say she suspected the army. 'It's the LTTE,' they had insisted, asking her to say the same in a statement. She had refused. They asked her to identify the killers from farcical parades of criminals. Even now, every few weeks she was summoned to the army camp, often after dark. She went with her mother or uncle each time, which some soldiers said they didn't like. Once, they'd sent her mother home and kept Sangeeta for hours, asking repeatedly about the Tigers but never saying anything about Daya's murder. Madhusan was on her lap, but they'd said she was still young, and that if she 'cooperated' with them, as they put it, they would let her off lightly. After a few hours, she pinched Madhusan hard. His bawling gave her an excuse to scurry home.

Now, as they sat in Mugil's house, Sangeeta said, 'Sometimes I think that I'm worse off than a widow. Same situation, more problems, but no help from NGOs or anybody.' She was used to it now, she said.

In the north, there were around 59,000 households headed by women like Sangeeta, Mugil and Amuda. They included widows, women with incarcerated husbands and several who were not even sure if they were widows because their husbands had simply disappeared.

'How many women can the NGOs help?' Sangeeta asked almost to herself. 'We'd better look out for ourselves.'

She opened the school notebook they used as an accounts ledger, in which Mugil had noted the expenses on the left-hand page and sales on the right. Sangeeta added up carefully, counting on her fingers as always. They had made more than usual, thanks to a new snack recipe Sangeeta and Mother had come up with the previous day. They had stuffed spiced sprats and caramelised onions into sesame-dusted buns. All seventy of these were sold, and they had received more orders. She asked Mugil to start charging 25 rupees instead of 15 for each piece.

Mugil laughed. 'You plan to become a millionaire with this business or what?'

When Mugil slept on her straw mat at night, with Tamizh splayed on her stomach and Maran snoring softly next to her, she sometimes wondered how things would be if her kids were raised by Divyan, if their roles were reversed. Would Divyan have been able to keep them healthy and fed? Would he, too, feel like he was pretending to be someone else? She asked Sangeeta if she thought her husband would have been a good single parent.

'I'm dead or I'm in detention?'

'You're off. Dead.'

'Then he'd struggle. Widowers don't get any compensation or help, do they?' she asked. 'Which doesn't make sense. We know how men are … they are more helpless than us.'

Looking at Sangeeta's animated face, Mugil found herself wishing again that her own sister were more like this young woman, bright and full of life, engaging in conversation. But there was never a discussion with Amuda that wasn't peppered with complaints about insomnia or exhaustion. Since they were girls, Amuda had been expected to be weak and Mugil strong.

'I guess some people just make better victims,' Mugil said.

Having finished with the accounts, Sangeeta went to the kitchen to knead the batter for the rolls and crumb some bread. Mother would join them soon, and in two hours the prepared *vadais* and tuna rolls would be wrapped in newspaper and tied with twine. The house was always quiet at this time, with Maran still in school and Tamizh napping. On such afternoons, time slowed down, and the women worked in silence. As Sangeeta and Mother cooked and the aromas of spice and jaggery peanut balls wafted through the rooms, Mugil tended to things that had nothing to do with being a mother. She combed her hair, did her laundry. She read the grimy day-old newspapers the cool-bar owner gave her—it was a ritual that she felt nurtured the part of her everyone else wanted gone.

Sangeeta cynically called her friend's reading unproductive 'timepass', but it helped keep Mugil's mind sharp. In some elemental way, it connected her to the world where real life unfolded. Her own existence was a tightly knit routine of work, eat, worry, sleep. Elsewhere, people protested, went to court, fought elections, wrote poems, reunited with their families. Men got visas, women married them to get visas, politicians lied, children died. Even the circus of geopolitics fascinated her: India was confused; China was the new ally; the US and UK were diplomatic enemies of Sri Lanka, passing resolutions against it; the UN threatened the president with an international investigation into war crimes; the president booed and promoted his brothers in government; his brothers looted the country and abused the UN. The newspapers said which areas had been demined, where a new army camp had been established, where Buddhist monks had attacked mosques, where the defence secretary cut ribbons for newly built 'ancient Buddha viharas', where a startled soldier had shot a child. In another time, men would have been sitting around in tea shops discussing these events, trashing politicians and sharing news. But this was the era of cameras and spies, so the tea sessions were replaced by brooding silence.

She read out some important stories to Mother. Prabakaran's childhood house in the Valvettithurai coastal town, which he had left as a teenager, was found destroyed. The house had been badly damaged in army and Indian Peace Keeping Force operations in 1987, four years after the family had left. The army had been guarding it, and the newspapers speculated that the soldiers had been gradually demolishing it, a rumour that grew quickly after the war ended, when southern tourists thronged to see the house. The army denied the accusation, but some generals mentioned wanting to avoid the house becoming a shrine for Prabakaran. Mother said the papers only showed how the country was becoming more hellish, but Mugil wanted to know what was happening. Every day threw up an unforeseen challenge, and she wanted to know how each of these events came about.

If not for the papers, Mugil would not have known why Divyan, who was supposed to come home the previous month, never arrived. What she learnt was that the Sri Lankan prime minister had made a statement to the media that the police in the South Indian town of Trichy had found several lorries full of ammunition, which they had linked to a Tiger sleeper cell. The prime minister had declared this to mean that the LTTE was regrouping, a 'serious security threat'. Immediately, plans to release former combatants were shelved. A few weeks later, the Trichy police denied finding any such ammunition or LTTE sleeper cells. Soon after, the Sri Lankan prime minister said he was 'mistaken'. Divyan's release, along with that of all the other detainees, however, remained cancelled.

Sangeeta often asked when Mugil would go to see Divyan. The couple spoke on the detention landline every other day, but Mugil hadn't been to see Divyan since she had moved to Point Pedro. The bus fare to Vavuniya was around 400 rupees each way, and there were always other pressing expenses. But the real reason was that she didn't feel much need to see him. Mugil couldn't admit this to Sangeeta, who sorely missed her late husband. Days would go by without Mugil once missing Divyan, except perhaps when she wanted to tell him a funny story or use him as a sounding board. Neither of her sons had asked about their father since they left camp.

For two years, Mugil had made all the decisions for her family. And they were not led by Divyan's obsessions: loyalty, vengeance, duty. Without the structure that stitched these concepts to her life, she was running free. She was doing things her way, and despite the creeping fears and daily insecurity, she felt strong. Her choices were her responsibility; she didn't have to convince anyone else or follow some moral code. Her home and the relief of coming back to it every day and deciding the shape of her hours were things she had never had before. Not during the war, not before it. These were days of rebuilding. There was much to fight against but also a lot to work for. She was a single parent, and she focussed on her children like never before. When Tamizh had nightmares, she consoled him with a song, but never any songs of the revolution. The old tunes filled her brain, their lyrics enchanting, bleak, romantic. But her sons would not hear them. She kept them, and herself, away from former cadre. Maran was now in the first grade and Tamizh had grown three inches taller. They did not need the weight of the past on their shoulders. The cycle had to end somewhere.

After they'd come to Point Pedro, Mother had visited Prashant at his detention centre in the Chettikulam school. Mugil still remembered the news Mother brought back for its resounding peculiarity. Her brother had apparently been excited about being assigned kitchen duty, because it gave him access to more chicken than he otherwise got at meals. He had also told Mother that the inmates had been served the auspicious Sinhalese dish *kiri bath* on the anniversary of Prabakaran's death. He had sung to Mother the Sinhala-language national anthem, which he had been taught there. After that, he had been sent to take a short 'leadership' course in the dreaded Boosa prison complex in the southern city of Galle. The family hadn't heard from him since then. To Sri Lankans, Boosa was synonymous with torture and indefinite detention, and Mugil worried about her little brother.

It was almost three o'clock and the snacks were cooling in the kitchen. Mugil washed her face and changed, getting ready to pack the *vadais*, buns and rolls in the newspapers she had been poring over. The packets had to be delivered to the shops by four—teatime. Before Mother left to pick up Maran from school, she told Mugil that she had heard of some neighbours hiring a mini-van to visit the Poonthottam detention camp. 'You can share the cost and go with them to see your husband,' Mother said. 'Boys need to see their father, *ammani*.' Mugil nodded and left on her bike. She had deliveries to make.

21.

July 2011

INDRA LAY IN bed watching the fan turn at its lowest speed. July in Nuwara Eliya didn't warrant fans, but the hum helped her sleep. A childhood in tea estates was not cosy, but it made you a weather snob. Her family complained far too much when it was warm.

The last time she heard from Sarva, he had called from the Riyadh airport. He had just arrived from Colombo, and his first words on the phone were about the tremendous heat. 'Yes, you're a prince straight from *Ing-Land*,' she'd teased. He hadn't called again after that, and she had no number for him.

Indra turned to the window. A fog hung low on the tea bushes outside. The purple dawn was turning pink. The steady drizzle was a hush on the kitchen's asbestos roof. She tried to recall Sarva's hurried words from that last phone call.

It had been afternoon for her. 'Each call is costly, Amma,' Sarva had said. 'But I am all right, there are twenty-five of us in this batch.'

She had asked him if things had gone smoothly at the immigration desk at Colombo. 'The officer had been fixed, but I still had to give him 100 dollars extra.' Sarva had borrowed these dollars from Shirleen, who had waited outside Colombo airport till he boarded.

Indra had asked if he'd eaten. 'On the flight. I had two non-veg boxes!' He seemed giddy with expectation. He didn't know where the group would go next, only that it would be constantly on the move. 'I'm out of the wretched country, that itself is amazing. Now my luck will change, you'll see. I'll come for you soon, Amma. Our time will come.'

She had started to cry, saying she was praying for him. 'Take care, child. Eat well, child. Your mother is fine, don't worry about me, think of your health and safety. Everything will be fine, be careful'—she had spoken in loops. He said he had to hang up, others had to use the phone. 'Try not to cry all the time, okay?' He was teasing, but that had set off more tears and they didn't stop all day. She forgot to cook lunch, and when John asked about it, she sent the maid out to buy chicken lunch-packets.

Indra now sat up on the bed. She had been worried about Sarva but wasn't sure exactly how long he'd been gone. On the wall a calendar displayed a grinning tea picker with a big nose ring and bad teeth. Flipping back two months, Indra pressed a finger to 4 May, the day Sarva left. Ideally, she would have crossed out the date as a reminder, but she didn't want to leave a clue for the TID. She had been careful not to note the date down anywhere. Was that why she had lost track of time?

The days were a blur, the events embarrassingly fuzzy. For a month after Sarva left, plainclothesmen had visited repeatedly, demanding to know where her son was. Fed up, she had gone to her aunt's house in Jaffna. She had planned a round of visits to temples and family but was instead mired in a dispute with the tea estate company over a house lease. She was drowning in debt from Sarva's trial and departure. Waiting for a bus one day, she had suffered a stroke and been hospitalised for weeks. Her aunt had helped with the bills, but eventually John had Indra discharged before she had fully recovered. They could not afford more expense, and hoped rest and prayer would heal her. She was on stronger blood pressure medication now, but did not trust her health anymore. She called it a cursed time. Body, mind, spirit—all were failing.

It was early July now. Two months and not a word from Sarva. Indra went to the kitchen, grabbed some holy ash and smeared it all over her forehead. She prayed furiously, '*Pullaiyar appa, Pullaiyar appa,*' rocking back and forth. Her eyes were shut tight.

She chanted till the words drowned out her fear, till her blouse was drenched in sweat.

She finally leaned back on the kitchen counter. Her shoulders slumped. All the energy seemed to leave her body, dissipating like the fog outside. She was sure something had happened to her son. She sensed a dread, solid and pulsating in the pit of her stomach, calling her to action. It was all too familiar.

JOHN OFTEN SAID Indra spent more time saving Sarva than raising him. It wasn't easy to rear a good child in bad times, she would reply. She had rescued Sarva from disease, riots, the police, and the ravages of a country always on edge. But there was one incident she rarely brought up, although the memory of it had plagued her since Sarva's detention. It was the unspeakable reason for his arrest in 2008, and it continued to be an obstacle in her attempts to prove his innocence. All the NGO men and women she met had asked about it, noticing a gap, something that didn't add up. She had answered them vaguely, remembering what not to say.

It was 2002, the year of the ceasefire. Sarva had just finished his naval engineering exam. While he waited for the results, his brother Deva asked him to help at their video centre in Negombo. Deva was due to get married in a few months and wanted Sarva to fill in for him while he was busy with the wedding plans. Indra was relieved; if Sarva had stayed in Nuwara Eliya, she would have had to foot the bills for his aimless motorbike trips.

The Negombo video centre and Internet cafe was in the main market, and was doing reasonably well. The brothers shot weddings, parties, store openings, and child-naming ceremonies. The month after Sarva joined, another young man, Sujeevan, turned up asking for a job. He was from Vavuniya—a cousin of a friend of a friend of Deva's—and was on the run from the LTTE's clandestine conscription drive during the ceasefire. He begged them to help. He didn't want to be snatched off the streets by a white van, he said, and be forced into training. He was the same age as Sarva, twenty-four.

'We can't afford him,' Deva said. 'We can't save everyone.' But at Sarva's coaxing, Sujeevan was employed at half salary as a camera assistant. He turned out to be a fast learner and, as a bonus, cooked fabulously. The brothers congratulated themselves on this perfect hire.

After three months, Deva went off to prepare for the wedding. Sarva joined him a week later, leaving Sujeevan in charge of the shop. On the night after the wedding, Sarva received a phone call from the tea vendor near the video centre. 'Your cameras and computers are being taken away! Sujeevan says you asked him to do it. But he's loading them in a car, so I felt suspicious.'

Sarva rushed to Negombo, but it was too late. All the equipment, worth about 800,000 rupees, was gone. His brother squarely blamed Sarva for the robbery—he was the one who had convinced Deva to hire Sujeevan, befriend and stupidly trust him. He was the one who left a thief in charge.

Sarva filed a police complaint and a few days later the police used Sujeevan's vehicle registration to track him down in a lodge in Negombo. When Sujeevan opened the door of his room, the Tamil inspector swung hard at his face. 'Stealing from your own, are you, you ungrateful bastard?' In Sarva's presence, Sujeevan confessed that he had sent the equipment to someone in north Vavuniya. He said it was to pay for his freedom from the Tigers. As soon as he mentioned an LTTE connection, the police made excuses and backed off. 'This is not our jurisdiction,' the inspector said. Sarva didn't entirely understand what Sujeevan meant by 'payment for freedom', but he took the man's details—name 'Thiru', dark, fat nose, short, sometimes wore spectacles, close to LTTE commander Paulraj—and decided to go retrieve the equipment himself.

Indra forbade him: 'There's only a slim chance you'll get the stuff back, and there's a greater risk of something happening to you.' But Sarva felt too guilty, and too upset that his trust had been betrayed. Indra begged Deva to accompany Sarva, and when he refused, she decided to go along herself.

In Vavuniya, a town in a southerly section of the north, Indra and Sarva stayed at his schoolmate's house. For days, they searched in vain for Thiru. Gradually, Indra began to regret coming; it had been rude to leave Deva's new bride at home alone. When Sarva put Indra on a bus back to Nuwara Eliya, she made him promise to stop his search in a week. On each of the next five days, he called Indra with nothing to report. On the seventh day, Sarva's friend called. 'Kutty is missing,' he said, using Sarva's school nickname. The friend had gone to the police, who guessed that Sarva might be at the LTTE base camp—that was where most missing boys were found in those days. The police couldn't do much to help.

Indra rushed to Vavuniya with her youngest son, seventeen-year-old Carmel, in tow. From the bus stop, she went straight to the LTTE base and demanded to see her son. The men in the office were nonchalant; they had heard such parental demands a hundred times. They said they would check and asked her to return the next day. The following day, they sent her away again. This went on for a few days until Indra snapped. Before she could think about the consequences, she was sitting stubbornly on the red earth in front of the office gate, leaning on a wooden pole and abusing the Tigers. She asked every passer-by if he or she had seen Sarva, her son, an innocent boy these people had gobbled up. She cried openly, beating her chest, refusing to drink water or eat. When exhausted, she slept face down on the mud. Carmel stood by silently, protesting with his mother. Some people tried to give Indra some glucose or lemon juice, but she pushed it aside. Several Tiger members begged her to stop creating a scene, but to no avail. After almost two weeks, Mohan, a senior leader, came and sat next to her. 'Your son came to us willingly,' he said.

'Nonsense. I know my son,' Indra shouted.

'Stop telling everyone this is "forced recruitment". Your son is the one who came looking for commander Paulraj.'

He spoke calmly, sure of himself, as if he knew Sarva better than Indra did. She had heard about the Tigers' sense of entitlement, their blindness when a person refused to serve under them. She already despised Mohan and his indifference.

She said Sarva had not come to join the Tigers, but to find some stolen video equipment.

'He was hungry, and we fed him. He was talking to some Tigers, maybe he changed his mind. Many young men do this, they want to serve their community.'

She did not care if Sarva changed his mind, she yelled, she did not care if he joined willingly or by force. She wanted her son back in her house. 'I will die if you don't give me my son back,' she swore.

Mohan sighed, saying that Sarva had already begun training in Kilinochchi. 'There's nothing you can do now.'

Straightaway Indra went to Kilinochchi, relaunching her hunger strike and public shaming at the camp office there. If Sarva had joined the Tigers voluntarily, she wanted news of her raving in the streets to reach him, to wreck his resolve. She wrote letters addressed to Sarva and asked young Tiger cadres to hand them to her son if they saw him. She wasn't sure if any of the notes reached him because there was never a reply. Many families had suffered this way when their children were snatched from them. Indra had dreaded this catastrophe for years—every Tamil mother did—yet she could not believe that it had struck.

The Sri Lankan government and the LTTE had signed a ceasefire agreement with Norwegian facilitation in February 2002. It threw open the A9 highway, and gave journalists, NGOs and government officials a glimpse of the fortified Tiger-held regions for the first time. But, as Indra realised when she came to the Vanni to look for Sarva, there was no real pause in the fighting. As peace talks were being arranged, the LTTE staged assassinations, used the loosened border controls to rearm itself and, most aggravatingly for Tamil families, recruited massively. The forced conscription of children spiked alarmingly.

After a month demanding to see Sarva in Kilinochchi, Indra became afraid that Carmel too would be sucked into the movement. She took her youngest back home. There, John and Deva could do little to pacify her; they offered no ideas, no help. The weeks of starvation had ravaged her digestive tract and she was laid up in bed. Every time she got better, she went looking for Sarva, roaming Kilinochchi, Mullaitivu, Vavuniya, pleading with anyone remotely senior for his release.

Once, someone told her Sarva had been sent to Palestine for training. This wasn't as far-fetched a possibility as it seemed to Indra; Hamas had indeed trained some Tamil militants in the eighties. Another combatant told her she should be proud; Sarva was being trained to be a trauma doctor. Yet another said he had been sent on a foreign spying mission. Lies, she thought, all lies. The more they refused to let her contact him, the surer she became that he was being held against his will.

Driven by her manic will and a vision of Sarva's untimely death in battle, she continued her campaign for more than a year. She shouted from the streets of Mullaitivu that the LTTE may spew great philosophy about the Tamil motherland, but their 'hearts must be made of stone to let a Tamil mother struggle so'. She was blind to the dangers of challenging the Tiger leaders, of abusing them in a place where they wielded absolute power.

John was distraught at her mud-smeared skirt, unkempt hair and raccoon eyes: 'Do you think they will listen to a *pichchakkari*, a shabby beggar?' Her sisters were sure she would be shot to death. 'What option do I have?' Indra would scream. Were they suggesting she give up? Being a middle-aged woman and a mother made her bulletproof, she said. As she turned up at LTTE offices every few weeks, some people in the Vanni began to recognise Indra because of her antics. When she returned one day to Nuwara Eliya, a Vanni newspaper printed a news item headlined '*Pillaiyai thedi vantha thaaiyai kaanavillai!*' The mother searching for her son is missing!

Eventually Indra was able to meet Commander Paulraj through an acquaintance, a friend whose brother was martyred in the Mullaitivu siege. Indra had gone to see Paulraj with the martyr's mother, so the commander listened patiently. It was the first breakthrough she had had in a year. He offered Indra a glass of lemonade, which she refused. She wasn't taking any chances. He said she should trust them more and that he would 'speak to the higher-ups'. He gave her a room in the female combatants' camp and asked her to wait for news from him.

Indra stayed in the camp for some weeks, too nervous to consume much more than a bun and a bottle of soda every day. Paulraj spoke to her often on the hostel landline, telling her not to starve, and continuing to assure her that he was doing his best to get Sarva out. One day he sent a junior around with a note written by Sarva: 'I'm happy here, Amma, please, go home.' The girls she had befriended in the camp—they said Indra reminded them of their own suffering mothers—passed the note around, analysing its authenticity. Even if it was in Sarva's hand, they said, it was probably written under duress. They advised Indra to step up her campaign and threaten the authorities, attack them where it hurt the most.

During the ceasefire, the LTTE was conducting a public relations offensive to win the sympathy of international media and aid agencies; the Tigers wanted to undo their proscription by the US and Europe. 'So many white people come and go with cameras now, Amma,' one the hostel girls said. 'You should do some drama in front of them.' So Indra bought a bottle of poison and waited. When some foreigners—activists, peace-talk negotiators or journalists, she didn't know—were in the camp one day, Indra ran out of her room. Waving the poison in the air, she swore to drink it if she did not see her son in ten days.

One of the foreigners in the camp was from the Sri Lanka Monitoring Mission, or SLMM, an independent body whose Nordic members oversaw the execution of the ceasefire. They had recently denounced the LTTE's forced recruitment. The SLMM representative got Indra to file a report with them and launched a formal search for Sarva.

Two months on, SLMM said they had found evidence that Sarva had been conscripted and witnesses testifying to the fact, but they had not been able to trace him. A local newspaper, otherwise sympathetic to the LTTE, wrote a story on the trauma of motherhood during the war, featuring Indra. A combination of the SLMM search and the press report appeared to have pressured, or irritated, the Tiger leaders, because on 24 November 2003, when she was back in Nuwara Eliya for a few days, Indra received a note asking her to go to Mullivaikal. She could have one day with her son.

Sarva was unrecognisable. He seemed taller, his neck thicker. His biceps pushed against his shirtsleeves. His hair was cropped in a crew cut so close that he had no more curls. Indra had nursed a tiny hope that he would've escaped the physical training, but as he stood in front of her, muscular and coal-dark, she knew that wasn't the case. She had brought Deva's infant son along to illustrate a point: did Sarva even know that his brother had a baby?

They had not seen each other for a whole year, but Sarva behaved as if meeting in this way was perfectly routine. He held the child in his arms and smelled its head. He hugged Indra tight, but she recoiled. Despising the iron feel of his body and the pistol at his hip, she slammed her fists on his chest and pushed him away. The months of patience, anxiety and illness boiled over. In a sudden rage, she ripped his green checked shirt down the front. How could he leave his family and live with strangers? she shouted. She fished out his letter, tore it into pieces, flung it in his face. She slapped him hard.

'You don't have any love in you!' she screamed. Did he know how sick his mother had been? Did he not miss his family, not want to see his nephew gurgle and to play with him? Did he not want to get married and have his own babies? 'What are you doing? You never wanted all this,' she cried.

In the cottage where they were meeting in the Kaithady camp, some men in uniform stood watching, including Uday, Sarva's immediate supervisor. Looking at him, Indra sobbed that she didn't understand why they needed her son if the government and the LTTE had signed an agreement to stop fighting. 'And don't you have hundreds of other willing soldiers?' Sarva held Indra back, shushing her. She was an emotional mess, more so because her son seemed so unruffled. His face was placid, his voice soft. He described his training: the swimming, shooting, and code-reading workshops; he told her that the leaders said he was smart but needed to be more obedient. He likened it to a nine-to-five job. Indra wondered if her son had been briefed to say these things; she wished she could undo the brainwashing.

After some time, a young combatant invited Indra for a meal at the canteen. With hundreds of others, Indra sat with Sarva and watched him wolf down a mountain of rice. She could not eat. Was he really happy here, was this what he wanted, was this his future? She did not want him carrying a gun; people did not do such things in her family. Where had he even got such an idea? She wondered if she had ever romanticised the LTTE and their cause while raising Sarva. She had cursed the Sinhalese, certainly; she might have wished aloud for a country where Tamils could be free. But had Sarva seen enough hate to think of vengeance in this slow, dispassionate, organised way?

Sarva's generation had grown up imbibing the fears, wishes and bitterness of the elder members of the community. Even though his family had lived outside the Vanni, he had been surrounded by films, books, songs, myths, superstitions, schools and political and religious leaders—all of them talking only of fears and threats. In her helplessness, Indra blamed herself, but the dining room was filled with young Tamil men training to be combatants. Many had experienced a recruitment that was as ambivalent as Sarva's, somewhere between forced and voluntary.

In this era of conflict, it was nearly impossible to distinguish between propaganda and threats; the two worked together: a barrage of messages simultaneously seducing, inviting, demanding, arm-twisting and threatening. When Indra was young, people her age thought about political protest or pursued an existence indifferent to the issues of the day, but after the rise of militancy, Tamil identity—as projected by the Tigers—had become acutely embattled. The air was heavy with calls to sacrifice. Victimhood morphed into martyrdom, non-participation became betrayal. The idea of Tamilness was community action, not silent suffering. Militants had usurped the voice of Tamil protest in Sri Lanka, and the LTTE, by murdering or sidelining all moderate groups, had emerged as the most prominent catalyst of political awareness. Their militarised language whipped together the images and sentiments of masculinity, feminism, equal rights, Tamilness and bravery to impel men and women to action.

When facing discrimination, youngsters were expected to be enraged. When the doors of opportunity shut on them, they were meant to retaliate. It was common for the poor to become combatants, and for middle-class men like Sarva to join the LTTE as officers, propagandists, spies, and intelligence strategists. But as a parent, Indra saw this as a personal failure. She could not believe Sarva wanted this, she was sure he must have lost his mind. To her, this had robbed her of the life-loving child she had raised.

After lunch, she begged Sarva to go with her. 'Enough of this, *kanna*! Throw this life away! Come back home!'

Sarva was quiet, and Uday answered for him: 'He can't go with you, amma.'

Sarva and Uday escorted her in a van to the old Tiger base in Kilinochchi. When Indra was not looking, Sarva rummaged in her bag and filched his nephew's bib. They took her for a glass of tea at the Pandian Hotel, which had opened after the ceasefire. She asked Sarva tearfully why he had ignored her when she was in the Vanni, demanding to see him. Again, it was Uday who replied, saying that no one had told Sarva that his mother was looking for him.

'All parents want their children back,' Uday said. 'We thought you'd soon give up.'

'Have you lost your tongue?!' Indra yelled, looking at Sarva. He kept his eyes on the floor.

When they dropped her near the stop for the Nuwara Eliya bus, Sarva hugged his mother desperately. When Uday stepped back to let them say their goodbyes, Sarva held Indra's hand and secretly traced some words with his fingers on her palm. Indra was too flustered to make out the letters. Listen to me, he urged, and hugged her again. In her ear he whispered, 'Get me out of here somehow.'

Elated that her visit had changed her son's mind, Indra went back to Paulraj and demanded that he send Sarva back home: 'He's told me he wants to leave.' The commander wasn't convinced but offered to send Sarva home on a long period of leave. After that, he said, it was up to them. Indra thought she heard the implied suggestion that Sarva desert the LTTE while on holiday.

Sarva was supposed to come home on leave a month later, but the A9 highway was often closed. In 2003, the LTTE pulled out of peace talks. The ceasefire was crumbling; the Tigers would soon be blamed for violating it 3,000 times and using the lull in fighting to rearm and recruit.

In January 2004, one and a half years after he went to Vavuniya, Sarva came home. He took a bus from Kilinochchi to Colombo and was picked up at the bus stand by Deva and John. When he left Vanni, Sarva said, he had been ordered to wait in Colombo for his first assignment. As soon as he admitted this, Indra packed a bag for him and got Deva to buy him a ticket to Kuala Lumpur. Deva was going to spend a year in Malaysia to start a travel business with a friend, and it was decided that Sarva would leave with him. Indra wanted him to escape abroad to shake off any Tigers that might be tailing him.

'They will still look for me,' a nervous Sarva insisted. 'They will want me to do things.'

'You don't have to do them,' Indra replied determinedly.

On 24 January 2004, Sarva left with Deva for Kuala Lumpur, where he stayed for a year helping his brother, but keeping a low profile. He learnt to cook and clean, and watched TV interminably. Malaysia was a networking hub for the Tigers; its chief arms procurer, Kumaran Pathmanathan, operated from there, and cadres often trained at a aeronautical centre in Perak owned by a Tamil. Sarva rarely left the house, and when he did, he pretended to be a non-Tamil Indian.

That year, the rejuvenated and rearmed Tigers struck harder than ever before in Sri Lanka, assassinating Foreign Minister Lakshman Kadirgamar, a Tamil politician, in Colombo. Indra read about Tamil youths being scooped up by the hundreds and thrown in jail. She broke 500 coconuts in a temple, thanking God for pulling her son out of the storm just in time.

INDRA HAD AVERTED a catastrophe when she prised Sarva out of the Tigers, but the ghosts of his time spent training as a militant were persistent. The past caught up with Sarva in 2008, with his detention. During his interrogation, Sarva recognised a man Inspector Silva asked him to identity: a fellow trainee in the LTTE. It was he who had informed the TID about Sarva's history, and provided the distinguishing characteristic that gave him away: his three false front teeth. During the LTTE training, Sarva had guilelessly showed these to his comrades as a trophy from a childhood fall. Their supervisor suggested Sarva use the gap behind his dentures to hide the Tigers' standard issue cyanide vial. During Inspector Silva's nightmarish interrogation, Sarva had looked at the informer standing against the glass window in the same room and—to avoid an incriminating confession—denied knowing him. Sarva had wanted to charge at him for his betrayal, crash through the high window, and send them both plunging to their death. But even if he'd had the nerve to do that, he could never know why the man had snitched, whether he had succumbed to torture or bargained for his freedom. In every official statement since Sarva's detention, Indra stuck to his version of events: he had been forcibly recruited and trained by the LTTE, but he had never worked for them. To appease her conscience, she also held on to Sarva's whispered plea in the Vanni, asking her to get him out of there.

Every other period of Sarva's life was investigated, and was wide open to scrutiny, but the LTTE years were locked up in a pact between mother and son. They told one story but, between them, there existed several layers of truth. When Shirleen or Jehaan asked her about it directly, or other sceptics needed clarification, Indra would look at her feet, and evade, deflect, swallow. She believed it was the only way to protect Sarva. If she admitted to his having spent one and a half years with the Tigers, forcibly trained and bordering on voluntary service, the state would not spare him. They would not care that she had almost starved herself to get him out. The activists would not—could not—have helped as generously as they did if they'd had to put 'received arms training under LTTE' in his file. She was petrified that they would be indifferent to the state's torturing him in 2008 because he was sullied by militancy. Worse, they might think he deserved it.

Even in the greyest of conflicts, systems and people tried to put matters into black and white, for moral comfort, for their own safety. Without assurance that her son would get a fair trial or humane treatment in Sri Lanka, Indra had produced a palatable narrative that might evoke the easiest empathy for Sarva, and therefore a chance of survival. She didn't know when she could discard the weight of distortion, when or to whom the whole truth could be told.

As she waited for Sarva to call her from another airport in 2011, on his way to the US, Indra was afraid that the storm had engulfed him after all. He had left Sri Lanka in May. It was July now. He had called once. Perhaps a Tiger spy had snared him, or a TID officer, or some criminal gang. What could she do from Nuwara Eliya?

Indra had known the risks of sending Sarva abroad with an agent of human smuggling, but she had drawn courage from the many young men who had made the trip successfully. So many of them had reached the US and, albeit after a great deal of struggle, had become foreign citizens with happy, wealthy households. But nobody mentioned the months of impenetrable silence before they got there. By miserable experience, she knew that when her son went incommunicado, trouble was close at hand.

22.

August 2011

IT WAS AN ordeal to coordinate dates, times and money with fifteen women around Point Pedro, and Mugil was not surprised that once she'd agreed to visit the detention camp with this group, she would be the one stuck with the logistics. She was good at maths, she didn't have a time-consuming infant to deal with, she knew people, she owned a phone—there were myriad reasons for them to leave it up to her. Sangeeta's brother offered to drive them to the camp for half the market rate, but she would have to arrange a van.

Most people she asked seemed to have SUVs which they leased to international NGOs at unaffordable international NGO rates. Owners of private minibuses plying through Point Pedro didn't see any profit in carrying only fifteen women when they could make much more by packing in fifty people each way. Bigger private buses were available, but they were sixty-seaters. Mugil could easily have mobilised that number, but she didn't want to manage that large a group. The army would then get involved; emergency regulations were still in place and large gatherings had to get army permission.

Seeing Mugil flailing, the cool-bar owner gave her a number for a van rental company that usually catered to tourists. They would have vans for fifteen people, 'but the owners are Muslims,' he said apologetically. 'Make sure you bargain properly.'

There was a popular perception among Tamils that Muslim traders and businessmen had become the largest profiteers after the war. In truth, however, the government-driven economic revival of the north largely benefited those with political connections—Sinhalese, Tamil or Muslim. Among the less connected, more Muslims than Tamils appeared to have obtained licences or set up shops in the north; this was because Muslims had not been recently displaced, many spoke both Sinhala and Tamil, had a cultural affinity for certain trades that were now flourishing in the north and, most significantly, possessed capital, thanks to Colombo businesses and decades of foreign remittances from relatives in the Middle East. Most Tamils, on the other hand, traditionally preferred agriculture, fishing, government work, or employment in the legal and banking sector.

The less trade-oriented and now war-affected Tamils simply put the relative success of many Muslims down to racial shrewdness and opportunism. *Rendu muham kaatuvangal*, people tended to say: the Muslims are two-faced. Mugil was prejudiced, too, but believed she had a valid reason. For months, she had noticed truckloads of rusty wheels, bicycles, trishaw parts, engines, doors and windows being carried along the highways. One day, seeing a child's dress entwined in a wheel, she realised that the trucks were carrying the things her people had desperately discarded in Mullivaikal at the end of the war, before crossing over to the army. The Mullivaikal area was a high-security zone now, and few Tamils—from across the north and east—had recovered their belongings. Those who did manage to enter saw a bleak scene: the possessions of hundreds of thousands being divided into mountains of metal, wood and perishables. The place was being cleared of evidence and the scrap dealers were largely Muslim. Mugil could not forgive them this callousness. 'Grave robbers,' she called them.

So when she called Yaqub Ibrahim—the name on the visiting card the cool-bar owner gave her—she did not expect help. Yes, they had vans, Yaqub said on the phone, but if she had her own driver, she would have to pay a deposit.

'Why? I'm not going to vanish with your van,' she said, infuriated already.

It's just to be on the safe side, he said, and then asked, 'You're all women?'

Mugil told him they were all going to the Poonthottam detention centre and immediately bit her tongue. She had not thought of it before: why would this Muslim help the families of former Tigers? This Yaqub sounded young, one of his office addresses was in Puttalam, so she guessed he must have been one of the 75,000 Muslims the Tigers expelled from the north in 1990. He would have been a child then.

There was a long silence. Mugil was about to hang up, when Yaqub replied. 'Okay, I can make an exception. If you come back in five hours, you don't have to pay the deposit.'

Surprised but trying to push her luck, she asked for a discount on the day rate. Yaqub refused initially but then spoke to someone behind him and finally slashed the cost by 10 per cent. 'One of our friends in Jaffna will give you an old van. Don't turn on the AC,' he said.

The next Sunday, when the women left for Poonthottam, one of them noticed on the windshield a sticker carrying an inscription from the Quran.

'Muslim vehicle,' the lady sighed. 'They own everything nowadays.'

Mugil didn't respond.

AT THE DETENTION centre, the women's IDs and bags were checked and they were asked to wait in the visitors' hut. Mats were laid on the floor and the women sat down in rows. Mugil had worn an ankle-length skirt and a long-sleeved blouse. She always worried that her arms were too muscular. Tamizh was on her lap, his arms tight around her neck; all the uniformed soldiers made him tense.

Divyan walked in with the others. He looked as if he had been sleeping and had hurriedly thrown on his shirt; he had buttoned it wrong. He wore a washed-out sarong. He also had a thick beard.

They were told they had fifteen minutes. Divyan sat opposite Mugil. Tamizh crawled onto his lap and hugged him.

He misses his father, she said. She gave Divyan a new shirt and shaving kit. He took them, hardly looking at her face.

'You didn't bring Maran,' he said, part question and part complaint.

'He won't sit still. I thought we could talk.'

'Mmm.'

She ruffled the plastic bag in which she had brought his clothes. 'Are you eating well?'

He shrugged. '*Naaku seththu pochu.*' My taste buds are dead.

It was the same answer he used to give on the phone through all the months he had been in detention. She had expected a different conversation when they sat face to face. Around them, the other families seemed to be chatting away, using every second in those fifteen minutes to provide detailed updates about extended family, house issues and money problems.

'How are you, Thambi?' Divyan asked Tamizh, who smiled shyly. 'Are you being naughty and troubling Amma?' Tamizh shook his head, and said his brother was the one always being naughty.

Divyan asked if Maran was doing well in school.

'He's good at maths, but his Tamil and social science are very poor.' She didn't care if he was doing badly, he was in the second grade. They were talking about everything but the things that mattered.

'Is something wrong?' she asked.

'Why? Nothing. We can't talk about it here.'

Next to Mugil, a woman hugged a young boy and started crying. In the far corner, a man who looked about Divyan's age held his newborn close and repeatedly offered his index finger for the baby to clasp. Every time the infant's hand gripped him, the man grinned at his young wife.

'How is your snack business doing?' Divyan asked.

'It's okay. Sangeeta … have I told you about her?'

'No.'

'She's a smart girl. The army shot her husband, *paavam* …'

Divyan finally looked her straight in the face. 'Don't speak like that here. I am the one who has to go back inside,' he snapped. 'I will be released, who knows when, but sometime soon I hope. We will talk at home.'

On the way back to Point Pedro in the van, the road was lashed with the kind of downpour they hadn't seen in weeks. Mugil slid the window shut and stuffed a handkerchief along the sides to prevent the rapid dripping from flying onto Tamizh. The child was asleep, and she wished she could be as content as he looked. She had the impression that Divyan was angry about her visit. He had never been a talker, but he had practically growled at her this time. Even in 2009, during the worst period of his detention, he had been reserved when she visited from the refugee camp but always affectionate, never on the offensive as he had been today. He had spent two years in detention now; perhaps it was getting harder to focus on freedom.

Some of the other women in the van had had better visits and were sharing what their brothers or husbands had said. There had been a 'mental' major general until six months ago, and since he had been replaced, the number of violent interrogations had dwindled. Still, there were monthly interrogations of some inmates, whom the army encouraged to spy on others.

They had morning assemblies, where an inmate would read the headlines from a newspaper. A woman's brother had described the news as 'what the president said, what he did, who he met'. They would sing the national anthem in Sinhala, stumbling through the words. The rest of the day, they sat around talking, sweeping, sleeping. There were some old magazines and dailies to read.

Most of the time, they watched pirated CDs on an old television set, Tamil movies made in south India and shot in Chennai, Switzerland or New York, love stories with uncontroversial heroes and curvaceous fair-skinned heroines. One of the men had told his sister, 'All those *scenes* are also there, so many *scenes*.' He meant sexually suggestive dialogue, shots of midriffs and cleavages, as well as innuendo, which had always been edited out by the LTTE censor board in the Vanni's makeshift cinemas. The man had said that *Boys*, a raucous movie about four oversexed teenagers, featured a hot girlfriend character who had been entirely removed in the Tigers' cut. During a satirical court scene where the boys are let off terrorism charges, the inmates had apparently hooted and clapped. One of the inmates had stupidly asked the soldier in charge for

Ezham Arivu, an Indian movie renowned for its Tamil nationalism; that had not gone down well. The inmate was isolated for a week. The men also watched Bollywood movies with the soldiers, neither group really understanding the Hindi dialogue but enjoying the landscapes and songs.

'Yes, very good,' one of the women said wryly. 'We are breaking our backs building houses and raising our children and they are sitting and watching movies.' She announced that the detention camps, or *thaduppu*, had now been renamed 'rehabilitation centres', offering a new life, or *punarvazhvu*. In keeping with the nomenclature, workshops in carpentry, welding and construction were offered in addition to Sinhala language lessons. Computer classes were in the works.

But one element remained unchanged: no NGO or civil body was allowed inside, and all the classes were administered by the army. There was no trauma counselling or psychological therapy. The ICRC made many requests for entry, but all were rejected. Some men had admitted to feeling humiliated by the basic skills being imparted. 'My husband was a bike mechanic and farmer, you know?' a woman said. 'Just because he was in the movement, these fellows think the only thing he knows is how to lob a bomb.'

After a while, the exhausted women started to nod off. Mugil went to the front of the bus and used a newspaper to wipe the fogged-up windshield. She asked Sangeeta's brother, who was driving, if he wanted some buttermilk or water, which she had brought along in Sprite bottles. After glugging down some chilli-infused buttermilk, he asked how she felt after seeing her husband: 'Calmer or more tense?' She didn't know. 'Any idea when they'll send him home?' She wasn't sure of that either.

'Remember how they told us before the elections that they'd free the refugees from the camps?' she asked. The parliamentary elections had been held in 2010. 'You think we'll have to wait for the next election before they send the detainees home?' That would mean another five years.

'But they know our people didn't vote for the ruling party,' Sangeeta's brother said. 'We voted for the Tamil National Alliance, and we always will.'

'So?'

'So, the president has realised he doesn't have to do anything for us because he doesn't need us to win.'

ONCE THE EMERGENCY regulations were lifted, Mugil's brother returned home from detention camp. The two events were perhaps unconnected, but Mugil always thought of them together. Both were much anticipated; neither went the way she expected.

Prashant slept and ate at Mother's house but spent every waking hour with his nephews and niece. In his florid way, he said it was a relief to bask in the daylight innocence of children after a long stay in a dark hell. He had boundless energy in playing with them and they responded with devotion. They wanted to spend the nights with him, wanted him to walk them to school and to their tutors afterwards, wanted to tag along when he was sent on errands by Mother. Chitthappa, Chitthappa, Chitthappa—Maran and Tamizh asked for him as soon as they woke up. Mugil wondered if they were somehow casting Prashant in the role of their father. They still turned to her when hurt or hungry, but they admired Prashant and craved his presence in a way she'd never seen them do with anyone else. Within days, Maran had begun to imitate his uncle, expressing a desire to grow up and be treated like a man. He wanted trousers instead of shorts. He told Mugil he would bathe and dress himself. When she walked into the house from the market one day, she saw Maran standing over Tamizh, speaking sternly. 'I'm the elder one, so you have to give me the book. When Chitthappa is not around, I'm the man in the house. Give!' Amazingly, Tamizh meekly handed the book over. Perhaps there was something about boys, even this young, that she didn't intuitively grasp. They seemed to explore new sides of themselves under Prashant's paternal influence. She began to encourage him to come over, not just to babysit but also to take over some parental responsibility. He said he had all the time she needed; it wasn't as if he had a job.

Prashant's joblessness was not for want of trying. He had finished the three-month army-mandated leadership workshop where, among other things, they had taught him some nautical science. He had a knack for mechanical things, and he had fewer injuries than many other young men from the Vanni. The Rajapaksa government encouraged highway and building construction, making it the fastest-growing industry in the north. Sangeeta's brother had recommended Prashant to a road construction supervisor. But in a few weeks it had become clear that this contact wouldn't lead to a job. The largely Sinhalese contractors seemed more comfortable hiring and communicating with Sinhalese labourers, even if those workers had to be driven up from the south and given accommodation. This was a source of much anger among the local Tamil population, who had lost property, jobs and homes and now had next to no opportunity to be part of the biggest infrastructural development projects in their own neighbourhoods.

Like many other young men, after a couple of failed attempts, Prashant stopped applying for jobs in construction. 'I have a fighting chance only with our own people,' he declared, but the private sector was just as cliquish. He applied to be a salesman at a new department store in Jaffna, but the owner ended up hiring five relatives. A bank wanted a night security guard for one of its ATMs, but Mugil advised Prashant to steer clear of any contact with the police. She was afraid he would be held responsible for any robbery he couldn't prevent; too many former Tigers were being accused of turning delinquent. She begged the cool-bar owner to give Prashant a job as a waiter, which the elderly man did, at decent wages. But after tea-sipping soldiers casually questioned the owner about 'the new *Kottiya*', he told Mugil he could not afford the risk of being shut down.

When Prashant was finally hired as a cleaner at a new guest house near the Jaffna beach, he was fired after two months. The management had expected him to work twelve-hour days all week and did not like his frequent requests for leave. 'You don't even have a wife or children, so why so many days off?' they asked. Prashant couldn't bring himself to tell them he was on probation. He was required to sign an army register at Point Pedro once a month, but unscheduled head counts were often held to prevent former detainees from absconding.

The army also used the register of returnees as a sort of blacklist. Whenever there was a burglary, a murder, an unlicensed meeting, a skirmish in a neighbourhood, former detainees on the list were called to the army camp or police station. Alibis and excuses were scrutinised and houses searched for arms. The process often took a whole day. If someone didn't turn up—even for good reasons like illness, travel or work—his or her employers and family were harassed. It was difficult to hold down a full-time job while being watched so closely.

Government jobs, too, had interminable waitlists that could be overcome only through bribery or political influence. Through a friend, Prashant met and sought help from a local journalist who wrote for the weekly *Thinappuyal*, known to be run by former LTTE arms trafficker Sivanathan Kishore, now a politician. When Mugil discovered this, she was livid. Kishore was close to state intelligence agencies. She warned Prashant not to trust people like him: former Tiger leaders who had ingratiated themselves with the ruling regime. Some had even joined thuggish political parties like the Eelam People's Democratic Party or EPDP, a pro-government Tamil outfit, which was riding the construction boom in the north with a lucrative sand-mining business across the Jaffna peninsula. Thanks to the state, the party had a free rein to wreak havoc among Tamils. A typical abuse of power involved the navy restricting fishermen's access to the sea while the EPDP dug up the beach. The party men—co-opted Tamils and former LTTE and non-Tiger militants accused of crimes such as rape, arms smuggling and murder—bullied poor civilians, kidnapped people for ransom, and worked with military intelligence to spread fear. To seek political help was to enter a murky, opportunistic world a desperate man like Prashant could never fully comprehend.

Prashant eventually paid a Jaffna placement agency 3,000 borrowed rupees to find him a position as a driver or handyman. Until they called back, he decided to make do with part-time work in a motorbike repair shop, being paid per puncture fixed. It was barely ten rupees a day.

Mugil saw her brother grow more bitter by the day. Any news about 'normalcy' or 'rapid economic development' pushed him over the edge. He would throw aside the newspaper and kick the mud. 'The Northern Revival is improving lives, it seems!' he would say, spitting the words, referring to the state's economic plan for the war-torn northern province. 'Their lives or our lives?' At other times he moped around the house, no more the energetic playmate of his nephews. He grew unpredictable and moody.

At dinner one day, as he squished the pink rice *pittu* with some banana, he reminisced about the simple life they had led in the Vanni. 'We didn't have much, but we felt safe, and we were happy, no?'

Mugil nodded. 'But it feels like it was so long ago. I hardly think those days will come back.'

'I believe they will if we want it,' he said. Mugil rolled her eyes.

Another day, as they were walking back with him from a friend's funeral, Prashant broke down. He had been carrying Tamizh piggyback and had to set him down on the street. 'I just can't go on, I just can't,' he said, burying his face in his hands. 'I had to give away several others, Akka, I had to give names,' he said. 'I could not bear the pain.' He had focused on the future to endure the humiliation, he said, but the future was nothing but broken promises.

It was only these episodes that gave Mugil some indication of what her brother might have suffered in the camp. His only instruction on his return home had been for his family not to ask him about detention. He sometimes said he could never forget or forgive the treatment meted out in the first year, but rarely elaborated. Instead, he kept a diary. He wrote in a thick college notebook every afternoon after lunch, the words flowing so swiftly from his pen that the dots and lines of the Tamil characters were forgotten. Long sentences, many exclamations, words furiously underlined. Nothing scribbled out or corrected. Sometimes it was as if he couldn't see the blue lines on the page: the sentences drooped with the fatigue of remembering. On one page, he drew the missiles the LTTE engineering department had taught him to design, perky arrows labelling the illustrations. On another, he listed all the artillery shells that he had identified in the war zone. He squeezed rhyming couplets into the margins. Every day, he picked a fresh topic to write about: the disabled, the former combatants, orphans, disappearances, the president, the army, Tiger turncoats, prayer, mothers. 'Detention' was the most extensive section, running for almost twenty-four pages. It began thus: 'If I had to explain how I felt in front of him, I would use this word: eunuch. No one will believe me, but I <u>know</u>. I <u>remember</u>, and it twists inside me like a knife mauling my organs.' He referred to the entire army, the Sinhalese people, state representatives, all with the single disrespectful male Tamil pronoun *avan*. Him, he, his. 'He is not capable of mercy'; 'He gave us food, but we were empty shells with full stomachs'; 'It was his plan to keep me away from my family so that I see no hope'; 'He is teaching me carpentry but his repetitive questions about hidden weapons continue'; 'He gives me two choices in a leader: the evil general who gave orders, and the evil mastermind.' And the line that occurred repeatedly: 'It is his plan to finish me.' It was fiercely personal, yet Prashant seemed conscious of an unknown reader at times: 'You should have seen the toilets—they were not fit for dogs, perhaps that's why they gave them to Tigers.'

He was on his fifth such diary when Mugil found them all hidden in the back of the kitchen cupboard. She read some of his writings on and off, but it rekindled too much of what she was trying to forget.

Prashant wanted to submit his diary as testimony to an independent committee that he hoped would investigate war crimes. Global civil society organisations, the Tamil diaspora and the UN had been demanding such an unbiased investigation since the end of the Sri Lankan civil war. Assuming it would be similar to South Africa's Truth and Reconciliation Commission, Prashant wrote a diary entry lauding the format of the TRC but questioning its method of redress: the criminals of apartheid were shown mercy, but he did not want to forgive his abusers. 'All my generosity has died with the thousands of victims. It might be petty of me, but real justice is punishment for all.'

When he read it out loud to Mugil, she argued with him. She wanted severe penalties for the politicians and upper ranks of the military but forgiveness for others. 'Think as a Tiger soldier yourself,' she told Prashant. 'We were foot soldiers, teenagers. Should we be punished for what our leaders asked us to do?'

Prashant insisted that the Sri Lankan army was different. He recalled videos of soldiers shooting the naked bodies of suspected Tigers, laughing about the shapes of women's corpses as they piled them in the backs of trucks. 'They enjoyed killing us,' he said.

'Lower your voice, I don't want the children hearing this.' Some days earlier, when Maran had asked to go to the beach, Prashant had asked him to bring his toy gun along to 'shoot the navy base down'. Mugil did not want her brother's venom poisoning her sons.

'Don't overprotect them,' he said.

'They're babies!'

'They should know anyway. They'll be feeling the humiliation soon.'

'Be practical about the justice you're asking for,' Mugil continued. 'If we ask for all of them to be killed, the government won't even start an investigation.'

'They've started, no? A practical, useless committee.' Ignoring the calls for an independent probe, the Sri Lankan government had launched a domestic investigation into the events of the last phase of the war. Called the Lessons Learnt and Reconciliation Committee (LLRC), it was made up largely of retired government employees, including some who had publicly defended the state from allegations of irresponsibility during the war's final stages. Since May 2010, the panel had been sitting in several districts in the north and east, calling for testimonies. People were speaking on record about Tiger atrocities and forced recruitment. Some NGOs wrote letters detailing the army's illegal shelling of no-fire zones and hospitals, but without witness protection, most individuals were afraid to accuse the military openly while still living under their authority. It was clear from the beginning that the circumstances under which the LLRC was set up would skew the findings in favour of the government. In the two years since the war, after Rajapaksa had been re-elected and his coalition voted back into parliament, the state had become more autocratic. It had removed presidential term limits and any remaining independence from the police, provincial governments and human rights commissions.

But Prashant was especially hurt by Tamils who pointed a finger at the Tigers. 'The army may have destroyed the Tigers, but our people are destroying the Tigers a second time,' he said. He had been to see Prabakaran's childhood home in Valvettithurai—there were rumours that Tamils had helped demolish it. 'Where is their sense of respect?' he asked, his pitch rising further. 'And why all this talk about forced recruitment? They are talking the government's language.'

'It is not a lie, though,' Mugil said softly.

Prashant's eyes flashed. People must be getting paid off to trash the LTTE and court the military, he said, and if Annan were around to see Tamil women talking and flirting with the army, he'd have them shot on the spot. 'You would not have been spared for speaking so ungratefully, Akka,' he said.

Mugil listened, astonished at how easily he insinuated that she flirted with the army. Did all men speak this way? No, Sangeeta's brother was exasperated, too, but not vengeful. Why was Prashant struggling so much harder? What had they done to him in the rehabilitation camp?

When combatants surrendered in droves, their families worried they would all face trial and execution. But when the government spoke in softer terms, of disarming, demobilising and integrating former combatants into society, they had expected some psychological and employment help. However, the Ministry of Defence ran the rehabilitation camps to privilege security concerns over counselling. No distinction was made between the leaders and ordinary cadre—all were interrogated repeatedly about sleeper cells, weapons stashes, and global underground networks. For the heavyweights in detention, cooperation was proportional to freedom. Some had found places in the cabinet. For lower-rung cadres like Prashant, rehabilitation was plumbing and welding workshops and Sinhala patriotic song lessons. One nationalism to stamp out the other.

Prashant was still itching for a fight because he had not had the opportunity to adapt. Straight from the war zone, he had been slammed into detention, prodded and thrashed for information for more than two years, treated as a terrorist, punished as a national shame, and then sent home. It wasn't a surprise that he blinked in the glare of the real world. He could not accept that life had changed permanently, that they could not go back to PTK, that they would never be able to demand the equality they had once dreamt of, certainly not as they did in their uniforms in the Vanni. There was no battle, no leader for him to cheer, but the conflict raged on the streets every day. He had come home in a climate of increasing militarisation—surveillance, accusations, threats. There was a trigger for his outrage, a reminder of his impotence, at every corner.

When he spoke of politics, his body quaking with frustration, Mugil's greatest fear was that he would rip through their family's veneer of calm. They had toiled hard to move on, battling the same challenges that defeated Prashant. He resented being vulnerable to arrest; but instead of lying low his instinct was to provoke. In the evenings now he didn't lounge in the side yard with his nephews but hung out with men of his own age, who were also struggling to find work. Somebody was always coming to Mugil's gate, calling for Prashant. 'What do you do with them?' Mugil asked once.

'We have things to discuss. We share the same pain,' Prashant replied.

'And what, your family won't understand? Tell me what it is, I'm your older sister.'

'I don't want to talk about it to you,' he said.

'Someone told me they saw your group walk right past a soldier in the market. Just cross the street and walk on the other side, no? Why are you challenging them?'

Prashant didn't say a word.

She walked up and put a few rupees in his shirt pocket. 'I know it is not easy, *da*, it is tough for me, too. Every few days, something happens to my head and I want to explode, and punch their faces, but I remind myself of my boys, of you all.'

'Why?'

'I don't want to get into trouble.'

He looked in her face with absolute incomprehension. 'Is that all you think about?' He seemed to be searching for more words, but a friend called him again. 'We'll talk later,' he said and walked out the gate.

Mugil knew that he was with an idle, discontented group of returnees from various rehabilitation centres. Some had a new drinking habit, but Mugil didn't worry about Prashant taking to drink. Her brother had railed against alcoholism more than anyone she knew. 'The soldiers try to corrupt us by inviting us to drink with them!' he would fume. Raised in the prohibition years of the LTTE-controlled Vanni, Prashant thought of drinking as a solely Sinhalese vice. To his mind, the growing alcoholism among Tamils after the war was a symptom of cultural erosion. Mugil was concerned about the resultant domestic abuse and what a waste of money it was, but as long as Prashant's stereotypes kept him sober, she didn't bother asserting her views.

Some of Prashant's friends were also planning an escape to foreign countries—borrowing from moneylenders against ancestral property or at heavy interest, leaving aged parents or young wives to repay their debts for years while the men settled down with visas in faraway countries which their families could not even find on a map. Prashant had not yet brought this up, but it was only a matter of time. He was a ticking bomb now. She would rather he were gone. If this was how the men returned from detention, she would have her work cut out for her with Divyan.

23.

September 2011

AT THE RIYADH airport, after he had called his mother, Sarva called Malar. There were tears, blown kisses, assurances, encouragement and a rehashing of their dreams of freedom. Outside an airport bookshop, he had stared at a world map in the window display: the big and small countries, great expanses of ocean, squiggling rivers, red-dot cities and the blue roads that joined them.

He had then flown a great distance—far enough for the language and the shape of people's faces to change, for the air itself to feel different, for the women to be as beautiful as they were back home but more knowing. He wondered at how a red-eye flight could introduce him to a populace with skin only a shade lighter. The final destination was America, he knew. But he had not even dreamt of the worlds in between. A couple of air tickets, a bus perhaps, some tolerable struggles, and then a stealthy dash across the Mexican border: this is what he had imagined. He had heard of the Indonesia boat route and the Nepal flight route, but not the less common route he was being led along.

For months after Sarva left Sri Lanka, he couldn't tell where he was when he opened his eyes in the morning. That it was South America was all he grasped. He was made to shift houses every few days, travelling to different towns, each divided by a short bus trip from the next. The agent's 'chaps'—there were so many, all seemingly recruited for their apparent lack of scruples—took Sarva to neighbourhoods whose jumble of poverty wasn't too different from the tea estate slums he had grown up around. People from all over the world were jammed into tight neighbourhoods of disrepute; here anyone could slip into safe anonymity.

The dingy apartments he was put in were packed with runaway Sri Lankan Tamils, from mousy fishermen to urbane students. They all had a depressing reason for leaving and a vague dream of success abroad, neither of whose details Sarva wanted to know. Early on, he decided he didn't want a fellowship of misery; he switched to what he thought was his arrogant face and stuck to monosyllables. It was bad enough that they smelled each other's fear all day.

On some mornings, a chap arrived with a box of food, usually a type of burger, chicken dish or subdued biryani. On the days he didn't come, they starved. Most of the time the men slept or daydreamed. The new sobbed into their arms at night; others chatted nostalgically about their childhoods. If there was power, they watched TV, a feature surprisingly present in every house. They stared at the local programmes that looked just like Tamil and Sinhalese soaps, dramatic and emotional, but with actors and newscasters speaking rapidly in a musical foreign tongue. To avoid the TV and stretch his legs, Sarva sometimes paced the building corridors. The man in the one-bedroom downstairs said he spoke Portuguese. The old woman next door said she spoke Spanish. Just like back home, he thought.

It was funny how much he thought of home when he was running from it. When he left Sri Lanka, he felt as if he might go anywhere, to a trillion possible future homes. Yet, a squalid room once again became his universe. If he left it, anything could happen. Unknown police could subject him to unknown laws or ask him the two questions he had to avoid at all costs: 'Where are you from? Do you have a visa?' He yearned to phone home but had no local currency. He considered speaking to some locals but didn't know the language. He wanted to go on the street, but stories of deportation had worn away his courage.

The agent Siva rarely came, and when he did, he subjected

everyone to the same wilful neglect and pretentious care. 'I'll get fish for everyone tomorrow, okay?' he'd say. 'I used to be like you all, so I feel your pain,' or 'One must lose something to gain something.' It mattered little that Sarva called him *anna*, knew Siva's relatives in Negombo, or that Sarva's brother was Siva's friend. The discount Deva had wrangled from Siva actually seemed to cause some resentment. 'The money won't go far,' he would often say. 'Your brother thinks I owe him something, but expenses are going up, so I'll do what I can.'

On his ninth or tenth move, emboldened by some others who were openly accusing Siva of fraud, Sarva demanded to know the larger plan. It had been five months, about time he gave up on the futile formality.

'I'm trying my best, you ingrates!' Siva said. The Mexico–US border was heavily manned and he hadn't found a coyote, one of the Mexican people-smugglers he could pay to take them around the checkpoints, walk them across the Arizona desert, and put them in a shelter from where agents would take them to claim asylum. The US anti-smuggling laws and Arizona state's aggressive anti-immigration policies had hardened criminal penalties for smuggling, and to compensate for the risk, coyotes were demanding 3,500 dollars, twice the amount Siva had accounted for in the fee he charged Sarva and the others.

The room was quiet. The migrants had not imagined such a dangerous journey. The hundreds of miles of physical barriers, security infrastructure and highway checkpoints along the US–Mexico border left only the southwest desert as the entry point. But the scorching, waterless desert itself was a daunting natural barrier: about 250 people died every year crossing it. There was a slim chance of making it across even with the coyotes, and going without them would be suicide. Until the men coughed up more money to pay the smugglers, Siva said, they would stay in Latin America, constantly moving base to avoid suspicion.

Siva's self-importance was grating, but this was the first nugget of real information. 'Don't worry, I won't send you to the places in South America where you could get shot,' said Siva. 'But *veliyila pona, ponathu thaan*.' If you go out, you're gone.

'Where are we going next?' Sarva asked.

'Peru. To a town just across the border.'

Pucallpa was a bustling modern town with a broad brown river, but Sarva's gang was taken straight to a shantytown on its edge. Here they were handed over to a stocky middle-aged Tamil man who wore faux gold chains and oversized football jerseys, like the rappers in Carmel's YouTube videos. The fat rolls on his neck glistened with sweat. He was one of Siva's senior chaps, in charge of receiving new men or taking some away every few days. To any questions from the men, he never said more than 'I will have to ask Siva.' The chap existed for this reason, to be the dampening buffer between the agent and the hopefuls. He had a room in the same house, where he spent the nights with several women he called his girlfriends. The younger men were impressed, but Sarva was sick to his stomach. His disdain built up for weeks till it exploded in a string of accusations: 'You act like this is a hotel and you're on vacation! This is a brothel for you! You forbid us to call our families and you are not even working on our situation.' The chap left the house with a smirk and didn't bring food or water for four days.

When he punished them, Sarva thought, it was to rub in their powerlessness. Everyone in the house had paid millions. Immigration was a transaction, but the chap treated them like they had been trafficked for prostitution. 'Our madam,' someone called him on those hungry days, and the name stuck.

A little over a month later, Sarva and two others were picked to leave. The chap boarded a bus with them. Sarva read the board, but the name didn't mean anything to him. When the bus reached its final stop after a day's journey, the chap asked them to wait till after midnight for their next step.

At two in the morning, he started to walk and the others followed. They reached a wide highway and skulked along the dry undergrowth at its side. 'A few kilometres down is the unpatrolled section,' the chap said, where they would cross the border.

'To where?' someone hissed.

The chap pointed to the darkness beyond. 'Ecuador. It's that country.' Sarva had not heard of it. 'Just remember you don't have a visa,' the chap said. 'So if someone comes to check, be *paavam*, innocent, say you're lost.'

It seemed like a lame excuse, one the border police might have scoffed at a hundred times. But they nodded; they had no other plan. Perhaps they would take a flight to America from Ecuador, Sarva thought. He would call his mother and Malar from there.

He made it across to Ecuador without incident, but for another month he continued to take buses, cross highways, run across fields in a mad scramble, crawl under barbed-wire fences and jump borders between Ecuador, Peru and Brazil. Throughout this time, he was unable to call home. In Peru, he fell down a flight of stairs and hurt his back again, ran out of money, and even got mugged. In Ecuador one night, gun-toting thugs looking for Siva broke down the door of the abandoned restaurant where they were sleeping. They shouted abuse in a blend of Spanish and English, saying over and over that that bastard Siva owed them money, that they would cut all their balls off if they didn't tell them where he was hiding. None of the boys knew where Siva was, but they were gagged and tied, thrown in the back of a car, and abandoned in a dumpster. Later that night, when Siva rescued them, the petrified young men rained abuse on him, but he was unmoved. All he said was that he would send them somewhere safer.

They were sent next to Santa Cruz, Bolivia. The group was split up and Sarva was taken to a two-room tenement in the outskirts. Eight others were already there, having arrived on different flights from Colombo through various transit points; they were fresh off the boat. The youngest among them, a twenty-one-year-old Jaffna university student called Bharati, was the only one smart enough to have brought a world map. Sarva pored over it, finally able to visualise the continent and borders he had been ripping through for months. When he found Bolivia nestled in the centre of South America, he counted upwards, towards the USA. If he continued to travel as he had been doing, nine, possibly ten countries lay between him and his destination.

Gradually, as had happened at every other safe house, some men started to leave with the chap, many of them taking boats or flights to Canada. Finally only Bharati and Sarva were left. Bharati was not like the others; for one, he had brought books and a pen along with his map. And at night, while Sarva tossed on his mattress, Bharati scribbled away in his book. 'What are you writing?' Sarva once asked. 'My thoughts,' Bharati replied, in absolute seriousness. After some time, Sarva borrowed a pen and some paper from him. He wrote letters to Malar, one every day, kept neatly folded in his wallet with 3,000 Sri Lankan rupees. His wallet used to have a small picture of her, too, the one with her in the yellow sari, but he had been nervous about one of the agents getting to it. He had avoided even mentioning Malar, and though he made repeated requests to call home, he didn't ask to call his girlfriend. He could not bring himself to throw her picture away, so, in Ecuador, he had swallowed it with a glass of water. He wrote about this in one of the letters, adding that Malar now literally resided in his blood.

By this time, Sarva had begun to lose sight of the future. It had been seven months. He was not sure where he was going, only that he could not go back. If he landed in Colombo and took one step near customs, he would be dragged into a dark basement without windows once again and have an iron rod shoved up his arse. He was so sure of it he could smell the petrol bag fumes squeezing his lungs. It was 2011, three years after he had been picked off the street, two years after the end of the war, but all that would matter to the antiterrorism police were the years Sarva trained to be a Tiger. No time, no action, no court acquittal had been able to undo that.

During the horrible idle hours, his mind whirred, hypothesising. Suppose the UN or some independent body went to Sri Lanka and investigated the war crimes perpetrated by both sides, the Tigers and the government. Suppose they threw some people into jail and provided counselling to reform others. He hadn't killed anyone; he had never even held a gun after his training. Assuming that he was forgiven, would he go back? Or going a step further, suppose the LTTE issue didn't matter at all, and the TID forgot about him. Would he go back?

He posed these questions to Bharati, who had left Jaffna after two occasions when men in white vans attempted to kidnap him. Two of his university friends had been jailed for trying to gather funds for the regrouping of the Tigers—he said they had actually been collecting donations to buy mosquito nets for refugee families being forcibly settled in the Vanni jungles. Two other university students had simply gone missing after a game of cricket on the school grounds opposite the Jaffna library. Bharati said he could not go back. 'Actually I *would* not, even if I could,' he added in that determined way of his, enunciating every Tamil syllable. He had a zoology degree and a good grade, but he was sure he would not find a job. Moreover, his parents had sold their house to send him on this journey, dreaming that he would settle down in America and then fly them over. Going back home was not an option. Listening to him, Sarva wondered if the young man didn't have every reason to want to drive a knife into a Sri Lankan soldier. The crime would be huge but the sentence had already been served.

Sarva couldn't return either, not to a place he knew would never pardon his crime. He might as well have stayed in the Tiger ranks, Sarva thought sometimes, instead of letting Amma persuade him to quit. It was not out of the ordinary to serve in the Tigers; they had recruited thousands like him. He, too, had felt the rage, the helplessness, the desire to level the uneven playing field.

Throughout the years of his youth, the idea of militancy had presented itself to him repeatedly. He told Bharati about the time when, eleven years old and living in Chavakacheri, he had lost the key for his bicycle and was trying to break the wheel lock with a stone. Two female Tigers with double braids had passed by, asking if he needed help. He nodded shyly. 'In exchange you better join the movement, okay?' they had laughed. When his bike was unlocked, he sped away, but their faces always caught up with him. They were not threatening or scary, he had thought then, just young girls doing an honourable job.

At other times, he had desired retribution. Like that day when he was fourteen, standing in the Vavuniya bus station with his aunt, looking at a soldier kicking a youth, pounding his boots into the boy's face till he was bleeding, till his mother was wailing, throwing herself on her son, cursing the soldiers in stricken Tamil.

Every so often, such a scene had confronted Sarva, forcing him to take a stance. In or out. Family or community. Anger and pride pulsed through him. This mix of emotions had burnt fiercely all through his life: in his childhood, when his one-day-old sister died and he was sure the Sinhalese nurses had been neglectful; as a young man, when he roamed the streets unemployed; during his darkest years in prison.

There had been so many reasons to pick up a gun. If not for Amma pulling him out of the school in the Vanni and sending him to Hatton, perhaps he might have turned to violence when still a teenager. She tried sending him abroad, but when that didn't work, she encouraged his work as a seaman, which kept him out of the country. Even when he signed up with the Tigers, she had forced him to abandon them. Had he seen this fugitive life coming, he might have stayed with the LTTE.

'At least I would have made a real contribution,' he told Bharati.

'You're being nostalgic,' Bharati scoffed. 'They were there for thirty years'—longer than the span of his life—'and they did nothing but leave us in a mess.'

A COUPLE OF months after Sarva arrived in Santa Cruz in eastern Bolivia, Siva made an appearance. Ever since the night with the thugs, Sarva's patience had been wearing thin.

'Why am I still here?' he demanded.

For the first time, Siva answered the question directly. He said that everyone else had paid him properly. 'You have paid me half.'

That was the agreement, Sarva said, a discount in exchange for a favour from his brother.

Siva looked annoyed. He took his phone out, opened the calculator, and made as if he were doing complicated arithmetic. Finally he clucked. 'Yes, one million rupees. I need at least one million more from you to pay people to get you safely across. And I won't be making a profit.' Looking at Bharati, Siva said, 'That goes for you, too.' Until he got that money, they were staying where they were.

The next day, the boy who usually brought lunch told Bharati they would have to fend for themselves. Siva would not provide food anymore. Sarva kicked the wall in frustration and injured his toe, but in a few days, when hunger struck, he left his room. He went downstairs, walked a few blocks, his hoodie up, hands deep in his pockets. If someone asked, he would say he was lost, just as he had been told to do earlier. Or he would give Siva up, tell the police he was being smuggled and would disclose all the details in exchange for his freedom. Sarva and Bharati went in and out of small shops all day looking for work. They did the same the next day, and for a whole week, circling further away from the hideout, and returning beaten every night. Finally, they found a job cleaning a deli and taking the garbage out. They didn't tell the employers they were illegal immigrants; but perhaps the shop owners guessed the risks involved, since the wages were so low. Sarva and Bharati worked alternate days at the same job and were able to make just enough to buy food. Both were aware that their pay would never add up to the amount Siva wanted. 'Even if we sold our kidneys,' as Bharati put it.

When Siva next visited, he was transformed. He spoke to Sarva respectfully, apologising for the fight on their previous meeting, but still not offering to pay for their meals. Most suspiciously, he revoked the prohibition on using a telephone. He offered the use of his own iPad to Sarva. 'It must have been ages since you spoke to your mother.' He then went out for a smoke.

Sarva was sceptical, but he logged on to Skype and looked for Malar. Luckily she was online. There was shouting, crying, many questions, few answers, disbelief and concern. He asked her to tell Amma where he was. With Sarva still online, Malar called his mother on her phone. Amma was in Nuwara Eliya, she said, and Carmel was there with a laptop and Internet connection. Sarva buzzed his little brother on Skype.

'Why haven't you called your mother in so long, child?' Amma cried immediately. 'Are you all right? Where are you?'

He let her get the questions out of the way before saying he was in Bolivia.

'Olivia? Where is that?'

'In Latin America.'

'Is that America?'

Sarva laughed, but until a few months ago, he himself hadn't known any better. 'It is still far away, Amma. I don't know how long it will take.'

She didn't seem to know what to say. 'Show me your face.'

The connection is not fast enough, he lied. His emaciated face would worry her. She would also ask to see his room. She was sitting on the living room sofa with Carmel, her face tired but beautiful, and Sarva's own surroundings felt too shabby to share.

'Is Siva good to you? Remind him I asked him to take care of you. He used to eat so often in our house.'

Sarva said he would let Siva know.

'Are you eating well? Do you need money, child? Tell me the truth.'

How could he tell her he needed yet more money? He was trying not to blame his brother for this ruinous turn of events. 'I'm eating fine.'

She launched into a long story about her calling Jehaan and Shirleen, seeking their help to find him.

Finally, he had to tell her. 'Amma, can you send one million? Siva is demanding more now. Without it, he won't take me further.'

Immediately she sounded anxious. 'Is he treating you badly? I will speak to Deva.'

'Please don't. It will make things worse. If you can arrange it yourself … If not, I will … I don't know. I'll have to see.'

'No, no. I will do something. Don't worry, child, I will do something, okay?' and Sarva believed she would.

When he hung up, Bharati got on Skype with his parents, who also assured him they would send money 'somehow'. It dawned on Sarva that Siva had anticipated exactly what would happen. The agent had planned for a long silence that, once broken, would prompt a wire transfer of one million rupees.

24.

January 2012

ON A JANUARY afternoon in 2012, Divyan's guards asked him and twenty others to get into a military truck. As they drove out of the Poonthottam rehabilitation camp, a blue tarpaulin was draped over the back of the truck, so they wouldn't know where they were being taken. One man, sure of a mass execution, wished he could have seen his family one more time before the end. Others came to different conclusions about their destination: they were going to Boosa prison to be tortured or to another camp for interrogation. Divyan closed his eyes and forced himself to sleep, a skill he had taught himself in two years of imprisonment. It kept him sane and, most importantly, unthinking.

A few hours later, the tarpaulin was lifted and the man next to him shook Divyan awake. 'Your place is here,' he said. They were at the Point Pedro bus stop. Divyan got off the truck, bemused at this anticlimactic return home. He didn't know where to go from there. He had to call Mugil on a borrowed phone.

She came on her bike to pick him up. She was radiant as she pedalled towards him, not like the mouse he had seen on her visits to the camp. She asked him why he hadn't told her in advance of his homecoming. He said he only knew when he got off the truck. They did not have any more words and smiled in acknowledgement.

He folded his sarong and took the handlebars, while she moved to the carrier at the back. She did not remember the last time she sat pillion. It was a willing submission to a role she had not enjoyed for two years. He did not know where to go, and she gave him gentle directions.

'The shirts and sarongs I gave you at the camp?' she asked as he pedalled.

'They got left behind. They didn't tell us to pack. Children are home?'

'I sent Amma to bring them from tuition.'

At home, Tamizh clambered all over his father, but Maran hugged him uncertainly. He asked when Divyan was going back. 'Maran!' Mugil slapped his arm. But she wanted to know, too. Divyan said he didn't know.

He found out that evening when, as instructed, he went to the police station and put his name in a register. They sent him to the army camp nearby, where he signed next to his name on a list. Return next week to collect your release certificate, they said.

'That must mean I'm here for good,' Divyan announced at home.

Mugil arranged a reunion party. Sangeeta brought sweet *kesari* and chicken rolls while Mother made fish *kozhambu*, saying he must have missed Tamil food. 'The Sinhalese don't use tamarind like us, I think.' Amuda brought a large bottle of chilled Fanta from her shop fridge. 'Isn't that someone else's?' asked Prashant. 'Oh shut up, I'll replace it tomorrow,' she snapped. Mugil found herself talking endlessly, trying to bring Divyan up to speed with everything. Mother was grinning at everyone and Prashant, for once, did not leave to see his friends.

After everyone had retired for the night, Divyan lay down next to Maran and Tamizh on the floor mats in the living room. Mugil sat next to him. 'Prashant is behaving very strangely, and he won't talk about it to me. Can *you* please tell me? I need to know what happened in the two years you were gone.'

Divyan told her about his time in detention. They beat him, asking questions over and over: where are the weapons, who has left the country, who was funding the Tigers, what are the plans for regrouping, who was his supervisor, what did they train him to do?

He told them he had joined when he was twenty, was a fighter for two years until he was injured and put out of action. It was all true, but only part of his story. He had been asked about spies—he had given some names. They had asked about armouries, he directed them to a couple. 'I said just enough for them to be satisfied.'

'How old were you when you finished training?' they asked one time. A month later, they asked what year it was when he finished training. Divyan guessed they were checking for inconsistencies. He stuck to the same story from beginning to end; he did not add or omit anything. He told them his first LTTE name, Dileepan, and not the later ones. He did not interact much with the other inmates, not wanting to divulge details that someone could blurt out during their interrogation. It was impossible to make friends when they were all so vulnerable and being pitted against each other. To his relief, the physical torture stopped after the first year. He explained how he meditated for hours and fell asleep at will. He had to rid his mind of aggression, file away his edges. He thought of the children and wanted to make it out sane.

'I used to think that this family's only blessing was that all four of us survived,' he said on the night of his return. 'But now, this house … Is this luck? Or is this the dowry payment you escaped earlier?' He was teasing, but Mugil said it did feel like a gift her Father had given her.

It had been only a year since his father-in-law's passing, but to Divyan, it felt so deep in the past, an experience reduced to two images: his touching the old man's feet before surrendering in Putumatalan and Mugil saying that her father had passed away. Only Mugil and Mother, and perhaps Maran, retained the memory of his death. There had been no funeral. There were no ashes to scatter or grave to visit—the one under the barbed wire at Manik Farm was inaccessible.

In the impressive house that was now theirs, Mugil would've liked to hang a framed picture of her father on the wall with a garland and an oil lamp, but not a single photograph had survived the conflict. Because Father had died from an illness in camp, he had perhaps not even been counted in the UN estimate of 40,000 civilians killed in the last war. With no evidence of his death, it was as if he had never lived. Mugil held her father's life and death in her head, carrying on without the healing release of a mourning. Thousands of Tamils had not been accorded that dignity.

'You have done so much, Mugil,' Divyan said. 'I'm here now, I will take over.'

'Enough, just sleep now,' she replied. She wanted to preserve somehow this supple promise on his first night back, before it decayed like everything else around them.

Divyan faced the same barriers as Prashant when it came to finding employment, but he fought harder. One word spun in his head, a term of abuse usually hurled by annoyed fathers at their good-for-nothing sons: *thanda-sor.* He couldn't simply subsist on his wife's earnings, and he couldn't bring himself to sit at home. So he took a bus every morning to a highway under construction and sat with the sarong-clad men at the roadside. A contractor would come by, size them up, pick five or ten of them, state a wage and put them to work for the day. Divyan told people he was a skilled mason, but he did semi-skilled or unskilled labour for 700 rupees a day: breaking stones, pouring hot tar from a perforated tin drum, carrying pails of concrete. Some days he wasn't picked and came back empty-handed.

In the beginning, Divyan imagined that the bigger the road, the greater the job opportunity; but the main four-lane highways used machines for most tasks. One day he saw a lumbering contraption with dusters spinning rapidly against the road, and it struck him that he couldn't even get a job sweeping the streets. The work he did get was hard on his back, which had been injured when he slipped several discs, but he continued doing labour at least twice a week.

When he was not working in construction, Divyan occasionally helped Mugil out with the snack business. She did not dare invite him to join them; he was too proud to partner with women. After her experience with Prashant, Mugil hadn't counted on a purely happy reunion with her husband, and just as she had predicted, the gratitude exhibited on his first night back was short-lived. Divyan would not cook meals when she was out at work or confer with her on family decisions. Much as she was glad he was home, his return had immediately eroded her independence and authority around the house. Their boys sensed it first; they hardly listened to her anymore. Tantrums were thrown around her, and a doe-eyed love once lavished on Mugil was reserved for their father. In return, Divyan was wonderful with them, spending more hours than she could on their homework and meals. But Mugil knew it would not be enough for her husband; he would not derive his self-esteem from parenting or housework.

The work—or lack of it—began to scrape away at Divyan's determination. If only he could get a driving gig: it was decent work, his back could take it, and with the great numbers of tourists and NGOs, there was a constant demand. He had done it for ten years in the Vanni, but now he needed a new driver's licence, for which he required a national ID card.

The women had until then been using provisional IDs that the police had given them. Divyan submitted applications for ID cards at the government agent's office for Mugil, Mother, Amuda, Prashant and himself. He took Prashant along and gradually the two began to spend all their time together, going to the wood shop to buy a door, to the placement offices and to the bus depot to get annual passes made. He told Mugil he was setting her brother right, giving him mature advice about getting a job and dumping his gang of wastrels. One day, she walked in on them sitting in different corners of the room chatting. Maran and Tamizh were playing around them, and she could only hope the men were not talking about detention. '*Kathaikarathileye irungal*,' she said smiling: just keep chatting.

Tamizh was nearby. '*Yengal inatthai azhikkarathileye irukkangal!*' he responded, his eyes glowing mischievously: just keep wiping our race out.

As she heard the words spill from her five-year-old's lips, Mugil felt punched in the gut. There it was, everything that she had protected him from, dancing in front of her. Divyan and Prashant were grinning as if this was simply an entertaining quip from a precocious child.

Mugil called Divyan outside and told him that this was the most violent thing a father could have taught his son. 'Don't you want him to be different from us? Why are you saying this shit in front of him?' Divyan said his sons were not going to grow up hearing only fish patty recipes.

Mugil walked out of the house and went straight to Sangeeta's. 'These men, they're going to get my boys killed!' Sangeeta consoled her, saying that would not be so easy as long as Mugil was around.

'No, but they've completely sidelined me,' Mugil cried. 'They're always whispering together and won't tell me what they are talking about. I mean, it's not like I grew up wearing bangles and flowers!'

'It was bound to happen, *akka*; they like to take charge.'

'But why behave as if I'm a good-for-nothing? Did I not protect these children from everything in the refugee camps, did I not take care of my mother, did I not find the bungalow he's stretching his legs in? Thankless!'

Mugil said they had hardened towards each other, but she couldn't bring herself to yell at Divyan. 'He's never had it easy,' she said. All his life, he had pursued clear goals, and now the loss of control was making him flounder. The military remained in their neighbourhood because, despite all evidence to the contrary, it was convinced that the Tigers would regroup. Just as she wanted the military to back off and let them breathe, Mugil wanted Divyan and Prashant, too, to rethink some of their Vanni-brand Tamil nationalism and move beyond the battle talk. Hadn't her community lost enough people, sacrificed enough children? She, too, had once found inspiration in sacrifice, but she bet that today, despite all the bravado about another uprising, few would send their own kids to fight.

The men didn't think alternatives existed, but they did, albeit imperfect ones. Some Tamil parliamentarians demanded greater political autonomy for their northern province, for the president to promote reconciliation by sharing power. Mere elections were not democratic enough; the Tamil-dominated province should be allowed the autonomy to legislate with regard to land, law and order and economic development. Equal rights and more autonomy—for both the Tamils and the Sinhalese—had been intrinsic to the separatist movement. For decades, negotiations had failed because the Sri Lankan and Eelam leaders refused to compromise. Finally now, the federal language, earlier silenced by militancy, offered the possibility of peace. Tamils referred to such moderate politicians as *samadhanavaadhis*, but some also considered them compromisers, cynics, Western mouthpieces, Indian stooges or anti-Eelam weaklings. Because the president and Parliament would not even discuss demands for autonomy lest doing so became a step towards the bifurcation of Sri Lanka, people like Divyan thought it futile to work through the system for great equality and freedom.

'You know, I think he does not see our boys as children but as future little warriors. How am I going to change his mind?'

'Just give it time, *akka*.' Sangeeta's back was turned, but Mugil saw the slumped shoulders. 'For now, at least you have someone to share responsibilities with.'

Mugil slapped her forehead and held her friend's hands. 'Sorry, Sangeeta, I didn't mean to make you feel ... I am lucky he's alive, it's true.'

'*Chi*, *akka*, not like that! Are you mad? I'm not missing a husband ordering me around!'

Sangeeta's smile was taut. Mugil wanted to kick herself for coming here to whine about her problems, but who else did she have? In the years without her husband and brother, it had become their habit to turn to each other for comfort. Mugil thought Sangeeta was the strongest fighter she knew—she was the kind of woman the Tigers used to say were equal to any man—but it had nothing to do with battle or training. She was able to keep a cool head despite being so alone, raising three children, being harassed by soldiers, living with the nightmare of seeing her husband killed in broad daylight. She had not put a foot wrong in her life, and yet she had perhaps suffered more setbacks than Mugil. She broke down with Mugil sometimes, agonised by the lack of closure in her husband's death and her vulnerability. She often wondered what would happen to her children if she, too, were bumped off one day—not a far-fetched concern given the times. But she never let it detract from her resolve to forge ahead.

If Mugil had to design a poster for a Tamil fighting force today, she thought, she would have it feature a photograph of Sangeeta, with her daughter and son standing next to her and the baby on her hip. Behind them she would put Sangeeta's brother, the supportive man behind this powerhouse of a woman. For the poster's background, she would use the image of the white dove that hung from a calendar in their living room. '*Suthanthira paravaigal*,' she would write under the picture, and pin it on trees and walls: birds of freedom. These were the warriors she felt her community needed to admire today: the people toiling to make peace work.

Sangeeta had lately stopped coming over as often as she used to. Mother guessed that she didn't want to be seen as the lonely widow meddling in a happy family's affairs. Mugil narrowed the reason down to that dumb movie night. Some weeks earlier she had gone to watch the Indian Tamil movie *Singam* with Amuda and Sangeeta on a borrowed laptop at a neighbour's house. While Mugil was lost in the movie, Divyan had called her phone repeatedly and she had not heard. When she returned home, he had charged towards her, bellowing, demanding to know where the hell she had been. She had turned her face and lifted her elbows up, sure that he would slap her. Later that night he had admitted to being angry—it was her fault for having been careless—but he was hurt that she thought he would hit her. 'Don't you know me?' he asked. She couldn't tell him that she didn't anymore. His temper had eclipsed everything else about him.

After Mugil told Sangeeta about this, the younger woman stopped coming by for meals or a cup of coffee or to bathe her children by the well. An air of formality had crept into their relationship.

In her house, as Sangeeta feigned normalcy, Mugil sensed that their friendship was hanging by a thread. They were good business partners, and perhaps that was all they could be now. Mugil shouldn't bring her household problems here anymore. This was not the family reunion Mugil had waited more than two years for. With the returnees, love too had hardened, turned brittle.

MARAN DECLARED THAT he wanted to go 'out'. This was code for him to go to the beach after sunset with Mugil, just the two of them. They held hands and crossed the main road, across which stretched yards of white sand and moonlit ocean.

There was nobody else around. Mugil sat on the sand while Maran dug holes he said were bunkers for crabs. He never went into the water, so she let herself relax, staring into the purple sky streaked with retreating orange. It was late in the evening, and she heard fishermen launching their boats beyond the sea wall, heaving and pulling between rhythmic grunts and song. It was May 2012, exactly three years after the end of the war, and the fishing restrictions had finally been lifted in this area. Hearing fishermen call out after all this time and seeing their boats bob in the distance on the waves was reassuring, a return to an ancient profession and the beginning of hope for some.

When Maran was done playing, they went to a nearby shop and bought cotton candy. Maran always ate two: the first one flattened into a finger-sized ball and swallowed like a toffee and the second eaten in all its fluffy glory, the pleasure drawn out till they reached home, before Tamizh could see his brother's treat and throw a tantrum. It amazed Mugil to see how much joy and contentment just two rupees could buy.

They were walking down the long street home when Maran spotted his grandmother ahead. Mother was returning from the bus stop where she now sold rolls and buns from four in the afternoon till the last minibus stopped there at eight in the evening. The snack business had slumped several months earlier—the items cost more to make than the shops were willing to pay. Since the women didn't make enough profit for three, Mugil quit. Since then, Sangeeta cooked and Mother hawked at the bus stop closest to her house. She sat beside the plastic stool on which stood her basket of snacks, next to another woman selling tea from a flask. This was clever teaming: a bite of a spicy roll made the customer yearn for a glass of tea, or the sweetness of the tea would call for a salty bun. They made about 200 rupees a day, but it upset Mugil to see her aged mother become a street vendor.

'Paati!' Maran yelled and ran to his grandmother. He took the stool she was carrying. It was his height, but he lugged it home chivalrously. When Mugil caught up, Mother handed her the last oily tuna roll.

'Apparently that tea lady's daughter found a husband in England,'

Mother said. 'She is enrolled in English classes now.'

'Is he a citizen?' Mugil asked, smiling at Mother's revived interest in neighbourhood gossip.

'She says he got asylum eight years ago. Looks genuine, but you never know.' Mother was wary of weddings that doubled as emigration plans, especially after her niece had gone off with a one-way ticket to marry a Tamil man in America, only to discover that he was an illegal immigrant.

Mugil asked when the wedding would be.

'This fellow can't come back to Sri Lanka, so the girl will go after three months, have a wedding ceremony there and stay in England.'

'Lucky Aunty can go to England for the wedding.'

'Where? She can't afford to go. This is as usual, give your daughter away, get a photo album.' When Tamil refugees abroad got married, parents in Sri Lanka made all the arrangements, often also choosing the bride, but could rarely afford to attend the wedding, which had to be conducted in the foreign country because the groom couldn't re-enter Sri Lanka. The parents would receive pictures of the celebration by post or email.

'How much is she giving as dowry?'

'One and a half million only, because the girl is fair, quite pretty. Also, they bluffed that she knows English already.'

They reached Mother's house, and as Mugil waited for her to pack some leftover gooseberry curry for dinner, Amuda hobbled out of her nearly defunct shop in front of the house. The solar panel was shot and her fridge ruined by sporadic power cuts and wildly fluctuating voltage. She kept the store open now only to sell off the dusty stock of stationery and biscuits and to show the loan NGO that she was trying—and failing—to repay the debt. Seeing Mugil in the yard, Amuda looked surprised. 'Why aren't you home?'

'What do you mean?'

'Divyan Atthaan and Prashant are holding a memorial at your place. I thought you were also part of the plan. They came and took lots of candles and chart paper from me.' Mugil still looked confused, so Amuda repeated herself. 'They are holding a memorial for, you know—today is 18 May. You didn't know?'

Mugil sighed. 'No. They didn't tell me.' It was the three-year anniversary of the end of the war. The men were commemorating the death of thousands, including Prabakaran. She shouted to Mother that she had to go. Dragging Maran, she marched to her house.

When she barged into the living room, the scene was set. Stuck on her wall was a familiar image drawn with her sons' crayons: a pair of large eyes with teardrops. Under it, in Divyan's hand, were the Tamil words *Eela Tamizh maaveerargale, ungal thyaakam endrum unarvom!* Martyrs of Tamil Eelam, your sacrifice will be forever remembered!

Under it were two lists. On the left, names of their closest colleagues in the Tigers who were no more—Mani, Mugil's first unit friend, was at the top. On the right were civilian friends and relatives who died in the war—Father headed the list.

'I hope I haven't left anyone out,' Divyan said.

To the side of the lists, Prashant had attempted to sketch Prabakaran's face, but the only recognisable features were the stern moustache and the camouflage cap. Around the face he had written a lengthy poem about the leader. Another poster showed a hand-drawn map of Eelam in red, black and yellow, with the roaring tiger and AK-47s of the LTTE symbol at the centre. All of them had etched this tiger perhaps a hundred times as children, and it was as accurate as if it were traced. Tamizh was on the floor, setting small birthday candles around three tall ones, ready to be lit. 'One for each year that has passed,' Prashant said.

Mugil had burst in to stop the memorial, but she didn't feel the parched-mouth panic anymore. In the three years since the war, this was her first remembrance ceremony. The friends on the list, whom she had avoided so much as mentioning all this time, were not simply colleagues but her compatriots from a time that felt more real, more theirs. A year or even a few months earlier, she might not have recalled these times so fondly, but remembering itself was considered an act of terrorism these days and she had grown weary of criminalising her thoughts. She did not want to fight again, but she wanted to cry aloud for the ones they had lost.

This was not allowed in the country they lived in today. That morning, Divyan and Prashant had been called to the army camp along with other former combatants. It was another head count, a reminder that they lived under surveillance. When, at dusk, they were finally allowed to leave, the men came straight home to defy the rules. 'If they won't let us do it publicly, we thought we would just do it in private,' Prashant said.

The government had christened 18 and 19 May, the dates of the end of the war, as Victory Days. The anniversaries were public holidays, celebrating Sri Lanka's second independence, its freedom from terrorism, a moment of glory for the troops. In the army barracks all over the north and east and in Colombo, they installed twelve-foot billboards to memorialise the young soldiers killed in the war, and congratulated their parents with garlands at large public events. TV channels played patriotic songs all day.

Meanwhile, private funerals for Tamils killed in the war were not permitted, and Tamil commemorations got people arrested. Thousands were aching for closure, but the military police turned down requests for group prayer or community memorials. Any gatherings—political, social or religious—were banned in the north during the holiday, and at whim on other days. The army cracked down on a meeting of Hindu temple trusts in Jaffna organising a special *puja* on the anniversary. Mugil's Amman temple priest was told that coconut smashing was not to be performed on 18 and 19 May. A church in Mannar had organised a service on 18 May, but soldiers arrived early that morning to prevent any prayer or service.

The government was bulldozing graveyards and banning Tamil memorials to the departed as it set up Sinhalese ones. It removed the tombstones from an enormous Tiger war grave near Kilinochchi, turning the land into an army football field. At the Mullivaikal lagoon, the site of the last stage of the war, a memorial marked military victory. On blocks of granite, a triumphant soldier stood holding a gun over which a dove flew. His other hand held the Sri Lankan flag. The granite base was guarded on each side by a stately stone lion, the national animal of Sri Lanka and the symbol of the Sinhalese race. The lagoon was now out of bounds, taken over by the army, which was building a posh eco-resort there.

All the landmarks of the Vanni as Mugil knew it were either being erased or converted into tourist destinations. In Mugil's PTK, where former residents were still not allowed to resettle, an open-air war museum had been set up about five kilometres from the junction. Soldiers guarded it, and former residents were told the area was still riddled with mines, so Mugil had never visited. If she had, she would have seen, arranged under a long tin shed, captured Tiger weaponry: torpedo shells, experimental submarines, mid-sized amphibians, GPS devices, smart mines, and assorted guns. Rusted parts of a tank displayed on the dust; a row of 'suicide bomber boats' gleaming under the sun. She would not have been able to read the legends under each exhibit because the museum was curated solely in Sinhala. This ramshackle museum was intended to demonstrate to southern tourists the calibre of the enemy their army had been up against for thirty years and had finally outsmarted.

Beyond the museum, as far as the eye could see, were ruined houses and beheaded coconut trees, the only remnants of a bustling town. Tourists were not permitted to see the demolition, and were hustled to another shrine to victory close by. On the road from there to Mullaitivu, a four-storey-deep bunker used by Prabakaran was one of the first to be open to tourists. Smartly dressed soldiers gave guided tours to Sinhalese groups, pointing to the 'bulletproof war room', the bathroom, the tunnel that led to the back of the building and into the forest. Nearby, a less popular attraction was a swimming pool in which the Sea Tigers, the naval wing, supposedly practised diving. 'Olympic-size pool!' the guide soldier would announce with a flourish.

In this environment, a Tamil memorial to loss or silent grief was deemed a travesty, as something unpatriotic. But how long could they pretend that the war killed nobody, stole nothing?

As Divyan and Prashant sang LTTE songs, Mugil lit the candles. She felt she finally understood why her men wanted to record, cherish, and talk about the past, about the Vanni all the time. They were afraid of forgetting. As survivors, they felt the burden of proof, the need to carry sights, sounds and events lest history erase them. That night, when Divyan and Prashant told her sons stories of the Tigers, she didn't stop them.

25.

August 2012

OF ALL THE time he had spent as a child at his grandparents' Jaffna house, Sarva remembered the summer afternoons best. On those languid days, the heat seemed to expand the hours. Lunch done, Paati would clean the kitchen while Thatha would relax in the curve of the wooden easy chair in the foyer; meanwhile Sarva would follow ants and chase lizards in the back garden. Only Paati's promise of *saami kadai*—Hindu myths of heroes and gods—brought him indoors. For him, they were great adventure stories and, for his grandmother, the perfect fairy tales to lull a child to sleep. She would lie down on the polished black floor, glassy and cool as the surface of a lake, and her gravelly voice would tell the stories of baby Krishna and his mother, Yashoda; Prince Rama and his wife, Sita, exiled in the jungle; Shiva and his shape-shifting wife, Parvati. His grandmother narrated with her eyes closed, and Sarva listened, lying on his back, staring at the ceiling, his head luxuriating in the soft homeliness of her cotton sari. Majestic lions, trampling elephants, verdant forests and cascading waterfalls crashed into the room. Seas were swallowed, mountains lifted like umbrellas. Deer turned into men, horses flew. The quiet house burst with otherworldly magic.

Paati preferred to tell epic stories of powerful gods and goddesses, but the ones Sarva recalled most vividly when he was older were short tales about minor characters: the giant warrior Kumbakarnan who fell into a sleep so profound an army could not wake him; the demon Raktavija, who could not be slain in battle because from every drop of his blood rose another demon; the boy Ekalavya, who loved archery so much he cut his thumb off for his teacher. They were not typical gods or heroes, but people and demons whose odd powers and obsessive desires led them into surreal situations that were as riveting as they were tragic.

One such story was that of King Trishanku, who loved the idea of heaven so much that he desired to go there while still alive. He begged powerful sages for help, but they all said this would breach the laws of the universe. Disgusted at his attachment to physical existence, some of these wise men cursed him to suffer from disease and an early old age. Finally, only the powerful sage Vishwamitra promised to attempt the impossible. He performed powerful rituals and prayers, but the gods were enraged. They told Vishwamitra that a human, however devoted or good, could not be allowed into heaven. The arrogant Vishwamitra defied the gods and started to meditate so strongly that Trishanku began to ascend to the heavens. When he had almost reached heaven's gate, the gods retaliated. 'Fall back to earth!' they said, and Trishanku began to fall, his body upside down. Vishwamitra regretted challenging the gods, but to keep his promise, he stopped the king's descent midair. And there Trishanku would hang upside down for eternity, between the earth he left and the heaven he craved.

During similarly languid days in Bolivia, suspended between his destination and the country he had fled, Sarva thought of Trishanku and his regret. Jehaan and Madhavi had warned Sarva about the perils of trusting a smuggler, but he had not listened. How could he have known there would be no end to his bad luck? That his life was doomed to suffer setback after setback? Amma had paid another million rupees to Siva's associate in Colombo. That was in July 2012. It was August now, and Sarva was still in Santa Cruz, not New York or even Mexico or Arizona. 'Things are not as easy as you think,' Siva said. Circumstances had changed, the US government was stricter about immigration, he needed another million from Sarva. Meanwhile he brought other men to the apartment, fresh off the flight from Colombo, their hope still unbroken. Sarva despised their optimism. When they spoke with him, he could not help telling them about his long journey, Siva's frequent demands for money and the starvation penalty for speaking up. He described the night with Siva's creditors, exaggerating the size of the guns involved. The next time Siva came to the apartment, the new men surrounded him, refusing to pay upfront for anything until he showed them a clear plan of action. Sarva saw them panic and lose their cool. He felt like a wolf among pigeons.

A life in the shadows had taken its toll on Bharati, too. Whereas once he'd stood on the threshold of a new life with a boldness that impressed Sarva, the long months of waiting had whittled away at this young man's resolve. He hardly ate or slept and missed his parents with the intensity of a toddler. The burden of their having sold their house, pinning all their hopes on him, hung heavy over his head. It prevented him from changing his plans when all he wanted was to go home. He told Sarva that if he had understood what leaving Sri Lanka really meant when he boarded the plane, he would have taken in more of his native country, committed his house and street to memory, inhaled the smell of the sea more deeply. He craved the flavour of tamarind fish; it was unbelievable that he would miss that taste forever. He had not gone to his favourite Rio ice-cream parlour in Jaffna before leaving, not hung out enough in the union room at university, not said goodbye to all his relatives and friends. He had lived in Jaffna all his life, and was he never to see it again? How could that be?

As Bharati teetered on the edge of making the dangerous decision to fly back to Sri Lanka, his concerned parents sent money through the agent, asking their son to live more comfortably, to eat better, to work fewer hours at the deli. Siva delivered only half, around $400. And Bharati used all the money to purchase a smartphone and a SIM card. He began to speak to his aged mother every day. She read the paper out to him, telling him about suicides among Tamil youth in Sri Lanka and about the absolute military control over his university, whose dean was now a government appointee. She spoke about how his aunt in the Vanni lost her tobacco farm because the government did not recognise the deeds to her property. She said his father had been smart to have sold his land early, before it was seized by the government for the 'northern revival' development projects. Long-displaced Muslims were coming back to Jaffna, and Sinhalese to the other northern districts, his father said, but almost half of Bharati's classmates had left or were in the process of leaving. There were no jobs, a former military general was the governor of the north, and disappearances were at an alarming high. Bharati was soon cured of his desire to return to Sri Lanka.

Thanks to the new phone, Sarva, too, was now able to call home more regularly. He spoke to Amma at least once a week and to Malar every day. She was already becoming a distant memory, the ghost of everything good that was slipping out of his grasp. They always discussed the same things: the moment they would meet again, their simple wedding, how they would live, how many children they would have, how they would love a daughter more than a son. She told him about the pressures at home: she was twenty-nine, nearly five years past the average age of marriage for a Tamil girl. Her father had shared her photo and astrological chart with marriage brokers for prospective grooms, and she was afraid one of them would be a match. Sarva would ask her to trust the strength of their love; it would prevail over everything, he said.

To Bharati, however, he admitted he was numb with the prospect of losing Malar. 'What do I have to offer? A broken body and this apartment with Siva?' Sarva had to act before more eligible men came along for Malar. He needed to make a good life and bring her over. As soon as possible, he had to leave Bolivia, and get somewhere close to where he had set out to be.

Bharati had a suggestion. 'Why are we stuck on America?' he asked one day. When Sarva said that was the agreement with Siva, Bharati clapped his hands. 'That!' he shouted. 'That is what is going to change now.'

Bharati's parents had met the family of one of his friends from university who was on the army blacklist. The young man had fled the country with an agent around the same time as Bharati did, but his agent had sent him to England. In six months, he had been granted asylum. Since Bharati's reasons for leaving Sri

Lanka—political instability, fear of persecution and attempted kidnapping—were exactly the same as this friend's, he thought he, too, might stand a good chance of finding asylum in England. He suggested Sarva join him.

'And who's going to take us there?' Sarva asked.

Bharati's mother had already spoken to his friend's agent, Kannan. For 1.2 million rupees, Kannan was ready to take Bharati and Sarva to London.

Sarva was not sure how they could leave Siva. But Bharati said Kannan knew Siva and such transfers happened all the time. Kannan would 'buy' Bharati and Sarva from Siva. 'Like slaves,' Sarva added. Amma encouraged him to go ahead. Deva had not said a word or paid a rupee; he had not acknowledged any responsibility for his friend Siva and his brother's year of torment.

'It's just the two of us now,' Amma said. 'We should go ahead with whatever seems best to you.'

Once the move was decided, it was simply procedural. Siva did not care about losing them, as long as he got his money. Over the next month, Amma sold all of her gold jewellery, which made enough money to pay both agents. Siva got the half-million rupees paid by Amma to his associate in Colombo. Another 600,000 was handed to Kannan's man, the rest being payable after they reached London. 'This Kannan seems to be more honourable than Siva,' Amma said.

The dream shifted continents. Bharati and Sarva were taken to a house near the airport. Kannan's people brought food every day. Sarva tried not to think that another year might be lost to anticipation.

AS SARVA CHANGED his plans, Malar found the courage to tell her family about their relationship. She built him up to be the whole package, selling him on the basis of his good family and British dream, but not mentioning the torture, the Tiger years or the jail time. Her parents were concerned about her age and Sarva's unpredictable future. Yet, a love marriage held some appeal: if the groom loved the bride enough, there might not be a dowry.

'You will make sure your mother doesn't ask for much, no?' Malar asked Sarva.

Sarva was not sure if he could; a dowry was unavoidable. But he suggested that Malar meet his mother. 'You both live in Nuwara Eliya,' he said. 'She was impressed when you last met. If she likes you enough, maybe she will not ask for much.'

'Does she know about us?'

'No. But it will be fine.'

The next Sunday, Malar spent the afternoon at Amma's house. That evening, she told Sarva on the phone that his mother had been sweet to her; they discussed Sarva's situation and had tea and pakoda; they parted with smiling hugs.

When Sarva called his mother after a few days, he knew immediately that Malar had been a victim of his mother's misleading civility.

'So, she came, that girl. On Sunday,' Amma began frostily. 'To have tea with me.'

'Yes. Malar. Good. What did she say?' He kept his voice upbeat.

'She must have already reported it to you, no? You talk *every day* apparently. She seems to know more about you than I do anyway.'

'*Aiyo*, Amma.'

'I did not expect this from you, Sarva. After everything I have done, you just want to torture me again.'

'Why? How am I torturing you? She will be perfect for me, for our family.'

'Your brother's wife also thinks she is too good for me. I should at least have one daughter-in-law I can be close to.'

'You can be close to Malar, Amma. She is caring, she is a family girl.'

'I have protected you from all sorts of things. After everything, don't think I will let you get swept away by some love affair.'

'What are you saying, Amma? What does this have to do with all that?'

'They will not be able to give us anything! After everything I have spent on you, can a mother not expect at least a girl from a good family?'

'I don't want a penny from Malar's family.'

'You don't get to decide that,' Amma shouted. 'Sarva, they're from the sweeper caste! They're so much lower than us!'

Sarva was losing patience. He made exasperated noises.

Amma started to cry. 'I raise you, protect you, everything. And then some girl just swoops in?' She went on, wondering why Sarva needed her for everything and then made this life decision on his own.

'You are the one who encouraged me to meet her.'

'I curse the day. Couldn't you wait for me to find you a girl from our community?'

'It will not be easy, Amma. Malar knows everything about me. She accepts me.'

'She's not doing us a favour! You are a catch for anyone.'

'Yes, good luck trying to find a princess for this broken item.' His voice choked.

Amma changed tack. 'Don't worry, my child—in a few years, when you are in England, everything will be fine. Then your mother will find you a nice girl from a decent family. Just end this, okay? I know you must be lonely, so she is a good friend. Okay? A good friend, that's all. I know my son will not hurt me.'

He switched the subject to his father's struggle to get retirement benefits.

Sarva felt like a fool for thinking Amma would accept Malar and ignore the caste difference. He should have known; she would find hierarchy even in a box of apples. She was trying to compensate every single day for her own marriage to a lower-caste man.

In addition, there was the dowry. In his community, there was rarely a way around it. It was compulsory, a convention that had become more entrenched with mounting expenses among young men's families during the years of the conflict. Particularly among Indra's Vellalar caste, brides were expected to bring a house. Malar would not be able to afford this, and Sarva didn't want to demand it of her. Yet he knew that his convoluted journey had left his mother with a heavy debt—close to five million rupees. He knew she had counted on his marriage to ease that burden. It was why she felt so betrayed—abandoned in her effort to fix their family. At that moment, he hated his mother for the hold she had on him, and for the sacrifices that hung over his neck like a sword.

THANKFULLY, SARVA HAD other urgent concerns to distract him from family drama. The journey to London was fixed for October.

Kannan had three instructions for Bharati and Sarva before they boarded the flight. Once inside the plane, destroy your passport. At the immigration counters, lift your hand up high and say, 'Asylum.' Do not speak English, no matter what.

The instructions sounded mysterious and crucial, and Sarva was annoyed at Kannan for mentioning them at the last minute. The one about English sounded most bizarre. If they were going to the UK, should he not speak the native tongue, however little he knew of it? But thinking of the 600,000 he had paid Kannan, Sarva decided not to jeopardise his chances.

On 24 October 2012, when their flight landed at Heathrow, Sarva and Bharati looked at each other across the aisle and smiled. They had decided to go their separate ways, each bearing the burden of his past alone, without additional encumbrance, increasing both their chances of being accepted into this new country. They were not sure when they would see each other again.

Sarva disembarked and took the train to the airport terminal. He had a small backpack holding a toothbrush, toothpaste, a comb, a towel, blood pressure medicines from Bolivia, underwear, a couple of T-shirts, a pair of trousers, business cards from Jehaan, the Nonviolent Peaceforce and the ICRC, his Sri Lankan ID and the finger-sized idol of Pullaiyar that had been with him since prison.

He joined the long immigration queue. When it was his turn and the officer reached out to receive a passport, Sarva raised his own hand and shook it. 'No,' he said, stressing the word, trying hard not to break into more English.

The officer froze, his face hardened. 'No. No passport,' Sarva repeated. He had done as Kannan had instructed: on the flight he had ripped his passport to shreds and flushed the little maroon book with the Sri Lankan insignia down the toilet.

The officer said something about deporting him; he was already motioning to the security guards.

As uniformed guards walked towards him, Sarva abandoned the English rule. 'No! I can't go back to Sri Lanka!' he screamed. 'They kill me! They KILL me!' To his own surprise, he started to cry.

The guards pulled him away from the immigration desk. Sarva yelled: 'They kill me. No go back to Sri Lanka, please!' He was sobbing by now, unable to say the words properly, but it didn't loosen the grip of the guard's fingers around Sarva's forearm.

'Asylum!' he said, suddenly remembering. The word felt strange on his tongue. The officers didn't seem to have heard. He said it again and again. 'Asylum, sir, asylum.' Why did it sound like Tamil? He had practised it throughout the flight, muttering it over and over, but now it sounded wrong.

He was taken to an office with frosted glass doors. As the officers shut the door and sat down, he said 'asylum' a few more times. Each time more meaning was shed from the word, until it was just a yelp.

'Language?' one officer asked. 'Tamil,' Sarva said. They called an interpreter. The man looked South Indian. Great, Sarva thought. An interpreter who would only half-understand him. He wiped away his tears and prepared to narrate the incidents he had described many times by now.

He had landed at three in the morning; they started speaking to him at seven thirty. With breaks, the interview went on for over ten hours. Questions about how he got to London, why he had left Sri Lanka, why he could not go back. They asked him about the smuggler who had helped him, and Sarva told them about Siva, not Kannan. If they were going to investigate and arrest someone, he wanted it to be Siva. They ran Sarva's bag through a scanner and took his fingerprints. They left the room and returned every few hours with more questions. The fear Sarva had initially felt was fading, replaced by a dull anxiety. The procedure calmed him a little. The investigators wanted to know about him, not trap him. They might not be treating him as they did passengers with passports, but they were not going to beat him.

At dusk, the guards took Sarva out of the airport. The sky was threatening rain. Cold needles in the air pricked his bare arms; he had not worn a jacket. He was guided into a car. After a few minutes' driving, they reached a police station. There, they said they were arresting him for 'illegal entry'. Did he have a lawyer? When Sarva said no, they made a few calls. In an hour, a female lawyer and a male interpreter arrived. Through the interpreter, the woman asked him about his journey there and took rapid notes. 'Don't say anything,' she finally said, almost echoing Kannan. 'Whatever you say now or in court could be used against you later, so just say "no comment" to everything.' Another phrase that meant more than it seemed to. Sarva memorised it.

That night, he was kept in a cell in the police station. He fell asleep wondering where Bharati might be.

The next morning the police took him to a court. As they clapped handcuffs on his wrists, Sarva's heart raced. He stood in front of the judge, and the interpreter said he was being tried for crossing the UK border without the requisite travel documents. The judge ordered an immediate deportation, but his lawyer argued that he deserved better.

Sarva watched her struggle to convey his situation properly: the impossibility of his return, the certain death that awaited him in Sri Lanka. He was sure he could be more convincing himself. Her inability was going to get him killed. So despite the lawyer's clear instructions not to talk, he spoke up.

'Please, judge,' he said, folding his hands, emphasising each word. 'I can't go Sri Lanka. Full trouble for me. Please, don't send me back.' He wanted the judge to see his desperation.

The lawyer used the opportunity to quickly add that Sarva's was a case of genuine persecution. She quoted from the UN Refugee Convention, to which the UK was a signatory and which compelled its agents to shelter people facing political persecution abroad, and which put Sarva's safety and freedom above the immigration laws he had broken.

The judge took note and sentenced Sarva to two months in prison. Not understanding what that meant, Sarva resumed begging to be let off.

The woman sitting below the judge explained, 'You have to do it so that the asylum process can start.' From the lawyer's exuberant handshake outside court, he gleaned that they had won. He would not be deported.

The police took him back to the station and gave him lunch—a box of fish and chips. As his tongue searched for any taste other than oil and salt, Sarva marvelled at how just twenty-four hours had changed the course of four tormented years. Perhaps the catalyst was the new country, or maybe his luck had turned. It was incredible that this government would actually consider letting him stay to keep him safe. He was not a citizen or voter, not educated or affluent. He felt like a liability, but law or morality seemed to have conspired to let people like him sneak into this world. What gall he had leaving Colombo, expecting countries he knew nothing about to just take him in because he arrived at their gates. He was better off than Trishanku, in that sense, because he was not turned away; he was allowed into the heaven he sought. He felt grateful for the unspiced fish and the absence of malice.

That evening, as he sat with two large white men in a cell at the East Acton prison, Sarva's whole being was soaring, as if at the end of a crazy circuitous run. This was jail, too, but it felt like a five-star hotel. It had bathrooms instead of pee spots. His cell had a thin mattress for him to sleep on. At mealtimes, he was asked if he had a preference: vegetarian or Halal or ordinary. He felt free, not imprisoned. The TID could do nothing to him here. No Siva could suspend his life in places that ate away his dreams. If he did everything right, Sarva might never see Sri Lanka again.

26.

November 2012

AS THE FAMILY gathered for dinner one cold November night, Mugil asked the boys to go wash their feet at the well. She gave them a few minutes, letting them splash around. When they didn't come inside after her third call, she went to the side door. The boys had settled around a full bucket, playing with paper boats. Tamizh's ship was from the Sea Tigers and Maran's was from the Sri Lankan Navy. They were shouting Shooo! Dish! Boom! Bam!—the noises of missiles attempting to drown the other's ship. Tamizh's T-shirt was already soaking wet.

Mugil told them they could play after dinner. As she turned around, Maran asked if she knew how the army would order a retreat in Sinhala. She shrugged.

'Okay, I'll ask my teacher tomorrow,' Maran said.

Mugil said it was unlikely the teacher would know.

'I will ask my new teacher,' he insisted. 'She will know.'

Mugil started to ask who this knowledgeable teacher was, but Maran ran to the kitchen with Tamizh, paying her no attention.

It slipped her mind until a few nights later, when she put the boys to bed. She asked Maran if he had found the word he was looking for. He hadn't. 'Anyway, what is so special about this new teacher?' she asked.

'I don't know,' he said sleepily. 'She is not like us.' It was only after Mugil spoke to Amuda's son, Maran's senior in school, that she discovered that the new teacher was one of the two recently recruited Sinhalese women. For the first time ever, Sinhala had been made compulsory in Tamil-language schools in the north. It was announced as part of the government's postwar commitment to trilingualism.

Schools in Sri Lanka had always been segregated by ethnicity—Sinhala, Tamil, Muslim. Universal free education meant that the population was over 90 per cent literate, but children grew up with little opportunity to interact with different communities. The best schools in the country were state-run, and a handful of these taught in English to multi-ethnic classes; in the rest, the language of instruction was exclusively Tamil or Sinhala. A small urban upper class—that cut across ethnic groups—spoke English, but the majority of Sri Lankans remained monolingual and did not share their formative years with people from other communities. Intimate relationships between people of different ethnic backgrounds were rare; it was common for a Sinhalese person never to have entered a Tamil or Muslim house for a home-cooked meal, and vice-versa. Inter-ethnic marriages were violently opposed and couples that defied the family diktat were often ostracised.

The only Sinhalese most Tamils met were policemen, soldiers or government officials, none of whom inspired much affection. After the Tigers forced the Muslims out of the north, these two Tamil-speaking communities drifted apart as well. As long as militancy existed, most Sinhalese never set foot in the Tamil-dominated north. Disastrously then, with rare exceptions, the only continuous interaction between different communities had been through conflict. Militants, the government and extremists of all types used this gulf between peoples to further fan hate and suspicion.

After 2009, the government created a Ministry for National Languages and Social Integration to undo this systemic ethnic polarisation. It mandated that all government officials be fluent in both Sinhala and Tamil, and also introduced native-language lessons in schools. In the policy's implementation, however, deep biases privileged Sinhala. Tamil schoolchildren in the north now had to study Sinhala but Tamil was not mandatory in Sinhala-language schools. Moreover, from what Amuda's son was saying, his Sinhalese teachers did not speak any Tamil at all. As a consequence, he was learning Sinhala poetry and stories by rote, but he could not string words together to make an original sentence.

As the boy ran off to his after-school class, Mugil sat on the threshold of Amuda's shop. 'What nonsense is this?' she said. She didn't understand why they could not hire bilingual Tamil or Muslim teachers. 'How will these teachers explain Sinhala to our children?'

'I'm just grateful our children didn't get the soldier teachers,' Amuda said. In schools in Mullaitivu and Kilinochchi, military personnel had been appointed as Sinhala teachers. They were known to take class in uniform and conduct 'leadership workshops' for the higher grades. The armed forces gave out scholarships, distributed books and stationery, organised field trips and sports meets. A military wing called the Civil Security Department had entirely taken over the administration of nursery schools in the Vanni. The change was unannounced, and many found out about it only when kindergarten teachers started receiving their wage slips from the Ministry of Defence. While people saw this as militarisation, and an attempt to exercise total control over the population, the Ministry of Defence claimed that these were philanthropic activities aimed at reconciliation and development.

When Amuda and Mugil were in school, the Tigers—the military of their time and region—visited their classrooms, too, spreading propaganda. Schools in the north, especially in the Vanni, had always been militarised. Now, the occupying force had changed from the LTTE to the Sri Lankan army. Much had changed, but nothing really had.

'Where did they get these Sinhalese women from?' Mugil asked.

'From one of the new colonies, must be.'

In the decades that the sisters had spent in the north, they had seen few non-Tamil households. The war had divided the island demographically. The last of the Sinhalese and Muslim families in the north had been driven out by the Tigers in the eighties and nineties respectively, and Tamils moved in droves to the north to escape persecution by the state or Sinhalese mobs. Mugil was thirty when the war ended, and having always lived in the north, she had never met or talked to a Sinhalese civilian.

Since late 2010, however, Amuda and Mugil, like most Tamils, had heard about poor Sinhalese families from the south settling in the northeast. They noticed little shops with Sinhala signs cropping up, women in Kandyan-style saris, the newly set-up Sinhala-language schools and now Sinhalese teachers in Tamil schools—small changes but significant ones because these were formerly unfamiliar sights.

The influx of outsiders had caused friction. Tamils returning from refugee camps found Sinhalese families on their land. Many of these Sinhalese settlements were fenced in and guarded by military personnel, perhaps to protect them from angry Tamil locals. People accused the government of inviting—even incentivising—southern families to relocate north and put a dent in the otherwise nearly homogeneous Tamil population. Defence Secretary Gotabaya Rajapaksa responded that the Sinhalese were moving of their own accord and asked why any area should be dominated by Tamils. If the country was to be truly united, he said, all citizens should be allowed to live in any part of the country. 'Do we stop Tamil people from living in Colombo?' he asked once.

Politicians from the Tamil National Alliance, the most prominent coalition of Tamil parties, however, countered that many more Sinhalese had now returned than had left, and that the Colombo analogy was disingenuous. Tamils there didn't get allotted land or houses from the state as the Sinhalese did in the north.

There was an avalanche of land disputes in the local courts. Some challenged the new Sinhalese takeover of Tamil land, but a majority of ownership claims were against the military. As the war wheeled to a finish in the summer of 2009, sixteen of the nineteen brigades of the Sri Lankan armed forces—more than 100,000 troops—were stationed in the north-east, mostly on the Jaffna peninsula. To accommodate them in high-security zones, land had been commandeered from Tamil civilians without consent, due process or compensation. Close to one-fifth of the Jaffna peninsula was now occupied by the armed forces, while the land claimants were sent to thorny forests or shabby refugee camps.

By mid-2012, thousands of Tamils were protesting this indiscriminate land grab. As the military expanded, Mugil, like thousands of others, found that she had no claim over her property. When some refugees were permitted to settle in uncontested parts of PTK, her family wondered if they, too, should try to recover their land. Mugil was against it—for a few months now, she had been thinking about the missed boat to India, wondering if staying had been her worst decision ever. She had made her peace with not going back to PTK; she did not know of a single case of a Tamil successfully claiming land back from the military. Amuda, too, said she had neither the resources nor the energy to start again. As the eldest in the family, Mother advised that they 'let it be'.

Divyan promptly disregarded their advice. He was tired of manual labour and had failed to find a driving job. Seeing other families apply for permission to cultivate their land, he wanted to follow suit. Prashant was the only one to support him. Mugil suspected that her brother meant to use their land as collateral for a loan. Prashant wanted to emigrate to Saudi Arabia with three of his friends on fake passports, and needed to pay the agent in advance before his planned departure in November 2012.

When they were alone, Mugil warned Divyan about Prashant's plans, but he wasn't worried. 'He can have any designs on the land he wants. We don't have to think about that,' he said. 'I just want to go back home.'

She asked him not to be nostalgic. 'PTK will not be the place we knew. You will not be able to bear it.'

'We can build it up slowly. It's not like we are strangers to hardship.'

Mugil reminded Divyan that they had bought the plot in 2005. 'What if the government says that it is not legitimate?'

Divyan twirled his hand in a 'what to do'.

'What if there is a Sinhalese family on our land? Or some army camp?'

'*Che che*, nothing like that will happen.'

It had happened to almost everyone they knew. A few of Mugil's acquaintances from near Nilaveli in the east had complained to the district officer that Sinhalese families had unlawfully occupied their land—in a village where Tamils were excluded. The officer said the new colony was legal. The divisional secretary had assigned plots of land for cultivation and residence to the Sinhalese families, following orders from the Eastern Province governor, a former military general. In Mannar in the west, too, when 285 Tamil families were displaced from Mullikulam village in 2008, navy officers had moved in, and subsequently their families. When the refugees protested this illegal takeover in 2009, a few were offered compensation and replacement homes elsewhere, but their access to the sea and to their fertile ancestral farms was lost.

'We're not special, you know,' Mugil told Divyan.

'Since when did you start giving up without even trying? Is it not worth trying?'

Mugil didn't reply. Her hopes were frayed, but she didn't want to dash his.

Divyan wrote to the village officers in both Point Pedro and PTK, giving the address of their plot of land. A couple of weeks later, at the Vavuniya revenue office, an official told him that no land documents remained for the area; the Tigers had burned all the records for the Mullaitivu district. The government had also issued a land circular ordering that land lost during the conflict would be used for security purposes and 'development activities'. As Mugil had feared, any purchase or sale made during the conflict was considered void and made 'under terrorist influence'. The officer said that if Divyan had any of his own government-certified records, perhaps some appeal could be made in court. Otherwise the land would be deemed unclaimed. The new records would say the owners were not traceable.

'But we're claiming it now!' Prashant shouted. 'How can you say there is no owner when we are standing in front of you?'

The officer said these were his instructions. Unless there was proof of ownership, the government would keep the land.

Divyan looked askance at the officer. Their family had left everything behind, including their documents, when they ran from place to place in the war zone. As the officer turned to the person waiting behind them in line, Prashant's frustration boiled over. He pounded the desk, shouting abuse at the Tamil official, calling him a lapdog of the president. Some other disgruntled petitioners in the queue joined in, venting their anger.

Divyan expected to be thrown out, but the officials paid little attention, looking as if their mouths were sewn shut. They were powerless against the will of the military and the regime. Prashant's was surely not the first tantrum they had seen. With no written record, Divyan was just one among hundreds of thousands who had been kicked off their own land. He was not special.

WHEN HE GOT home, Mugil did not ask Divyan how it went at the revenue office. Instead, the next day, she told him that Sangeeta had decided to move to India. Some days later, Mugil said she had contacted an uncle in Chennai in southern India and he had invited them to visit. A few weeks later, she said the uncle was ready to put their family up for a few months should they want to move there. If they wanted to stay in the government-run refugee camps for Sri Lankan Tamils in Tamil Nadu state, the uncle advised they go to Trichy, where the tents were kept in better shape.

Divyan was unresponsive to these hints, so Mugil finally asked him directly: did he want to leave Sri Lanka?

'Leave here?' Divyan asked. 'Permanently?'

She told him it had been a recurring thought ever since the military had taken over school administration. She wanted a different childhood for her sons, one that did not involve the normalisation of guns and armies. India, easily reached by boat and just half an hour's flight away, was the only foreign country they could afford to emigrate to. Divyan knew all this; they had talked about it under fire at the Mullivaikal lagoon. Their future was no more certain now, but at least the family was together, in one place. She wanted to revisit the idea.

'You're the one who didn't want to go last time,' Divyan said.

'Everything has changed,' she said. Couldn't he at least think about it?

They had only received their new Sri Lankan IDs the previous month, he pointed out.

'I don't feel connected to this anymore,' she replied, pointing to the ground. With the last patch of her beloved hometown snatched from her, she was living in someone else's house, in someone else's country.

Some nights later, when Maran and Tamizh were asleep in their parents' laps, Divyan said he was ready. 'We will have to borrow a lot of money somehow,' he said. But his face glowed. 'I have heard that the Srirangam temple near Trichy is beautiful.'

27.

November 2012

WHILE SARVA SERVED his jail time for entering the United Kingdom illegally, his immigration lawyer applied to the UK Border Agency on his behalf. Wheels turned to start his asylum process, and after two months and four days of incarceration, he was released.

He was driven to a refugee facility in Cardiff, Wales. When Sarva asked where that was, the van driver pointed to a picture of Princess Diana on his dashboard.

'Diana, do you know?'

Sarva nodded, he did.

'She was the Princess of Wales. I will show you the castle on the way.'

Sadly, the castle was behind an enormous stone wall, but the Cardiff Sarva saw through the van window intrigued him. The capital city of Wales was quaint and bustling with tourists and students. On signs outside pubs, offices and shops was the image of a red dragon standing on its hind limbs, clawing the air with its right front paw. If it held a sword, he thought, it would look uncannily like the Sri Lankan flag's golden lion, the symbol of Sinhalese pride. He stared at the street names—they had English lettering but he was unable to read them. 'What is that?' he asked, pointing to CAERDYDD.

'It's Welsh for Cardiff,' the driver explained. 'In Wales, the language is Welsh.'

'Wales is not England?'

'No!' The driver laughed. 'And don't you dare call a Welshman an Englishman!'

Sarva was impressed—he had assumed everyone in the UK spoke English. 'Then this place is like Jaffna in my country,' he told the driver. 'I am from Sri Lanka, but I speak Tamil, you know.' The driver, who worked for the agency, said he had driven hundreds of asylum seekers from a dozen countries, and he rarely met a Sri Lankan who was not Tamil.

The driver dropped Sarva off at Lynx House, a transitional shelter for asylum seekers. As he shouted 'Good luck!' and drove away, Sarva decided that when—if—he settled down in the UK, he would drive a taxi for a living. The roads in this country were silk.

The sheer number of refugees at Lynx House astounded Sarva. In jail, he had met thieves, burglars, chronic violators of traffic regulations, trespassers and other petty criminals. But here was a horde of the biggest rule breakers: men and women who had shed their citizenship to creep across the border of a developed nation. In every room, brown, black, white people sat: a country of outsiders, their eyes shining with immigrant hope. How many nations had given them reason to flee to this alien land? What were their wars? Whatever they had run from, here they could count on three meals a day at the canteen, TV programmes in the common area, health care at the nurse's station. Sarva had expected competition among the refugees, like hundreds of creatures converged around a shrinking watering hole. Instead, he felt camaraderie.

Sarva shared room 113 with four others. Prathipan, a diffident thirty-six-year-old plantation Tamil from Sri Lanka, was a handsome hypochondriac with a propensity for marathon naps. His sinuses were agitated by winter and summer alike, and the joke in their room was that Prathipan was born wearing his turtleneck sweater. He soon became Sarva's wingman and confidant.

His second roommate, a gaunt Pakistani farmer with endless legs, had two unpronounceable *q*s in his name; Sarva just called him Pakistani. He was in many ways Prathipan's opposite. He was never in the room, rarely wore more than a shirt and trousers even on the coldest of days, and resisted Sarva's boyish charm. They conversed in broken English, neither much bothered by their incomplete understanding of each other. There were two more refugees sharing the room—a gay student from Libya and a middle-aged Chinese man—but both were moved to another location before Sarva had been there two weeks. For days after they were gone, Sarva kept up the crude mockery of an imaginary character that was a combination of their former roommates: a gay Chinese man. It was this running joke that would eventually win Pakistani's affection.

During his twenty-eight days at Lynx House, Sarva befriended five other Pakistanis and a Sinhalese couple with a toddler. Sarva was surprised about the latter. Why would a Sinhalese man want to leave a nation that was tailor-made for him? In time, he found out: the Sinhalese husband was a vernacular journalist who had been threatened for writing pieces critical of the government. The last article had been on the demolition of mosques and churches by a new hard-line Sinhala Buddhist group called Bodu Bala Sena. As a devout Buddhist himself, he had written about his shame when Buddhist monks had attacked people of other faiths. The police had raided his house, and a few weeks later he had left Sri Lanka with his wife and child. Sarva liked the couple but he didn't bring up his own reasons for leaving.

The canteen was Sarva's classroom for learning about life in the UK: he could drink cold water but not hot water straight out of the taps. He learnt to chew with his mouth closed and eat dinner at six thirty in the evening, not nine. To fit in at the dining table, he tried to master cutlery. It was embarrassing when a European child smiled to see him slyly use his left index finger to nudge the last of his peas onto his spoon. Shoes were not taken off at the door and were even permitted on the sofa. He discovered the power of 'please', 'would you' and 'thank you'. Accompanied by a smile, these words worked like magic on the icy administrators of Lynx House. In his room, however, Sarva lived as he always had: barefoot, speaking loudly and sitting cross-legged on the floor. He missed home for its small freedoms.

Lynx House had strict rules, but it was nothing like prison; inmates could wander in the city as long as they returned by early evening. On his walks around Cardiff, Sarva would call his parents from a telephone booth. Amma had had another hernia operation and was in and out of hospitals. She was relieved that he sounded upbeat and assured him that she prayed for him every day. His father came to the phone, too, these days, asking him to describe the roads, buildings and people of England. He advised Sarva to polish up his spoken English. Before his father hung up, Amma would grab the phone to issue her stock instructions: eat well and don't call 'that girl'.

Sarva did call Malar. Her parents were urging her to meet eligible boys and choose a husband. He tried desperately to dissuade her from giving in to the pressure. He sang paeans to the good life in the UK and the luxuries of the developed world, such as furnished houses, automatic doors and microwavable meals. Men opened doors for women, and she could wear stylish clothes without worrying about what society might think. 'Imagine, you will be living in comfort here with me,' he would say. They couldn't speak long, so he took to plastering her Facebook wall with images of pink hearts, teddy bears and roses. He emailed her videos of love songs and pictures of himself in romantic poses. Prathipan said that love was Sarva's full-time job.

SARVA WAS SOON allocated independent accommodation in Swansea—with Pakistani and Prathipan, to his delight. They were to share the house till the agency reviewed their applications and called them for an interview. They were not permitted to accept paid work or leave town for more than five days at a time. Till their asylum application was reviewed, the National Asylum Support Service would pay their rent. Additionally, each received a cheque for £150 by mail every month, to be cashed at the post office. The arrangement sounded practically hedonistic to Sarva.

They moved in on 16 January 2013. Number 77 Prince of Wales Road was at the top of a street with an almost thirty-degree incline. It was supplied with a moody heater, a TV that never came on and sofas whose cushions held the imprint of the previous tenants. In the kitchen, the vent above the stove was broken and the carpet reeked of mould. The two-storey cottage was perhaps only a few decades old, but it had suffered severely from the coming and going of its temporary inhabitants.

There were two great marvels in the house, however: glorious hot running water in the bathrooms and a separate room for every man. Sarva picked the single room on the ground floor, Prathipan the triangular one on the landing, and Pakistani the attic. Two Eritreans already occupied the master bedroom. One of them, a scraggly young man with a bouncy walk and goofy grin, introduced himself as Takloum. The other, whose name Sarva didn't catch, became The Other Takloum.

Most of the houses in the vicinity were rented to the UK Border Agency for refugee occupancy, and the only remaining locals were working-class. The street was clean but bore tell-tale signs of neglect. The dustbins on the pavement bulged with overstuffed garbage bags, and the odd beer can rattled about. Mattresses, TVs and patio tables discarded on the pavement vanished in minutes. The street was bookended by a small car park and an abandoned cinema. The house was a fifteen-minute walk from the bus station and a ten-minute bus ride from the community centre for asylum seekers. Most grocery shops, phone booths, video arcades and hair salons in the area were run by immigrants. In this refugee cocoon, Sarva was not expected to speak English or to understand the currency. If he was lost, someone brown would appear on the street and help him out. He disappeared into the neighbourhood's heterogeneity.

Before he left Lynx House, the Sinhalese couple had given Sarva the numbers of other Sri Lankans who had been sent to Swansea. After spending the first week scrubbing his house and familiarising himself with the town, Sarva called a young Tamil family that he knew lived nearby. They had moved to Swansea a few weeks earlier. Bagi Annan welcomed Sarva to the town and invited him to come over for lunch that very day, if he had the time. 'I'll tell my wife to make extra,' he said. 'It must have been a long time since you ate our food.' It had been two years.

After shopping for everything from soap, bed sheets and towels to kitchen basics with their first benefit cheques of £90 each, Sarva, Prathipan and Pakistani walked to Bagi Annan's house. His wife, Kajini, opened the door and her jaw dropped. 'Oh,' she said. It was clear she had expected only one guest. 'Which one of you is Sarva?'

The lunch of sweet-and-sour fried brinjal and chicken biryani was the beginning of a friendship that became Sarva's lifeline over the next few months, as he learnt to live without the certainty of sunlight. Kajini and Bagi Annan were asylum seekers, too, with the same limited means, but they opened their doors to him, soothing his restless spirit with their calm domesticity. They were from the Vanni, and their son, Niru, now four years old, had been delivered in the thick of war in a bunker half-filled with muddy water. Perhaps it was the circumstances of his birth, his age, or his resemblance to Sarva's own nephew, but the doe-eyed boy brought Sarva the kind of solace even his mother's voice no longer provided. Niru reciprocated, singling Sarva out as his favourite uncle, imitating his guffaw and calling him over when he wanted to play horse or tell him a secret. Sarva told Kajini she was the sister he had almost had. He occasionally cooked for her, in gratitude for all the meals she invited him to. She presented him with a picture of Lord Shiva and Parvati, which he hung in his room next to his Shiva calendar.

Once a week, when they had to sign in at the community office, they staged a relay. The unlimited day ticket on the bus cost £5, and after Bagi Annan and Kajini had used it, they called Sarva to come to the bus stand, where they handed him the travel card. When he returned, he gave it to Prathipan, and he in turn shared it with Pakistani. To make the most of the day ticket, all errands in the city—visits to the post office, refugee council or butcher—would be scheduled on the same day. The community centre had recommended a local physician who worked with immigrants, and Sarva spent an hour at the clinic every week receiving physiotherapy for his feet and back.

The group lived like intertwined creepers, awaiting the same fate, though no one shared his story with the others. Bagi Annan and Prathipan knew from Sarva's injuries that he had suffered some form of physical abuse, but they never knew the details. Bagi Annan and Kajini did not describe what they had endured in the war or how they had escaped the Manik Farm camp and escaped to the UK. Prathipan had an iPad that he had bought when he was a student at an obscure university in England, but he did not explain why he had overstayed his student visa.

Lynx House abounded with examples of refugees stealing scenes from another person's history, refining and practising it for the asylum interview. They had all heard the cautionary tale of two Iranian roommates who were best friends and had shared their stories with each other. The one who was interviewed first by the UK agency had told his friend's story as his own. When it was the other man's turn, he was accused of lying and denied a visa. It was only when he challenged the ruling in the courts that, a year later, the decision was reversed. Everyone wanted a visa, Sarva's group agreed, and people would not hesitate to spice up their history with someone else's horrific experience. It was best to be careful.

Sarva and his friends spent most of their time in supermarkets, reading price labels, prowling for new discounts and offers, such as a jar of mayonnaise with every bottle of ketchup or a two-for-one offer on packets of rice. Sarva knew that Poundland was where he could get the most enormous bottle of shampoo or body lotion for only a pound. Tesco had the spicy chillies and pungent red onions essential to his Sri Lankan curries. The chicken was fleshier at the local Arab shop than at the big stores. Basmati rice and vegetables were cheaper at Lidl and the 99 pence store had the best deals on cheap sweets and chocolate, of which Sarva ate fistfuls when he was hungry. The housemates shopped together like a family. Their purchases differed according to culture and dietary habits, but in a matter of weeks everyone settled into an even pattern determined solely by the £5 daily allowance from the NASS.

Sarva had a phone now and called home daily. He saved small amounts from his meagre dole and sent them to Malar so she could pay her phone and Internet bills. Their conversations these days always degenerated into a fight, broken only by a heavy silence or tears. A prospective husband had visited Malar at her house. 'I couldn't help it, Mummy just invited him,' she said.

'Okay, so why did you have to serve him tea and snacks?' he had demanded. She explained that she couldn't insult her parents in front of guests. She assured him she would love no one else as much, that he was her soulmate.

'It's not all that,' he said. 'You are tired of waiting for me.' In his angst, he was rude about her family. She hung up. They did not speak for weeks after that.

To overcome his insomnia and impending failure in love, Sarva drank cheap readymade cocktails ('It's only juice,' he told Kajini) with Prathipan till he passed out on his bed around dawn. He would wake at noon, drink a mug of milk, and check the mail to see if he had a date for his interview. He whiled away the rest of his time going for walks, thinking about Malar or visiting Niru. Days and nights blurred together. Finally, one snow-lashed February morning, he received a letter calling him to an interview on 11 March.

HIS BODY BUZZED, his back throbbed, his sleeplessness worsened. The interview was a month away, but Sarva was tense with anticipation. His lawyer was overjoyed. 'I don't want to get your hopes up,' she said on the phone. 'But an early interview is usually good news.'

There was a party at no. 77. Prathipan invited three Sri Lankan Tamil women from the neighbourhood, Kajini brought her sister, brother-in-law and their children visiting from Luton, and Bagi Annan supplied soft drinks (there would be no alcohol in front of the women). As the guests arrived at midday, filling the kitchen and living room, Sarva started on his elaborate version of *koli kozhambu* and *elumbu rasam*, chicken curry and bones soup. He delegated the onion chopping, garlic smashing and tamarind squeezing to the other men and he cleaned the large bird. Niru darted around the house playing train with his cousins. Kajini teased that Sarva's idea of good food was copious amounts of oil, cream and dried fruit. The women itched to take over—'Turn the heat down,' 'Cut the tomatoes finer,' 'Put the lid on'—but the men banished them from the kitchen.

When he finally served lunch at five o'clock, the famished guests attacked the soggy potatoes and spicy chicken with gusto.

The housemates joined them. 'Sarva, my brother! Asylum for you!' Takloum toasted with a glass of Pepsi. Sarva widened his eyes and shook his head, dramatically mouthing, 'No! Ssh!'

By dusk, the men had shut themselves in a room with a bottle of brandy. The women wished Sarva luck and left. Kajini hung back at the door. 'There were twelve of us here today,' she said. 'Some have been in the UK for years, but only *you* got an interview. I am praying every day. God will take your side.' She asked a sleepy Niru to give Sarva *maama* a hug and kiss.

'*Akka*, it will happen for you also soon,' he said, guiltily.

'I sure hope so,' Kajini sighed.

Sarva had downplayed it all day, but he knew that for everyone he had fed, an interview was nothing short of a miracle. He didn't want to rub it in their faces. He had been edgy about the evil eye, about envy corroding his good fortune. He had no experience of being the lucky one in the room.

WHEN HE HAD a moment alone some weeks later, Sarva called Malar and quickly hung up. A missed call of two rings meant 'Call me back when you can.' One ring meant 'Call me now!'

'?' she texted. This broke protocol, but it was the first time since their fight that she had responded at all. Through her silence, he had drunk himself silly, sobbing in the bathtub for hours, wondering if God had knowingly thwarted his suicide plans with the interview letter, blaming his mother for the strain on his affair, cursing President Rajapaksa for making it impossible for Sarva to even visit Malar in Sri Lanka. With one text from her, hope was restored.

'Have interview in two weeks,' he texted back, then chased it with an 'I love you soooo much.'

After about three hours, during which he had imagined their entire life together—the wedding, the happy family and children, economic success—she called. 'Hello?' she whispered.

'Mummy is near you?' he asked, always his first concern and annoyance.

'No, she has gone to the neighbour's but she could return any moment.'

'I got my interview letter!' he squealed. It was thrilling to say it aloud, with the appropriate high pitch of achievement. He had reserved the excitement only for Amma and a handful of friends.

Malar did not reply.

'Hello? Mummy has already come back?!'

'No,' she said, and went quiet again. Sarva wanted to fling his phone at the wall.

'Okay,' she said finally. 'I will pray for you, like I do every day.'

'Thank you. At least you still care for me,' he snapped, unable to help himself.

He heard her sigh in exasperation. 'Please, Sarva,' she said, switching to English, as she did when she wanted to be romantic. 'You are in my heart always.'

'Then why are we apart?' Sarva pleaded. 'Talk to me. I will get the visa, I'm 90 per cent sure! Tell your parents you will come to the UK, you will have a home with me.'

Malar said she could not come, could not wait, her parents didn't like him, she could not disobey them, but her love had been true.

'After everything I went through, I was done in by love! I'll tell the interviewers that!' Sarva laughed bitterly. 'I don't like to point it out, but I sent you money, Malar … We had a plan …'

'Mummy is coming,' she said hurriedly and hung up.

So that was how it was going to be. When the interview letter arrived, Sarva's first thought had been that he would tell the interviewer he was engaged and intended to bring his fiancée from Sri Lanka to the UK. He had heard that the agency always asked about family back home, and he had planned on proudly telling them about Malar, showing them her picture. He even had a letter from Father R. attesting to his having seen them exchange rings in Hatton. But that plan was trash, she was trash—all promises and all betrayal. Sarva tried not to give his mother credit for her 'bad feeling about this girl'.

EVERY DAY, SARVA lay on his bed, going over imaginary situations in which he found the words to make Malar change her mind. Or other scenarios in which he'd never met her and was single, a wild bull, free to be with a different woman every day. Once, when Sarva ranted about how he did not care that Malar had betrayed him and how he would never fall for feminine wiles again, Prathipan asked him if he knew what he was going to say at the interview.

'What is there to say?' Sarva said. 'And is there a point in all of this?'

Prathipan suggested that he meet Giri Anna, an asylum consultant. Giri Anna had advised hundreds of Tamil asylum seekers for close to a decade, vetting their stories of persecution for gaps, adding or refining believable elements for those whose applications he considered weak. This elderly man had arrived in the UK as an asylum seeker himself in the early eighties, fleeing the riots in Colombo. Now, he ran six grocery shops and two hotels in London.

A few days later, Sarva met Giri Anna at his house just outside Swansea. Sarva suspected that Giri Anna might have helped the Tigers smuggle men abroad—rarely did a penniless, uneducated Sri Lankan Tamil migrant become so wealthy without cooperating with the LTTE—but he did not ask.

Giri Anna knew that interviewers watched like a hawk for inconsistencies, suspicious documents, and lies. Consultants like him helped applicants tell their experiences coherently, sharpening the relevant bits and cutting the flab. They encouraged them to exaggerate or blur details as required. A woman who had lived in five villages in Jaffna and the Vanni, for instance, would be advised to focus on the Vanni days. The fear of kidnapping would be revised to look like a narrow escape from an actual attempt. The state oppression of the Tamils was real, but as thousands sought asylum in the UK, consultants helped enhance individual experiences to improve the odds. They filled gaps, but left just enough of the rough edges for the story to seem convincing. 'Only a lie sounds perfect,' Giri Anna said. 'The truth is always a little vague.'

Most asylum seekers thought they had to convince the interviewer they were victims, he said. They tended to focus on their horrific past experiences. But in countries like Sri Lanka, where the war had ended, interviewers expected testimony about recent atrocities and the threat of future attacks. So Giri Anna advised a student refugee to elaborate on his friends' disappearances—to demonstrate the grounds for his fear of deportation. He asked a harassed Tamil journalist to include in his statement unrelated incidents of his wife's sexual harassment at a police station.

Sarva was told to list the number of times the police had harassed his mother after he had left Sri Lanka. While all asylum claimants had fled state violence, a visa was granted only to those who were at risk on their return.

Giri Anna was sure the agency knew that former Tigers were the most obvious targets of the Sri Lankan government today. He claimed that after the end of the war, conscripts, child soldiers and rehabilitated former combatants had become better candidates for asylum in the UK than civilians. The agency would shun those who had been convicted of human rights abuses or had occupied leadership positions where they might have been involved in war crimes, he said, but it recognised that in an ethnic war of three decades, there were many helpless pawns.

After listening to Sarva and looking at his documents, Giri Anna insisted that at the interview, he talk about his LTTE days. 'You have a much greater chance with your truth,' he said. 'They won't send you back knowing you will get killed within five minutes.' Staggering through these fine distinctions between truth and falsehood, Sarva decided to tell all.

28.

November 2012

MUGIL SHOULD HAVE known that thoughts about leaving were contagious. As soon as Divyan agreed to emigrate to India, Amuda decided to join them, a prospect that, to her own surprise, gladdened Mugil. Their children had grown to be closer than their mothers had been as siblings, and separating them would have been difficult. But a larger party meant greater expense and more elaborate plans for departure. They needed to raise 100,000 rupees for each family.

They could borrow what they needed from a moneylender. Mugil was acquainted with some people in Jaffna and Point Pedro who helped former combatants through remittances from the Tamil diaspora that once supported the Tigers. The whole transaction would be informal, just like during the war. But Mugil and Divyan discussed it, and decided to avoid any former Tiger associates. It was better to let those old relationships lapse.

They ploughed through their possessions for anything of value. Mugil had her bicycle, furniture and steel utensils; Amuda had her fridge and house. All of it was put up for sale. For the first time since the end of the war they were looking for permanent solutions to their problems.

After his disappointment with the land records, Prashant, too, came up with a way to leave the country. He would work on a ship somewhere, for which he would not need a fake passport; his naval science certificate helped him get the requisite travel document for working at sea. He would have to get to Saudi Arabia at his own expense and, once there, he could work without pay for a year at the Yanbu port, gradually reimbursing the agent who got him the job. The agent had taken Muslim men to the Gulf this way for years. Ever since hard-line Sinhala Buddhist mobs started demolishing mosques and attacking Muslim-run shops and malls, many more young Muslims had been looking for work abroad. Prashant would soon depart with a group of forty men.

Mugil thought this a dangerous plan, especially since the agent would keep Prashant's travel documents, but her brother was not one to worry. After a lot of drama and tears, he got Mother to sell her gold wedding chain for enough money to buy him a ticket to Jeddah. With that, his emigration plans became firm.

Only Mother would be left behind. There was no question of her going with Prashant, and she hated the idea of India. She had visited South India briefly when Father worked in a quarry there and had found it unbearably filthy. There were more than 100,000 Sri Lankan Tamils in India, living in more than a hundred camps across the southern state of Tamil Nadu, including special high-surveillance camps for those considered security threats. Mother had heard grim stories about the dirty refugee tents, the infamously brutal and corrupt Q Branch anti-terrorism police, the strict evening curfew, and the lifelong requirement for a residence permit to be stamped every six months. She believed India was not hospitable to Sri Lankans anymore. The strain of finding a respectable job and a decent house to rent would be too much at her age.

She didn't dissuade her daughters, though. They would be better off leaving before they got embroiled in some mess here; India would let Mugil and Amuda breathe easier. Mother's elderly cousin was setting up a house in Patthampattaram in PTK, and the old women would be fine together, she said.

Mugil fought every day to change her mother's mind—how could she stay behind alone? Did she not realise that once her family left Sri Lankan shores, there was no coming back? She would never be able to see her grandchildren again. If Mother became ill, they would not be able to come to her. And, god forbid, if she died alone, who would visit her grave? At that point, Mother shut Mugil up by saying there would be no point visiting if she were already dead. 'You stubborn old goat!' Mugil shouted. 'Your brain has shrunk with age, you are making dumb decisions!'

In any case, there was their estranged sister in Mannar, Mother said. 'She'll at least come to see me when I'm dead.'

'Don't count on it,' Amuda replied.

Eventually the sisters let it go. Perhaps Mother wanted to die in the same country as Father. Maybe she wanted to spend her last days in the Vanni. Or maybe she was just tired of taking care of them.

On 24 November, Mother cooked the last elaborate meal she would make in a long time. It was a seafood extravaganza: crab prepared three ways, fish fried and curried, shrimp steamed with drumsticks, and sprat chutney. She said it was because Prashant was leaving for a desert, 'and who knows when he will taste fish next'. To an explosion of laughter from the others, Prashant told her that Saudi Arabia was surrounded by seas and that he would be working on a ship. Mother was sheepish, but the meal was perfect.

The children had been told about their uncle leaving forever. The younger ones made drawings for him; Maran drew a ship, Tamizh a smiley face, Kalai an infinite spiral. Amuda's oldest gave him a stiff hug.

When the day came, Prashant packed a single bag and left the house with Divyan. The family stood at the gate, waving and crying, but Prashant looked excited.

Divyan accompanied him and two of his friends to Colombo, from where the three would take a flight to Jeddah. A travel agent in Wellawatte found them affordable tickets for 30 November, in five days' time.

Prashant insisted that Divyan return to Point Pedro instead of wasting his time in Colombo. When Divyan said his goodbyes and took a bus back, he thought about how desperately the family had wanted to stay together during the war and when he and Prashant were in detention. The reunion had been brief, and somehow this final parting seemed preordained.

DIVYAN WAS OUT working on a bridge and Mugil was in the kitchen when Prashant called her mobile phone in the early evening of 1 December. When she saw the missed call half an hour later, she tried to call him back, but her prepaid phone card didn't have enough credits for the call to go through. She ran to Amuda's house and used her phone, but there was no answer. The sisters were worried sick; Prashant had not answered his phone since Divyan had left him in Colombo. He should have boarded the flight to Jeddah on 30 November. How was he calling from his phone a day later?

Mugil bought more talktime the next day and called and called. Prashant's phone was always switched off.

Three days later, around dusk, two plainclothes policemen walked into Mugil's house. They went straight into her living room and called her name. Startled, she ran in from the side yard. When she saw them, the crew cuts, the hard eyes, the large forearms crossed in front of their chests, she knew what it was about. It was happening to her family now.

They said they were from the TID. The local policeman accompanying them explained that Prashant had been arrested under terrorism laws. He and two others had drawn an LTTE flag on a red cloth and hoisted it up a flagpole.

Mugil wasn't able to understand whether Prashant had done this in Valvettithurai before he left or in Colombo the day after he got there. Of course things were unravelling now, when they had found a way out. It had to be her brother who put a spanner in the works. She kicked herself for letting Prashant out of her sight on 26 November, Martyrs' Day. She had thought his Saudi plans would restrain him.

She asked where he was, if she could see him.

'Don't look for him, we have him,' they said. They warned her not to leave the house for the next few days.

After the TID left, Mugil fished Prashant's diaries out of the kitchen cupboard and found the drawings Maran had saved from their secret memorial in May. She burned them in the backyard in a pile of dried leaves.

The next afternoon, the TID officials came again. They searched the house and, finding nothing, interrogated Mugil about Prashant. She told them they perhaps knew more than she did, that her brother had been in the LTTE once but had already served time in the rehabilitation camp. When she told them he was even let out early for good behaviour, they chuckled.

They asked for Divyan, who was out working. They went to Mother's house, posing to Amuda the same questions they had asked Mugil. Both were asked if they had ever been in the LTTE. Both said they hadn't.

Divyan went to the Valvettithurai police station the next day to be questioned. The police asked him for the details that had come to define him now—his LTTE days, when he surrendered, how long he was in the rehabilitation facility. He showed them a copy of his release certificate. They reminded him that he had better not leave town.

Divyan was furious with Prashant, who knew how keenly the police watched for signs of militant dissent. He knew that Prashant's sentiments were mere nostalgia, but the authorities wouldn't make that distinction.

The state that came down hard on former combatants and those still obsessed with the Tigers did not invest time or money in rehabilitation and counselling in the detention camps. It had wasted opportunities to win the trust of the Tamils. Instead, it criminalised any recollection of the past. Memorials and commemorations were classified as acts of terrorism, warranting detention without bail. For the past few years, the government had been raising the bogey of an LTTE resurgence, with rarely any evidence to justify the mass detentions and curfews that followed. President Rajapaksa's regime needed an excuse to exert more control, curb more freedoms and claim more power, and what better way to do that than the tried and tested paranoid fear of the militants' regrouping? Severely oppressed, some Tamils did reminisce about the LTTE. But few, Prashant included, had the will, capacity or need for another conflict. The state, however, just didn't want to acknowledge this.

The interrogations, house searches and threats then were to be expected. Mugil and Divyan knew the drill and submitted meekly to it. By now, they knew not to ask questions. There would be no answers, only repercussions.

Five days on, a different set of TID officers parked their pick-up van near Mother's house. They summoned Mugil. Divyan, too, was at home, but guessing what would happen today, he did not accompany her. His presence would only exacerbate the situation.

As Mugil left for Mother's house, Maran ran after her. Divyan did not stop him; a child might soften the TID's heart.

When Mugil reached Mother's gate, she noticed Prashant sitting inside the van. The door was only half open, but she saw the outline of his face and the edge of his rubber slippers. His handcuffs glinted in the dark. One of the TID officers asked Amuda to pack a bag with a few of Prashant's clothes. Turning to Mugil, he said her brother had admitted to keeping five brushes and red paint in the backyard of Mother's house. Could she get them? They were what he had used to paint the LTTE flag.

When she returned from the backyard, Mugil saw one of the officers speaking to Maran. 'Yes, Chitthappa used to draw the flag,' her son was saying. He then looked inside the van. 'It is wrong, no, Chitthappa?'

The officers took the brushes and the bag of clothes and drove away. Maran clambered on to Mugil's hip and started to cry.

Mother sat down on the threshold. 'The ground is swallowing us up,' she said.

ᘓ

FOR A WEEK after the incident with the van, there was no word from the police. It was a confusing, sleepless time. Accusations ricocheted between the family members; the fragile thread of optimism that had united them snapped. Mother pulled her hair out and threw a fit about being left with nothing, that her children did not give her a moment's peace, that she would rather take a whole bottle of sleeping pills than remain in this hell anymore. She left for her cousin's house in the Vanni.

On 17 December 2012, fifteen minutes before midnight, there was a knock on the door. Mugil opened it. Divyan woke to the TID officer's loud voice telling Mugil, 'Come with us!' When Mugil stepped outside, Tamizh leapt into her arms screaming. Divyan pleaded that there were children at home. Could they please spare her? She had done nothing wrong. Mugil's eyes were on the ground, her shoulders drooping; she looked resigned. She waved sadly at her sons. '*Amma* will come back soon, okay. Be good boys when *amma* is not there,' she said.

'We will bring her back tomorrow,' an officer promised politely, as if it were the truth.

At one o'clock the next afternoon, two officers came to the house. They gave Divyan a letter that said Mugil was being detained under PTA, the anti-terrorism law. During his interrogation, they said, Prashant had revealed that Mugil had served with the Tigers. 'She was a child then,' Divyan wanted to say. 'What has she done now? Does four years of being a good citizen mean nothing?' he wanted to ask. 'How can you trust a man who will fly an LTTE flag?'

But he couldn't. The words would not form in his mouth; he seemed to have forgotten how to argue. Instead he begged. 'Please, can I see her? Please, don't do anything to her, she has small children …'

Unmoved, the officers handed Mugil's mobile phone to him. 'She won't be needing that anymore.'

After they left, Divyan dropped off Maran with Amuda and took a bus to the Valvettithurai police station with Tamizh. Every officer there asked him for his details repeatedly, going back to his youth, to his Vanni days, to his time in detention. At any moment, he expected them to accuse him of drawing an Eelam flag or singing a Tiger song, or none of that but throwing handcuffs on him regardless.

He and Mugil had switched lives. He spent that night and all of the next day outside the police station, on a bench with three women waiting to see their husbands. Tamizh did not demand food or water. A TID officer told Divyan he was wasting his time. 'Go bring some clothes for her to take to Colombo,' he said.

When Divyan returned with the bag in the evening, Mugil was already in a van that stood in the parking lot. She was handcuffed and bent over with exhaustion.

Divyan called her name almost at the same time as Tamizh screamed, '*Amma*!'

She looked up and shuffled toward them on the seat. She beckoned to Tamizh to come, awkwardly extending her handcuffed hands. Tamizh and Divyan started running towards her.

Surprised, the van driver quickly slid the door shut, forcing Mugil to pull her hands in. The windows were tinted and she disappeared from view.

'Go inside, ask inside! Go, go!' the driver told Divyan, blocking him from the door with one hand and pushing him towards the police station with the other.

In the station, the TID officer told Divyan he could see Mugil in a couple of weeks, but only in the TID head office in Colombo. 'I'm sure you know where it is,' he smirked.

29.

March 2013

THE DAY OF the asylum interview was one of the windiest Sarva had seen in Cardiff. On the radio, the disc jockeys were astonished at the raging winds and complained about the bitter cold of minus one degree Celsius. On the twenty-five-minute walk from the train station to the UK Border Agency office, his cheap rubber-soled shoes slithered on the ice. His jacket billowed and wrenched him backwards, an uncooperative sail. Speeding snowflakes felt like pinpricks on his face. Pedestrians on the other side of the road were almost running, propelled by the wind; one young woman was walking backwards to stay stable. Seagulls swooped down from the tops of multi-storied buildings, playing, letting their wings catch the chilly gusts. Sarva took his jacket off to regain his balance, folded his hands in front of him, bent his head and trudged ahead like a bull.

The interview was scheduled for nine that morning, and Sarva arrived at the glass and red-brick building half an hour early. He waited in the lobby with other tense applicants. One of them was shivering in the cold; another rocked back and forth. Everyone avoided eye contact. Sarva had taken the five-thirty train from Swansea. He had not had breakfast or coffee. No one offered him any here. Mobile phones had to be left at home, so Sarva picked up the nearest newspaper, *The Western Mail*, 'the national newspaper of Wales'. A quarter of the front page was plastered with an advertisement for English-language classes. He kept it aside and, like the others, stared absently at walls adorned with posters about immigration. He tried to divert his attention to a mental image of Pullaiyar, the god of wish fulfilment. He wished that, for just this one day, his nerves would not hamper his speech. 'Bless my tongue, Pullaiyar! Bless it, bless it, bless it!' he chanted. Another part of his mind ran through his time in Latin America as if on fast-forward. What if they asked where he had been before coming to the UK, why he didn't come here directly? What if they wanted a list of the places he had passed through? He was afraid that all his illegal border crossing would count as a black mark against him. What if they cared more about his breaking the law than his problems in Sri Lanka?

By nine thirty, Sarva had been to the water cooler in the corner five times. He had to pee but didn't dare go to the men's room, in case the interviewer came out to call him when he was inside.

At nine forty, a white middle-aged man in a suit walked into the lobby and gestured for Sarva to follow him. Sarva slapped his thighs, hopped up and scurried after.

In the clean white office, the interviewer pointed Sarva to a chair beside a table. He himself sat to Sarva's right and pulled his chair in. 'Does he have to be so unsmiling,' Sarva thought. They had spoken a few days earlier on the phone to cross-check documents, and he knew he would be hearing a brusque tone. The craggy-faced interviewer pointed to a computer monitor where a streaming video showed a young brown man who introduced himself in Tamil as the interpreter. The agency had accommodated Sarva's requests for both the interviewer and interpreter to be male and for the proceedings to be recorded.

First, the interviewer collected the documents Sarva had brought, asking about their relevance and for the notarised English translations. Sarva had to remind himself to wait for the interpretation before he answered, even when he partly understood the interviewer. The Eritreans had advised him to stick to his mother tongue and not shift between languages. 'However okay you think your English is, you might be saying something wrong, and he will put that on record, and later you'll have problems.' Sarva tried to follow Takloum's wise advice.

When all twenty-eight documents had been discussed and verified, the interviewer called a break. Once he was gone, Sarva sat back in his chair. It had gone without incident so far; the documents were the easy part. His palms were sweating and his mouth was dry. He had to be on his toes but was worried he would let himself down. He sipped from the glass of water in front of him. In the clinical whiteness of the room, he felt as if he were about to undergo exploratory surgery.

The interviewer returned after twenty-five minutes. 'Happy to continue?' he asked. The interpreter on the monitor translated this into Tamil. 'Yes,' Sarva replied. He smiled politely and wondered if that was inappropriate.

'I have been sent a witness statement by your solicitor,' the interviewer said, showing it to Sarva. 'Do you recognise this?'

'Yes.' His lawyer from Elder Rahimi Associates had recorded a statement with his account of the detention, trial, imprisonment, emigration and arrival in the UK, in chronological order.

As the interpreter started to translate the next question, they were disconnected. When they retrieved the connection, the video went down. From then on, the interpreter was just a voice. He repeated the question: 'Does this witness statement contain all of the reasons why you are claiming asylum?'

'Yes.'

'I notice that you mention an older brother. Where is he currently?'

'He's in Colombo now.'

'Does he work in Colombo?'

'Yes.'

'Has he had any difficulties with the authorities?'

'Yes. He had a problem when I was in jail. He was abducted and beaten. He sold his travel shop and gave that money to his abductors.'

'When was he abducted and released?'

'I don't remember the exact date. I think after 2008.'

'Why was he abducted?'

'Because I was involved in the LTTE, he was abducted by the TID. But they took his money, so it may have been partly for extortion that they abducted him.'

'Who abducted him?'

'Probably the government authorities.'

'Do you know this for sure?'

'I think … because they questioned my brother about me, where I was. Only government authorities knew that.'

'Has he had any further trouble with the government?'

'I don't think so. Not to my knowledge.' Sarva knew part of the assessment would be to check if his family was still being harassed in Sri Lanka, but he was irritated at having to speak about his brother. Deva had backed off from helping Sarva or his mother, and it was difficult to show concern for him now. He was relieved when the interviewer got off the subject.

'Okay. You joined the LTTE in 2003, correct?'

'In 2002,' Sarva corrected him.

'Do you remember the date?'

'May 2002.'

'Are you sure it was 2002?'

Sarva was dead sure until a few seconds ago, but now he felt doubtful. 'I think 2002. But I forget dates these days.'

The interviewer tried another tack. 'What year did Sujeevan steal your stock from your shop?'

'2002.'

'What year did you go to the Vanni to retrieve it?'

'2002.'

'Your witness statement says it is 2003. Is this a mistake?'

'I can tell you it was 2002. I may have given 2003 wrongly to the lawyer. When we spoke, I was in tension because of my problems. That may be why I gave the wrong date.' The interviewer's face was unreadable. Sarva had done dozens of interviews since his detention—the violent kind, the sympathetic, investigative, superficial, cynical kind—but this was by far the most dispassionate.

'Why did you join the LTTE?'

'I was forced to join them,' Sarva said.

'Your statement at paragraph thirteen says that you were quite taken with LTTE ideas. It makes no mention of your being forced to join. Can you clarify?'

'Initially they took me by force. But because they gave me some lectures on their ideology, I was attracted to that. After they gave me the lectures, they took me for training.'

'Then how were you forced to join the LTTE?'

'They asked me to either get the training or work for no pay on their farm as punishment.'

The interviewer took notes. Sarva knew he had given muddled responses—he had not sounded believable. He was not lying anymore, but the reality of his two years in the LTTE was not black and white, not easily compartmentalised as voluntary or forced.

'You were trained in the use of weapons, is that correct?'

Sarva said yes.

'Which weapons?'

'Initially the AK-47, and different AK families. And also physical training and working as a sentry, checking people. We also had lessons on politics. This is the basic training for three months.'

'I want to talk about the AK-47. How many bullets did the AK-47 hold?'

'Thirty rounds.'

'How many in the magazine?'

'Twenty-nine. It has been a long time. The numbers may be wrong.'

'What is the effective range of an AK-47?'

'Three hundred metres.'

'How many settings does an AK-47 have?'

'Auto and single. There is a switch. One for auto, one for single, and a safety.'

'Does one switch do all three, or is there a separate switch?'

'One switch.'

'Which side of the gun is the switch on?'

Sarva imagined holding the gun. His right hand moved. 'Right-hand side. Because it is made for right-handed people.'

He had not thought or spoken about these details for years. Jehaan, Shirleen, Randy, his lawyer Mr Vel, his friends in Swansea—he had told none of them about the LTTE apart from the bare fact of his conscription. He had been too afraid of being abandoned and having to pay forever for his mistake. Not even Amma knew about his having become a willing trainee for a while, let alone his proximity to AK-47s. The truth was dangerous in Sri Lanka, but here he knew that lies were the things that could get him deported. For the first time, moreover, he felt safe enough to confess.

'Where is the cleaning equipment kept for an AK-47?'

'Underneath the front—the barrel. There is a rod. There is something for cleaning the barrel kept in the butt of the gun.'

'How would you adjust the sights of an AK-47?'

'There is a clip on the AK-47. You can adjust it to one hundred, one hundred and fifty, two hundred, three hundred metres. Like that … I used AK-2 more. But I have seen the AK-47.'

'Oh. Are your previous answers in relation to an AK-47 or an AK-2?'

'There is no difference between the two. The only difference is we can fold the butt in AK-47, not in AK-2.'

'Where did you use the AK-2?'

'During the basic training.'

'What training did you receive as a commando?'

'It was very intensive, more than physical training. I was taught how to be patient in the field. They gave instructions on heavy weapons, it was more detailed. More crawling, training on rifle positioning. In basic, we ran for six kilometres, in the intensive, we ran for ten.'

'Why were you chosen for this extra training?'

'I was so good in the basic training, so I was selected.' Sarva instantly worried that he sounded proud about being picked. He was sure the interviewer would wonder how he could simultaneously have felt proud to be in the Tigers and yearned to go back to his family.

'Did you volunteer for this extra training?'

'I was compelled to go with them. They told us that we had to continue.'

'You were sent to Colombo to work as an operative after a further three months of intelligence training. Is that correct?'

'Yes.' That was the condition under which he had been released to go home to his mother. The leaders in the intelligence unit had asked him to wait at home for an assignment.

'What were your instructions in Colombo?'

'Initially, I was told that if I was given a parcel, I had to pass it to someone. Activities like that.'

'Were you part of a particular cell or subsection of the LTTE at this point?'

'No. When I went to Colombo, after three days, I went to Malaysia. I didn't work in Colombo for the LTTE.'

'How did you feel about the LTTE after living among them and training with them for all this time?'

'I feel the LTTE safeguards the culture of the Tamils. The Tamil community does not chastise the LTTE. Only, say, 20 per cent of the people do not recognise it. But in some cases, I disagree with the Tigers.'

'What about the LTTE do you not agree with?'

'I don't think they should make people join them by force. I disagree with them on that.'

'When you left Sri Lanka, were you still working as a member of the LTTE?'

'I left the LTTE when I went to Malaysia in January 2004. My mother sent me to Malaysia for fear of my life. I stayed with my brother there.'

'Why? Why did you leave the LTTE?'

'I wanted to live in peace, happily with my family.'

'But by leaving the LTTE, you had to leave your family. This confuses me.'

'While I was with the LTTE, they would not let me see my family. I was not allowed to visit for two years while I was with them in the Vanni.' Sarva thought of that day when Amma had come to see him at the Tiger base, her distraught face on seeing him in uniform. In the documents with the interviewer, there were three letters from her addressed to politicians and Tiger leaders, begging for her son's release.

'Have you actively taken part in an LTTE mission?'

'No.'

'Have you killed on behalf of the LTTE?'

'No.'

'Have you assisted anyone else in any way to kill on behalf of the LTTE?'

'No.'

The interviewer said that he knew of LTTE trainees who worked abroad, making contacts, collecting money and so on for the LTTE. 'Did you ever behave in this manner on behalf of the LTTE?'

'No. After I left the Vanni, I had nothing to do with the LTTE.'

'When did you leave the LTTE?'

Sarva realised that he was being asked the same question in different ways to check for contradictions. 'January 2004. After that I went straight to Malaysia.'

'Date you returned to Sri Lanka?'

'I don't remember the month. It was 2005.'

'You were in Malaysia all of this time?'

'My brother had a house there. I was staying with him.'

The interviewer asked if Sarva was willing to take a short break. When he left the room, Sarva breathed deeply. He felt weak, his hands limp. He had not ever been closer to the truth than in this room.

After the break, they talked about his detention. There was something from this period, too, that Sarva had told no one.

'You were tortured during incarceration, right?' the interviewer asked, adding that there was no need for Sarva to repeat all the details in the witness statement. He only wanted to know specific methods of torture used. 'For example, you were placed in a chair and hit from underneath. What were you hit with?'

'They hit me with something like a thick rope. I was blindfolded, so I could not see …' Sarva was feeling suddenly feverish, he wanted to say it before he lost his courage. 'Sir, I asked for a male officer to interview me here. If female, I would not be able to tell everything I want to tell you …'

'Tell me.'

'I was … sexually abused …' His hands were cold, he felt so ashamed. 'Sexually … tortured.'

The granite face of the interviewer softened. 'Do you want to tell me how you were sexually abused?'

'I was blindfolded and tied to a desk and ... they took off my clothes. I was made to kneel down and everyone came and ... I don't want to describe.' He began to sob.

The interviewer gave Sarva a glass of water. He took notes and said he didn't need to know more. 'You told these men that you did not receive training from the LTTE. Is that correct?'

Sarva struggled with the lump in his throat. 'Someone had already given them information about me. Initially, I did not tell them I had been to the Vanni or received any LTTE training. After they beat me, I told them that I was given forced training. I had to.'

'Did you sign any confession?'

'They tortured me to sign a few pages. Some had writing, and some were blank. I didn't sign them.'

'Were you asked to be an informer for the government?'

Sarva said he wasn't.

For the next few minutes, they clarified a few confusing statements in the documents. The interviewer pointed out that the seaman's book stated that Sarva was six feet ten inches tall. 'You are not that tall, can you explain?' Sarva was five feet nine inches; he was not sure why they had given him a giant's height.

When the interviewer asked about family in Sri Lanka, Sarva spoke about the TID's continued harassment of his aunt and mother in Colombo and Nuwara Eliya. Tears streamed down his cheeks and his nose leaked. Just a week earlier, his mother had been shoved by plainclothesmen as they entered the house. She had fainted and had to be taken to the hospital.

The interviewer wanted to know about the petition against the New Magazine prison authorities. Sarva explained that the Sinhalese prisoners were used to 'kill' the Tamils. 'Our clothes were taken off and we were beaten.' The attack had been reported in the newspaper with photos. There was also a medical report of the injuries he had sustained.

He was asked if he had any lingering medical conditions.

'A lot,' Sarva replied. Because of the beating on his feet, he had trouble walking. He also suffered from insomnia and post-traumatic stress, for which he took sleeping pills. He was receiving physiotherapy and medication from the government-appointed doctors for immigrants.

'We will finish now, okay?' the interviewer said. 'Do you want to add anything?'

Sarva folded his hands. 'Please, I can't go back … If I go back I will be killed. I want to live in peace with my family.'

'Why do you wish to remain in the UK?'

'Because … because it is a free country. I expect my life to be protected here.'

They shook hands and Sarva walked out of the office. The sun was finally out, and the snow had ceased. More people were out on the street.

Walking back to the Cardiff train station, Sarva wished he had elaborated on his jail time. He should have better explained the institutional discrimination, the volatile environment he was running from. After the interviewer had brought up the torture, Sarva had lost his composure. He had uttered the words to an absolute stranger. It had sucked away every bit of his energy. He hoped he would never have to talk about it again. The answers about the LTTE had been messy, but Sarva knew he could not have done better. Little was redeemable in that part of his life, but if Giri Anna was right, it would not matter.

By the time he boarded the train back to Swansea, a weight was off his shoulders. He allowed himself to feel a flicker of optimism. He took his shoes off and stretched his aching legs under the seat in front of him. From his window, he saw stripes of snow between the tracks, like the back of a zebra. Slums passed, then the retirement communities, and the undulating acres of grey farmland, waiting for summer before they burst into colour.

The coffee cart came by, and he spent three whole pounds—more than half a day's stipend—on a cappuccino and chocolate-chip muffin. When the coffee man left with an effervescent 'Enjoy!' Sarva felt a rush of belonging.

30.

April 2013

'HELLO, AMMA. I got the letter from the Border Agency,' Sarva had said on 30 March. 'It is thin.' A thick envelope meant a rejection letter along with all the documents he had given the agency. A thin one would contain a simple letter of acceptance and instructions about how to collect his visa.

Indra had prayed out loud. 'Open it now!'

He had fallen silent on the phone. Then he read: he had been approved for asylum; he would live in the UK with a refugee visa for five years, after which he could be considered for permanent residence. He was free.

Kaalum odale, kaiyyum odale, Indra told all the activists and relatives when she called them to share the unbelievable news—she had lost the use of her limbs when she heard. Some of those she called did not pick up the phone; she laughed that they must have expected another Sarva crisis, another appeal for help for the fifth year in a row.

A round of promised temple visits and much relieved crying later, Indra readied herself for the next challenge: finding Sarva a suitable bride. She had to ride the wave of good fortune. She had to engineer a match before her son turned into a lovelorn teenager again, in some stubborn relationship with a girl who was all wrong.

Sarva had collected his visa and been efficient about immediately securing a full-time warehousing job in an Indian-run factory that manufactured plastic lids. He would soon leave the Swansea asylum house and move to Luton, near the factory. He was ecstatic but also heartbroken: Malar was gone, he would have to say goodbye to darling Niru, leave behind his friends who were still checking their mail every day for an interview letter. Sarva was restive when it came to living among people who couldn't fathom the warped world he came from.

But Indra didn't allow him to mope about the break-up. 'These are normal setbacks, *kanna*,' she consoled. 'You have to learn to take them in your stride.' She believed a marriage would help him heal, induct him into life as it should be.

On the evening of the Tamil and Sinhala traditional New Year in mid-April, Indra tried to call Sarva. She was in Colombo and had seen an astrologer that morning about a potential match. To speak to her son about it, Indra needed to use Viber—a new free Internet phone application Sarva had introduced her to—but found that her data pack had run out. She yelled out to Rani that she was stepping out of the house for a phone refill and would buy some spinach if she saw a fresh bunch. She walked to the stationery store just around the corner from the apartment.

The shop was one of the oldest in the area, and behind the counter were the owner's teenage son and daughter. There were no other customers, and the daughter was chatting in whispers with her girlfriend. Another boy, slightly older than the rest, seemed to have dropped in from the adjacent grocery store to pass the time. When Indra walked in, she found them all laughing about something on the small television on the counter. She asked the owner's son for a 1,000-rupee Internet coupon.

As the son rummaged in a box, the older boy teasingly asked the girls in Sinhala what they were talking about.

'Not about *you*,' the owner's daughter replied in Sinhala, giggling with her friend.

'I know, I know,' he laughed, and then added, 'You girls don't have school? *Anh*, I forgot! Happy *aluth avurudhu*!'

The daughter wished him a happy New Year back, but her friend was quiet.

'What, your friend won't wish me?' he teased, half in English and half in Sinhala.

'Maybe she doesn't celebrate it,' the daughter said and the girls giggled again.

'Why? What are you?' the boy asked. Looking at the owner's son, he repeated the question. 'What is she? Muslim?' He looked at the friend again. 'Why won't you wish me?'

Surprised at the turn in the conversation, the friend slung her handbag on her shoulder and got ready to leave.

'Okay, don't answer,' the older boy said. 'Show me your ID card, then we will get to know everything about you.' He looked for approval from the owner's son, but the boy was uneasy. The girl got up and shook her head at the owner's daughter, as if to say she would see her later.

The Sinhalese boy continued his discomfiting flirtation. 'What are you hiding? Show me your ID, show it!'

Indra took her coupon from the owner's son, paid for it, and left the shop.

ON THE NIGHT of New Year's Eve, Tamizh kept on whining throughout the bus journey from Point Pedro, protesting because he had to share a seat with his older brother. Maran threw screechy tantrums, demanding Divyan's phone, and when he got it, played the snake game till the battery died. At one point, when the boys started to punch each other, a groggy Divyan twisted Maran's ears and shook Tamizh by his shoulder. 'I will tell *amma* that you pinched me,' Maran wailed, but cried himself to sleep after that.

At quarter past nine the next morning, they reached the Pettah bus stand in Colombo. It was swelteringly hot. At the enquiry desk, Divyan asked for the bus routes to Borella, where the TID office was located. 'There's one leaving in five minutes across the road,' a Tamil man at the counter said.

'That is CTB, no?' Divyan asked. He rarely used the state-run

Colombo Transport Buses because most of the conductors spoke only Sinhala. 'What about private?'

The man at the desk told Divyan the bus numbers. 'Some routes have changed because of road repairs.'

Later in November that year, Colombo would be hosting the meeting of the Commonwealth heads of government and a makeover was under way. The Urban Development Ministry was absorbed by the Ministry of Defence and Gotabaya Rajapaksa, the president's brother and the defence secretary, had launched a massive beautification drive to showcase the prosperity and peace of postwar Sri Lanka. With military precision, the seaside capital was being transformed: roads were relaid, pavements extended, high-rises commissioned, street-side hawkers and small shops swept away. Low-income houses were razed and public playgrounds suddenly cordoned off. The army now manned parks, malls and beaches. Giant-sized cut-outs of a waving president or his brother beamed at people from virtually every junction. Lawns everywhere warned the grubby public not to walk, play or sit on the manicured grass. Modern, growing, messy Colombo was being reshaped into a thing of sterile beauty.

Carrying Tamizh in his arms, Divyan walked with Maran to his preferred snack shop, run by an elderly Muslim woman. The single table fan in the shop circulated warm air. Sitting on a bench by a window, the boys ate biscuits as he sipped sweet tea.

Outside, Pettah market gleamed in the sun, its sea of DVDs, clothes, mobiles, toys, and electronic goods flowing through and around the private and state bus stations. The capital always overwhelmed Divyan, but Pettah put him at ease. Tamil-speakers ran most of the establishments, and there was a comfortable familiarity and anonymity in the chaos. But this time, the men who sold fake designer T-shirts and handkerchiefs along the pavement were missing, the lottery ticket sellers were gone. A road divider had been heightened and extended along the length of the road to prevent jaywalking. Passengers, shoppers and businesspeople milled to the one zebra crossing, compressed on either side of the road, waiting impatiently for the walking man on the traffic light to turn green.

As Divyan watched, a teenager suddenly darted across the

street before the light changed. Divyan expected the parted sea to converge immediately, for the men and women to shed restraint and follow the rule breaker. Instead, a policeman emerged from nowhere, slapped the boy hard, and dragged him away by his collar. The other pedestrians seemed nailed to the spot.

Divyan's shirt was plastered to his back with sweat. He asked the shopkeeper for a jug of water to wash his face. Maran and Tamizh saw parotta curry being served at other tables and asked for some. It was 50 rupees a plate, but Divyan had only 300 rupees left in his wallet, which was the bus fare back. He told the boys their mother would be waiting for them, and they had better hurry up if they did not want to miss her.

Three months had passed since Mugil's arrest, and this was the second time Divyan had been permitted to visit. The first time, a week after her arrest, he had travelled to Colombo for a thirty-second meeting, only enough time for him to give her some clothes and for her to kiss her sons. Since then, he had applied for the ICRC's visitation aid for families of detainees—they paid the bus fare and gave him an ICRC card to show the police. Today he would have at least ten minutes with Mugil. They took a bus to Borella and walked to the TID office.

Unlike the white colonial buildings the government preferred to build, the office of the Terrorist Investigation Department was an unappealing boxy monstrosity. To Divyan, it was like solid fear. As he walked in, the tittering boys became absolutely silent. When he signed into a register and waited on a bench in the corridor, they hugged his legs. There were about twelve other families. One of them acknowledged Divyan with a smile to Tamizh.

Divyan remembered his own detention like it was yesterday; he was terrified of what he was about to see on Mugil's face.

Half an hour later, she was brought out of her cell and put next to Divyan on the bench in the corridor. The two policemen took a step back but did not leave. Mugil's eyes were on the floor. Tamizh threw his arms around her neck and sobbed. Maran complained that *appa* had pinched him on the bus.

'What is this?' Mugil scolded Divyan mockingly. Her left cheek was marbled blue and red; she had been hit hard, probably just the day before. Her hands were free, but her wrists were bruised by rope. Divyan put his hand on her knee. She flinched.

He gave her a plastic bag with a change of clothes, underwear, a pair of rubber slippers, and a packet of sesame balls that she liked. They spoke in a wary code.

'The kids are too much,' he said.

'What do they eat?' she asked. 'Rice, chicken, dal?'

He nodded. He cooked what he knew.

He said he had not worked for weeks because he didn't know where to leave the boys. Since Mugil's and Prashant's arrest, Amuda had asked Divyan not to come too often, not to impose familial responsibility on her when there was little familial affection left. 'I guess she has worries of her own,' Mugil said.

She asked hesitantly if Divyan had gone to see Prashant. Maran, who was listening to their conversation from her lap, piped up, '*Appa* says he doesn't care if Chitthappa rots on the TID fourth floor.'

'Your brother is an out-of-control big mouth,' Divyan spat. She sighed.

'You're okay, no?' Divyan did not ask directly about the TID or the detention. She made a show of being all right, smiling painfully.

'There are eight other women with me in the cell,' she said, as if that were somehow an answer.

Neither spoke of when she might return; they could not know. She asked him what would come next. 'They may offer rehabilitation,' he said. 'Just take it, accept everything. We can't do court and all.'

A policeman grunted for them to finish. Maran refused to let Mugil go, simply repeating no, no, no, dragging the syllable out in desperate complaint. Tamizh asked her when she would come home. Mugil threw a worried look at Divyan. He told her she had better leave.

After Mugil was taken back inside, Divyan asked an officer when he could visit again. Stay in touch with her on the phone, the officer snapped, there is no need to keep coming.

Heading back to Pettah on a bus, Tamizh and Maran stared out the window, dazed. They would be fine once they were home,

Divyan thought. They would forget to ask for their mother in a few days. On his next visit, he would have to find someone to look after one of them. This family trip was too draining and made Mugil anxious.

BACK AT PETTAH, Divyan looked for a bus to Jaffna, from where he would take a minivan home. Behind him, Maran and Tamizh leaned on other people's luggage, their heads lolling drowsily in the afternoon heat. Other passengers stood in irate stillness in the queues. Plumes of diesel smoke hung in the warm air. Flies burrowed into the apples in the fruit shops at the entrance. Perspiring Muslim shopkeepers announced the price of grapes, plums and mangoes in Tamil and Sinhala. Their assistants walked around enticing passengers with plastic packets of chilled mineral water.

As Divyan fished his wallet out to see about the possibility of buying some bananas for lunch, the fruit sellers hurriedly started to shove their baskets of produce inside their shops and pull the shutters down. Some of them darted across the bus station and exited from the back. At first, Divyan thought it must be time for daily prayer. But some men were climbing into parked buses to hide under the seats. One Muslim shopkeeper hissed in Tamil, 'Again they have come!'

Divyan craned his neck to see what had provoked this reaction, but he heard it before he saw it: Sinhala shouts that rose and fell like a slogan. A chorus of voices: 'Stop the butchers!' 'Ban Halal!' 'Stop favouring Muslims!' '*Jai* Sri Lanka!'

The voices came closer till a procession appeared on the street, about 200 metres from where Divyan stood. There were around fifty people, most of them male, and dressed in white. Some wore T-shirts displaying the words NO HALAL within a crossed red circle. Leading them were a half-dozen saffron-clad Buddhist monks. They filled the pavement.

The leading voice—sounding like a sharp clap—was that of a Sinhala Buddhist monk. He looked around forty years old. His thick shoulders shone with sweat. His eyes popped, and spit sprayed from his mouth as he bellowed. When he punched the air above him, the rage seemed to shoot from his feet up to his clenched fist. On occasion, he roughly pushed back the saffron robe slipping onto his hairy arms. Behind him were a handful of other monks who looked equally angry.

The mob marched into the bus station. Divyan ordered Maran and Tamizh to stay close. Some in the group carried wide banners with curling Sinhala letters and exclamation marks. There were two small English banners on the side. 'No Halal!' one said in black paint. 'Stop Muslim takeover of Sri Lanka!' the other said. A few men split from the group and ran towards the shops that were shutting rapidly. They shouted for the owners to come out. They were yelling in Sinhala, but Divyan recognised the abusive words they were using to refer to Muslims. He knew the Sinhala Buddhist extremists were now attacking mosques and turning on the Muslims. He had not seen this new hate until this moment.

One of the mobsters thrust his agitated face so close to a youth that their noses almost touched. He was spewing abuse, and his hands scrunched the young man's shirt collar. Cornered against a sack of coconuts, the young man let his body go limp and kept his eyes on the ground. A No-Halal T-shirt wearer smashed the glass of a bus bearing Arabic lettering and then ran into a nearby mobile shop and tore the displays down. Another one ran to a closed shutter, unzipped and pissed in front of it.

After a few minutes, the lead monk waved his hands at the scouts and the group started to leave. Five policemen, who had been watching until then, followed them, deep in discussion.

For several minutes after, the station was still. People spoke in whispers, shaking their heads. The shopkeepers did not return. Soon, as if at the flick of a switch, the buses started to come alive. The drivers revved the engines and the conductors called to passengers to hurry up and get in.

A Brief History of the Sri Lankan Civil War

SRI LANKA HAS a multi-ethnic population of more than twenty million. Apart from the majority Sinhalese community, it is home to a long-established Tamil minority in the north and east; Tamil-speaking Muslims; Indian-origin Tamils brought by the British to work on tea and coffee plantations in the central hills; Burghers of European descent; and Veddas (aboriginal people). Between the sixteenth century and 1948, the Dutch, the Portuguese and the British successively colonised the country. In the wake of Indian independence, the British left Sri Lanka in 1948, leaving behind fractured ethnic communities.

The country's recent history has been defined by a fierce twenty-six-year civil war, which came to an end in May 2009. The United Nations estimates that the protracted ethnic conflict left up to 100,000 dead, although the number could be a gross underestimation. The war also displaced several hundred thousand people, stunted the island nation's economic growth and intensified ethnic hatreds. It was one of Asia's longest-running civil wars.

After taking the reins of the country after independence, the Sinhala Buddhist majority, which had long resented the British bias towards the Tamils during colonial times, began implementing discriminatory policies against minorities. In 1956, the government replaced English with Sinhala as the country's official language and ignored Tamil, which was spoken by nearly 30 per cent of the population. In 1972 a new constitution declared Buddhism, the faith of most of the Sinhalese, the country's official religion, and the greatest duty of the state the protection of Buddhism. In the following years, university admission procedures and government employment practices were repeatedly amended to deny opportunities to young Tamils.

In response, several armed Tamil nationalist groups emerged in the north during the 1970s. They were poorly armed and funded themselves through petty crime and robbing small banks. But two events in the early eighties expanded their membership. In May 1981, Sinhalese policemen and protesters set fire to the Jaffna Tamil library. The building burned for over a day, filling Jaffna town with the smoke of 97,000 Tamil books and rare manuscripts as they turned into ash. In July 1983, Sinhalese mobs provoked by the Tigers' killing of thirteen Sri Lankan soldiers rioted in Tamil neighbourhoods in the capital city of Colombo and other towns, killing Tamils. The death toll is still hotly contested; the government maintains that only 400 died, while others put the number at around 3,000.

Thousands of Tamils began fleeing the country, seeking asylum in the UK, Canada, Norway and India. Hundreds of others picked up guns. The Liberation Tigers of Tamil Eelam (LTTE), founded by Velupillai Prabakaran in 1976, emerged as the strongest and most ruthless of these Tamil militant groups. The Tamil Tigers, as they were also known, demanded Eelam, a separate nation for Tamils in the north and east.

The south of the country was simultaneously lashed by a leftist insurgency led by Sinhalese peasants and youth under the banner of the Janatha Vimukthi Peramuna, or JVP. The two JVP insurrections and the state's answering crackdown killed almost 15,000 southern youths. More than 7,000 were jailed for terrorism. By the late eighties, that leftist insurgency had been quelled.

But for the next three decades, the Sinhalese-dominated Sri Lankan army and the Tamil Tigers continued to clash. The extended fighting saw vicious suicide bombings; the assassination of several high-ranking ministers and political figures in both Sri Lanka and India, including Sri Lankan President Ranasinghe Premadasa and former Indian prime minister Rajiv Gandhi; and audacious guerrilla attacks on key government installations and the international airport in the capital Colombo. The only relief: periods of ceasefire brokered by Norway. Notorious for recruiting child soldiers and establishing their own laws and taxation system in controlled territories called the Vanni, in Sri Lanka's northeast, the Tigers were also known to be the only militant outfit in the world to have a navy and air force. Over thirty countries branded them a terrorist organisation and banned them.

After four peace talks failed and both sides grossly violated the ceasefire, the Sri Lankan armed forces launched a military offensive in Tiger-held regions in 2006. By 2008, the government had forced every international and independent body, including the United Nations, to evacuate the war zone, leaving about three million Tamil civilians caught between warring Tigers and the Sri Lankan military. The UN estimates that between 40,000 to 70,000 civilians were killed by the army, and some by the LTTE too. Over 2.5 million people were displaced. By 19 May 2009, the LTTE chief Prabakaran had been killed and the LTTE eliminated.

When the war ended, some hoped that Sri Lankan society would rebuild and grow. Instead, the next five years saw the country's prospects diminished by a government that sought to consolidate its power and limit the rights of its citizens.